TENDER MERCIES

Books by Lauraine Snelling

Hawaiian Sunrise

A SECRET REFUGE

Daughter of Twin Oaks

RED RIVER OF THE NORTH

An Untamed Land   *The Reapers' Song*
A New Day Rising   *Tender Mercies*
A Land to Call Home   *Blessing in Disguise*

HIGH HURDLES

Olympic Dreams   *Storm Clouds*
DJ's Challenge   *Close Quarters*
Setting the Pace   *Moving Up*
Out of the Blue   *Letting Go*
Raising the Bar

GOLDEN FILLY SERIES

The Race   *Shadow Over San Mateo*
Eagle's Wings   *Out of the Mist*
Go for the Glory   *Second Wind*
Kentucky Dreamer   *Close Call*
Call for Courage   *The Winner's Circle*

TENDER MERCIES

LAURAINE SNELLING

BETHANY HOUSE PUBLISHERS
MINNEAPOLIS, MINNESOTA 55438

Tender Mercies
Copyright © 1999
Lauraine Snelling

Cover illustration by William Graf.
Cover design by Dan Thornberg,
Bethany House Publishers staff artist.

Published by Bethany House Publishers
A Ministry of Bethany Fellowship International
11400 Hampshire Avenue South
Minneapolis, Minnesota 55438
www.bethanyhouse.com

Printed in the United States of America by
Bethany Press International, Minneapolis, Minnesota 55438

Library of Congress Cataloging-in-Publication Data

Snelling Lauraine.
   Tender mercies / by Lauraine Snelling.
      p.   cm. — (Red river of the north ; 5)
   ISBN 0–7642–2089–6
    1. Norwegian Americans—Dakota Territory Fiction. I. Title.
II. Series: Snelling, Lauraine. Red River of the north ; bk. 5.
PS3569.N39 T46   1999
813'.54—dc21   99–6410
                                             CIP

To all my teachers,
those unsung heroes in a person's life,
but especially Jen Southworth and Damon Peeler,
who pushed me toward excellence.
What gifts you were and are to me.

LAURAINE SNELLING is an award-winning author of over thirty-five books, fiction and nonfiction for adults and young adults. Besides writing both books and articles, she teaches at writers' conferences across the country. She and her husband, Wayne, have two grown sons, four granddogs, and make their home in California.

September 1887
Blessing, Dakota Territory

Good riddance."

Pastor John Solberg stroked an impatient hand across sandy hair that no longer covered an ever broadening forehead. He watched one of his parishioners twitch her way out the door of the schoolhouse, where she'd trapped him. Good thing she hadn't heard him.

"Why, Lord, why? Is it written somewhere that the local pastor is fair game for every woman with a marriageable daughter? You know I'm not the only single man around here." Talking out loud with the Lord had become the norm for him in his solitary life. After all, when he knew Jesus was right beside him, why not carry on a conversation with Him out loud?

Between getting ready to teach twenty-seven students from the ages of five to fourteen in a one-room shoddy all day and his pastoral duties, lonely wasn't a word in his vocabulary.

Usually.

He eyed the loaf of fresh bread that waited for him on the side of the desk. That was one good thing, those marriage-seeking mamas almost always brought a gift, and most often it was food of some sort. As did his neighbors. Yesterday he'd found an apple pie on his kitchen table. The accompanying note had invited him to supper on Sunday at the Knutsons'.

Now if there were more women around like Kaaren Knutson—not only lovely like a cream-colored rose but with a sweet spirit to match and wisdom far beyond her years.

Like Katy.

He closed his eyes, the better to see her on the backs of his eyelids. Katy Bjorklund, with laughing blue eyes, an endearing Norwegian accent since she'd only come to America last year, and a heart always ready to help anyone in need. He'd thought her the perfect candidate for a pastor's wife.

Katy thought of him only as a friend.

On May 27, 1887, he'd officiated at the marriage of Katy Bjorklund to Zeb MacCallister.

Weddings were usually such a happy time for him, but not that one. From the time Zeb MacCallister rode into Blessing, Katy had eyes only for the stranger. Pastor Solberg had learned a valuable lesson from all that. If you don't want to get burned, stay away from the stove.

"Lord, forgive me," he murmured into his cupped hands. "Must I be so base as to think of her still? You know I have given her up. Why do the memories yet haunt me?" He pushed himself upright. "If you have a wife for me—now I'm beginning to wonder—let her be a gentle Norwegian girl who will fit right in with these dear people of mine."

He almost smiled at the thought of referring to the bread-bearing mama as "dear."

The jingle of harness caught his attention. He glanced around the schoolroom, knowing that all was in readiness for his pupils who would start in the next week. But it never hurt to check.

"Whoa there." The clomp of horse hooves ended at the same time the harness stopped jingling.

He would know that laugh anywhere. His heart felt as if a giant hand had squeezed it once and then again.

Katy.

Why hadn't they put two doors in this building? With no way of escape, he pushed himself upright and pasted a smile on his face.

"John? Are you here?"

"Y—." He cleared his throat. He could hear the slow drawl of her husband answer some question. Was there a third person out there? "Yes, I'm here. Come on in."

He flipped open a book and stared down the pages. The print danced before his eyes.

The door burst open, and Katy Bjorklund MacCallister entered, laughing at something Zeb had said. Spring rushed in with her.

"John, we have someone for you to meet." She glanced over her shoulder. "Come on, Mary Martha. You must meet one of our best friends."

Solberg groaned inside. *Have I acted so convincingly that she has no idea?*

"Good afternoon, Pastor." Zeb MacCallister removed his wide-brimmed hat as he came through the low door. If he hadn't, the doorframe would have done it for him. "Sorry to bother you, but my Katy insisted."

The slow molasses drawl clogged Solberg's ears. *Why can't the man learn to speak properly? Or at least faster.* He felt like snapping his fingers to encourage the words to come more rapidly.

"Mary Martha MacCallister, I want you to meet Pastor John Solberg." Katy did the honors with her usual flourish.

"My sister is visiting from Missouri," Zeb added. "We would have introduced you sooner, but with you being gone and all . . ."

Mary Martha? Couldn't they make up their mind when they named her? "I'm pleased to meet you, Miss MacCallister." His voice sounded stiff, even to his own ears. *Probably good I have been gone. I needed that time with my family, and marrying off a sister was pure delight. So now I'm back and . . .* The day seemed to have brought nothing but annoyances.

"Ah've heard so much about you."

She talked just like her brother. He glanced up from studying the hem of her skirt to see eyes that appeared to be laughing. At him? "Yes, well, welcome to Blessing. I hope you'll enjoy your visit. If you'll excuse me, I have somewhere I need to be."

Liar. He almost turned to see who was sitting on his shoulder. He moved toward the door, ushering them before him.

"Hey, Solberg, you in there?"

Saved by a Bjorklund. The irony of it all.

"You caught me, Haakan. Come on in."

"How you doing, Pastor?" Haakan filled the door, ducking under the frame as a matter of habit.

Since today seemed to be one of honesty, John admitted to himself that maybe if he had the broad shoulders and arresting blue eyes of the Bjorklund men, perhaps Ka—er, a young woman of his own choosing would be more disposed to accept his advances. Often he felt he lived in the land of giants when around the men of Blessing. Including Zeb MacCallister.

"Why, Katy, Zeb, how are you? And Miss MacCallister?" Haakan smiled at each in turn. "What brings you to town?"

"We thought to show Mary Martha around some." Katy sent a troubled glance Solberg's way. "Now that Pastor Solberg is back, we—I thought—I guess . . ." She stammered to a close, glancing from the minister to her sister-in-law and back to Haakan.

See, another one. I didn't expect this from my friends. Is there no safe haven?

Haakan nodded. "Ingeborg said if I saw you, I was to tell you that the coffeepot is always on and the ladies will be hosting the first quilting meeting of the fall on Saturday. That's a good chance for you to finish meeting everyone." He directed the last sentence to their visitor. "Right, Pastor?"

"Ah, right." John took another step toward the door. He felt as though the room were trying to smother him. Something was.

"Good. Then we will go to Penny's and swing by your house on the way home," Katy said.

The look Katy gave Pastor Solberg clearly said she was not only puzzled but concerned by his actions. His mother would have burned his ears over such boorish behavior but . . . *Please, Lord, get me out of here.* When they finally got outside, John sucked in a breath of air as if he'd been underwater and about to drown. As if from a far distance, he heard the others saying "good-bye" and "see you soon," but for the life of him, he couldn't respond. Instead he raised a hand in farewell when Zeb had his womenfolk back in the wagon and was clucking his horse to back up.

"Are you all right?" Haakan asked.

"I will be." John sucked in another breath of cold air and felt his head clear. Now he'd have to apologize. "You in as bad a need of a cup of coffee as I am?"

"You know me. I never turn down an offer like that." Haakan held out a paper-wrapped packet. "Especially since Ingeborg sent you some molasses cookies fresh from the oven." He nodded toward the loaf of bread John had tucked under his arm. "You had time to bake along with getting ready for all those children?" The twinkle in his eyes said he knew otherwise.

"Just another matchmaking mama." John stepped back inside the schoolhouse and snagged his coat off one of the pegs in the cloakroom. "Won't take too long to get the coffee hot. I sent Thorliff over to rattle the grates and fire up my stove. You know how hard I have to work to keep ahead of that young man, don't you? I surely do appreciate Ingeborg sending him over to help me get the schoolroom ready for classes." He closed the door behind him and turned to see the wagon raising a dust cloud down the road to the store. Yes, an apology was definitely in order. What an oaf he had been. After all, she was only a visitor here, and the Lord commanded them to welcome visitors. *As angels unawares* . . . He checked a groan. He hated failure.

"I don't envy you." Haakan shook his head. "Sometimes the questions that boy asks . . . He is always thinking, that's for certain. Just the other day he asked me why, if God wrote the Bible, did most of the books in it have other men's names on them?"

"What did you tell him?"

"To ask you."

"And I suppose when he asked where babies came from, you told him to ask his mother."

"You bet your britches. I did good on how the steam engine works though, and why the hailstorms skipped over the farms here in Blessing."

John looked up at the man walking beside him. "What did you say to that?"

"God made it so, and so it is. That was my mor's answer to any question she didn't know the answer. Worked with me."

Solberg groaned and rolled his eyes. "You know, it's farmers like you who keep us ministers and schoolteachers in business." He opened the door to his sod house. An orange tiger cat rose from its place on the rug in front of the stove, stretched every rippling muscle, and purred its way to the door to wind around the legs of the men as they divested themselves of coats and hats. The freeze the night before and the wind from the north seemed as if they'd skipped right over fall to winter.

When the coffee was poured and they'd both sat down—Solberg in his rocking chair—the wind could be heard pleading around the eaves to join them.

Haakan blew on the coffee he'd poured in his saucer to cool. "I sure ain't looking forward to winter this year. I must be getting old."

"Ja, and my legendary tante Irmy lives right next door."

"Really? When did you sneak that one by us?" Haakan looked up over the rim of his cup. Reaching for one of the cookies now on a plate, he dunked it in the coffee and slowly blinked his eyes in bliss. "Now this is the way an afternoon ought to be spent."

"And how is that?" Solberg broke off a bit of cookie and fed it to the cat waiting at his knee.

Haakan waved a cookie. "Hot coffee, cookies, talk with a friend. What more can one ask for?"

Putting all thoughts of his earlier visitors aside, John studied the man before him. "I know it's about chores time, and you didn't come pick up the children because they aren't here yet. I don't want to seem inhospitable but . . . why are you *really* here?"

Haakan examined the rim of his coffee cup. The silence between the two men stretched, the cat's purring vibrating the stillness. Haakan looked up. "Now, you know I don't take no part in gossip?"

Solberg nodded. "No fear of my thinking that." He waited, watching as wrinkles chased each other across Haakan's forehead and then turned to chase again.

"And that I ain't an interfering man?"

Knowing the question needed no answer, John waited.

"Well, I just don't think it's right, that's all, and I don't know what to do about it."

Hurrying one of the Bjorklund men was like trying to push water uphill. What in the world was Haakan referring to?

"W hy did Bestefar die?" Five-year-old Andrew Bjorklund propped his elbows on the table.

"Ah, child, the questions you ask." His bestemor, grandmother Bridget Bjorklund, brushed a lock of snowy hair from her forehead with the back of a floury wrist. She reverted to Norwegian, unable to even *think* of an answer to such a complex question in her meager English. "Have a cookie," she replied, giving herself more time to think.

"Mange takk." Andrew could eat a dozen cookies—if anyone would let him—and then sit down to a full dinner without slowing down. Overnight he'd turned into all ankles and wrists. Since he grew up with both languages, he could switch back and forth with ease. He stared at his grandmother, waiting for an answer to his question.

Just thinking of her beloved Gustaf brought the sheen of tears to Bridget's eyes. "His heart grew tired and quit one night while he was sleeping."

"Didn't he want to live anymore?"

"Some things we don't have a choice for. When God calls you home, you go, whether you want to or not."

"Like when Mor calls me from playing with the baby pigs? And if I don't hurry and get here, she will use a switch on me?"

Bridget rolled her lips together to keep from smiling. The serious look on her sprouting grandson's face warned her that he really wanted answers. He wasn't just dawdling to keep from his chores or some such. "Not quite. See, you could still keep on playing—"

"And get in trouble?"

"Ja, but when God calls, you are gone"—she snapped her fingers, snowing flour and bits of sour cream cookie dough down on the table—"just like that."

"Like when the hawk took my little chicks away?"

"Well, not exactly, but close. But dying does mean they won't come back alive again."

"Um." Andrew reached for another cookie, checked his grandmother's face for agreement, and at her nod helped himself.

When he looked up at her, his blue eyes so much like his grandfather's, she felt her heart turn.

"Did you say good-bye?" he asked.

"No." A simple word to cover a world of regret. Had Gustaf needed her, and she slept? Had he said good-bye, and she didn't answer? What she wouldn't give to hear his voice again, even if only asking for a cup of coffee. To see his boot marks across a clean kitchen floor, to sweep up curls of wood from his incessant carving, to hear his laugh, his wonderful laugh that made everyone around him laugh too. However, in the later years he had become more serious, bent over by the troubles of farming on land that wasn't large enough to support his family, thus watching his sons leave for the new land. Never to return.

She left a fluff of flour under her eye when she backhanded away the tear that overflowed. *You should be done with the crying now, you crazy old woman. After all, dying is part of living.*

"I don't like to say good-bye."

"Ah, Andrew, neither do I." She stopped rolling the cookie dough. "But you see, God didn't offer me a choice."

"Going along is better than saying good-bye."

Bridget stared at her grandson. So often she had thought that very thing. Why didn't God take her too? "Have another cookie, and then you must go bring in the wool for carding. I hung the fleeces out on the clothesline, and they should be dry by now."

Andrew nodded and reached for another cookie. "I wish I knew Bestefar. Thorliff did."

Bridget wiped her hand on her apron and brushed his curly blond hair off his forehead. "You have such a gift for saying the right thing. Go, now, before there are no cookies left for the others and I have to start all over again.

"Put your coat on," she called just as he started to slip out the door.

His chuckle, a younger version of his grandfather's, floated over his shoulder before he closed the door.

Bridget dabbed away a bit of lingering moisture and went back to rolling out sour cream cookies. With Astrid down for a nap and no one else in the house at the moment, she returned to dreaming up plans for her boardinghouse. If she could get the men to build it, that is. Supper last Sunday evening had turned into a heated discussion, she recalled.

"And so, if I am going to stay here in America, I need to have something of my own," she had said, looking from one astonished male face to another. *Where had they been when the women were talking about her boardinghouse? Men! Did they never listen until you took them by the ears and . . .*

"But, Mor, isn't helping Penny and Ingeborg enough work for you?" Her last remaining son, Hjelmer, rocked back in his chair.

She wanted to tell him to sit on the chair the right way so it wouldn't break, just as she had those years when he was young, but right now she knew better than to start an argument over something like that. "No." There, she'd said it.

"But you are busy from the time the rooster crows until the lamp runs low on kerosene." Haakan nodded to the yellow circle of light cast by the lamp in the middle of the table.

And who do you suppose fills the lamp again? Through the years she'd learned to keep thoughts like that to herself.

Ingeborg nodded when Bridget looked to her for assistance. "It seems to me that if Bridget wants to own a boardinghouse, she should do so."

"It isn't as if we don't need one in Blessing. You all know I've been thinking along those lines myself." Penny, Hjelmer's wife, was already expanding her store in town into an eating establishment too. She looked directly at Hjelmer, as if daring him to disagree.

He dared. "But, Mor, aren't you too old to start something like that now? After all you are—"

"After all, I am your mor, and I still have the strength in

these hands"—she held them up and looked to her son—"to wash and cook and bake the bread you are selling in the store."

"Not me," he mumbled under his breath, but she heard him anyway.

"Ja, you. You might be the big-shot banker in town, but you still got black under your fingernails like any other blacksmith." She watched as he checked his hands. When he closed one fist, she knew she'd hit on his weak spot.

While Hjelmer had always been a good blacksmith, he liked handling money better. But the bank hadn't been in business long enough to pay him much, so when someone needed a blacksmith, he donned his leather apron again and fit wheels, repaired machinery, or shod the local horses.

"If it is the money worrying you, I will sign a note and pay it all back just like anyone else. I ask for no favors." She glanced at Penny, who had talked with her about how things like that were done in America, and got a brief nod in return, along with a swift glimpse of the dimple in the young woman's cheek. Penny had learned much with the opening and running of her store.

"Ja, well, the board of directors will have to vote on a loan and . . ." When Hjelmer grew agitated, his accent deepened.

"Okay, let's call a truce here." Haakan laid his hands flat on the table.

"You think this is not a good idea?" Bridget turned to look at him, her knitting needles lying idle in her lap.

Upstairs the children could be heard playing Thimble, Thimble, Who's Got the Thimble. Andrew's laugh rose above the rest.

If we build a boardinghouse, I will no longer live here where I can hear the children. The thought caught Bridget unprepared. Her shoulders slumped. Perhaps they were right. Maybe she was too old to think of such a thing.

The slamming of the kitchen door brought her back to her cookie baking. She slid the last pan into the oven and checked the firebox. After adding two more sticks of wood, she set the round lid in place and dusted off her hands.

"Where do you want these?" The fleece were longer than Andrew was tall. He looked like a walking mountain of fluffy sheep fleece.

"In the parlor by my spinning wheel. You can fold them against the wall."

Andrew did as he was told, then returned to the kitchen. "Astrid's awake."

"How do you know? I haven't heard her cry."

Andrew shrugged. "She is."

Just then a whimper preceded a weepy, "M-a-a-a."

"Uff da." Bridget hurried into the bedroom behind the kitchen. Astrid sat in the middle of her mother's bed, her cheeks bright red and round as apples. She held up her arms, a sunny smile breaking out as soon as Bridget picked her up.

She felt the child's diapers and, since they were dry, whisked her over to the pot in the corner. Sliding down diapers and soaker, she sat Astrid on it. "You be a good girl and go now."

"Mor?"

"She's at Tante Kaaren's."

"Drink?"

"As soon as you go." Bridget picked up a flannel square from the pile on the bed and began folding while she waited. She held one to her face, inhaling the fragrance brought in fresh from the clothesline. Soon they would no longer be washing diapers in this house, if the look on Ingeborg's face at times was any indication.

Trying to understand why God sometimes failed to bring more babies to a home was about like trying to understand why Gustaf had died so unexpectedly. God was God and, as such, beyond understanding.

But He could work miracles, and getting the men to build her a boardinghouse might just be a bit easier than parting the Red Sea. "Uff da," she muttered again, folding another diaper.

"I done," Astrid sang out. The odor emanating from the corner said as much.

"You sit still. Have to wipe." Bridget pulled one of the rags from the edge of the diaper pile. After wiping the little girl's bottom and setting her on her feet again, she dropped the rag in a bucket kept for that purpose. More to be washed. Maybe Hjelmer was right. She should stay here and help care for the babies.

"Gustaf, what am I to do?" But, like God, her beloved husband didn't answer either.

N ow don't go getting all het up over it."

"But I don't understand." Katy shook her head, setting the golden curls flowing down her back to bouncing. "John is never abrupt like that. He was downright rude." She shook her head again, this time more with sorrow than indignation.

"Maybe he had something on his mind." Zeb MacCallister propped a lean shoulder against the post holding up the porch roof that aproned his house. From this vantage he could see the corrals that surrounded three sides of the two-story main barn like a woman's skirts. In the paddock to the west, Manda had one of this year's crop of colts, haltered and on a lead line, following behind her like a docile dog. He knew for a fact she'd just begun to work with the young one the day before. Talk about a gift—that ornery young girl could gentle an animal faster than anyone he'd ever seen.

"Zeb, are you listening to us at all?"

"Sure enough, sugar." His drawl, laced with warm molasses, made both his wife and sister giggle. Only when he'd been somewhere far away in his mind did he slow his Missouri drawl like that. It gave him time to think. *What had they been discussing? Could it still be the way Pastor Solberg had cut them off?*

"Ah 'magine we'll understand sooner or later."

Mary Martha hooted at his roundabout comment. "Zebulun MacCallister, that is the most farfetched bit of boondoggling I've heard since I left home. I know you got the gift from Uncle Jedediah, but he's much better at it than you."

Zeb had the grace to look sheepish. "Yes, but he's been at it longer."

"I know exactly what was going on with the preacher. He's not still mooning over Katy, but . . ." Mary Martha had to pause at the gasp of horror from her sister-in-law. "Come on, Katy, surely you knew he was in love with you."

Katy shook her head, so golden beside these two with the dark curls. "Pastor Solberg was—is—one of my best friends, but I never . . ." Her look of horror grew. "I never did anything to . . . to . . ." Her gaze darted between the brother and sister, whose grins grew wider with her discomfort. "Zeb, you know I—when you . . ."

"Darlin', take it easy. I know you fell in love with me the first time I rode into the yard at Ingeborg's and that you are pure as gushing springwater, but you are such almighty fun to tease."

Katy swatted him on the back pocket from her position in the rocking chair.

"Tease me all you like, but I still think—"

"Solberg took me aside one day and warned me that I better take good care of you, or I'd have to answer to both him and God."

Katy flopped back against the chair. "He didn't!" Her Bjorklund blue eyes grew rounder. "You didn't." Heat painted roses on her cheeks to match the pink climber that dressed their porch.

"Sure 'nuff." He leaned forward to run a gentle fingertip down the bridge of her nose. Silly how after six months of marriage he still couldn't resist the urge to touch her. . . . He jerked his thoughts back in line. This was the middle of the afternoon, and if the laughter dancing in his sister's eyes carried any warning, he'd soon be the brunt of *her* teasing.

"Well, I . . ." Katy lapsed back into her native Norwegian when she couldn't find the right words in English.

"I have a feeling that Pastor Solberg may still be nursing his wounds," Mary Martha added. She smiled up at her brother. "First you take his sweetheart, then you parade your sister by him. Tsk, tsk, tsk. Poor man."

Zeb rolled his eyes. "Poor man indeed. He's got every

matchmaking mama in the countryside courtin' him in her daughter's stead."

"I rest my case." Shaking her head, Mary Martha continued. "Why anyone would want to be a minister's wife is more than I can guess."

Zeb gave her his "don't ask me" look and glanced out at the barn where thirteen-year-old Manda Norton, now Mac-Callister—he and Katy had formally adopted both Manda and five-year-old Deborah just before harvest—was jogging and stopping, the colt obeying her every move. Manda's sister had stayed over at the Bjorklunds' to play with Andrew and Ellie. The three would be going to school for the first time next week.

His thoughts wandered back to the days he and Katy had spent in Montana rounding up wild horses. The mountains drew him with their grandeur, and he knew Katy would go there with him if he asked. But they had a fine farm here and family and friends close for her to enjoy. Not that he didn't also, but he knew homesteading was harder for the women, and it was important for them to have other womenfolk nearby.

Manda had put away the weanling colt and was bringing out one of the young fillies he and Katy had rounded up from the wild horse herd. Now that he had purchased the heavy stallion, in a couple years he would have some fine workhorses for sale, a much needed commodity out here on the Dakota prairies, especially farther west where homesteaders were still breaking the sod. Here in the Red River Valley farmers were trying to improve their stock and plant as many acres of wheat as they could beg, buy, or lease. The coming of the railroad had made shipping easier, and the territory now produced more wheat than several of the eastern states combined.

Mary Martha watched her brother, the pride of him evident on her mobile face. While she'd give anything to get him to come back to the MacCallister homeplace in Missouri, she could tell he was happier here than she'd ever seen him. With the threat of the feuding Galloways finally over, Zeb was a free man and living that freedom with a joy that pleasured her heart. If only her mother would come west also, she could stay here. There was an excitement underlying life here on the prairie that she didn't find in Missouri, where folks still talked about *the war* as if it were last week.

"Katy, why don't you go put your feet up for a spell and take a bit of a nap?"

Katy's eyes snapped open, and she set the rocker to creaking again. "No, I'm fine."

"You may be fine, but your snoring near to woke the bees." Zeb turned from his study of the corrals and, taking his wife's hand, drew her to her feet. "Seems that young'un of ours makes you a mite weary."

"Zeb, the way you talk." The blush bloomed on her cheeks again while her other hand gentled her middle. She tried to catch a yawn but failed, and her eyes twinkled over the effort. "All right, if you insist." She turned to Mary Martha. "Wake me up in a little while, you hear?"

Mary Martha nodded, knowing she would let Katy sleep as long as she could. While Katy wouldn't admit it, anyone with eyes could see the telltale blue shadows under her eyes. The heaves didn't come just in the morning, and they should have been over by now. Once again, she wished her mother were there, her mother with all her years of wisdom, all the doctoring she had done, her herbs and potions.

Surely there must be a wise woman in this area. She resolved to ask Ingeborg at the quilting bee on Saturday. Pastor Solberg wouldn't be at the women's meeting, would he?

❧ ❧

Wagons and teams were tied up at all the hitching rails and more still coming when Mary Martha followed Katy into the church on Saturday morning. If Mary Martha heard one "velkommen," she heard twenty. Did none of them speak English?

"Come, sit over here by me." Kaaren Knutson patted the bench beside her at the quilting frame. "You do quilt, don't you?"

Mary Martha breathed a sigh of relief and nodded. "My mother made sure I knew all the womanly arts, even though my stitches aren't near as tiny or perfect as hers. She finally gave up on me."

"Ja, well, only a few of us here are so particular. We just

try to get the quilts done in time for the next wedding." Katy nodded to the wedding ring patterned quilt stitched onto the frame. "Sometimes we have weddings so close together we have to tie them instead of quilt."

"Lawsamercy." Mary Martha rolled her eyes heavenward and clutched her hands to her bosom, raising a chuckle from the woman with spun gold hair captured in a bun at the base of her neck.

"Now *that* isn't a phrase one would hear around here." Kaaren's smile invited one in return.

"I know. I haven't heard many of the sayings of home since I arrived. I knew that things were different in other parts of the country, but I don't believe I was prepared for *how* different." Mary Martha looked around the room at all the women chattering and laughing while keeping busy with their hands cutting, piecing, stitching.

"Ladies, can we begin now?"

"That's Penny Bjorklund. She owns the general store," Kaaren whispered.

"I know. We met her the day I arrived. Her husband runs the bank, right?"

"And the blacksmith shop. We all have a multitude of jobs around here. Whatever needs doing, someone either steps forward to take it on or gets volunteered. With as small a community as ours, we do for each other."

Mary Martha threaded her needle and took up the stitching line where someone else had left off. Wouldn't you know her predecessor had been of the *perfection* school.

Penny clapped her hands to get the group to settle down. When the din had hushed, she smiled and nodded. "Good. Kaaren, would you read our lesson and lead us in prayer?"

Kaaren smiled at Mary Martha and, pushing her chair back, got to her feet, Bible in hand. While she read in Norwegian, the woman on the other side of Mary Martha whispered the words in English for their guest. Kaaren had chosen part of the Sermon on the Mount, so Mary Martha knew what she read after the first lines were translated. *Blessed are the pure in heart, blessed are they that mourn. . . .* Her mother had read those same words so often, and no matter what her family had lacked, she always said they were indeed blessed.

From what she could see of these women, they believed the same.

Kaaren closed the Bible and looked out over the gathering. "We have been so greatly blessed with health, a good harvest, and with one another. Let us bow our heads and thank our God for what He has done. Then I will close." She bowed her head, and after a few shufflings silence fell.

Outside, the children could be heard laughing and playing, the older caring for the younger. Geese flying overhead sang their own wild song.

Like the others, Mary Martha found it easy to enumerate things to be grateful for. Her family out here with new nieces and a sister-in-law with whom she felt an instant kinship, Zeb's freedom from the Galloways, her safe trip here, a house of God to worship in. With that, a picture of the minister to this flock flashed into her mind. So much for a reverent attitude for prayer. Now that she'd had time to think about it, she was irked. After all, he had been terribly rude.

"Heavenly Father . . ."

Kaaren's words brought Mary Martha back to the moment.

"Thou knowest our hearts, thou knowest our inmost beings, and we thank thee that thou lovest us anyway, for we are thy children and the sheep of thy pasture. Keep us in thy will that we may bring glory and honor to thy name. In Jesus' blessed name we pray. Amen."

There were sniffles as the women echoed her "amen," and several had to surreptitiously wipe their eyes when they raised their heads.

"Thank you, Kaaren. As usual, you have given us food for thought and an opportunity to spend time with our heavenly Father." Penny's eyes looked a bit damp too.

On the surface we all look so fine, but I have a feeling that some of these misty eyes came because of hurts inside that no one wants to admit, me included. Mary Martha watched as Penny took control of herself again and beamed a smile around the room.

"Now, does anyone have anything to say about what has gone on in our meetings before?"

"Ja, what happened with the letter you sent to find out about Manda and Deborah's homestead?" Mrs. Valders' feather on her hat bobbed as she spoke.

"I still have heard nothing, so I sent another letter. I have a feeling Mr. MacCallister is going to have to make a trip out there to settle this thing. It would be his place now that he and Katy have officially adopted the girls."

"Ja, he's been thinking on that, but he had to wait until harvest was over." Katy looked up from cutting out bits of cotton one and one-quarter inch square to piece for the wedding ring pattern. "We hate to take the girls out of school, but they want to see their homeplace again."

"Can't say as I blame them." Ingeborg joined the conversation. "We'll take care of your chores while you are away."

Penny nodded. "I know cousin Ephraim wouldn't mind living out there again."

"On the matter of women's votes, you know, like we talked about before?" Wrenlike, Mrs. Dyrfinna Odell raised her hand as she spoke, glancing at Hildegunnn Valders as if to ask permission.

Penny nodded. "What is it you want to say?"

"I . . . I read that the men don't want our proposal even on the ballot. The *Fargo Argus* had a big article about it. The . . . the man who wrote it said God didn't make women to think well enough to make decisions like choosing our government officials."

"Ah, yes, the men are doing such a fine job themselves what with all the graft going on in President Cleveland's administration. And if you look into the Indian matters, the reality between what was ordered and what gets to those poor misfortunate beings is inhuman." Penny rolled her eyes and took a breath. "I better not get going on this, or I'll go on for hours." She shook her head again. "And that Louisiana Lottery they're trying to push over on us, oh!"

"So, I want to know how we are going to get our men to vote for women's suffrage."

"Oh, pshaw," Agnes Baard said with a shake of her head, "we just tell 'em no vote, no—"

"Agnes!" Penny had to roll her lips to keep from laughing out loud.

" . . . cookies to go with their coffee." Agnes finished with an innocent look on her face. "What did you think I was going to say?"

While some of the women snickered either into a handkerchief or behind their hands, others laughed out loud.

But through all this, the work continued as if minds and hands were two entirely separate entities. Mary Martha marveled at them, since she had to quit stitching to follow the conversations.

"While I know that some of you have met my sister-in-law, I'd like to introduce her to those of you who haven't yet had the honor." Katy stood and motioned Mary Martha to do the same. "Mary Martha MacCallister is here from Missouri to visit. Let's speak English as much as possible so she can join in. Now if the rest of you would say your names, she can get to know us all."

Katy sat down, making Mary Martha feel as if a spotlight shone right on her. She could feel her cheeks heating up as around the room all the women introduced themselves.

"We're going to give you a test at the end," whispered Kaaren.

"Thank you." Mary Martha sat down and whispered back, "If you made me pronounce them all, that would be hard enough."

"We are glad you are here," Penny added at the end. "Now, was there anything else?"

"Ja, but we didn't talk about this before." Ingeborg nodded toward Bridget, who was stitching on the quilt across the corner from Mary Martha.

"So, let's start now." Penny nodded to Bridget, who put a hand to her breast and rolled her eyes beseechingly at Ingeborg.

"No, you tell them," Ingeborg said.

Bridget got to her feet, clasped and unclasped her hands, and launched into rapid fire Norwegian. She finished in the same rush and sat back down.

"She wants to build a boardinghouse here in Blessing, but her son thinks she is too old. She wants to know what we all think." Kaaren hit the high points for Mary Martha.

"Why, the nerve of him. From what I've seen and heard of Bridget, she has the energy of one half her age. And from what

Penny said the other day, a boardinghouse would be a good idea."

"It is." Kaaren agreed. "I think Hjelmer is just being cautious."

"If Bridget decides to do this, we will help her." Mrs. Valders glanced around at the others, and they all nodded. "Contrary to other political situations, we have as much say at the bank meetings as the men do. She will most certainly be given the loan. After all, the men borrow money for machinery from the bank and for barns and such. Why can't a woman take out a loan too?"

"For the same reason they think we can't vote." The voice came from the group at the cutting table.

"Bridget, you need a savings account at the bank." Penny looked around for the approval of others.

"But I . . . I have no money."

"Of course you do. I sold those sweaters you knitted, the soakers, and the wool stockings. If I pay you in cash rather than dress goods and such, you could open an account. Then you will have a vote just like the rest of us."

A flutter of frowns crossed Bridget's forehead, disappearing into her snowy hair. When she nodded, she smiled at the same time. "I am in America now. I will try this new thing."

"Then we must sit down and begin to figure out what the building and furnishings are going to cost." Penny nodded as she spoke. "I have price lists from companies that will help us get an idea of costs."

"Uff da." Bridget shuddered. "I must be a crazy woman to think I can do such a thing. Maybe Hjelmer is right. I am too old."

"No, just as we broke the sod one furrow at a time, we will raise this new building one board at a time." Ingeborg leaned toward the bestemor of her two sons. "You can call it Bridget's Boardinghouse or The Bjorklund Boardinghouse. Either one will look good on a sign right on top of the porch roof so all can see it."

"Just don't serve any spirits there is all I say." A comment again from one of those at the cutting table.

Penny waited a moment before continuing. "If there is nothing else, then, help yourself to the coffee and cake whenever you want. We will serve dinner at noon like always." She made her way to the quilting frame and took a seat between Bridget and Kaaren.

"I'm glad to get that part out of the way." She reached for her needle. "Oh, Kaaren, one of the ladies asked if you would read to us again like you have in the past. Would that be all right?"

Needles flew as Kaaren read from the Psalms and then asked for any favorites. One woman asked for the story of Ruth, so Kaaren turned to that book.

Mary Martha let the sounds flow over her, wishing she understood the words. Women went about the business of quilt making, took care of the children, nursed their babies, and wiped away a tear once in a while, at the same time listening to what the Scriptures had to say. After she finished reading, Kaaren took her whimpering baby, Samuel, and, folding a blanket over her shoulder, set him to nursing.

When they broke for the noon meal, a male voice intruded on the female conversation.

Mary Martha knew immediately who it was even before she heard the "Welcome, Pastor Solberg, you are just in time." *Why is it that I know his voice already? It isn't as if we've been acquainted for a long time or anything. Why does just hearing his voice bother me?*

The thoughts raced as she schooled her face to neutrality, continuing her description of the homeplace in Missouri to Kaaren and Ingeborg. They were having a difficult time understanding the term hollow, or holler, as she said it.

"I don't know," Ingeborg said with a sigh, accompanied by a gentle smile. "Between our Norwegian accents and your Missouri drawl, our understanding of each other might be nothing short of a miracle."

"Zeb and Katy surely did work it out real fastlike. You should have seen them. Zeb went to the classes where our new immigrants were learning English so he could learn enough Norwegian to help out. We had many good laughs over that." Kaaren motioned Mary Martha toward the table where the food was set out.

"Kaaren and Agnes helped with the English classes and probably will again," Ingeborg said from her other side.

"Agnes helped out with what?" Agnes said, joining them.

When they reached the head of the line, they gestured for their guest to go first. Mary Martha turned toward the table and glanced over to another just in time to catch the glance of Pastor Solberg.

He looked at her as if she weren't there, as if he could see right through her.

She felt like waving her hand in front of his face just to get that look out of his eyes. But instead she turned to dish up her soup and buttered bread. Surely that must be the problem. The man had no manners. None at all.

And if that were the case, how on earth did he shepherd this flock, who certainly seemed to hold him in high esteem.

Was there something wrong with *her*?

4

"I'm going to school today. I'm going to school today," Andrew recited in a singsong voice.

"Not if you don't hold still. *Andrew Bjorklund*, I mean it." Ingeborg tapped her young son on the shoulder. She raised the scissors again. "I *am* trimming your hair, and you *are* sitting still."

"Ellie and Deborah are going too."

"Ja, I know."

"Pastor Solberg will be our teacher."

"True." She snipped a bit more off the left side in the back, leaving no curls along his neck. The top now lay in waves, but she knew as soon as the wind caught it, the nearly white curls would fly free again.

"I like Pastor Solberg." Andrew looked up at her.

Ingeborg rolled her eyes. "Andrew, sit still, or you will look very strange."

"Andew petty." Astrid studied her big brother with adoring eyes. "Me go too."

"No, you're too little." Andrew shook his head, flinched, looked up to the right to catch his mother's frown, and froze. "Sorry."

Astrid straightened her spine and glared at her brother. "Me go."

"She surely is a Bjorklund. Look at that jaw." Bridget scooped up the two-and-a-half-year-old in her arms and kissed her rosy cheek. "Astrid can help Bestemor bake cookies."

"Cookies?" She clapped her pudgy hands to her grand-mother's cheeks, then looked over her shoulder at Andrew. "Andew no cookies." The tip of her straight little nose rose in the air just a mite. Astrid knew how to act like a queen bee when she wanted to.

"You be good now. We don't want any bad reports." Bridget smiled at Andrew, who looked at her as if she'd grown two new sets of ears.

"I am always good."

Bridget and Astrid headed for the well house, giggles floating over their shoulders.

"Mor?"

"What?"

"I *am* good all the time, ain't I?" He looked up at her with eyes of Bjorklund blue, slightly darkened with the seriousness of his question.

Ingeborg whisked away the dish towel she had tied around his neck and kissed his cheek. "Most of the time, and I know you will do all you are asked at school."

"Mor. Hurry him up." Nearly twelve years old, Thorliff carried in an armload of wood and dumped it in the woodbox by the cast-iron cookstove. "We're going to be late, and we can't be late on the first day of school." The horrified look on his face made his mother smile. He brushed the bark and chips off his arms and the front of his sweater, one that Bridget had just finished knitting for him the night before.

"No, you won't. Lars is taking you. He has to go to town anyway."

"Good." He studied his brother. "You got your slate?"

Andrew nodded.

"Your lunch pail?"

Another nod.

"A handkerchief?" At the third nod, Thorliff pursed his lips and narrowed his eyes, studying his younger brother.

Andrew sat like a small creature in the grass when the shadow of a hawk flies overhead. At Thorliff's nod, the little boy let out a long held breath. He'd passed inspection. He leaped off the stool and ran around the table once, then again, singing out happily, "School today. School today."

Thorliff and Ingeborg exchanged looks of both pride and

laughter. Andrew had always been the one to make the two who had a tendency to seriousness smile and laugh.

I'm going to miss him. Ingeborg hid the thought carefully from her sensitive older son. *Thank God for Astrid. But she will soon be on the way too and then what? Why, oh why, don't you trust me with another baby, Lord? Have I been so evil in your sight? Do you not believe me when I plead for another child? What can I do to change your mind?*

All the while she kept a smile on her face and forced the clouds away from her eyes. Knowing in her head that God knew of His plans for her and convincing her heart were two different things.

The jingle of horse harnesses and a sharp bark from Thorliff's dog, Paws, announced the arrival of the wagon.

Andrew headed for the door, skidded to a stop on the braided oval rug, and spun around. He grabbed his lunch pail and slate off the table and headed back outside.

"Andrew."

Another screeching halt. This time he ran back to his mother, gave her a peck on the cheek, suffered through a hug, and danced out to the wagon.

Thorliff, who had grown so over the summer that the two of them stood nearly eye to eye, looked to his mother and shook his head. "Andrew, he gets kinda excited." With that he took his own things, tipped his head for a quick kiss on the cheek and a pat on the shoulder, and joined Andrew in the wagon box behind their uncle Lars. Hamre, their twelve-year-old distant cousin who had come from Norway the year before with Bridget, sat on the seat beside the driver. The family resemblance was so strong that a stranger would have thought the three were brothers. While he nodded at their greeting, he, as usual, said nothing.

Bridget and Astrid came out of the springhouse to wave them off, and Ingeborg did the same from the top of the steps. A running figure caught the wagon before they passed the barns. Baptiste, dark hair flying as he leaped in great strides, swung into the back of the wagon as it kept on rolling. Grandson of Metiz, the French-Indian friend of the family, and Thorliff's best friend, Baptiste would rather be hunting and fishing out on the land he loved. He suffered school for his friend's sake and because Metiz insisted that he learn to live in the white man's world. Thanks to Metiz and her grandson, the settlers of Blessing—mostly the Bjorklunds—had learned to live off the land too. Metiz taught Ingeborg about the healing herbs growing around them and how to use them.

"He almost waited too long, huh?" Bridget said, her basket full of eggs, a crock of buttermilk, and a haunch of venison Baptiste had brought them two days earlier. Astrid carried an egg carefully in each hand.

"Ja, that rascal." Ingeborg drew in a deep breath. Someone already had their smokehouse going—must be Metiz with the venison. This would be her first winter in the frame house Haakan and Lars had built for her on her three acres by the river. A haze lay across the land, blurring the edges of trees and the cattle out in the pasture. Geese and ducks sang their leaving song in the skies above, their V formations nearly clouding the sun at times.

Off in the field she could see Haakan waving at the passing wagon. Row after row of black soil rolled over from the blade of his plow as he and the team made their way back and forth across the wheat fields. All of the prairie land they owned was now broken to the plow except for the acres they kept for hay and pasture.

Ingeborg glanced up at the sky again. What she wouldn't give to take the gun this afternoon and go bag some geese, both for the meat and the feathers. They never seemed to have enough down for pillows and feather beds, and roast goose would be such a treat. If she were lucky, she might even get a deer. With all the land settled around them, the deer had become more scarce so close to home.

All good reasons. With the boys back in school, they wouldn't be able to hunt as they had lately, so . . . *so why not me? If Bridget is too scandalized by my britches, well, she . . . she can just live with it. So what if it isn't exactly ladylike.*

Haakan would roll his eyes and tease her about her need to be out in the woods, but as long as she didn't insist on working the fields, he'd allow her this. Kaaren would shake her head, but it would all be worth it to walk free in the woods and fields. Maybe she'd find a hazelnut bush or a bee tree.

She could feel the anticipation welling within her like a

spring newly uncapped. Freedom! Freedom from the hot kitchen, four walls, and hampering skirts.

But in the meantime, she'd better get the bread to rising.

We're going to need more desks, Pastor Solberg thought as he counted the children lining up from the smallest to the largest in front of the school door. A bit of a scuffle ensued toward the end of the ranks where the bigger boys vied for position. A wagon coming from the north promised more pupils. He'd have to talk to Olaf Wold and see when he would have time to build a couple more tables and benches, but for now they'd have to crowd closer together.

"Children, quiet now. Please count off." He nodded to Ellie Peterson Wold. "You begin—one."

"One." She glanced over her shoulder to Andrew Bjork-lund.

"Two." He looked toward the wagon. "Deborah will be three."

Two girls jumped from the wagon and raced toward the lineup. "Sorry," Manda Norton MacCallister panted as she skidded into her place in front of Thorliff.

"You're three," Andrew whispered to Deborah, loud enough for the crow flying above to hear.

"No, I ain't. I'm five," Deborah hissed back, stepping into place behind him.

"We're numbering off," John explained, hiding the smile that tugged at his lips. He'd learned early on that if he was strict and stern the first few days of school, he could relax and be himself later and not encounter any discipline problems. Sometimes that was hard, as right now. The little ones were so earnest. He glanced up to wave good-bye to their driver and was forced to try to hide his shock. Miss MacCallister had driven the children in. He finished his wave, grateful she couldn't see the heat rising up his neck. He'd been so rude the other day. The guilt of it flamed him every time the thought returned. He'd been ungentlemanly, let alone unpastoral. While she visited here, she was part of his flock and deserved respectful attention. He would have to apologize.

"Twenty-nine," called out fifteen-year-old Swen Baard.

"Thank you," Solberg called back, hiding his surprise that the Baard boys returned this year. Joseph had grumbled last spring about needing his sons in the fields, that they had all the book learning they needed. Agnes must have put her foot down.

"Since we have more pupils this year, we will be somewhat crowded until we get new desks, so I expect you all to treat each other with good manners." He dreaded the thought of having the older boys and girls sharing the higher benches, especially because of the teasing that went on with the Baard boys. He'd almost looked forward to their not being here this year.

He looked down at a tug on his coattails.

"Pathtor Tholberg, I brung you thith." Slender to the point of emaciation, Anna Helmsrude held out a bright red apple for him. "I picked it juth for you."

He wanted to gather the little girl into his arms and shield her from all harm. "Thank you, Anna," he said, his face as serious as her own. The Helmsrude family had more pride than possessions, but Anna insisted on bringing him presents. How would he ever find time this year to help her get over her lisp when he had so many students? *Dear God, help her get through another winter. She is so frail.* Praying for his pupils, as well as his congregation, was as natural as breathing. Listening for the answers took more doing.

He turned and led the way into the soddy classroom that was formerly the church and school combined. As the children passed the line of pegs along the back wall, they hung up their coats and set their lunch pails on the shelf built for that purpose, then made their way to the benches. Just as he feared, there were more boys than girls in the upper grades.

Baptiste and Swen eyed the same seat.

Thorliff raised his hand. "I can sit on the floor today and bring a chair tomorrow."

"I can stay home." The giggles that answered Baptiste's reply showed how the children had come to accept him as one of their own.

"Thank you, Thorliff, but why don't you go over to my house and get a chair from there for today? We'll work something else out tomorrow." Actually he'd thought of having Thorliff help him with the younger children. The boy learned quickly and was so far ahead of the others that keeping him busy took plenty of forethought.

As Thorliff left the room, the others settled in.

John Solberg glanced around the room. Most everyone had slates, and several had new books they raised with pride when they saw him looking. Those who read well were already studying the bookshelves, one of which held all new books he'd ordered over the summer. Other books had been sent by his mother, who had impressed the ladies of her church to consider Blessing School their mission for the year. He hoped to have boxes for the children to open and delight over once in a while.

"We will now stand for the Pledge of Allegiance and our morning Scripture reading, after which we will ask our heavenly Father to bless this school year." The older children got to their feet, and the younger followed suit.

Pastor Solberg pointed to the American flag hanging in the corner and put his hand over his heart. The older girls helped the younger children get the right hand in place, and they all stood erect.

"I pledge allegiance to the flag. . . ." John spoke slowly and clearly so that the children could follow easily. At the end he turned back to his class "Very good. We'll work on memorizing that for all the new ones here." He picked up his Bible and waited for the rustlings to cease. "Today we are reading from Matthew, where Jesus is talking to His disciples and a large crowd. 'He said, "Suffer the little children come unto me, and forbid them not: for of such is the kingdom of God." ' " John looked up at the serious faces before him. "You see, Jesus has a special place in His heart for little children, but we are all His children, some of us just older than others.

"Shall we pray?" He waited again until all heads were bowed, eyes closed, and hands folded.

"Heavenly Father, we thank thee for the life and death of thy son, Jesus the Christ. We are glad that He is here with us right now to bless our school and our hearts and minds so that we might learn quickly and behave in a quiet and godly manner. Be with us now, in Jesus' name. Amen."

Lifting his head he looked at his students and breathed a quiet prayer that God would give him the wisdom needed to guide these lives entrusted to him.

"You may be seated," he told them.

He took up his pad of paper and newly sharpened quill pen to write the children's names and ages, later to fill in their grade according to their level of learning. Some still spoke little English, but he had resolved to no longer talk Norwegian in the schoolroom. These children would learn to speak English if he taught them nothing else. It wouldn't be long before the weekly language classes for their parents would begin again also.

"I would like all of our new pupils to come forward and line up beside my desk. The rest of you may choose a book from the shelf and read to yourselves until I am finished." He ignored the two groans, feeling fairly certain which throats they came from. Baptiste would never say a word, but the Baard boys were not so reticent. He knew for certain who it was when their younger sister Anji hissed at them. He had a fair idea that Agnes would deal with them when they got home.

One by one he wrote down the names of the four youngest, asking them their ages and how to spell their names. He looked at Ellie. "It is Peterson or Wold now?"

"Wold." Her smile lit her face.

"So the adoption is final?"

She nodded. "Pa said so."

All but one passed with flying colors, and that was because he only spoke Norwegian. When John translated, the little boy did fine.

"Very good. Now, can you recite your alphabet?" At their looks of confusion, he said, "your ABC's?"

Andrew led the way. "A." He glanced at the other boy. With only minor prompting from the teacher, they rushed through to the end. "Z. That's the sound the saw makes. Zzzzzz." Andrew flashed a grin up at the teacher.

"You're right. And that's the sound of bees buzzzzing too." John smiled at each of them. "Now, how far can you count?"

Ellie went the furthest with twenty-nine. She'd shut her eyes to remember the last numbers, so when she opened them, the teacher smiling at her made her cheeks turn red.

"Very good. Now, you four may take your seats and write your letters on your slate. Anji Baard will help you if needed." As they filed away, Toby and Jerry White, soon to be Valders, stepped forward.

"We ain't had no schoolin'—"

"'Cept what our new mama gived us." Neither of the boys looked too excited about it now either.

"Can you spell your names?" They shook their heads. "How old are you?" Shrugs. John had talked with Hildegunn Valders, and they decided the boys were about seven and nine, Jerry being the eldest.

"I . . . I can count." At the teacher's nod, Jerry scrunched his eyes closed and rattled 1–2–3–4–5–6–7–8–10 without a breath.

"Nine."

"Huh?" His eyes popped open.

"Nine. Nine comes before ten."

"Oh, I forgot." He shut his eyes again, rapid fired through eight, added nine, and his eyes flew open again. "Ten!"

"Very good." Pastor Solberg looked up, hoping to catch Thorliff's eye, but the boy had his nose in a book. The whole soddy could blow down before Thorliff would know it. John had learned it did no good to call the boy's name. He wouldn't hear. So he laid a hand on Toby's shoulder and pointed to the boy on the chair. "You go ask Thorliff to help you and Jerry with your numbers and your alphabet."

The two did as asked, and John turned to three stairstep children standing before him, all looking so much alike except for their height that he'd have sworn they were cut from matching cookie cutters. They spoke only Norwegian, would have to have smile training, and the eldest, Mary, obviously didn't want to be there. When John quizzed them in Norwegian, they answered in monosyllables. The Erickson sisters made reticent Hamre Bjorklund seem like a chatterbox.

By dinnertime, Solberg had cabin fever as bad as the children. Since Indian summer had given them a glorious day, he sent them outside to eat and run off some of their boundless energy.

Eight new pupils. How would he handle so many children with such a variety of ages and education? Or lack thereof? Last year had been easy in retrospect.

A girl screaming from outside drew him flying to the door.

5

"M iz Bjorklund, there's a drummer here wants to talk with you."

"Thank you, Mr. Valders, I'll be right there. On second thought, send him back for a cup of coffee. He can show me what he's selling here." Penny Bjorklund glanced around her kitchen, which turned into a restaurant for the noon meal. She had just served dinners to eight men who worked on the track repair gang for the railroad. Several of them had become regulars, two wondering when there would be a place in Blessing for them to sleep.

They really did need the boardinghouse or a hotel. She thought back to the months she'd worked in the Headquarters Hotel in Fargo while finishing high school. And waited for Hjelmer.

"Mrs. Bjorklund?" The man paused on the other side of the curtain between the store and the Bjorklund home.

"Yes, come on in." Smiling, she looked up from clearing the last table. "How can I help you?"

A man not much taller than her five foot six inches edged through the door with his sales case first. Setting the carryall down, he removed his black bowler hat and glanced around the cheerful room. "Ah, now isn't this like home?" Hat over his heart, he nodded and almost bowed at the same time. "The man out front said I was to talk with you. Not Mr. Bjorklund?" The tentative note in his voice showed as wrinkles on his broad forehead. While he didn't appear older, his hair had begun to recede, making his prominent nose even more so.

"That's right, unless you need to speak to the banker or the blacksmith. Hjelmer is both." She brushed the last crumb into her palm and gestured to the straight-backed chair. "Have a seat, and I'll get you a cup of coffee. You take cream?"

He shook his head and sniffed the air. "Smells like home too. I ain't been home for a long time, you see, and this . . . this room and . . . and you, why, my Emma would think she was looking in a mirror." He slid into the chair Penny had pulled out and continued to look around, smiling at the things he saw.

While Penny poured him a cup of coffee and placed cookies on a plate, she followed his glance. Red-and-white gingham curtains at the window, a braided rug in front of the door and another in front of the cast-iron stove polished to a high sheen, woodbox newly filled, thanks to cousin Ephraim, white painted cupboards along one wall with a counter for her to work on. Two square tables and one round table with four chairs at each took up much of the room, leaving only a corner for Hjelmer's rocking chair.

They really did need more space if the business continued to pick up as it had been.

She set the food in front of the man. "You know my name, but . . ."

"Oh, pardon me." He half rose and ducked his head. "I'm Alfred Drummond, proud purveyor of Singer sewing machines, the latest invention to make life easier for America's women."

"Sewing machines?" Via some of the others who provided her with merchandise for her store, Penny had heard tell of some newfangled machine that could sew faster and stronger than anyone with a needle.

"Wait until you see how fast you can sew a seam." He talked around a mouthful of molasses cookie. "Making a dress takes no time at all. And strong, just like store bought." He slurped his coffee and dunked the crisp cookie again. "Why, you could carry a line of Singer sewing machines right here in your store, like you do the John Deere plows outside."

Sewing had never been Penny's favorite pastime, so when he said speed, he had her undivided attention. "How much are the machines?"

"See those curtains up there, why you could hem a house-ful in a short afternoon." He drained his cup. "If I could set one up and show you, I know you would be both surprised and pleased. Every woman in Blessing will want one."

Penny glanced at the clock. Anner Valders, who did the bookkeeping for the bank and sometimes worked in the store for her when cousin Ephraim was needed elsewhere, had asked if he could go home early today. Since he never asked for favors, she had agreed.

"I'm sorry, but I don't have time today. Will you be coming back through here again?"

"I can wait."

"Until tomorrow?" Hjelmer had gone to Grafton on the morning train, or she would ask him. There was no one else unless Ephraim came back early too.

"I could set it up in a corner of your store, and then if any ladies come in, they could come and see what I was doing. Surely you have some tea towels or sheets or something that needs hemming."

If he only knew. Her basket of sewing and mending had been mushrooming lately. Somehow she just never got to it. And with all her dinner guests, she needed more napkins every day, as well as tablecloths. Even though she knew the railroad men ate in cookshacks at long trestle tables and were lucky if the plates were clean, she made sure they had a taste of home in her kitchen. If only she had room and time to set up more tables.

If Bridget doesn't build that boardinghouse, I will. And hire her to run it. The thought made her catch her breath. That's what she would tell Hjelmer the next time the discussion arose. And since he already thought she had more than she could handle, he would be forced to agree to his mother's petition for a loan.

"Miz Bjorklund." Anner Valders' call from the store brought her back from her musings. She looked up to find Mr. Drummond staring at her. He must think her addled.

"Coming," she called to Anner, then nodded to the man at her table. "Come, I'll show you a place and bring you some muslin to hem for napkins."

"Thank you. You won't regret this, you know."

A long whistle blew south of town. As the train drew nearer, the floor began to shake, and the pots hanging above the stove rattled together. Since Valders was leaving, she would have to put the mail out too. And she hadn't set the chicken to roast for supper yet. They might be having pancakes again. She could always serve chicken and dumplings tomorrow to the dinner crowd.

"Mail's here," sang out the conductor. She heard the sack thunk on the counter in the store.

"Come, Mr. Drummond, I am needed in the store."

She showed the man where to set up his machine, provided the chair he asked for, and took over from Anner Valders in sorting the mail, inserting it into the slots with the names of the area families written below.

"See you tomorrow, then?" Valders untied his apron.

"Sure enough." Penny reached into the peppermint stick jar. "And take these to Toby and Jerry to celebrate their first day in school."

"I got me a feeling it's going to take more than peppermint sticks to make those two like school." He shook his head, stuffing the candy in his shirt pocket. Since he had lost an arm in a threshing accident, his pockets served almost as another hand. "Mrs. Valders' been working with them two, but they ain't much for book learning or even sitting still. I got to help them tonight with their numbers."

Even though his tone grumbled, Penny knew he was right proud of his two adopted sons who'd come in on the train during the summer and got caught stealing food from the store. Near as anyone could tell, how the two had made it this far in the world was one of God's special miracles, and that He'd brought them to Blessing when He did, another. Anner and Hildegunn had needed the boys as much as the boys needed a home.

Penny heard laughter and a buzz of conversation from the group gathering at the front door. She tossed several pieces of mail on the counter to be opened by herself later, then flipped the Mail's In sign and stepped out of the way of the customers. Many of them would pick up other things on their way out, so while Penny didn't get paid much from the United States Postal Service, she made out in the long run.

"Any cheese?" called Mrs. Johnson. "That Ingeborg makes the best cheese."

"Right here." Penny measured off three inches or so of the wheel. "This much?"

"About twice that." Mrs. Johnson, her girth increasing again, leaned her belly against the counter. "What's that man doing back there with some contraption?"

"He's going to show me how to use his sewing machine."

"Sewing machine? What's wrong with a needle and thread?"

"He says it is faster and stronger. I'll believe it when I see it."

Within minutes she was cleaned out of the last loaves of bread, the wheel of cheese was half gone, and the new order of headcheese spices sorely depleted. Butchering season was almost upon them. Good thing both Bridget and Hildegunn were bringing bread in the morning. And Bridget would stay to help her cook and serve the noon meal.

As the last of the customers visited their way out the door, Penny made her way to the corner with the sewing machine and the salesman, straightening merchandise as she went. The machine had a song of its own, but until she reached it, she wondered at the strange noises.

The man sat hunched over a shiny black machine that was trimmed in gilt and set on an oak cabinet. The intricate cast-iron legs were joined by a flat treadle that he pumped with one foot. The stitching portion hummed along as the hemmed muslin square flowed out behind it.

"Well, I never . . ."

Mr. Drummond picked up the napkin, snipped the threads with a small pair of scissors he wore on a ribbon around his neck, and handed her the napkin. "There you go." He nodded to a neat pile of squares lying on the board attached to the right side of the cabinet.

Penny examined the even stitching of the hemming. Both sides looked exactly the same. "How—I mean—what . . ." She shook her head, eyes widening in delight. "This is amazing."

"So it is." Mr. Drummond smiled, showing one blank space where a lower front tooth should have been. "I can guarantee that quilts, curtains, dresses, children's clothing—anything you do now with a needle and thread—will be done easier, faster, and stronger."

"Even sewing on buttons?"

His face melted into sadness. "Sorry, no."

"Blind stitching a hem?"

He nodded. "Yes, it can, but that's not a skill for beginners. However, when you own a Singer sewing machine, you will finish most of your sewing so quickly that those finishing touches will take only moments in comparison. Can I show you this from beginning to end?"

Wait until Ingeborg sees this. Penny shook her head slowly, one index finger on the point of her chin.

"But, dear lady, you've only seen one product. When you understand how easy this little gem is to operate, why, you must try it yourself."

"How much?"

He named a price that made her blink.

"But the beauty of this is that you only have to pay a little bit down, and the rest is only pennies a month. This plan makes it possible for every woman in America to have a Singer sewing machine in her own home. Think what this will do to ease the burden on your friends and family."

Penny held up a hand to stop his spate of words. "Easy, Mr. Drummond, easy. I see how this machine can help the women. I can see a hundred uses for it, but I can tell you right now that the people of Blessing are a thrifty lot and don't take too easily to new things."

"Do the men buy plows and mowers, binders and threshers?"

Penny had to agree.

"But not things like that for the home?"

"There haven't been things like that for the home."

"Ah, but they are coming, and this little beauty"—he laid a reverent palm on the wheel of the machine—"will revolutionize the way women sew clothing for themselves, their families, and their households."

"I know. Now I have to figure out how to do this."

"If you order one today, it will be shipped directly from the factory and be here in two weeks. Then I will return and train you how to use it so you can teach others." He rubbed a hand over his balding pate. "I saw those women eyeing me when they came in for the mail. Having a machine set up like this will increase your business and provide a much needed service for the women of Blessing and parts beyond. You will be the first store north of Grand Forks to carry the Singer sewing machine. Why, down in Fargo a woman is opening an entire store just to sell sewing machines. Can you believe that?" He stroked the machine as if it were a favorite horse or dog. "Of course she will soon be selling the latest silks and cottons, wools and linens. I can just see it—The Sewing Emporium."

The tinkling bell caught her attention. "Excuse me, Mr. Drummond. I have another customer." She hustled toward the front of the store. "Goodie, how wonderful to see you. Why, here you live almost next door, and it seems like forever since I've seen you."

"I . . . ah . . . haven't felt good the last couple of days." Goodie Peterson Wold dropped her gaze to her hands. "I lost the baby, you know." Her fingers twined around one another, as if by moving they would right the wrong that tore at the woman's heart and soul.

"No, I didn't know. Oh, Goodie, I'm so sorry." Penny put an arm around the woman's shoulders. "Did you call for Ingeborg and Metiz?"

"No, it happened too fast." Goodie sighed. "One minute I was rejoicing, and the next I felt this terrible cramp, and it was gone." Her head wagged from side to side, more perpetual motion. "I just want to give Olaf a son. He is so good to me and mine."

"But you will, surely." Penny forced a note of cheer into her voice. She who would give anything to be expecting, and God seemed to be looking the other way. "Is that why you missed the quilting bee?"

Goodie nodded. "Do you have any molasses? I been hankering for some gingerbread something awful."

Penny thought a moment. "Let me check." Knowing she'd had Ephraim wash out the molasses barrel, she went to her own cupboard and returned with a half-full jar. "This is all, but you are welcome to it."

"Thank you. You are a real friend." Goodie dug in her bag. "How much do I owe you?"

"Nothing. I've got some molasses cookies left. How about some of those to last until you get the gingerbread baked?" Penny laid a hand on Goodie's arm. "Besides, you look as if you need to lie down, not bake."

Goodie cocked her head. "What's that strange sound I hear?"

"Oh my, I near forgot. The sewing machine man is here." Penny called that over her shoulder as she went for the cookies. "Go on back and talk with him."

When Penny returned, Goodie and Mr. Drummond were talking like old friends, and the sewing machine hummed between them. Goodie's cheeks were pink again, and the sparkle had returned to her eyes.

Clearly she was in love—with a sewing machine.

Penny hoped Olaf was making plenty of money at the sack house, for it appeared he was about to purchase some new machinery.

"Can I bring Olaf back to see this?" Goodie looked from the machine to Penny and back again. "Why I could open me a dressmaking business right down the street from your front door. Blessing needs more businesses, just as you always said. Are you going to sell these in your store?" She looked around the room, every square inch of floor already filled, up the walls and things hanging from the ceiling.

Penny eyed the hand corn planter hanging from one beam and the carved saddle that rested on a small half barrel attached to the wall. She wished she'd dusted more recently. Ugh, the cobwebs. Some of the things had been there since her first order.

Penny listened while Mr. Drummond told Goodie about the sewing store opening in Fargo, all the while watching Goodie's face. Clearly the idea intrigued her.

Worries raced through Penny's mind. Was there room for two places to sell sewing materials in Blessing? Dress goods and the attending notions were a good part of her inventory. Penny nibbled on her bottom lip. If Goodie followed her dream, should she stop carrying the calicos and ginghams?

Or should she put the machines in her store? Where was Hjelmer when she needed him?

6

Freedom smelled like fall.

Ingeborg kicked into a pile of oak leaves still rich with the oranges and burgundies of newly fallen leaves. She wanted to lie down and roll in them, as she did when she was a child. The oak trees of Norway and the oak trees of Dakota wore the same painted fall dresses and rich perfume. A squirrel scolded her for intruding upon his territory.

Ingeborg laughed at his antics, then shifted the rifle to her other hand and broke into a trot. The geese would be settling down soon for their evening feed, and she wanted to be there before then. The wheat field south of the Bjorklund land, bordered by the swamp, was a favorite resting place. Any wheat that the thresher missed had sprouted again, thanks to the warm fall rains, and made perfect grazing for the geese.

She wished she had spent more time practicing with the shotgun so she could have brought it instead. It wasn't that Haakan really frowned on her using firearms. He just didn't quite understand why they were so important to her. After all, Baptiste and Thorliff, besides grazing the sheep, managed to supply much of their wild game and fish. Both boys were excellent hunters.

"So am I," she proclaimed, and the sound of her voice sent a crow flapping from the tree, his raucous voice announcing her presence. "Uff da," she muttered low enough for only her own ears. "I know better than that." *Every self-respecting deer in the country will hear that crow and head for cover. Ah well, it is geese I came for, and geese I will get.* Ignoring the game trails to the river, she settled herself behind a thicket of Juneberry bushes. There was still enough leaf cover to make a blind for her, and she'd wait until there were plenty of the Canada honkers on the ground. Big as they were, they made for easy hunting.

The haunting cries came close as a large V settled to graze, the swamp close enough to provide moisture. The heavy beat of their wings, the honking between the birds, and the beauty of their landing made her clutch the gun more tightly. Such magnificent creatures they were, with their gray bodies and black heads and necks. More continued to land, and those on the ground nibbled the tender grass shoots and picked the seeds of any standing grasses and wheat.

She felt guilty for her presence, wishing she could just sit and watch and listen to their chatter. Instead she slowly raised her gun and sighted. With six shots she had five geese and another couple that were wounded. With a beating of wings and honks of protest, the flock rose. She downed another on the wing with the last shell.

Ingeborg moved swiftly, dispatching with her knife the two that she'd wounded and gathering up the carcasses. She cut throats and held each up to bleed out. She'd have to build a travois like Metiz had taught her to get them all home. They were far too heavy to carry even with some tied across her shoulders. Farther out in the field more geese settled down.

She jingled the shells in her pocket. That was another good thing about britches. They had deep pockets. She could go for more, but then she would be so late getting home. Eight wasn't bad. Even Roald would have been impressed with that. But then Roald was long gone, and Haakan would be pleased because she was pleased. Even though he'd tease her about her britches, secretly—or not so secretly to an observant wife— he'd wish she wouldn't wear them any longer. Why were men so set against women wearing pants? Kneeling in the garden to weed was far easier without skirts and apron. So was driving the team during harvest, getting up and down the wagon wheels. All the while the thoughts ran through her head, she searched for straight saplings to use as poles.

Taking her knife, Ingeborg slashed down the two slender trunks she'd decided on and stripped off some thicker branches. Then using the twine she'd brought for this purpose, she tied those farther toward the tops on the saplings and wove more branches in to create a bed. Laying the geese on the woven bed along with the empty rifle, she took a pole in each hand and began the trip home, dragging the load behind her. Metiz had shown her how to fashion a harness for her shoulders, but the load wasn't that heavy nor the distance that far.

Paws announced her arrival, yipping and dancing beside her as she slowly trudged her way into the yard. Even though the temperature was falling, she'd worked up quite a sweat on the walk home.

Thorliff came running out of the house. "What'd you get, Mor?" Seeing the pile of geese, his mouth became a big O. Along with his eyes. "How many?"

"Eight." Ingeborg laid down the poles. "You want to help me pick them?"

"I'll get Bestemor." He headed back for the house.

The jingle of harnesses told her that Haakan was on his way in with the team, so she dragged her load over by the well house, where a wide bench was attached to the building for just this purpose. She slung the geese up on the flat top and leaned the rifle against the wall. Once they were gutted, the geese could be left to hang until plucked or skinned in the morning. She ran a hand over the breast of one of the birds, feeling the dense down that made for such warm sleeping in the winter months.

"Whoa." The jingling stopped, and one of the horses snorted. "Easy, boy."

"Haakan."

"Ja."

"Come see what I got." She stuck her head around the corner of the building.

"You been fishing?"

"No."

"What then?"

She could hear him removing the harnesses while the horses stamped their feet, impatient to be released in the pasture. Swiftly she gutted each of the geese and tied their feet together to hang them. Saving the gizzards and livers, she tossed the rest in a pail to feed to the pigs. Paws whined at her side, so she gave him a gizzard. Eight livers wasn't enough for all of them for supper, but chopped with eggs in the morning would taste good. The gizzards she'd chop into stuffing.

The screech of the gate, a slap on a horse's rump, more gate noises, then she could hear Haakan coming toward her. Quickly she hooked the tied legs of the last goose over the pegs in a board farther up on the wall and stepped back.

"You got all of those? And back home by yourself?" He put an arm around her waist, dragging her close. "Well done, wife." His hand slipped lower, and he patted her bottom. "Hmm, maybe these britches aren't so bad after all."

Ingeborg could feel the heat flame up from her neck. "Haakan Howard Bjorklund, how you talk." She turned in his arms. "Now we'll have a new goose down quilt to help keep us warm this winter."

"We do pretty well keeping each other warm." His mouth was only inches from hers.

She leaned into his caress, grateful for the deepening dusk. His kiss, first on the tip of her nose, then her cheeks, then her lips reminded her anew how much she loved him. And loved to be loved by him.

"Please don't wear these britches where other men can see you. They might get the same idea I had."

"I won't. But I do love to hunt." She laid her head on his chest, grateful for the strong heart she could feel thumping in her ear.

"Not a womanly thing."

She shook her head. "But we will enjoy roast goose to-morrow night, as will Kaaren and Metiz, and we'll give one to Zeb and Katy too." She counted them out. "I think I better go out again tomorrow night."

"Ah, my Inge, what would I do without you?" Haakan kissed her again, a gentle kiss full of promise.

Perhaps this time there will be a baby. Ingeborg kept the wish to herself.

After hanging the spoils of her labor in the well house to cool, the two made their way to the lighted windows of their house, the peal of children's laughter welcoming them home.

"I have a deacon's meeting tonight, so I better get myself

moving," Haakan said at the close of the meal. "Mange takk, Bridget. You are one fine cook."

"Good enough to run a boardinghouse, huh?" She smiled at him over Astrid's head, the child nestled in her lap.

Haakan rolled his eyes and shook his head. "Some people never give up."

"Not when this is such a good idea." Her reply snapped back, tempered by a smile but undergirded with determination.

"Well, the meeting tonight is for church, not the bank, but keep thinking about it so you can answer all the questions the board is going to throw at you." He stood and stretched, giving Ingeborg a smile that promised more later.

"It helps to have people in your corner." Bridget rocked her lap sitter.

"I know. Far as I can see, the idea is sound, and no, I don't believe you are too old. Hjelmer doesn't either. You caught him by surprise, you know."

Bridget patted her white hair. "The hair may look old, but the back is strong."

"I don't think your hair looks old," Thorliff said, looking up from the book he was reading at the table where the lamplight was the brightest. "But I want you to stay here with us. If you live at the boardinghouse, we won't see you so much."

Ingeborg nodded. "Leave it to Thorliff to hit the nail right on the head."

Andrew looked up from drawing letters on his slate. "What nail?"

Ingeborg shook her head. "That is just a saying. Now, where's Hamre?"

"Gone to the soddy." Andrew took up his chalk again. "He doesn't like to be with us much."

"Hamre did a fine job oiling the threshing machine." Haakan shrugged into his coat.

"But he doesn't like school." Thorliff glanced up again. "Says he wants to go fishing again on the ocean like his bestefar."

"Is that so?" Bridget looked to the boy at her side.

"Um." Thorliff went back to his book.

How he can read and still keep track of the conversation

around him, I'll never know. Ingeborg wanted to reach over and brush away the lock of hair, no longer so blond, that fell over Thorliff's forehead. Instead she looked up at Haakan. "Tell Pastor Solberg there's a goose here for him as soon as I pick it."

"Better yet, invite him over for supper tomorrow night." Bridget dropped a kiss on Astrid's gold-white hair. "I'll make lefse. He says that's one of his favorites."

Fighting to keep her eyes open, Astrid looked up at her grandmother. "Me help?"

"Yes, you can help. You can scrub the potatoes for Bestemor."

"And pick feathers from the geese to stuff in a pillow just for you." Ingeborg stroked the back of her daughter's head. "Right now I think we will take a little girl up to her bed."

Astrid shook her head, but everyone could tell the fight had gone out of her.

Ingeborg stood and lifted the child from Bridget's lap. "Come, little one, we'll wash your hands and face and go say your prayers."

"Prayers." Not fighting the idea of getting her face washed said more than the droopy eyes.

Laying her sleepy child in bed, dressed in a clean nightgown fresh-smelling from the clothesline, made Ingeborg smile. She folded Astrid's hands and began, "Jesus loves me."

Astrid repeated, "Jesus loves Ma."

"No, Jesus loves me. Say me."

"Me." The eyelids ceased to flutter, and her breath came in a sigh. Just like that Astrid was asleep.

Ingeborg watched her daughter, gently stroking the fine hair back from her forehead and breathing in the peace of the room. Being out in the woods made her think of freedom, but here with her daughter, all she could think was *Mange takk, heavenly Father. Forgive me, please, for always wanting more. You have given me so much, and I so often forget to say thank you. Please help me think to thank you before I want*. She studied the sleeping face of her daughter. So perfect. The room around her with a window that showed the stars pinning up the cobalt sky at night and caught the first rays of the rising sun at dawn. Astrid would forget the darkness of the soddy and remember the sun. "Ah, my God, my God, I am in awe. Like the psalmist,

I praise your holy name. You are my God, and I am your child. And that never changes, in spite of the foolish things I do." She heard Thorliff bring in another armload of wood down in the kitchen below them. The horse trotting out of the yard meant Haakan had saddled and gone. She could hear the clank of the stove lid being set aside for more wood to be used in the firebox. Andrew laughed at something. It didn't take much to make him laugh.

Ingeborg leaned forward and kissed Astrid's wide brow. "God keep thee, little one, safe in the palm of His mighty hand." She sniffed and drew a handkerchief from her apron pocket. "All of us." She left the room as quietly as possible, not wanting to disturb the peace therein.

But it followed her downstairs, drifting around her shoulders as she sat mending in the lamplight while Bridget carded wool from the fleece stacked in the corner. The rasp and scrape of the carding paddles sounded loud in the stillness.

"If you do indeed build a boardinghouse, I will miss times like these."

"Ja, me too. Makes me wonder if I am being a foolish old woman. So much here, and yet I want more."

Ingeborg threaded her needle with dark thread and started on Thorliff's pants, letting out the last bit of hem. He needed new ones, and when she got them, she would put these away for Andrew. At the rate he was growing it wouldn't be long. "Strange, upstairs I was just thinking the same thing." She folded the last bit of fabric over and stitched it with nearly invisible stitches. "But I don't think you are foolish at all."

"No?" Bridget nodded, her hands continuing to straighten the strands of wool with the carders. "I am thinking I might take Hamre with me, if that is all right with you. He can be a big help, and maybe he will be happier there."

"I don't think that boy will be happy until he has the sea sighing around a boat under his feet. His grandfather poured the love of the ocean into him from the time he was born, maybe before."

"I'm afraid you are right. But where is there an ocean around here?"

"There's Lake Superior in northeastern Minnesota, but if

he is like the other Bjorklund men, he will want to go west, clear to the Pacific."

"Uff da. So far away." The mound of carded wool grew in the basket at her side. Bridget stroked the long fine strands. "Your sheep give such good wool. Spinning and knitting it is a pleasure." Each kept busy with her own task.

"Is it wrong to want a place of my own?" Bridget asked.

"Don't ask me. I wouldn't give this up for anything short of heaven." The two chuckled together, knowing the trials Ingeborg had gone through to keep the land after Roald died. Roald had been Ingeborg's first husband and Bridget's second son.

"Mor, I'm hungry." Andrew crossed the room to stand at his mother's arm.

"There's milk or buttermilk in the pantry, and you know where the cookie jar is, unless you'd rather have bread and jam."

Andrew thought a moment, his brow wrinkling in the process. "Can I have both?"

Ingeborg laid aside her mending and started to get up.

"I'll fix it," Thorliff called from the kitchen table. "Come on, Andrew."

"Thank you, son. Now you'll have clean trousers to wear to school tomorrow, ones that cover your ankles."

Not long after the boys were in bed, the horse trotted back into the yard, greeted by Paws, who took his job of announcing visitors or family very seriously.

"We'll have frost tonight," Haakan said a few minutes later after putting the horse away. "I could already see it in some places, the moon is so bright." He hung his jacket and hat on one of the pegs on the wall by the door. "Olaf said to tell you that he has your rocking chair about finished, Mor." He glanced at Bridget. "And there are no arms on it, like you asked."

"Good. It is easier to knit and do other things if there are no arms, especially when working at the spinning wheel." She looked with pride at the wheel nearest to her, the one thing she'd insisted come from Norway with her. Gustaf had made it several years before, after they sold her other one to help the brothers buy passage to come to the new land. It was the last thing he had made for her.

"The coffee could be hot in a minute or two." Ingeborg snipped the last thread and folded the pants, laying them to the side. The darning and patching basket seemed to refill of its own accord, no matter how many things she finished in an evening.

"No, I'm coffee'd out." He leaned a shoulder against the doorjamb.

"So, what went on at the meeting?" The look of him, so relaxed with cheeks burnished by the cold, made her heart pick up its beat.

"They're talking of building a frame house for Pastor. He says he doesn't need it, but I think Hildegunn is after Anner to get it going. Says a man in his position needs more than a soddy."

Ingeborg chuckled. *That sounded like Hildegunn all right.*

"He's starting English classes again next week, so, Bridget, if you want to attend, I will take you."

She nodded her reply.

"Oh, and there are so many children in school this year, he wondered if there were some who could give a bit of their time to help, especially with the little ones. You think Kaaren might be able?"

"What about Mary Martha? That might keep her here a bit longer."

"True." Haakan dipped his head and gave his wife one of those "you're cooking up something" looks out of the corner of his eyes. "Ingeborg."

"What?" Pure innocence shone from her face but for the slight curve of one eyebrow.

"Just don't meddle." He sighed at the futility of his remark and rubbed his chin. "There's to be a debate between Walter Muir of the Farmer's Alliance and Porter J. McCumber, who's talking for the railroads. They asked to use our church. I want to ask them what they plan to do about the railroad gouging the farmers. The shipping price per ton went up again."

"Uff da. You'd think they're afraid they'll go broke." Ingeborg had read in the *Dakota Farmer* newspaper about the wealth being accumulated by the railroad magnates. The only company that seemed to care about the farmers was Hill's Great Northern Railroad, but the Great Northern didn't have any cheaper rates, just more sidings to load wheat. Not having to drive the loaded wagons so far did indeed help, but the cost . . .

"Olaf said wheat prices dropped again too. Sure glad we got ours shipped when it was higher. Between the flour mills and the railroads . . ." He shook his head. "Maybe we should just make cheese."

Ingeborg's good cheese was bought up wherever she sent it, with shopkeepers crying for more. She'd given up trying to deliver to the Bonanza farm, so they rarely saw Solveig, Kaaren's sister. She had married George Carlson, who ran the Bonanza farm just across the river from St. Andrew. Mrs. McKenzie at the Mercantile in St. Andrew even drove out to the farm to buy cheese on her own.

"We'd need a bigger well house for curing."

"I've been thinking on that. If we build it like the ice house . . ."

She could tell Haakan was off on one of his planning trips again. He nodded and left the room.

"Inge, where's a piece of paper?"

"We better have Olaf build a desk so we can keep track of things." Ingeborg set the sock she was darning aside and got to her feet. "That man, he couldn't find his way out of a gunnysack."

The chuckle she and Bridget shared didn't need words.

Later that night, curled up in the curve of his body, she let her mind wander again. Would this time together have brought them another child? She didn't care if it were a boy or girl, just so she could have a baby again. Although, it would be wonderful to give Haakan a son of his own.

Please, God, I want to give Haakan sons. Is that too much to ask?

7

"A h heard you could use some help."
Pastor Solberg stared at the smiling young woman with her two charges in front of her. Her green eyes sparkled like morning dew on spring green leaves. And her hair, the dark curls rioting down her back, was caught back on the sides with two mother-of-pearl combs.

She should know enough to bind her hair up, a woman her age, after all. He could feel the frown deepening between his eyes. "Well . . . ah . . ." *Lord, help me. What can I say? She's the last person I want here.* The crisp fall breeze chuckled in his ear.

"Good. I'm glad to be useful, as my ma always said. While I've not taught school before, I've worked with little ones, and—"

"And she is the bestest reader." Deborah, who hadn't run off as Manda had, stood next to Mary Martha like a fiercely protective guard dog. The look she aimed at the teacher warned that she sensed his thoughts.

"I . . . ah . . . thank you very much. Ah . . . if you . . ." *Mind, where have you gone? I'm stuttering like a child.*

Mary Martha looked as if she might begin to twiddle her thumbs any second. "Where may I tie up the horse?"

"I'll show you." Deborah gave her teacher a confused look, then shrugged and took the woman's hand. "This way."

"Morning, Miss MacCallister. You staying to help at school?" Thorliff left the game and came over to her. At her halfhearted shrug, he responded in kind before continuing. "I could take off the harness if you like. Then if we tied your horse on a long line to the wagon wheel, he could graze, if that's all right. That's what we do for church on Sundays."

"That will be right fine, and I appreciate the offer." Mary Martha let the children help her, and just as the school bell rang, Deborah brought her back to the front door where children were lining up.

Pastor Solberg stood at the doorway, nodding in answer to greetings from his students. He very carefully refrained from looking at Miss MacCallister.

A bubble of laughter rose in her throat and threatened to embarrass her. Why, the man was flummoxed. He'd been rude the other day and didn't know how to get out of it. The idea tickled her. If Zeb were here, he'd tell her to leave it alone, but he wasn't here. Pastor John Solberg was too solemn for his own good, leastways that's how she saw him. Surely there was a remedy for such seriousness.

But don't embarrass him in front of his pupils, a wise voice in her ear cautioned. She agreed. That would never do.

"See, my hand is better now." Deborah held out her bandaged hand. Her scream the afternoon before when she'd impaled her hand on a stick had set his heart to racing, much like it was doing now.

Silence fell as Pastor Solberg bowed his head. "Dear Heavenly Father, we thank thee for this day, the beauty we see and the joy we feel." *Heaven above, what did I mean by that?* "Bless our studies today and every day, and make us worthy of thy kingdom." The children joined in the "amen" and immediately moved into the schoolroom, hanging up their coats and dinner pails without any fuss.

They stood by their desks and waited for the teacher to make his way to the front of the room. "Swen, will you lead us in the Pledge of Allegiance?"

All hands clapped over their hearts, including Deborah's after Andrew changed hands for her.

"Oh. I forgot."

A giggle came from somewhere farther back but was cut off at the look Solberg sent the offender.

"I pledge allegiance . . ." The words were picked up in unison, and while there were still some stumbles in the middle,

"With liberty and justice for all" rang loud and clear.

"Anji, you have the Scripture reading?"

"Yes, sir." The girl opened the Bible on her desk at the bookmark and read. " 'Trust in the Lord with all thy heart and do not rely on your own understanding.' "

"Thank you. Everyone may be seated."

Mary Martha stood off to the side, feeling as though she were right back in the schoolroom herself. When she looked up at Pastor Solberg, he stared back. "Ah, Baptiste, could you run over to the church and bring back a chair or a bench? A bench would be good. Yes, that's right, a bench."

She could see the red creep up his neck.

"Thank you." She nodded to the children.

"Miss MacCallister has come to help some of us—you—with your lessons, so will you kindly welcome her?"

"Good morning, Miss MacCallister." The older children led while the younger ones stumbled over the words.

"Shall we try that again?" Solberg sounded more sure now, as if he, too, were getting his footing.

After the second time, Mary Martha answered. "Good mornin' to you too."

Anna Helmsrude smiled as though she'd just seen an angel. "Ain't thee purty?"

Now the heat was crawling up her own neck. She helped Baptiste settle the bench against the wall and took her seat, folding her hands in her lap. She'd have folded them on top of a desk, had she one.

And so she sat for the next two hours, watching Pastor Solberg conduct the classes, the older ones helping the younger, and having much too much time to think. Keeping a smile plastered on her face was taking more effort as the morning wore on. At recess, the children walked to the door and then burst into running as if catapulted from a slingshot.

"Is there something I can do to help, or did you just want . . ." She almost said "spectator" but refrained.

He looked up from his book, his face as blank as the blackboard behind him. "No . . . ah, yes, yes. I was about to ask you to review alphabet letters with the little ones."

She could tell he was thinking off the top of his head. "That will be fine. And then?"

He shrugged. "Their numbers?"

She had the distinct feeling he didn't know what to do with her. "Would you rather I come back another day?" *Or not at all?*

John Solberg scrubbed a hand across his head. "Look, Miss MacCallister, I have a confession to make." Both hands this time, one followed the other across his now mussed hair.

She waited. *Surely he hadn't murdered anyone or done anything so terrible to earn the look on his face.*

"I have to ask . . . beg for your forgiveness. The other day I was unbearably rude, and today I am not doing much better. You see . . ." He stopped. He'd said enough. Now it was her turn.

She gave him the same smile she'd blessed Deborah with, warm and sweet. "I see. Yes, you are forgiven, and now I hope you can allow me to work with the children. I am not without schooling myself, you know, and you asked for help. Haakan Bjorklund made a special trip to my brother's house to tell me so. Otherwise I would never have presumed . . ." Her words trickled off, her face needing a fanning, and he just sat there.

Flummoxed, that's what he is. While she didn't know the exact meaning of the word, old Uncle Jed used it often to show complete confusion.

I may have to take a buggy whip to Haakan Bjorklund. The thought of that made him almost smile. At least he could feel a little grin tickling the right side of his mouth. This woman knew how to make a point, and that point stabbed him right in the gullet.

"I said I was sorry."

"That was for the other day."

"Can it cover today too?"

Children laughing caught his attention. "Glory be, they need to come in from recess." He started to rise. "Could you please call the children in?"

"Yes, surely." And so she answered both his questions in two words.

He sank back down in his chair, and this time his hands straightened the sandy hair that started waving back well beyond his forehead.

Mary Martha stood at the door and rang the handbell,

which called the children in from play. The sun shone brightly, and the air nipped her nose, pleading with her to come and enjoy the fall. Winter would soon be on its way.

She glanced back inside the dim room. Even with the door open and the two windows that faced south, the long room was dark. While the women whitewashed the walls every year, the dirt floor seemed to absorb the light. Wouldn't it be better to meet in the church where there was some light?

"Mith MacCallithter." Anna looked up, her face a picture of delight.

"Yes, Anna?"

"Your dreth ith tho pretty." The little girl fingered the royal blue serge of the skirt. "Like the thky."

Mary Martha wanted to pick up the little girl and hug her. She was so thin, it seemed the sun could shine right through her. "Thank you, Anna. I think you are a poet in that little heart of yours."

"A po-et?"

"Yes."

When the shoving, giggling, and bustling stopped, she stepped aside and motioned the children into the room. Several of the older boys' ears turned red as they passed her. Manda smiled as if they had a secret, she and the teacher's helper. Mary Martha wanted to tweak her nose and make her laugh.

Manda did more scowling than laughing much of the time. And all the time she'd rather argue than agree. Far as Mary Martha was concerned, the young girl wrote the book on independence. But no one could ever fault her for being lazy or telling lies. Like her mother used to say, *The child is honest as the day is long.*

When everyone had taken their seats again, Mary Martha included, Pastor Solberg stood and began assigning tasks. Far as she could tell, he'd left her out again. And here she thought they had come to an understanding. While she usually kept her temper under control, she could feel it starting to fire up.

"And Miss MacCallister . . ."

She quit simmering so she could hear the remainder of his sentence.

"Could you please help these three children?" He pointed

to three who looked so alike she'd thought they were triplets but for the difference in size.

"Of course." *Now what does he want me to do?* She beckoned the three to come sit with her and looked up at Solberg for assistance. He was answering a question from another part of the room.

The three sat down, staring at her out of blue eyes that appeared to have looked at life and found it wanting. She now knew what that phrase meant.

"First thing, could you please tell me your names?"

They stared at her without moving. Finally the tallest one, a girl, said something. It was something all right, but all in Norwegian, and Mary Martha had no idea what she'd said.

"Oh." She sent a glance to the man in the front of the room that could have melted his shirt buttons. She should have sent Katy here instead of coming herself. But Katy still didn't feel well and was doing her best to hide it. Tomorrow she'd stay home where she belonged and help Katy. If this self-righteous such-and-such wanted help, he could just sing for it.

The three stared at her.

She glared again at Pastor Solberg.

He must have felt her consternation because he turned to her and said, "I'll be right there."

Mary Martha nodded. She could handle this, of course she could. She laid a hand on her chest. "I am Miss MacCallister." She spoke slowly and enunciated carefully. Then she pointed to each of them.

"I am . . ." She waited for the older girl to fill in the blank.

"Ingrid."

"Good." Her smile brought a hint of life to the girl's eyes. "Now say it all." She waved her hand as if she were conducting an orchestra. Nodding, she started, "I am Ingrid."

The girl followed her and earned a pat on the hand from a teacher who could hardly sit still.

She followed the same routine with the others.

"Very good." John Solberg had joined them, and she hadn't even noticed.

"Why didn't you tell me they didn't speak a word of English?"

"I thought I'd be right over."

Now what could she say? A few names came to mind, none of them complimentary.

He turned to the children and spoke in Norwegian.

She wished she knew what he'd said.

"I explained that we only talk English in school, that you will be giving them English lessons, and that they are to repeat what you say. I can always send Thorliff or one of the others over to help you. I'd start with some useful phrases if it were me."

At a call from another student, he turned back to his classroom.

Mary Martha smiled at her three charges again, wishing she would get a smile in return. No children should be so solemn. She could hear the little ones piping their *ABC's*. How much easier that would be. Her mind searched frantically for necessary phrases.

"Pastor said I should come help you." Thorliff appeared at her elbow.

"Ah, good. When I say a phrase in English, you say it in Norwegian so they understand it. Then after they repeat it, I will write it on the slate."

"And I can write the Norwegian on another slate."

"You better ask them first if they can read and write Norwegian."

Ingrid could, but her sisters, Marta and Clara, shook their heads.

Mary Martha's stomach did a flip-flop. Why hadn't she stayed in Missouri? She sent another glare in the direction of the teacher, silently threatening him with death and destruction. To her charges she sent a smile that she hoped conveyed some form of confidence.

"All right." *Please, Lord, show me what to do, how to help these children. Please, right now. There's no time to waste.* "We'll begin with 'good morning.'" She nodded to Thorliff, who repeated both her phrase and the instructions in Norwegian. When they looked back at her after talking with Thorliff, she smiled and repeated, "Good morning."

Their response was less than enthusiastic, but they answered.

She continued with "hello," "good-bye," "please," and

"thank you." Some of those she had picked up from Katy. While they went back and forth, she racked her brain trying to decide where to go next. After reviewing one more time, she switched to the alphabet, printing the letters on a slate.

By the time they were all excused for the dinner recess, she felt as if she'd been run over by a twelve-up hitch of horses pulling a loaded freight wagon. Manda and Deborah brought her dinner pail over to her.

"You can eat with us if you like," Manda said.

"Teacher said we could go outside or eat inside, whichever we wanted. What would you like?" Deborah tucked her hand in Mary Martha's.

What would she like? She'd first like to strangle Pastor John Solberg, and then she'd like to go home and take a three-week nap, that's what. Instead, she smiled and brushed a strand of hair back from Deborah's cheek. "Outside would be wonderful."

One good thing, she thought on the drive home that afternoon, *I'm learning Norwegian about as fast as they are getting the English.* The other thing, Solberg had invited her back. He *had* thanked her for coming, and Ingrid had almost smiled. That last was what made her determined to keep going. That and Anna Helmsrude. *If I sewed her a new dress, could I give it to her somehow without causing a fracas? Guess I need to talk with Ingeborg.*

That evening she and Katy finished up the dishes and took their handwork into the parlor, where Zeb sat reading the *Grand Forks Herald* newspaper in the lamplight. When they were settled, Mary Martha asked, "So then, what do you think I should teach them next?"

"Go on with what you started and add names for the subjects in school. Then teach them simple things like 'go outside,' 'come inside,' 'sit down,' 'stand'—you know, the commands Pastor Solberg uses all the time. 'Open your books,' 'put your things away,' and everyone's favorite."

"What's that?"

" 'Class dismissed.' "

"I always liked that one best." Zeb joined the conversation.

"Why don't you read to us?" Katy smiled at her husband. She turned back to Mary Martha sitting beside her on the settee. "While I speak English pretty good now, I can't read it much."

A snort from her husband made her flap her hand at him.

When Mary Martha caught the look the two exchanged, she felt a lump in her throat. What would it feel like to have someone love her like Zeb so obviously loved Katy?

Zeb began reading, and Mary Martha listened while she hemmed the dress she'd been sewing for Deborah. She'd finished the one she made for Manda before school started. He read about the new elevator being built and the Lutheran church having a harvest festival. There was a renewed push for support of the Farmer's Alliance organization, asking all the farmers to join so that their voices could be heard before the Territorial Assembly. Walter Muir, one of the leaders of the Farmer's Alliance, had written an impassioned editorial, more like a diatribe, against the railroad, the elevators, and the flour-milling consortium for their efforts to gouge the farmers.

"Those buzzards," Zeb muttered after reading an editorial about the statehood party and their push for one state, with the capital located in Pierre.

"So what is wrong with that?" Mary Martha knotted her thread and clipped the end. "There now, Deborah can wear that tomorrow."

"It would make the state too large to govern efficiently," Zeb answered, "besides which, we in the north just think different from those in the south. They can't grow wheat like we do here in the Red River Valley."

"Just so they let women have the vote," Katy said, changing the subject.

"Katy, that is nothing but a dream, and not a good one at that. Women don't need to vote. That's what their husbands are for."

"And what about women who don't have husbands?" Mary Martha raised an eyebrow. "Who do they have to speak for them? Besides, it isn't just about the vote. Women should be able to purchase land in their own name and dispose of their own property."

"They can do that now. Look at Ingeborg and Kaaren."

"Yes, but there's also Manda and Deborah. That still isn't

settled, and you know..." Katy looked up from her needle-work.

Zeb held up a hand. "How about if I just read this, and we not get into a war over it?" He folded the paper and set it on the round table near his chair. "Better yet, I'm going to check on the stock and go to bed before you two tear me limb from limb." He flexed his arm as if they'd been tugging on it.

"Coward," Mary Martha said, just loud enough for him to hear.

"I do not understand why men are so stubborn," Katy said after he left the room. "Letting us vote doesn't mean they can't vote."

"They're just afraid that women might get smarter than they are." Mary Martha's grin held a hint of devilry. "Leastways, that's what I think." She waited for Katy's scandalized look to change to a chuckle. "You sure you wouldn't rather go work with those poor children tomorrow and let me stay here? After all, you speak Norwegian and English both, and you know them all, besides."

Katy shook her head. "I'd rather work with Zeb and the horses any day. Who would want to be cooped up in that soddy hour after hour?"

"I thought of that too. Wonder what we can do to make it brighter?"

"I'll ask at the next quilting bee. Somebody there will have an idea."

The next morning Mary Martha arrived at the schoolhouse armed with a list of things she wanted her three charges to learn. By the end of the day, she'd elicited smiles from the two younger girls. Ingrid was another matter.

"Marta said that Ingrid said she was too old for school any-way," Manda informed her when school was over. She had the horse all harnessed and the wagon hitched up by the time Mary Martha had put her things away and said good-bye to Pastor Solberg. "Can I drive?" Manda asked.

"Yes," Mary Martha said and swung up, using the wheel for a step, then settled on the wooden seat. "How come?" she asked, referring to what Ingrid had said.

"She thinks Norwegian is just fine." Manda slapped the reins. "Giddyup horse. We got plenty to do at home."

"She's only thirteen."

"Same as me. I'd rather be home too." She sent a pleading glance sideways.

Mary Martha shook her head. "Don't look to me. Ask your mother—er, Katy." She caught herself. While Deborah called Katy Ma, Manda still didn't. "Besides, it isn't how old you are but how much you know."

"Horsefeathers."

"Manda, Ma don't like cussin'." Deborah leaned across Mary Martha's lap to glare at her sister.

Katy wasn't in the kitchen when Deborah and Mary Martha entered. She wasn't in the parlor either.

"Ma?" Deborah called.

"In here." A weak voice came from the bedroom.

Mary Martha felt a hand clutch her heart. Something was wrong for sure. She knew she shouldn't have gone to help at the school.

8

"Y ou got any idea where I can spend the night?" Mr. Drummond asked.

Penny thought a moment. "Olaf Wold, who runs the sack house, lets people put down a pallet there if there's room. His building might be kinda full right now though, with harvest just finished. If he says no, then you can try Pastor Solberg in the soddy by the church."

"How come there's no hotel or boardinghouse in this little town?" Mr. Drummond shook his head as he spoke. "You want to grow, you got to get people to stay here. Then they'll like it so much they'll want to come live here."

"Tell that to the bankers," Penny muttered under her breath.

"Is there a place to eat?" At the shake of Penny's head, Drummond sighed. "And I missed the last train to either Grand Forks or Grafton, didn't I?"

"You can join us for supper. It's only what's left from dinner." She wished she'd kept her mouth closed. She'd forgotten they were going to have pancakes because the noon guests cleaned up every bit of food she had. If she'd had another pie, it would have gone too. "Or rather, it's pancakes tonight, but I can promise you they'll be filling."

"We can talk more about the sewing machines you want to stock here in your store?"

She arched an eyebrow. "I do?"

"You most certainly do. In fact, I'll give free lessons to anyone who buys a machine from you in the next three months.

What with Christmas coming up and all, maybe I should go talk with the men. They'd all want their wives to have an easier life, wouldn't they?"

"Don't count on it. Norwegians, especially those around here, could cut a dime in half and give you eleven cents change." *Where is Hjelmer? He surely should have been back by now.* She heard the clatter of wood in the woodbox and knew her newfound cousin Ephraim was back.

"Bet those same Norwegians know a good deal when they see it."

"They do at that. Go over and talk to Olaf, and I'll have supper ready in half an hour. Tell him I sent you." When he leaned over to pick up his case, she added, "You can leave that here. No one will bother it. Put it back by your machine."

After the door bell tinkled behind him, Penny went back and looked at the sewing machine again. She laid a reverent hand on the wheel and turned it just enough to watch the needle go down and up again. *I want one, and I want every woman around here to have one. So how do we do that?*

She picked up their own mail and, tapping the letters against her finger, turned the Closed sign over and pushed aside the curtain to their quarters. Laying the mail on the small table by Hjelmer's chair, she removed her canvas store apron and put on the calico one she'd hung over a hook in the pantry. Then humming to herself, she retrieved the flour, buttermilk, and eggs she needed for supper. After slicing thick ham steaks off the hindquarter, she laid those in the pan to begin frying.

"You need anything else?" Ephraim asked from the doorway. His wet hair carefully slicked back showed that he'd already washed up.

"No thanks." She paused. "You know where Hjelmer is?"

"Out in the blacksmith shop, drawing on something. I think he's got an idea that he's cogitating."

"Oh." No wonder he'd been so quiet.

"He was out to Haakan's earlier to talk to his ma."

"Uh-oh." That could be good or bad. Shame she and Bridget hadn't gotten the loan request made out yet. Things down on paper always looked more possible than just talk. She thought to the sewing machine sitting in her store. That fancy machine would help out like nobody's business in setting up the boardinghouse.

"Would you go tell him supper will be ready in a few minutes?"

"Sure 'nough."

"Mrs. Bjorklund." Mr. Drummond knocked at the back door.

"Come on in." She moved the frying pan to the back of the stove and lifted the round lid. After adding a couple of sticks of wood, she pulled the frying pan to the hotter part, took the square griddle down from the row of iron hooks Hjelmer had fashioned for her, and set it to heat.

"Do you mind if I show Mr. and Mrs. Wold the machine after supper? She is so excited about it, and Mr. Wold is plenty curious."

"Why not? Maybe Hjelmer would like to see it too. He likes machinery of all sorts." *And if he gets interested, I will carry them in the store for sure. Why am I dithering like this? Either I carry them or I don't. It is not Hjelmer's decision to make.* But she knew the reason. She always talked big ideas like this over with him.

"The Wolds want me to come for supper too, if you don't mind."

"No, go on. I'm sure Goodie has something better than pancakes cooked up."

When Hjelmer didn't come in, Penny sent Ephraim to find him, but it looked to Penny like Hjelmer ate supper without any idea what he put in his mouth. He passed the syrup when asked and nodded when she asked him if he wanted more pancakes. Ephraim gave up talking after a couple of attempts, but Penny persisted. She needed his opinion, not just an "um."

"Hjelmer?"

"Um." He cut his ham and put a bite in his mouth.

"The blacksmith is on fire."

"Good, dear, that's good."

She watched as her words sunk in.

"Ring the fire bell!" He shoved back his chair only to see the other two at the table burying their laughter behind mouths full of pancake. Taking his chair again, he glared at Penny. "That wasn't necessary. A simple 'Hjelmer' would do."

He shot Ephraim an accusing look, as if he'd encouraged Penny.

Ephraim shook his head and glanced over at the stove. "Any more of them pancakes? They're right good."

Penny got up and slid the griddle back on the hotter part of the stove. "In a minute." She glanced back at her husband, who wore that distant look again. What in the world was he thinking on so hard?

When supper was over and she'd poured the final cup of coffee, she set the dishes to soaking in a pan of soapy water on the stove and went to stand in front of her husband, now sitting in his chair. The faraway look hadn't left, even though Ephraim had. "Hjelmer, please, I really need you to listen to me." She waited, then raised her voice and touched his arm. "Hjelmer, are you all right?" Maybe something was really wrong, and he didn't want to tell her.

"What is it?" The snap in his voice brought forth one of her own.

"I'm just asking you a question!"

"So ask!" He glared.

She glared. And clamped her hands on her hips. "What is the matter with you?"

"Nothing! Can't a man do some thinking in his own house?"

"Yes, if his wife can ask a question and get a decent answer." She felt like stamping her foot—on his.

He sighed and rolled his eyes. "All right. What is it?"

He wore *that* look, the one that always drove her crazy. "Oh, forget it. I'll make my own decisions, and you can just go . . . go jump in the river."

"Fine." He flung himself out of his chair and out the door. The screen door slammed behind him.

Penny sank down in the chair he'd just left. All she'd wanted was one minute of his precious time. Was that too much to ask?

"Yoo-hoo." Goodie Wold, formerly Peterson, called from the back door. "Penny? You ready to see the machine?"

"Come on in. I'll light some extra lamps." She lifted a filled kerosene lamp down from the shelf and set it on the table. Then taking a long slender piece of cedar from the jar she kept for this purpose, she lighted it in the burning lamp and held it against the wick of the new one. When the wick caught fire, she broke off the burnt bit of cedar and laid it on the cold edge of the stove to reuse. After adjusting the wick, she set the chimney in place and smiled at her guests.

"Where's Hjelmer?" Olaf Wold, his receding hair giving him an even wiser look, asked as he took one of the burning lamps.

"I'm not sure." She felt like saying "God only knows," a phrase her tante Agnes often used, but she refrained.

"Is he coming to see this wonder machine?" He sent his wife a gently teasing look.

"Now, don't you give me that," Goodie answered. "I could even patch your gunnysacks with this. Or you could."

"Let alone your pants." Penny picked up the other lamp and gestured toward the curtain dividing the kitchen and the store.

"And shirts. She can make you a new coat or turn one you have in no time." Alfred Drummond joined the conversation.

"When I think how much faster I could sew clothes for all of us, I . . . I just get goose bumps." Goodie rubbed her arms.

"Maybe it's the cold weather." Penny hated feeling like a grump, but hard words with Hjelmer always made her feel that way afterward. Why couldn't she learn to not say things she would be sorry for later?

They moved other things aside to set the lamps where they could see easily, and Mr. Drummond took his place on the chair Penny had provided. As he went into his spiel again, Penny listened carefully. It all sounded much too good to be true, but she had the stack of hemmed napkins to testify to the speed with which this little machine stitched.

"Penny?"

"In here."

Hjelmer made his way to the group in the corner. "What's this?"

Penny bit her lip enough to leave marks. "If you'd been listening," she hissed, "you would have known."

"Oh, well, I . . ."

Her look quelled his excuses.

"Welcome. Mr. Bjorklund, I take it?" Drummond got to his

feet and reached a hand across the machine. "I am Alfred Drummond, representing the greatest little machine yet invented—the Singer sewing machine, designed to make your wife's lot easier, in regards to sewing, that is."

He faltered at the look on Hjelmer's face. Arms crossed over his chest, eyebrows straight and chips of ice floating on his Fjord blue eyes, Hjelmer wore that "show me" look.

Penny wanted to kick him in the ankle. Would nothing go right tonight?

"My husband believes new machinery for the fieldwork is one of the most important things of our time." Her tone was so coated in honey, the bees would stick to it.

He sent her one of *his* looks.

"Why, I know he is dying to try this out for himself." She turned to him, her mouth smiling and her eyes daring him.

"Good, good. Let me show you how it works first, and then you can try it." Drummond took his seat again. "You know they have had industrial machines for the clothing factories for some time now. But this little Singer is the first one designed for the home, and you can pay for it with only pennies a month."

Penny divided her watching between the demonstration and Hjelmer's face. Soon his love of machinery took over, and he leaned forward until he was eye to eye with the flashing needle.

When Drummond held up the seam of two pieces of muslin and tried to pull them apart to show the strength of the stitching, Hjelmer reached for the sample before Goodie got her hand out. He turned it both ways, tugged on the sides, and shook his head.

"Amazing." He studied it some more.

An "ahem" from Goodie made him start and, with an apologetic shrug, hand it over. He turned his attention back to Drummond. "Can it sew canvas for the binders? Tarps, leather?"

Drummond paused. "Well, it all depends on the strength of the needle." He turned a screw and removed the needle. "You buy these separately. I always carry extras."

"So if something happens to the machine, where do we get parts?"

Penny picked up on the "we." She and Goodie exchanged glances, neither of them looking to Olaf. They didn't need to.

His "mm" and "uh-huh" already indicated his approval.

"Can you show me the innards of the thing?" Hjelmer asked, his fingers tracing the shell of the machine as if he could divine what went on inside the casing.

"Certainly, sir." Drummond took out a leather packet with several sizes of screwdrivers, a brush, and a polishing cloth. "I teach new owners how to clean and oil their machines so that they will last. Just like keeping up farm machinery, this little beauty needs care."

"Where would we order parts from?" he asked again.

"The Singer Company in Boston. They can put them on the next train, far as that goes." He looked to the two men. "While I have a woman starting a store in Fargo that will stock machines, materials, and notions, I would be right happy to have someone do the same in this area, especially if'n that could include a repair service. Not that these little beauties need much repair, but, you know, just in case."

Hjelmer scratched his chin. He glanced at Olaf, who wore the same deep-thinking expression.

Penny's fingers itched. She wanted to try out the machine so badly, yet she hated to disturb the moment.

She stroked the stack of napkins, thinking of all the hours she'd spent hemming napkins, dish towels, sheets, pillow-cases, curtains—all that besides clothes. Goodie moved to her side and picked up one of the squares, leaning closer to the lamp and turning the napkin around.

"Take a heap a learnin', I'm thinking."

Drummond shook his head. "Not at all. Once you get proficient at using the machine, I can even show you how to blind hem."

"Like skirt hems and such?" Goodie turned her head, giving him an "are you sure about this" look. Her right eyebrow cocked while her fingers kept up an exploration of the hemmed napkin all on their own.

"Most surely." Drummond sat back down, creased a narrow fold in another piece of muslin, then folded a wider hem. "Just like you do, right?" The women nodded. "Okay, then you fold again, this time the body of the garment so you have this line to stitch on." He indicated the edge of the first fold. He set the material in place, lowered the presser foot. "Now you take four stitches." He turned the wheel manually rather than pumping the pedal with his feet. "Then give a little twist with your wrist, catch the body with one stitch, and return to the four on the edge." He did several more to show the pattern, lifted the presser foot, and snipped the threads.

Penny cringed at the amount of thread he wasted.

He smoothed the right side of the sample, and sure enough, all one saw was the one thread, and so even that it looked almost like a decoration.

"Well, I never." The awe in Goodie's tone echoed in Penny's mind.

"May I try it?" Penny had to clear her throat to keep from whispering.

"Of course, dear lady." Drummond got up and indicated his chair. "You just set yourself down there and give it a try. Then it will be your turn." He included Goodie with a smile.

He gave Penny instructions on how to work the treadle. "You can use one or both feet." Then he handed her a piece of material. "Now, with this handle back here, you lower that presser foot, then set your needle, and begin rocking the treadle with your feet." He turned the handwheel for her.

With a couple of tentative toe pressings, she got the rhythm, and the needle flew across the fabric, leaving a line of stitches in its wake.

"Well, I never." Goodie breathed from over Penny's shoulder. "Ya done it."

"It takes some practice to sew curves and angles and such, but I will teach you all of that. You'll be sewing up a storm before you know it." He patted the machine as though it were a favorite dog or horse—or wife.

"My turn?"

Penny hated to get up. She wanted to learn more immediately. She liked the song the treadle made and the whir of the needle. The speed amazed her. *Every woman needs one of these.* She couldn't get the idea out of her mind.

Goodie stood up a few minutes later with the same look of delight and awe. If this was the way Hjelmer felt when he first saw the binders, no wonder he nearly went loco.

"How soon can you have us one?" Olaf asked, cupping his elbows in the opposite palm. He rocked back on his heels, then dug in his pocket for his pipe.

Hjelmer looked up from studying the gears to Penny's face. "Make that two, and you better send an extra so there's one to sell. I know Haakan will want one for Ingeborg."

Penny smiled at her husband, but it did no good, he'd gone back to studying the gears.

Later, after Mr. Drummond left with the Wolds for his bed in the sack house, Penny turned out the one lamp and set the other beside Hjelmer's chair. He looked up from the mail he was slitting open with a letter opener he had made.

"Here, this one's for you." He handed an opened envelope to Penny.

She studied the handwriting and the postmark. Iowa. Who would be writing to her from Iowa?

W hat happened?" Mary Martha rushed through the bedroom door.

"Ma-a." Deborah flung herself in her new mother's arms.

"Gently, little one. There's no need to cry." Katy patted the little girl's back. "Here, let me sit up."

"No, you just lie there and tell me what happened." Mary Martha sank down on the edge of the bed by Katy's knees. Blue and purple shadows beneath Katy's eyes looked like bruises on her pale face. *How much weight has she lost? She looks like a ghost. Why haven't I been more observant?*

Deborah lifted her tear-stained face. "You ain't gonna die, are ya?"

Katy smoothed the sandy wisps of hair back from her daughter's face. "Why, whatever made you think that?"

" 'Cause you look like my real ma did." Deborah dashed the tears away with the backs of her hands. "She was sick something awful."

"Well, I'm not 'sick something awful.' I just didn't feel well and thought I better lie down so I would feel good when you got home from school. Why don't you go get me a drink of water? Ask Manda to fetch a fresh bucket from the well. Cold well water would taste so good right now."

"I will." Deborah pushed away and darted from the room.

"What really happened?"

"I . . . I found blood. Mary Martha, I don't want to lose this baby." She clutched her sister-in-law's hand.

"Now, lots of women have bleeding before the baby comes.

You just take it easy for a couple of days, and it'll be gone. You'll see. My ma takes care of lots of women. She's the midwife for our parish, and I've heard of all kinds of different things. You can always send for Ingeborg or Metiz, too, you know." *Please, God, let this be all there is. Oh, I wish my mother were here.*

Katy shook her head. "No, no need to bother them. You already made me feel better." She started to roll to her side to get up, but Mary Martha laid a hand on her shoulder.

"You are to take it easy for a couple of days, remember?"

"Surely that don't mean lying around like this. I got supper to make. Zeb will be home soon, and . . ."

"It won't be the first time my brother has eaten my cooking, and it surely won't be the last. How about you go over Deborah's letters and numbers with her while I see about the supper? And if I can get Manda in here, she needs review on her times tables."

"She'll be down working with the horses."

"I know. That girl would live at the barn if'n we let her." Katy lay back with a sigh. "I hate feeling like this. There's so much to get done before the winter comes. I thought to begin banking the house today."

"Ah 'spect my brother can do some of those things, you know? And if he brings up a wagonload of straw and manure, Manda and I can pitch it up against the house."

"You ever made soap before?"

"Many times. And dipped candles too. During the war we didn't have kerosene or oil, so we melted down some old beeswax and had the purtiest candles you ever saw. I was just a little girl, but I could dip candles just fine. We had a mold one time, but when some scalawag Yankee soldiers raided our place, they stole anything they could. We had to make do or die after that."

"Where was your pa?"

"Off to war. He come home without an arm, leaving both it and his will to live on some battlefield." Mary Martha shook her head. "He never was the same loving papa again. Near to broke my mother's heart, but she's a strong one. Kept right on caring for the farm and anyone who needed help until Papa finally got some better again. Zeb's been doing the work of a full-grown man ever since he was eight or ten."

Katy propped herself on one elbow when Deborah returned carrying a cup full of water. She tried to drink, but instead the water dribbled down her chin, making the little girl giggle.

"This is silly." Katy handed the cup back and pulled herself upright, crossing her legs under the covers. After drinking, she cocked her head, listening to the thunk of wood dropping into the box and the clattering of stove lids.

"That's Manda." Deborah snuggled herself against Katy's side. "She said for you to stay in bed, and she would make supper."

"What about her chores?"

"She done them."

"Did them." Mary Martha couldn't resist correcting the little one's grammar.

"That's what I said." Deborah used both hands to brush from her eyes the wisps of hair that had come loose from her braids.

The two women exchanged smiles as Mary Martha got to her feet. "You say your numbers and letters now for your ma, and I'll go help in the kitchen. Tell her what all went on today at school too." She patted Deborah's head gently and headed for the door, pausing before going through it. "You need anything else?"

"Just permission to get up," Katy said.

"Since that's not likely to happen, lie back and enjoy the rest."

"She's going to die, ain't she?" Manda slammed the last lid back in place.

Mary Martha shook her head. "You and Deborah. Why, no. Sometimes mamas just need a little extra help in the early months."

"My ma was just like this, and she died."

Mary Martha wanted to wrap her arms around Manda and hold her close, but the rigid shoulders and squared jaw told her that wouldn't be appreciated, nor even tolerated. She sighed. "Let's just pray for her and make her take it easy around here, and she'll be fine."

"God don't much care one way or t'other." Manda filled a

kettle with water and set it on the hot part of the stove.

"Why, yes, He most certainly does. Whatever gave you that idea?"

"We prayed, but Ma died anyway, and I prayed lots when Pa didn't come home, and it never did any good at all. So why spend all that time prayin' when you could be doing something instead?"

"I pray while I'm doing."

"You don't close your eyes and fold your hands like the preacher says?" Manda looked at Mary Martha as if a heretic had wandered in.

"Sometimes, but not always. The Bible says to pray unceasingly, but if you kept your hands folded and eyes closed all the time, your family would starve to death. I think God means us to live our lives like He would have us and keep on talking with Him, just like you and I are talking now." She could tell by the look on Manda's face that she had a long way to go to get any convincing done. "You just think about it. If Jesus is right in our hearts, He knows our thoughts."

"Durn."

Mary Martha couldn't resist. She laughed and grabbed Manda's arm, pulling her into a hug. "Ah, child, He loves you so much, and so do I."

Manda relaxed into the embrace for a moment before pulling away. "I got to get to peeling some spuds."

Letting her go, Mary Martha caught a sheen in Manda's eyes. *She's really frightened. Dear God, what all did these two lambs go through before Zeb found them?* While her brother had given her snips and bits of his two years on the run, they'd never sat down and talked about how he ended up with a ready-made family. One of his comments stuck in her mind. *"Mother wouldn't let me do anything else but bring them along."* She knew for a fact her mother had been living in Missouri on the homeplace, for that's where she'd been too.

And here the girls were facing again the fear of losing a mother. *God, please take care of Katy, for the sake of these two girls, if not for Zeb and the rest of us.* Mary Martha took the knife from Manda. "I'll do this. You go on and work with the horses, like you usually do. I thought to fry up some steaks cut off that pork shoulder. What do you think?"

"Uh-huh. I'll go dig some carrots then." Manda left without looking her aunt in the eye.

If she's embarrassed about a near tear or two . . . Mary Martha shook her head. Katy had a lot to deal with here—new husband, a baby on the way, and two girls who needed help making up for the years the locusts ate. *God, you promised to do that for us, and I sure do hope you plan to take care of this little problem here. To me, these are big problems, but to you, they're nothing at all.*

As she peeled the potatoes and sliced the meat, she kept sending up the petitions, grateful she didn't have to close her eyes and fold her hands, as Manda thought.

Katy joined them for supper, and with her presence and laughter, the big cloud that had been smothering the house picked up and floated away. Zeb, the girls, and Mary Martha herself joined in, each trying to outdo the other in outrageous stories.

"You won't tell Zeb, will you?" Katy whispered after the girls left for bed and Zeb had gone out for a last check on the animals.

"Not if you will."

"I will, but not right now. Let me see how things go and—"

"And that's not fair a'tall."

"I know, but this is woman's worry, and he's got enough of his own."

Mary Martha shook her head. "I don't know."

"If it's as you said, then I'll be fine in a day or so, and he would have worried for nothing."

"I'll stay home tomorrow, and then we'll see."

Katy shook her head this time. "No, then he'll know something is wrong. You go on about helping at the school, and I'll take it real easy here, and everything will work out right for everybody."

Mary Martha now figured she knew what a fly felt like when trapped in a spider's web. "You promise?"

Katy nodded.

"And you'll tell him yourself if the bleeding keeps up more than a couple days?"

Another nod.

"It's not like Pastor Solberg couldn't do without me." *Half the time he tries to pretend I'm not there anyway.* But she didn't tell Katy that, knowing the young woman would blame herself. *And it's not her fault he is being so standoffish.*

"Where's Katy?" Zeb asked, hanging his jacket on a wall peg.

"I sent her to bed. She's looking a mite peaked." Mary Martha put the last dish up in the cupboard and hung the wet dish towel over the oven handle.

"Good. I thought so too." He leaned his hips against the reservoir on the stove. "So, how did school really go today?"

"I think that while Pastor Solberg wanted help, he didn't want it to be me." She straightened the dish towel again. "I seem to make him very uncomfortable."

Zeb's eyebrows disappeared under the lock of hair that fell across his forehead. "Really?"

"Now don't you go getting any ideas. Or I won't go back."

Zeb held up his hands in surrender. "No ideas. Not a one will cross my mind. I am going to bed, since that seems to be the safest place in the house right now."

Mary Martha thumped him on the arm as he walked past her. "Just remember, *baby* brother, I didn't come here looking for a husband, and I plan to go back home before Christmas, so I won't be helping out too long with the school. Besides, the thought of being a pastor's wife is one of my worst nightmares." She even shuddered for emphasis.

"Wait till after Christmas to go. Ma and Uncle Jed can do without you for one year. They can go to Eva Jane's house instead of them all coming back to the farm."

"We'll see."

"And who said anything about you being a pastor's wife anyhow?" Laughter floated back over his shoulder as he left the room.

Mary Martha banked the stove and wandered off to her room, stopping to check on the girls on her way. They slept soundly in the double bed they shared. Manda had an arm thrown over her sister, protecting her even in sleep. "Father, bless them and hold them in the palm of your hand," she whispered, refraining from tucking the covers in more snugly.

After her prayers and crawling into bed, she promised herself that she would ride over and talk with Ingeborg after school the next day. Mary Martha finally drifted off to sleep but not until banishing from her mind a thought of Pastor Solberg as he smiled at little Anna Helmsrude.

At least today I have my assignments, Mary Martha thought as they neared the school. While she'd wanted to stay at home, Katy insisted she go. *"Those children need you more than I do,"* she'd said. And Mary Martha had a hard time arguing. For the first time in several weeks Katy had color in her cheeks, and she did indeed look rested.

But I'm still going to Ingeborg's. Deborah can go with me, and Manda can hitch a ride with someone else or walk. She just wished she could do something about the butterflies rampaging about somewhere in her middle.

"Mith MacCallithter, you came back." Anna ran across the school yard to stop beside the wagon.

"I surely did that." Mary Martha swung over the wheel and used it for a stepping stool.

"I'll take care of the horse for you." Thorliff and Baptiste met her as she stepped on the ground.

"I'll take care of our horse," Manda said, scowling at the two boys.

"We'll help."

Mary Martha watched the exchange, making sure her face remained serious. Laughing would only make Manda more churlish. She felt a small hand take hers. Looking down, she had Deborah on one side and Anna on the other. Their faces smiling up at her made her grateful she'd listened to Katy. Anna, for one, did truly need her. Today they would begin work on her lisp.

She swung their hands as they made their way to the soddy door, where Pastor Solberg was about to ring the bell. She glanced up in time to see a puzzled look wrinkle his forehead, but then it was gone. *What is bothering him today?* Not that she cared. Unless he banished her from the school yard or some equally farfetched idea.

She settled in with the three Erickson sisters, Thorliff again acting as interpreter. But her Norwegian was improving about as fast as their English, so the lessons were much easier. For all of them.

Clouds racing before the wind greeted them on their dinner recess.

"Storm coming," Baptiste said, studying the western sky. Cotton bole clouds stacked the horizon, not the gray ones skittering above them. When they covered the sun, everyone shivered.

Mary Martha took her dinner pail and sat with the children on the south side of the soddy.

"How come you talk tho funny?" Anna looked up from her folded sandwich.

"I live in Missouri. After we eat, I'll show you where that is on the map. Down there, people just talk different than you folks do up here. Maybe 'cause it's warmer, we like to talk slower."

"Oh. Are you going to thtay here forever?"

Deborah leaned closer on the other side. "Manda says we're going to hog-tie her to keep her with us. Her and Pa."

Mary Martha shook her head, her laughter rising like a lark's song on the wind.

Pastor Solberg had gone home for a book he'd forgotten when he heard her. He glanced up to follow the sound and saw her surrounded by the younger girls and Andrew, who never left Ellie's side. The bigger boys and Manda were setting up to play Ante Over, tossing a ball over the schoolhouse roof.

Mary Martha stood, then taking the hand of the child beside her, she pointed toward the open area in front of the shed. They all followed her there, and a circle game commenced. For a change there would be no hurt feelings from the little ones because the bigger children wouldn't let them play.

When he rang the bell, Mary Martha's cheeks were red from the wind, her laughter still echoed in his ears, and he couldn't keep his eyes off her. Whatever was the matter with him, he wondered.

Some time later, when Anna stood to take her turn reading aloud, a snicker caused heads to turn. Anna ducked her chin and held the open book to her chest. Red crept up her neck and washed her pale cheeks.

"Quiet!" Pastor Solberg felt like leaping to his feet, but Andrew Bjorklund beat him to it and headed for the White boys, one of whom had a hand over his mouth.

"Andrew, please take your seat." Solberg kept his voice even but firm.

Andrew stopped, looked at the teacher, then back at the boys, who now sat straight as if the snickering had never happened.

"Andrew Bjorklund, sit down!" hissed Thorliff.

Andrew took another step toward the boys, then turned, shot a glare over his shoulder, and took his seat again.

"Thank you." Pastor Solberg nodded at him. He turned to Anna. "You may continue. You are reading better all the time."

But her voice could barely be heard now, and when she came to an *s*, her lower lip trembled.

Mary Martha looked from the child to the teacher and back again. What could she do?

When Anna finished reading, he nodded. "Very good. Now you may go, and Miss MacCallister will help you. All right?"

Anna's head bobbed like a heavy flower on a tired stem. "Thank you."

"Toby, Jerry, please remain seated. The rest of you are dismissed." Pastor Solberg waited as the children stood quietly and walked to the door. Once outside, shouting and laughter told the world that school was out.

"I'll see you tomorrow then?" he asked Mary Martha.

She paused before following the children outside but didn't even glance at the two remaining in their seats. "That will be fine, thank you."

She was glad she wasn't in the boys' position. The stern look on the pastor's face said they were in for it.

Once outside the schoolhouse, Mary Martha called out, "Thorliff, and everyone going that way, you want a ride?"

As they all clambered into the back of the wagon, Manda took her seat beside Mary Martha. "I'll drop you off at home first if you want."

Manda shook her head. "No, this is all right. We won't stay long, will we?"

"No. Too much to do at home." Mary Martha could hear Thorliff scolding Andrew.

"You don't get out of your seat without asking permission first."

"But . . . but they . . . they made Anna almost cry."

"I know, but the teacher will take care of that."

Mary Martha clucked the horse forward just in time to hear a mutter from Andrew.

"They better not do it again or . . ."

10

S o, we can't both sell sewing machines."

"I think that's about right." Hjelmer looked up from the book he was studying. He and Penny had just finished supper a couple of days after the sewing machine demonstrations. "But there are several ways to look at this." He leaned back in his chair and tented his fingertips. "If you decide to carry the line, you will need more room. The store is full to overflowing as it is."

"But I already have the dress goods and notions."

"That's another point. You also serve dinner to more people every day. Today you had to sit a second serving because the tables were full the first time, and you can't bear to turn anyone away."

"Well, they were hungry, and there is nowhere else in town they can get a meal." She gave the bread dough she was kneading a solid thump when she turned it. The kneading rhythm began again. Push down on the dough with the heel of the hand, roll the top edge of the dough inward, and push again. One could work off all kinds of resentments kneading bread. The madder the kneader, the lighter the bread.

She turned to give her husband a "don't mess with me" look. "If Bridget could get her boardinghouse going, *that* problem would be taken care of."

"So, which would you rather do? Serve dinners or sell sewing machines and teach people how to use them?"

Penny nibbled on her bottom lip. "Both . . . neither."

Hjelmer smiled at her in the lamplight. "And that right

there is the problem. You have to make up your mind before you can go any further. Now, Goodie is single-minded. She could use part of the sack house for space if she needed. She is excited about the machine, and Olaf could become a repairman if he wants."

"From the gleam in your eye, I thought you might want to do that."

He wrinkled his brow. "I could. From the looks of it, Singer has done a fine job of creating a good machine. But . . ." He raised his hands in the air. "Like you, I already have more irons in the fire than I know what to do with." He shuffled through the mail from the day. "I think part of that problem may be solved though." He picked up one letter and raised it in the light. "You remember me telling you about Sam, the darkie who worked on the railroad with me, then we shared a house in St. Paul?"

Penny nodded. "I'm listening." She rolled the dough into a ball and laid it in a crockery bowl, putting a dish towel over the top. After setting it on the reservoir where it could rise all night, she started cleaning up the flour mess. The rustle of paper told her that Hjelmer was taking the letter out of the envelope. The wish for another letter like the one she'd received earlier flitted through her mind. Months before she had written to an address cousin Ephraim had given her in the hopes of contacting the brothers and sisters she hadn't seen nor heard from since they were all separated on the death of their parents. Oh, how she had wanted a family of her own. Her brother two years younger had written from where he lived in Iowa with a distant relative of the family. He had always wondered what happened to her and hoped she would answer back. She had, the very next day.

"Listen to what he says," Hjelmer continued.

" 'Dear Hjelmer,
I hope you remember me, as we worked on the railroad together. You said then that if I ever wanted to move to a small town in Dakota, to let you know. I have decided that is what I want. I have some money set by, enough to bring my family with me. I would like to buy a farm or work for someone until I can do that. If you know of anything there, please write to me.'

"He ends by giving the address." Hjelmer looked up, folding the letter at the same time. "What do you think?"

"I think you have plenty of work for him here. Haakan will need another pair of hands with the lumber milling and the ice house, besides the farm. Ingeborg is talking about building a bigger well house so she can make and sell more cheese. She might need more help. I'd say there's plenty for him to do here."

Hjelmer nodded slowly, his tongue stroking his front teeth. "There's one problem."

Penny dusted the flour into her hand and brushed her hands over the wash pan. "What's that?"

"Sam is Negro, black Negro."

"So?"

"Some people might hold that against him."

"Oh, for pity's sake, not here in Blessing."

"You think not? Look how some of them reacted to Metiz."

"Yes, but . . . but . . ." A frown creased her forehead. "Isn't this different?"

"How so?

"She—Metiz—is half Indian. And you know the horror stories people had heard about Indians. Besides, no one feels that way any longer now that they all know her. She's helped so many of them, even when they were less than gracious." She removed her apron and hung it on a hook by the back door. "So, what are you going to tell him?"

"To come and work for me but be prepared for some mistrust." He shook his head. "We didn't have a problem like this in Norway."

"We solved your problem, now what about mine?"

"Have you talked this over with Goodie?"

Penny shook her head. "I've been so busy I haven't had time. For all I know, she ordered the whole package."

"What about Drummond?"

"He said he'd be back next week and hoped I could have made my decision by then. I didn't feel I could ask him about Goodie."

"But you ordered your machine?"

She nodded again, then yawned and stretched. "So, when are you going to begin building Bridget's boardinghouse?"

Hjelmer stopped, setting out the ink bottle and paper. "I wish I'd never heard the word boardinghouse."

"Ingeborg is donating the land."

"How did you hear that?"

"She told me." Penny walked behind her husband and began massaging his neck and shoulders in the way she knew he liked. "And there's much of the lumber curing since last winter. She figures she could start with a two-story building like their farmhouse and then add on later."

Hjelmer shook his head. "It's not as easy as you women try to make it out to be."

"If someone, say, Olaf, wanted to do this, would there be as much of a problem?"

"Olaf can't cook."

"No, but Goodie can, and besides, you know that's not what I was talking about."

The ink blotted the sheet of paper. Hjelmer said a word not normally used in their home. Sometimes she heard it from the blacksmith but not in the house.

"Hjelmer Bjorklund!" She pinched his shoulder rather than rubbing it. *This thing with the boardinghouse is really bothering you, and I just don't understand why.* She soothed the spot she'd pinched. He hadn't even noticed . . . or so it seemed.

The words flowed from beneath his pen, and while Penny wanted to tease him a little, she refrained. After all, this was a business letter, and she knew how much he would rather be repairing machines than fitting wagon wheels. Shrinking the iron rims to fit the wooden wheels took a lot of time and firewood. He never had liked doing that much.

A thought stopped her ministering fingers. "Sam can do some of the blacksmithing for you, right?"

At his nod, she breathed a sigh of relief. A yawn caught her by surprise and made her jaw crack. "I'm going to bed. You coming?"

"Soon." He signed his name with a flourish and blew on the wet ink. "There. That can go off tomorrow, and most likely they'll be here within the month. Or at least Sam will." He turned and pulled her onto his lap. "You pinched me."

"You said something you shouldn't have."

"One word."

"When we have children, you want them to talk that way?"

"They better not."

If we have children? Each month brought another letdown. Once she'd been late and had high hopes for two days. Tante Agnes kept saying "all in God's good time," but Penny knew that Agnes herself suffered from not having more babies. But more babies was surely different than no babies, wasn't it?

"You've gone away from me." Hjelmer used two fingers under her chin to bring her gaze back to his. He looked deep in her eyes, his own warm and compassionate.

She felt a stirring deep inside her. The warmth grew and tingled all the way to the tips of her fingers, calling them to stroke back his hair and circle his ears. She stood and tugged on his hand. "Come on, Hjelmer, let's go to bed."

⚜   ⚜

"If I were you, I would talk this over with Goodie right away," Hjelmer said in the morning as he finished his last cup of coffee. They'd already heard Anner Valders open the door to the bank. The hinges on the screen door needed oiling.

"I plan to." Penny leaned over the oven door and stuck a straw into the chocolate cake she had baking. Four loaves of bread were rising in their pans. She shut the oven door and dropped the straw into the fire. Glancing at the clock, she figured another five minutes and the cake would be done. Once it cooled, she could frost it, and with the pies Goodie was bringing, they should have enough dessert for dinner. Yesterday Hjelmer hadn't even had a taste.

But when Goodie came, Penny was tied up with a customer in the store. By the time she broke away, Goodie had left her pies and bread and was gone again.

I'll have to go over there later this afternoon. But the day went by so fast that they were sitting down to supper before she knew it.

"Did you talk with Goodie?" Hjelmer had been equally busy, not even taking time for an afternoon cup of coffee. Talking, with all the noon guests around, was impossible. After the diners hurried on their way, Penny was left with a mountain of dishes to do, besides run the store.

The next day Olaf brought the bread and pies over instead of Goodie.

"We won't be needing any tomorrow," Penny said as he set them on the table. "What with that debate and all, I'm closing the Bjorklund restaurant for the day."

"Good idea. Besides, everyone will be bringing food for the dinner, right?"

"The railroaders can just come and join us all." Penny stood up from stirring the baking beans. "Olaf, what do you . . ."

But he shook his head, slowlike, and backed out the door.

"Now, whatever is the matter with him?"

Moments later, a knock at the door brought her running. "Good—" She stopped. "Bridget, how good to see you and Metiz. It's been ages."

"We brought half a wheel of cheese—that's all Ingeborg has right now—and there's a box of eggs too." Bridget turned to the wagon, and the three of them carried the things inside.

"You want we stay to help?" Metiz asked, her black eyes snapping. Short and getting shorter with each winter, her face wrinkled like an apple left in the barrel in spring, hair graying but still thick and full of life, Metiz gazed out on the world through eyes that saw far beyond the surface.

"Would you?" Penny pushed a pan back on the stove. "The tables need setting, the—" The bell over the door in the store tinkled. "Back in a minute." She heard Metiz say, "Something bothering Penny," as she brushed aside the curtain. Now how did she know?

By the time she'd helped Mrs. Vegard choose material for two new dresses, along with the lace and notions to match, all she could think of was getting dinner ready. She went to the door of the bank, where Anner Valders sat at the desk working on the books.

"Mr. Valders, could you please come mind the store awhile? I have to get the meal ready, and they're already lining up outside."

"Yes, surely." Marking the place with a slip of paper, he closed the ledger and, after setting it back on the shelf, walked across the room toward her. He no longer listed to one side, having gotten used to living with one arm after the accident during threshing last year. "Is there anything special you want me to do?"

"Well, we need coffee weighed out in one-pound bags, there's always dusting, and . . ." The bell tinkled again. Penny shrugged. "It's been like this all morning."

"I'll take care of it." He made a shooing motion with his hand. "Go now."

"Thank you so much. As soon as Ephraim gets back, I'll send him in." She headed for the kitchen, where the tables were all set and Bridget was mashing the potatoes. "Ah, you two are a lifesaver this morning."

"I told you I'd come regular, if you like." Bridget wiped away a bead of sweat from beside her eye, the potato masher waving in the air before being slammed back down into the pot of drained potatoes.

"How did you know I was going to mash them?"

"You had the masher all laid out." Bridget shook her head. "You got too much on your mind, child."

Metiz brought in an armload of wood and dropped it in the woodbox at the back of the stove. "What else?"

"The water bucket needs filling. They'll need to wash up before dinner." Many of her customers worked on the railroad in one capacity or another, mostly maintaining the tracks, so they were filthy from the dust and coal. The engineers rushed in for a plateful while Olaf filled the water tanks from the water tower.

With the three of them scurrying around, they made it just as the noon train blew its whistle up the track. Metiz was still slicing bread as Penny went to the door of the store and called her customers. "You can come round to the back now. Dinner is ready."

Bridget set a bucket of hot water out on the bench and one of cold. Bars of soap lined the shelf above the washbasins, and towels lay folded, ready for use. A sign read, "Please Dump the Soapy Water on the Flowers."

Washed and hair slicked back, the men lined up and found their places at the tables. There were three more waiting.

"If I bring you each a plateful, would you mind eating out here? There's just no more room right now."

The men nodded. One went to roll up a couple of wood

butts lying by the woodpile ready to split. Two more men came around the corner of the house.

"This where you get that good food I been hearing so much about?"

"You wash up there."

Penny heard the exchange as she returned with a plate in each hand. "Two more?" Her voice squeaked. *I'm running out of food again. How will I ever keep ahead?* At least she had plenty of baked beans and bread. There might not be any loaves for sale later, but that was just the way it was.

When the train whistled, four men stood to leave. Penny handed them their pie on a double-folded piece of brown paper, and out the door they went, dropping their twenty-five cents in the jar as they left.

When the kitchen finally cleared, Penny and Bridget looked at each other and laughed. Metiz shook her head. "You crazy." But her laughing eyes told them she was teasing. "I brought more knives, rabbit skin vests, and . . ." She raised a finger and slipped out the back door, returning in a few moments with a pack that she set on the table. "Moccasins." She set the things out on the hastily cleared table.

"Mittens too." Penny held up the children's-size mittens with the rabbit fur on the inside that would keep the child's hands warmer. "You do such beautiful work." Each moccasin had a design beaded on the upper portion. "Do you want me to pay you, or—"

"You take these, and I take flour, beans, sugar, coffee."

"That is good, but you still have not used up all the money you earned for the last things. You don't shop very often, and your bone-handled knives are valuable."

Metiz smiled up at her. "Only when need."

"Well, I'm glad we can work together like this, and thank you both for helping me. Now it's our turn to eat." Scraping the bottoms of the pans, they found enough for themselves and poured boiling water in the pots and pans to make cleanup easier.

When they were seated and the blessing asked, Penny turned to Bridget. "Wait until you see that new machine we found. It's going to change the way we sew."

"Sew? You mean this is a machine for us?"

"A sewing machine that sews faster than I ever saw in my whole life. You won't believe it. Mr. Drummond will be back next week, and I'm going to have demonstrations here so everyone can see it." She took a bite of her buttered bread and shook her head. "That little machine will turn out sheets and towels and napkins like you've never seen." She got up and fetched the stack of muslin squares from the shelf. "He did these in . . . in only a few minutes."

Bridget and Metiz each took one and turned it both ways, running their fingers along the stitching much like Penny had done.

"You watched the man do this?"

Penny nodded. "And, Bridget, you can pay for the machine in small monthly amounts if you can't afford the entire price. Hjelmer and Olaf both looked at it and talked with Mr. Drummond about repairing them. He said he needed repair places, although he promised the sewing machine hardly ever breaks. Just needs to be cleaned and oiled like any machine."

Bridget handed the muslin square back to her. "If it does what you say, I know I would sure like one someday."

Metiz laid hers down on the table. "Sew with deer gut?"

Penny chuckled. "No, I don't think so. The thread has to be fine to go through the eye of the needle."

"So Goodie has seen the machine work?"

Penny nodded. *And hasn't spoken to me since.* "And Olaf. I was so excited, I thought Hjelmer was never going to come home that night. If the salesman had one along to sell, I would have bought it right then. But I did the next best thing—ordered one." She glanced up to mentally count the days. "It should be here in six or seven days."

"My land, child, when you get an idea in your head, you're worse'n a runaway horse. What's the hurry?"

Penny couldn't say "to get ahead of Goodie." She studied the lines the fork tines drew on the tablecloth. Feeling eyes on her, she looked up to see Metiz' obsidian eyes zeroed in on her.

"What wrong?" The voice came gently.

Penny could feel tears burning the backs of her eyes and running into her nose. She sniffed. "Nothing." But she knew that wasn't true, and from the look she gave, so did Metiz.

"Ja, well, I better get on home. That horse has been standing out there for some time." Bridget looked around the kitchen. "Let's get going on those dishes."

"No, cousin Ephraim does that for me. He'll be along soon. He had to help the Johnsons with their butchering this morning."

"Haakan says it is not cold enough yet to butcher, but he hung the deer Baptiste got last night. The boys bagged some more geese too, but nothing like that load Ingeborg brought home. Eight Canada geese, fat they were. I kept the goose grease for our hands this winter. Nothing helps cracks on the fingers and lips more than goose grease."

"Oh, how I would love to serve goose one day. Ask if they get any extras to bring them my way. Maybe I should ask Ingeborg to get us a deer. I don't know when Hjelmer would have time to go hunting."

Metiz sat without moving, and every time Penny shifted, she could feel the old woman studying her. She kept her gaze from returning to Metiz, but only by concentrated effort. Finally she could stand it no longer.

"Would you like some of your staples today?"

Metiz shook her head.

Penny got to her feet, knowing the action invited her guest to leave. But she had so much to do, too much to sit here visiting the afternoon away. "Anytime you want to do some baking, Bridget, I can always use more. I've been bagging cookies, and the men take those with them. They'd take a whole pie, some of them, if I had it to sell."

"Maybe we should start a bakery."

Penny nodded at Bridget. "So many good ideas and so few hours in the day. That train going through here surely did make a difference." As they made their way toward the door, she snatched up one of the napkins. "Show this to Ingeborg and Kaaren and see what they think."

Metiz stopped with one foot on the wagon wheel. She turned to give Penny another one of her looks that seemed to go clear to the heart. "You do best."

Penny's next words caught in her throat. *But what is best? And for whom? And besides, Goodie knows the way to my house just like I know the way to hers.* Finally she said, "Ja, well, it goes both ways." She helped Bridget up into the wagon and stepped back.

Smoke curled out of the chimney of the house next door, not from the sack house. Just a quick walk across the field and she would be at Goodie's door. *But what do I say? I have done nothing wrong, have I? Then how come I feel like I have?* She waved good-bye to her departing friends. Right now, she wished they would stay.

Go on over there and talk with Goodie, she told herself, then took her order to heart and strode across the acre piece. But when she knocked on the door, there was no answer. She stepped back. Surely the fire would be banked if no one was home. Did that curtain move upstairs or was it the wind?

Maybe Goodie was sick.

Penny pushed open the back door and stuck her head inside. "Goodie, are you here?"

Nothing. Maybe she'd gone to get the children from school. Or was visiting someone.

Or maybe she didn't want to talk with Penny at all.

11

"Haakan, remember that matter you came to me about?"

"Ja, Pastor, I do." Haakan took his foot back down from the wagon wheel. "What about it?"

"I took care of it. No need for you to be concerned any longer." Pastor Solberg stuck his hands in his pockets.

"Mange takk. I do appreciate that. I just didn't know what to do."

"Well, I don't think he will be so rough with her again. Thank you for putting me in mind of it."

"Ja, since they stay outside of the community, I just didn't know what else to do." Haakan lifted his hands and let them drop again while he spoke. The silence between the two men slipped by, leaving a feeling of camaraderie behind.

"October sure is flying by, isn't it? That's that north wind warning us." Solberg glanced to the north, but the horizon held no storm clouds, only the haze of fall.

The horses stamped and blew clouds of steam into the cold air. The jingle of their harnesses made Haakan step back up on the wagon wheel. "I'd best be on my way. We're going to be butchering first thing in the morning. If you have nothing else to do, we can always use an extra hand." He swung on up to the wagon seat and unwrapped the reins from the brake handle. "See you then?"

"I might do that."

"Zeb and his family will be over to help, along with the Baards. It will be more like a party than a workday. And there'll be klubb for supper."

"Bribery it is then, eh?" Solberg stamped his feet. "I'll be there." His ears at least had warmed up—at the mention of the MacCallisters. That meant Mary Martha would be there. As if he didn't see her enough every day at school helping the Erickson girls and little Anna.

He waved again at Haakan and turned toward the soddy. The package under his arm would taste good with a cup of coffee. Bridget had sent him some lefse. The pencils and paper he'd purchased, along with some things for his cupboard, promised him an evening of pleasure. Preparing the Sunday sermon took several nights of studying, thinking, and praying for wisdom, then Friday night he wrote it out. If he waited until Saturday, there was no more time to rethink it, and besides, many times he was invited out to one of the farms to join the families in whatever they were doing. Like this invitation from Haakan.

The cat greeted him with a meow and a winding around the legs, then leaped up on the chair, kneading and purring. He knew the routine about as well as the man.

"Already need the lamp, don't we?" John took a spill from the can on the wall, then lighting it in the stove, he touched the lamp wick until it flared. His mother would say his lamp chimney needed washing, and she would be right. So many little things needed doing around here, things that he never got around to doing since school had started again.

After opening the stove draft, John laid a couple sticks of wood on top of the coals and watched while they caught. He should be out chopping wood, for the pile was getting low. Setting the lids back in place, he pulled the coffeepot forward and checked the reservoir. That needed filling too. But first the sermon. He buttered the lefse and sprinkled cinnamon and sugar on it, then he took his hot cup of coffee with the plate of rolled lefse and settled into his chair. The cat jumped on his lap, licked his chin once, then kneaded his way in a circle and curled up, his purr rattling the windows.

Solberg quieted his mind while sipping his coffee and enjoying the lefse. "Father God, you know I can't do this without you. I want them to hear your words, not mine. Please fill my mind with yourself so that this sermon, this service, radiates your love and forgiveness, Father, that we can continue to draw closer to you." He sighed. "How can I get them all into your Word every day? How can we survive without you?"

The cat purred on. The peace of the room seeped into his soul. He picked up his tablet and pencil and began to write. "Dearly beloved, I write this that you may know, and that knowing, you may have eternal life." He continued with the passage from 1 John, reading parts of it aloud, looking for other references about the value of taking in the Word. As he read them, he wrote them on his paper, closing his eyes and being silent before the Father.

When he finished, there were more of God's words on the pages than his, just the way he liked it. So often someone commented on how wisely he wrote, and he had to laugh. "Those are God's words, not mine." So often he said that. He read through the pages again, making some changes and thinking about what he knew of his people's needs.

He knelt before his chair and rested his forehead on his hands. As he held each of his flock before the throne of God, he asked for wisdom for some, love for others, and always a closer walk of faith for each. When Mary Martha came to mind, he shook his head. "Father, she irritates me so, and I have no idea why. She's so good with the children, and I should be grateful—believe me, I am—but one minute I think we could be friends, and the next she's gotten under my skin again. I don't know what to do." He waited, hoping God would give him a burst of wisdom right then. Instead he heard something that sounded like a chuckle but convinced himself that it was the sound of the wood coals falling in the stove. His knees creaked when he finally stood again.

He let the cat out, banked the stove, and made ready for bed. When the cat meowed, he let it back in and climbed under the quilt. Tomorrow would be a good time. He always had a good time at the Bjorklunds and came away feeling like part of the family. Everyone needed a family.

Which brought up another thought. "You know, Father, I thought you meant for Katy to be my wife, and that didn't happen. I really would like to have a family of my own." He waited, searching his own heart and mind. "But if that isn't in your plan for me, then so be it." *I know the plans I have for you, plans for good and not for evil.* The verse floated through his mind. "I know that, thank you." When he turned over, the cat resettled itself by his master's feet and commenced again to purr loud enough to wake the dead. Not that it bothered John one whit. His last thought was that he needed to get up early to split and stack his own wood before leaving for the Bjork-lunds'.

Two hogs were already scalded and scraped by the time he walked into the Bjorklunds' yard. The carcasses hanging from a tripod with a block and tackle steamed in the brisk air.

"On three now. One, two, three." Four men heaved another eviscerated carcass out of the scalding tank and onto a solid table where the scraping began.

"Thorliff, you and Baptiste bring in some more firewood. Got to keep this water hot enough." Lars motioned to the boys. The ring of ax on wood could be heard from behind the house where the Baard boys were hard at work splitting the butts.

"Howdy, Pastor." Joseph Baard looked up from scraping the coarse hair off the hog's hide. "You want to take my place here or help grind potatoes for klubb?"

"I'll scrape. How many hogs you doing?"

"Eight. Ten if we have time. I brought mine over here, eas-ier than moving all the equipment."

By the time they stopped for dinner, six sheet-covered hogs were hanging in the barn, the heads were boiling for head-cheese, and what seemed like miles of washed gut lay soaking in salt water, being kept to stuff with sausage meat, which would be ground the next day.

The men and older boys took turns at the woodpile, know-ing how much wood it would take to finish the day. While everyone had their own job to do, the teasing and laughter made the time pass like dry leaves blowing before the wind.

Solberg meandered over to where the women were forming the mixture of ground raw potatoes, fresh blood, flour, and seasoning into balls around a small piece of salt pork. Once formed and cooled, the fist sized balls were wrapped in cheese cloth and, when the women had made enough, set in an iron kettle over one of the fires to simmer for several hours.

"Hope you're making some extra," Pastor Solberg said.

"We always make extra. Why?" Ingeborg brushed a stray strand of hair out of her eyes with the back of a floury hand.

"Well, I wouldn't mind having some for breakfast, sliced and heated in milk. Mmm, tasty."

"Don't you worry. You'll go home with plenty." She glanced up. "Astrid, stay back from there. The men don't need a little girl under foot."

"I thought Anji had the little ones over at Kaaren's." Agnes looked up from where she and Katy were grinding potatoes.

"She does. This one must have slipped away." Ingeborg glanced around. "Thorliff, will you take Astrid back to Kaaren's and make her stay there?"

"Me stay here." The little girl's lower lip came out, and her Bjorklund blue eyes flashed.

"If she don't look just like her ma." Agnes stopped turning the grinder crank and pointed to the child.

"Are you saying I get that stubborn look?" Ingeborg rolled her eyes and her bottom lip too, innocence in action. "Astrid!" The little girl looked at her feet but the lip stayed firm.

"Ja, you could say that." Agnes and Kaaren, who, like Ingeborg, were in blood sausage to the elbows, nodded at each other.

"I am thinking that is where Andrew got that look too." Pastor Solberg's smile twinkled his eyes. He went on to tell them how Andrew went after the Valders boys when they laughed at Anna. "That Andrew, he is some champion of those he cares about."

"Ja, and Andrew cares about anyone and everyone who crosses his path. But especially those weaker than he." Kaaren wiped her chin on her shoulder. "That could cause him a problem sometime."

"If he hadn't sat down when I told him, he would have had a problem all right."

"Dinner's ready," Bridget called from the door of Ingeborg's house.

Thorliff scooped Astrid up under one arm and tickled her at the same time. "Come on, let's go get the others."

"There's hot water on the wash bench." Bridget pointed to the side of the soddy, where a long bench held basins and soap with towels hanging on pegs above. The women scrubbed first so they could help with the serving.

The first kettle of klubb steamed on the stove, filling the house with its hearty fragrance. With two tables set end to end and another in the parlor, there was room for everyone to sit down. Ingeborg, Metiz, and Bridget passed heaping bowls of klubb, potatoes, green beans cooked with bacon, mashed rutabagas, and fried green tomatoes, while platters of bread and bowls of pickles already lined the center of the table.

"Pastor Solberg, would you please ask the blessing?" Ingeborg smiled at their friend.

"Surely. Heavenly Father, we thank thee for this food thou hast given us, for the work of our hands, and the plenty of our harvest. We praise thee for such a glorious day and the joy of being together. Amen." When he raised his head, the first thing he noticed was Mary Martha across the table smiling at him.

"Thank you. Now, everyone, help yourself." At the head of the table, Haakan reached for the bowl in front of him, so the rest did also.

She has beautiful eyes. The thought made John Solberg's ears burn. He quickly took a slice of bread and passed the plate to his neighbor. With the food passing and plates being filled, the hubbub rose again, punctuated by laughter and the call to refill the bowls.

With amazing speed the bowls were emptied again, and as soon as the coffee was poured and Kaaren's eggekake devoured, the men filed out to begin the next round.

"You sit down now," Kaaren ordered Bridget, Ingeborg, and Metiz, "and let us serve you." She shooed them to the table and began opening pans to see what, if anything, remained. "They about cleaned us out." She scraped mashed potatoes out of the bottom of the kettle and retrieved three of the round sausages from the warming oven, where she'd hidden them earlier.

"Here, you can warm these up." Ingeborg passed over a bowl of beans. "This was about as close to feeding a threshing crew as we can get. Shame Penny and Hjelmer didn't come."

"She can't just close that store down whenever she feels

like it, you know." Kaaren pointed to a loaf of bread and signaled Katy to slice it.

"I know, and Saturday is usually the busiest day at the blacksmith, but it just don't seem right without them."

A loud screech from outside, followed by another, made them all chuckle. "Pig whistles."

"Pig whistles?" Mary Martha look up with a puzzled expression.

"They are cut from the windpipe of the pig where the sounds come from. Those screechings you hear are the children blowing through the pipe." Ingeborg pretended to hold a whistle to her lips and blow.

Bridget frowned and looked around. "I didn't see Hamre. Where is he?"

"He went in to help Hjelmer, left right after breakfast. You know he wants to go back to sea, but maybe we should talk to Hjelmer about letting the boy apprentice with him. He doesn't like farming much, and that would give him a skill." Ingeborg closed her eyes, the better to enjoy her first bite of klubb. "You know, I've been thinking of stuffing some of this into casings and smoking it. Might taste good along with cheese and bread."

"Our neighbors used to do that. You know, those up the hill beyond the Stav Kirke." Bridget smiled in remembrance. "Tastes a whole lot different."

"What spices did they use?" Ingeborg cocked an ear to hear what was going on in the other room where the smaller children were playing.

"Come on, Andrew, let's go outside," Gus Baard said. "I don't want to play with all the girls."

"Trygve isn't a girl."

"No, but he's so little, he's still wearing a dress. Come on."

Ingeborg smiled to herself. She knew the children were safe with Anji and Manda watching them, even though Astrid had gotten away from them. But then, Astrid got away from her lots of times too. One minute she was there and the next one *poof!* Just like dandelion fluff in the breeze. Andrew had been much the same. Only the good graces of Metiz' Wolf had kept him from being lost forever in the tall prairie grass. She shuddered at the memory. At least that was one problem they no longer feared. All the grass within a mile of the homestead was grazed short or the land planted in grain. No more buffalo grass taller than a big man's head, let alone that of a young child.

"What's wrong?" Kaaren asked, her hand on Ingeborg's shoulder as she poured more coffee.

"Just remembering. Sometimes it is good to think of the past and see God's hand upon us, saving us and guiding us. Things could have been so much worse. I couldn't have said that at the time, but now I can."

"Ja," Agnes agreed, "those first years." She shook her head. "Uff da, what we went through." She heaved herself to her feet. "I better go check on that kettle of klubb out on the fire." She waited a moment for her back to straighten. "You'd think I was an old lady or something."

Ingeborg's gaze followed her friend out the door. *She does look older. Never been right since that last baby. Lord, is there something I can do for her? If so, please let me know.* The two of them had many things in common, but one that broke both their hearts—no more babies. Agnes had lost hers stillborn, and Ingeborg miscarried after the plow accident, but the re- sults were the same. Barrenness.

She looked up to see Metiz studying her from across the table. "What?"

Metiz shook her head. "Nothing to do." Her shrug barely lifted her shoulders, but it said all she believed. If there was something wrong with Agnes, Metiz had nothing in her bag of simples that would help. The thought of that made Ingeborg sigh. If she and Metiz both saw it, something was indeed wrong. But what?

Kaaren went off to put the twins and Trygve down for a nap while Ingeborg did the same with Astrid. Then, since in- fant Samuel had begun to whimper, Kaaren sat down in the rocker to nurse him. With the youngsters sleeping, the older girls, led by Katy, attacked the dishes so the others could go out and keep on with the butchering. Hides were salted and rolled to be tanned and used for shoe leather, harness repairs, and anything else that needed tough leather.

Everyone headed home with fresh liver, heart, and kidneys if they wanted them. The feet would be pickled, the loops of sausage smoked, and the sausage patties set in lard-covered crocks. Once the carcasses hung a few days, they would be cut up with the haunches and side meat set in brine to smoke later.

Pastor Solberg carried his basket on his lap as the Baards gave him a ride home. He would have his klubb for breakfast as he'd wished.

"I appreciate the ride," he said to Joseph, the two of them sitting on the wagon seat. The rest of the family took up much of the wagon bed. They could hear Swen and Knute arguing at the back of the wagon, their feet hanging over the tailgate.

"You two stop that." Anji took her position as eldest girl very seriously. Her brothers swung the other way. Not much in life wasn't fodder for a good joke or laugh.

"Anji, leave them alone. They aren't bothering anyone." Agnes spoke gently, softly so as not to wake the little ones.

Solberg had to smile. His sister had treated him the same way.

"You goin' to the great debate next Saturday?" Joseph asked.

"I have the privilege of introducing the two gentlemen. You coming?"

"Wouldn't miss it. I got me some questions I want answered."

"You and all the rest of us." Pastor Solberg set his basket down on the floorboards and leaned his elbows on his knees. "Once Dakota Territory becomes a state . . ."

"Or two." Joseph hawked and spit over the wagon wheel. "I'm all for two states, meself."

"I'm not sure yet. That's one of the things I hope Muir and that politician—I keep forgetting his name—clear up. I know Haakan and Lars want to discuss the railroad and flour mills setting prices for both wheat and shipping. You given any thought to joining the Farmer's Alliance that Muir is so enthusiastic about?"

"Ja, in my mind that's the way to go. Like we done here in Blessing. You could call us a giant co-op the way we all work together, got our own train stop, sack house, and all. Pretty soon we'll have to build us an elevator, mark my words. And here we know that no one is cheating us. Sure a lot different than what I hear about other places."

"No doubt." Pastor sighed. "Progress is going to catch us whether we want it to or not. I just hope . . ."

Joseph waited before asking, "Hope what?"

"I wish I knew, Joseph, I wish I knew." *So much change so fast. Is it just me, or are the others also concerned?*

12

"A h, Goodie, could we talk for a moment before services?"
"I think not, you . . . you selfish hussy." Goodie Wold
spun on her heel and stalked up the stairs to the open church
door.

Penny felt as if she'd just been stabbed in the belly. She
could hardly catch her breath for wanting to check and see if
she was bleeding. To be called a name like that right here and
for no reason. At least none that she knew of.

"Are you all right?" Hjelmer caught up with her and took
her elbow, motioning toward the church door. "We need to go
in."

"I . . . I don't think I can . . . yet."

"Penny, we are going to be late." Now he increased the
pressure on her arm and took two steps toward the door.

She allowed him to lead her up the steps and into the vestibule, where Ingeborg and Haakan were greeting people.

"Penny, are you all right?" Ingeborg skipped right over the
how-do-you-do's. She took Penny's hand and smothered it
with her own.

"No, I—ah, yes." She looked around the shallow room.
Goodie must have already gone into the sanctuary.

"Hjelmer, what has happened?"

"Nothing, ah . . . ." He leaned close and whispered, "We'll
tell you later." Then he gently pushed Penny before him
through the wide doorway. They took seats in the back row.

"What do you mean 'nothing'?" she demanded.

Hjelmer shook his head. "You can't do anything about it

now, so just sit back and take part in the service." He kept his voice low, but still the Johnsons in front of them turned to see what was the matter.

Penny slumped against the bench back. *I should have gone over to her house again when I thought about it. Now this. What's the matter with Goodie? Is all this over the sewing machines, or is it something else? What have I done that could have upset her so much?* She wracked her brain through the opening hymn and could think of nothing. She searched the room, locating Olaf and his family in the third row on the far side. Was Goodie sitting rigid with anger, or did she usually sit that way?

The words of the Scripture for the day rolled right on by her.

When Pastor Solberg announced the political debate coming up, she nodded but went right back to searching her words and actions. Thoughts buzzed like angry bees but going nowhere.

She looked around again, this time for Agnes. If only she could talk with her. No one could calm her down like her aunt. She was three rows in front of them. No way to get a message to her.

Hjelmer took her hand and covered it with his other. Knowing his reticence about showing affection in public, she leaned her head against his shoulder for only a minute but clung to the warmth of his hands.

"Beloved, let us love one another, for love is of God."

The words flashed into her crazy maelstrom of thoughts. *But I thought I was. I did. I do.* She forced herself to pay attention. Would love be angry at a cut like that? She shook her head. *But I'm more hurt than angry. She's the angry one. Why? The real question is what do I do now?*

Tante Agnes would say pray, then go. *Go all right. I'll go on home and never speak to her again unless she comes and begs me!* She knew Agnes would mean go to Goodie, but Penny refused to entertain that thought at the moment.

"The Lord bless thee and keep thee. The Lord make His countenance to shine upon thee and give thee His peace. In the name of the Father, the Son, and the Holy Ghost. Amen."

When they all stood to sing the closing hymn, Penny slipped past the couple next to her and out the door.

Shaking hands and talking with people at the door, Pastor Solberg asked, "What happened to Penny?"

"She left," Hjelmer answered. His jaw was squared as though he had more to say but wouldn't.

"Is she all right?"

"We'll see." Hjelmer shook the pastor's hand and headed for home.

"What's going on there?" Ingeborg asked, coming right behind Hjelmer. "Did he say anything?"

Solberg shook his head. "Strange." He continued greeting his flock, shaking hands with the adults and patting the children on the head. Some of the older children sneaked by, anxious to get outside before they exploded. "Good morning to you, too, Swen, Thorliff, and Knute."

The boys waved and ran off laughing.

With each couple he said a few things, but all the time he could feel himself waiting. Waiting for Mary Martha to come out with Zeb and Katy. A group of girls gathered in one corner of the vestibule, giggling now that they were free of their parents.

But Manda stayed with her family, almost smiling at the pastor as he greeted her. "How are your horses doing? I heard good things about how you train them."

"Fine."

"They follow Manda around like she gots a rope on them all the time, but she don't." Deborah filled in the gap only to get a dirty look from her older sister. "Well, it's true."

He could feel her looking at him.

Katy laid a hand on Manda's shoulder and shook her head. "If only she worked as hard on her lessons, right?"

While he nodded, he looked up to see Mary Martha's green eyes twinkling like sun kisses on an emerald pond. "Good morning," he greeted her.

"And to you. That was a fine sermon. We all need reminding of His love—often."

"Mange takk."

"Velbekomme."

"And here I thought she was teaching English, not learning Norwegian." Zeb shook his head as he shook the pastor's hand.

"And you, my friend?" The arched eyebrow reminded Zeb

of his hours in English class so he could pick up some Norwegian to be able to talk with Katy more easily. "Seems to run in the family."

Zeb and Katy looked at each other and laughed as they followed others down the stairs.

Pastor Solberg could feel himself smiling all over as he turned to the next family. Although it took effort, he kept from turning to see what Mary Martha was laughing about as they visited with other friends.

"Mr. and Mrs. Wold, good to see you." As he shook their hands, he glanced from Goodie to Olaf. Something was wrong here too. Goodie's usual smile had gone into hiding, and her squared jaw made her appear almost formidable. Standing slightly behind her, Olaf gave a barely perceptible shake of his head. While Hans had gone to play with the boys, Ellie clung to her mother's skirts. That wasn't like her either. Generally she and Andrew fit together like two pieces of a puzzle.

When Solberg leaned down to greet her, she whispered in his ear, "My ma's been crying."

"I'm sorry to hear that," he whispered back. "You be a good girl, and that might help her." Ellie nodded, her face so serious that Solberg wanted to hold her close. Instead he shook her hand and patted her on the head.

How can I help all of you if I don't know what is happening? He let them go, wishing he could do something. He had a feeling there was a connection between Penny leaving so abruptly and Goodie fighting tears. Leave it to the children to be so honest.

Ellie's sober little face accompanied him home as he went to change clothes before heading to the Johnsons' for dinner. They'd invited him a couple of weeks ago. He wished he were going to the Hjelmer Bjorklunds' or the Wolds' instead. He was sure no one else knew of the problem, because someone would have told him. Maybe he should send Ingeborg over there. Or Kaaren.

"Ah, that is what I will do." He stripped off his clerical collar and white shirt, hanging them carefully on a wall peg, along with his black suit. He kept the suit and shirt for Sundays, weddings, and funerals, knowing that with his meager funds, replacing them wouldn't be easy.

He whistled for the horse he pastured out behind the parsonage, and within minutes he was saddled and bridled and on his way to see Kaaren and Lars. Frost still coated the grass in the shady places and the north sides of the fence posts. While the sun shone, the wind promised an even colder night.

"Winter's on the way, that's for sure." He patted the horse's neck as the animal snorted an answer. "The coat you're wearing promises a mean one, eh?" Another snort. John nudged him into a canter. No sense being late for the meal. That wasn't polite. "But, Father, while I don't know what is going on, I know that you do. Please speak to each person and remind them that your Word says to go to the other party, no matter who or what is right or wrong. Tell them to make it up. Friends are far more important than whatever got in the way."

The horse nickered as they trotted past the Haakan Bjorklund house and on to the next. Paws accompanied them partway, announcing their arrival before turning for home. Pastor Solberg swung off his horse at the gate to the fenced in yard and tied him to one of the posts. The roses had already been trimmed back and covered with straw for the winter, as had the other flower beds. Manure and straw from the barn banked the base of the house. Lars was a strong believer in being prepared, fixing things before they broke, and minding his own business.

John hoped the latter wouldn't be a problem in this case. He needed Kaaren's gentle wisdom. He knocked on the door, grateful to hear children's laughter inside. They could have all been over at Ingeborg's.

"Welcome, Pastor. Come right on in." Lars held the door open wide. Tall like most of the men in the area, Lars still limped from the loss of several toes in a freak late spring snowstorm a few years earlier.

"Thank you. My, it smells good in here." Solberg stopped just inside the door and sniffed appreciatively. Sophie and Grace, the three-year-old twins, ran to their father's legs, and Sophie smiled up at him. Grace, who was born deaf, studied him gravely. One had to earn a smile from the towheaded little girl with the gray eyes of her father.

"You are just in time for dinner," Kaaren called from the kitchen. "Won't take me but a minute to set an extra place."

She came around the corner, wiping her hands on her apron. Trygve toddled along with her, one fist clamped on her skirt for balance.

"Thank you, but no. I am on my way to the Johnsons', and I swung by here to ask you a favor." Solberg held his hat by the brim with both hands.

Kaaren looked at Lars, and he gathered the children together.

"Come now, let's go get washed up for dinner. I'll help you." He swooped his son up in his arms and, using his other hand, guided the two girls before him.

Kaaren led the way into the parlor and gestured for John to take the man's rocker while she sat in her own. "Now, what is it, and how may I help you?" She half turned to face him and folded her hands on the rocker arm.

Solberg leaned forward too. "I'm not sure—that is, I don't know what has happened, but I do know that we have some unhappy people. Have you seen Penny lately or Goodie Wold?"

Kaaren shook her head. "I haven't been out much, what with the butchering, and Trygve and baby Samuel both had a croupy kind of cough before that. Are they ill or. . . ?"

"Mostly *or*, but I have no idea what."

Kaaren waited while he collected his thoughts. "Penny left church today during the final hymn and looked about to cry all through the service. Goodie looked stiff as a barn beam, and neither Olaf nor Hjelmer said more than hello." He rocked a minute. "Oh, and Ellie said her ma had been crying. Out of the mouths of babes, you know?" He worried his bottom lip for a moment, then shook his head. "I don't know what to make of it, but I do know I cannot go barging in and ask them what's wrong."

"No, I suppose not." She smiled. "But you want me to?"

"They talk to you. Everyone does, either to you or Ingeborg. In this case, I thought your gentleness might be more effective." He ran a finger over the brim of his brown fedora. "Talking about it might just be enough."

"And if it's not?"

"Then we go from there."

The sound of the children laughing and talking with their

father made him smile. "They sound so happy."

"They are. And yes, I will do this, but unless I feel there is something you can do, I will not carry gossip."

"I know that, and so will they. That's what makes you the ideal peacemaker." He got to his feet, the rocker creaking a protest. "Mange takk." He gestured toward the table. "I'll take you up on your dinner invitation another time."

Kaaren rose also. "Anytime. You know that."

×⚘ ⚘×

By the time Solberg returned from the Johnsons', dusk was already graying the land. The wind had picked up as he'd predicted, making him grateful he'd worn his heavy wool coat. The half loaf of bread, slice of cake, and leftover beef roast wrapped and stored in his saddlebags would make a fine supper, even though he was still full from the food Mrs. Johnson had repeatedly encouraged him to partake of.

"I'll be four axe handles wide if this keeps up," he told the horse, who'd picked up his feet more quickly the closer they came to the soddy. He rode the horse into the shed, stripped off the saddle and bridle, rubbed him down, and dumped a can of oats in the manger. After checking to make sure there was water in the trough, he hung up his gear, then slung the saddlebags over his shoulder and headed for the dark house.

Once the lamp was lit, he found a message written on paper held down by the lamp in the middle of his table.

Pastor, please come. Our ailing mother is asking for you. She says her time is near.

The Bjerke family lived ten miles or more to the southwest of Blessing. John put the food into the pie safe off the pantry, poured some milk for the crying cat, and turned out the lamp. Who knew when he might be back.

He started to leave, then took the paper and pushed it over a nail he kept on the door for this purpose. That way anyone who needed him would know where he'd gone.

"Lord, if this is the time for her to go home to you, please make this as easy on her and the family as possible." He continued to pray while he resaddled his horse. The ten-mile ride out to the farm gave him plenty more time for that.

Could Mary Martha handle the whole class in the morning if he didn't get back in time?

13

Grandma Bjerke died an hour or so after he got there.

"Thank you for coming, Pastor, we sure do appreciate it." Knute Bjerke shook John's hand, his eyes still red from crying. "Mor did like to come to your church when we could." They had left the bedside and were sitting in chairs nearer the stove. The children had gone to sleep out in the lean-to in the bunk beds, so the house was quiet again.

"What day would you like the funeral?" John took the hand offered by Mrs. Bjerke.

"Would tomorrow afternoon be all right? I know you got school and all. I'll get the box built in the morning." Bjerke continued. "No need for anyone to help. We can get her ready and all."

"We thought to bury her out by the willow tree she loved so much," the woman said. She wiped her eyes with her apron once again. "She was right beautiful there at the last, weren't she?"

"Ja, when the saints get a glimpse of the heavenly host, they can't help but share a bit of that with the rest of us. We have the cemetery by the church, you know, if you want to bring her in there."

"I know. But she asked to be buried here, where we all worked so hard. She planted the willow tree and watered it till it got a good start. She was a hard worker, my mor," Knute said.

"We're just sorry we couldn't get to more of the doings at the church," Mrs. Bjerke said. "She would have loved the quilting and all, but it's just too far to go all the time."

"You did the best you could." John had held services for some of the local people several times at the Bjerke soddy. "Maybe we should think of having regular services out here, like twice a month on Saturdays. What do you think?"

"Would you do that?" The woman brightened. "We'll be building a frame house come spring, so there would be more room."

"If you could, pass the word around for the Saturday after this one. We have the political debate going on this Saturday, and I have to introduce the speakers. You're invited to that, you know."

"Ja, but that is awful far just to hear some guys argue about one state or two. We all know the mills and railroads are stealing us farmers blind, so what good will arguing about it do? They're a bunch of crooks, anyway."

John knew many of the farmers felt that way, so this wasn't any surprise. At least in Blessing they had Olaf weighing and grading the wheat, and he was honest as the prairie was flat. Even so, they'd had to argue with the buyers more than a time or two. No one in Blessing put rocks or dirt in the wheat sacks to make them weigh up heavier, as he knew went on in other places.

Silence settled gently in the room. *Father, comfort these people, as you've always promised to. Please lay your hand upon them and give them peace.*

"I sure do thank you for coming so quick." Knute rocked forward and propped his elbows on his knees.

"You're welcome. Do you mind if I read a bit of Scripture again and pray before I go?"

"Oh, please do." Mrs. Bjerke stifled a yawn behind her hand. "But you are welcome to stay the night."

"I need to be at school too early for that, but thank you." John thumbed through his Bible until he came to the Beatitudes. " 'Blessed are the poor in spirit, for theirs is the kingdom of heaven. Blessed are they. . .' " He continued reading, and at the end he repeated the verse " 'Blessed are they that mourn, for they shall be comforted.' " He looked each of them in the eye. "And that means all of us, for our Father comforts us moment by moment. Shall we pray?" He bowed his head and took in a deep breath, letting it all out so that he could feel his shoulders relax. With his Bible clasped in his hands, he began. "Heavenly Father, thou hast said we may come to thee in times of sorrow and thou wilt bring us comfort and peace. I thank thee for the life of Elmira Bjerke, for her years here on earth, and that thou hast now taken her home to be with thee. Bless her family as we mourn her passing yet rejoice in thy promise that thou hast prepared a room for her in thy heavenly mansion." He paused, sniffing himself at the sniffs he heard from his two companions. "She led a full life, Lord, one pleasing to thee, because thy Son died for her sins and ours. We thank thee and praise thee in the precious name of thy Son, Jesus Christ." They joined him in the "amen."

Knute then rose and shook the pastor's hand. "Thank you for coming." Grabbing his coat he excused himself and went to the barn.

Mrs. Bjerke pressed a packet of food into John's hand as he shrugged into his coat and wrapped a wool muffler around his neck. "I wish it could be more."

"Mange takk. I'll see you as soon as I can get back out here. I'll let school out early. That won't upset any of my pupils, I know."

She nodded. "I surely do wish we had a school close enough for our children. You think they'll build more schools when we get to be a state?"

"I think so, most likely before then, from what I hear."

"Your horse is ready, Pastor." The mister stuck his head in the door.

After saying more good-byes, John nudged his horse into a lope and headed for home, grateful that Henry, as he called him, knew the way home no matter how dark the night. At least it wasn't raining or snowing, but from the cold seeping into his heavy wool coat, the latter wasn't far away. By the time he staggered into his soddy, he had prayed for everyone he knew, planned the next Sunday's sermon, and thought of a new and easier way to help the little ones learn their letters and sounds.

The soddy was nearly as cold as he. "Father, you know a wife would have kept the fire going and been here to welcome me home. Don't you figure that would be a good idea?" He crawled into bed after putting another quilt on top.

There was ice on the water bucket in the morning, but he woke with another good idea.

While the schoolchildren were arriving, he put the question to his new assistant.

"Miss MacCallister, I have a favor to ask. An old woman died last night, and I need to help with the burying later this afternoon. Since it's better than an hour's ride, could you please conduct the last two hours of school for everyone? I know that's an imposition, but—"

"Of course."

He realized he'd been holding his breath. Almost stammering, he replied, "Th . . . thank you. Perhaps you could lead singing or read another chapter in *Oliver Twist*."

"Most likely both, and regular memorization?"

"That would be wonderful." He turned from looking at her to studying the children, some of whom were still walking toward the school. He and Miss MacCallister stood near the soddy, out of the way of the game of tag being played by the older children. The little ones played on the south side of the soddy, where the sun had barely melted the frost off the lower wall. A bench had been set there for the older folks to sit on when the soddy was still the church too.

"If it stays nice, would it be all right if we all came out here to read and sing?" she asked.

"I don't see why not." *Now why didn't I think of that? We could have brought lots of classes out here, especially since she came to help me.*

"Mith MacCallithter, I brung you thith." Anna stopped beside her, just close enough to touch the fabric of her skirt with a tentative finger. Mary Martha squatted down eye to eye with the little girl. Anna drew her hands from behind her back and handed her a well-polished apple.

"Thank you. That was very thoughtful." Mary Martha laid her hand along the little girl's cheek.

"I brung you one too, Teacher." She held out the other apple for him. "My ma thaid . . ." She stopped and looked to

Mary Martha and swallowed. "Thh . . ." She started, then changed the shape of her mouth, put her teeth together, and tried again. Ducking her chin a fraction, she made a hissing sound. "Sss-aid." Her grin nearly split her cheeks. "Ssaid . . . said apple-s are good for you."

Throwing all propriety aside, Mary Martha drew the little one into her arms and hugged her close. "Very good, Anna, you are wonderful."

"I did it. I . . . ssaid it right?" She laid her cheek against Mary Martha's. "You thmell tho nice."

Was that fear I just saw in her eyes? Mary Martha rose to her feet and took Anna by the hand. "That's all right. You can't do all the s sounds at once. We'll work on it some more." She wanted to skip and dance and swing her little pupil around in a circle. *God, thank you. She is trying so hard. Is it just that no one has time to help her, or has she been punished for not talking right? Do I ask Pastor Solberg to call on the family, or can I go? What do I do?*

"Very good, Anna, and thank you for the apple." Pastor Solberg patted the wispy hair trying to escape from the tightly braided French braids.

"You are welcome."

He left them outside and returned in a moment with the bell. As he rang it, the children gathered, falling into their regular places with only a giggle or two. But he heard the whisper.

"Teacherth pet."

Miss MacCallister heard it too. And since she was behind the culprit, she took one step, grabbed Toby White by the ear, and hauled him out of line.

"Yeeow. I din't do nothing. Let me go."

"If you didn't, your brother did. Which one of you was it?"

Jerry stared at her, his eyes round as teacups, his head shaking as if it might fall off his shoulders. "Not me. I din't do it. Uh-uh."

"Now, I know none of the others did it, because they have learned some manners, which I—" She broke off and glanced up at Pastor Solberg, who nodded. "Which we plan to teach you."

She didn't care that all the other children were listening so hard their ears flapped in the wind. She didn't care that she wasn't the *real* teacher. She just cared that little children should never be made fun of, especially when the action being mocked wasn't their fault.

Mary Martha and Pastor Solberg exchanged glances and, at his nod, exchanged places too. He took the young man in question by the arm in a grip that brooked no argument.

"Miss MacCallister, you may take the rest of the children inside and begin the day." His jaw was so squared, he could hardly talk.

Once they had gone inside, he hauled the young man out to the woodshed. "Now, Toby White Valders, you have a choice. I can take that stick over there to your backside, or you can take that ax and begin splitting wood. You will keep on splitting wood until I come out here and tell you to stop. Now, if you choose to split wood, I will not tell your mother and father about this second infraction, but if you choose the paddle, I will be forced to meet with them and explain exactly what you have done to warrant such an action on my part. Is this clear?" He gave the arm a shake for good measure. "What do you say?"

"The woodpile."

"Good choice. And after you are finished, you will apologize to little Anna. She is struggling to overcome her lisp, and if you struggle as hard to overcome your meanness, this will have all been worthwhile. Do you understand me?"

"Yeah."

"What?" The word cut the cold air like the tip of a buggy whip.

"Yes."

"Yes, what?"

"Yes, sir."

"Good. I'm glad you got that right." John dropped the boy's arm. "Now, show me how good you are with that ax."

After Toby had split a couple of pieces, Solberg nodded and returned to the schoolhouse. *Lord, please tell me I did the right thing. I cannot tolerate behavior like that in my school, and I know you don't tolerate it either. Help me to bring these children to an understanding of your precepts if I do nothing else.*

He paused in the doorway, watching as Miss MacCallister asked Swen Baard to read the morning Scripture. The boy's ears turned red, but he never stumbled over the words of Psalm 91. *Lord, please keep Anna in the shelter of thy wings. Keep all of us there.* He listened for the ring of ax on wood and, when it came, breathed a sigh of relief. He didn't want to have to spend the morning watching that young man split wood.

"Hamre, will you lead us in prayer?"

All the children bowed their heads and folded their hands. The silence, broken by a sniff or two and the ax slamming into another chunk of wood, lengthened. Someone shuffled his feet. Pastor Solberg began to wonder at the audacity of the young woman who had asked this other silent student to pray. Out loud, no less. Should he step in? He'd just about opened his mouth when Hamre cleared his throat and began.

"We come before thee Father God with hearts full of thankfulness. We thank thee for thy Son, for this world thy hands have made, for the air we breathe, and the food thou hast given us. Help us to do our best this day and every day. Amen."

John sought Mary Martha's gaze over the heads of the children. He knew his eyes must be shining as much as hers. All that from within the very silent young man who wore a chip on his shoulder the size of Denmark. And here he'd been afraid she had embarrassed the boy beyond measure. *Goes to show what I know, Lord. Thank you again for reminding me that you see the inward man, while we only see the outer.*

While the students took their seats, he made his way to the front of the room. Suddenly the day that had begun on a sour note sang of promise. "Thank you, Miss MacCallister, and all of you who helped this morning. We'll begin with reading for the fourth graders. Those beyond the fourth grade will please take out history books and begin reading at chapter five. Thorliff, you will assist Miss MacCallister as usual, and, Anji, would you please review the *ABC's* with the first graders?"

Everyone settled to their work, and the day continued, with John keeping an ear tuned for the ringing of ax on wood. Whenever he glanced Jerry White Valders' way, the boy seemed to be paying more attention than usual. While the stern talking the boys got the other day didn't seem to make much of an impression, it appeared this punishment certainly did.

After excusing everyone for recess, John went out to the woodpile. "If you think you have learned your lesson, you may be excused also, Mr. Valders. I hope I will never have to send you out here like this again."

Toby wiped the sweat from his forehead, even though the day was still brisk. "I hope not too."

"You will go with me now to talk with Anna."

The boy's face grew redder. "All right." His jaw clenched. He rubbed his hands on his pants and flinched.

Ah, most likely blisters. That will be a good reminder for a few days. Solberg could see that apologizing would be harder on Toby than the chopping. "Come along." He motioned Anna out of the game of Fox and Geese and stood with his hand on her shoulder so she had to face the boy.

"I . . . I'm sorry for making fun of you," Toby stuttered.

Anna looked up at him. "Thatth . . ." She paused, swallowed, and tried again. "That-ss all right." Her smile up at Pastor Solberg rivaled the sunrise. "I done it, huh?"

It was all he could do to keep from scooping her up in his arms and hugging her around in a circle.

Toby studied his boot toes, his ears red as the blisters on his palms, then looked up at the teacher. "Can I go now?"

John nodded, but before the boy could leave, Anna took a step closer to him. "I'm glad you comed here to live, and you got a Ma and Pa now."

"Th . . . thanks." The boy spun away and dashed off to the other side of the school building where the older children had teams of some sort and were yelling and cheering each other on.

"Can I go play now?" Anna looked up at Pastor Solberg, who nodded.

As she ran off, his gaze automatically searched out Mary Martha's. Had she heard? When she wiped something away from under her eye, he knew she had.

⚮　⚮

When Pastor Solberg left at one, Mary Martha waved him

off and returned to the classroom. "You have ten more minutes to finish your work, and then we will have singing," she announced to everyone. At the happy smiles before her, Mary Martha had to respond in kind.

Two songs later, she knew it for certain. The children loved singing as much as she did. When she heard the harmony begin to come from the taller students on the back benches, she could barely contain her delight.

"That was wonderful. Oh, if only each of you could stand where I am standing and hear how beautiful you sound. Let's do that one again, and this time let's do it as a round." She divided the class in three, with all ages in each group. "Now please stand." The scraping of chairs and benches took only a moment before they were all standing.

Mary Martha pointed to the first group and sang the opening note. At the right moment, she reverted to the first note and started the second group, and thus with the third. Three times they sang the song and ended with group three drawing out the final notes. A hush fell on the room.

"I know that's the way heaven will sound with all the angels singing," Mary Martha said softly, so as not to destroy the wonder of the moment.

"Now, does anyone have a favorite?" She pointed to Anji, who had raised her hand.

"Can we sing 'Blest Be the Tie That Binds'?"

"I don't think I know that one. Would you start it, please?"

Anji nodded and Mary Martha could see the red creeping up the girl's neck. But in a true soprano, Anji began to sing. "Blest be the tie that binds our hearts in Christian love. . . ." The others joined her, and Mary Martha hummed along. Some of them sang the ancient words in Norwegian, making the moment even more haunting. Again, a silence followed, more reverent this time.

"We sure sing pretty." Ellie looked up at her teacher. "Don't we, Miss MacCallister?"

"We sure do. You may all be seated." Mary Martha waited until she had everyone's attention again. "Do any of you play instruments of any kind?"

Swen Baard raised his hand. "I can play my pa's fiddle."

The Johnson girl volunteered she could play a few songs on her father's guitar.

"Hamre plays the mouth organ. He's good." Thorliff nodded to his cousin.

"Really?" Mary Martha looked over at the boy who appeared to be trying to melt under his desk. The look he shot Thorliff would have fried eggs. But he nodded when she asked him again. *Ah, if only we had a piano.* "Bring whatever instruments you have tomorrow, and we will have another music time. What do you think?"

"That was fun." Ellie Peterson Wold sighed. "I like to sing."

"I never had any idea you could all sing so well. We need to begin getting songs ready for the Christmas program." She thought for a moment. "Six weeks is all we have."

"Thorliff writes the program." Andrew turned to look at his big brother. "He writes good ones."

When Mary Martha looked toward the back row, she could see that Thorliff wanted to put a hand over his brother's mouth. Or in it. But his red ears told her he was pleased at the same time.

"Mor said it was the best play ever," someone else added.

"We s-sang 'Away in a Manger.' " Anna caught the s word this time before lisping.

"And I got an orange," another one of the younger group said with awe.

"I see." Mary Martha looked at Thorliff. "Are you willing to write another play for this year?"

He shrugged. "I guess."

"Perhaps we could write our own song too." Mary Martha looked around the classroom. "Have any of you ever made up a poem and a tune?"

Thorliff raised his hand. "My tante Kaaren has."

"Well, I have a feeling there are some in this very room who can do that too." She looked around, smiling at each of them. "So think about it, all right? Anyone have a favorite song we haven't sung yet?" They finished with "Yankee Doodle," and to their surprise and delight, Mary Martha had them all marching around the room behind her. When they took their seats again, laughing and puffing, she pulled out the stool and picked up the book they'd been reading.

"Now, where were we?"

"At the part where Oliver meets Artful Dodger."

"Ah, that's right." She flipped pages until she came to the right one, then with one finger holding the place, she looked across the upturned faces. "Now, you know we got extra reading and singing time today because you all worked so hard on your lessons." She waited while Thorliff translated for the Erickson girls. He was having to do less and less as they grew more adept in their new language.

She hoped their parents would come to the English language classes to be held at the church the next night.

"Now, then . . ." She began to read.

Soon the jingle of harness outside brought all of them back to the present day.

Mary Martha closed the book and stepped down from the high stool. "Class dismissed."

"How come it is so much nicer to be read to than to read myself?" Anji asked.

Mary Martha smiled at the question. "I don't know, but I agree."

As she shut the door behind them, she wondered how the funeral service was going for the Bjerkes. How nice it would be if Pastor Solberg could come back to a warm home and supper ready to be put on the table.

Mary Martha MacCallister, don't you go gettin' any such ideas. That's just not proper one whit. "But it would be the Christian thing to do," she said aloud.

"What would?" Manda swung up on the wagon seat beside her.

"N-nothing." Mary Martha clucked the horse forward. Whatever was the matter with her?

14

"Penny, surely you aren't still fussing about Goodie."

With a long fork in her hand, Penny swung from turning the ham frying for supper and shook hand and fork in her husband's direction. "If you think I'm going over there first, you got another think coming, mister."

Hjelmer tried melting through the back of his chair. Hands in the air, palms out, he shook his head. "Where did you ever get that idea from what I said?"

"I just know that's what you're thinking." *And your tone of voice. Why didn't you just pat me on the head?* She shook the fork again. "I didn't do anything to her, and she called me a selfish hussy. I don't even say that word. What's got into that woman is beyond me, and I tell you right now"—she shook the fork a third time—"she's acting crazy, that's what."

"Could you by any chance put the weapon down?"

Penny looked at her husband, then at the fork and back at Hjelmer. "Sorry." She set the fork on the warming shelf and wiped her hands on her apron.

"Now, you were saying . . ."

"Ah, it's not important." She brushed a bit of hair back off her forehead with the back of her hand.

"Come here." He beckoned with one finger.

"What?"

He motioned again.

She walked over to him, stopping in front of his chair. He took her hand and gently pulled her into his lap. "Now, start at the beginning, and maybe we can figure this out." Together they went over the last few days, starting with the arrival of Mr. Drummond and his marvelous machine.

"So?" Penny leaned against his shoulder.

"I wish I knew. I'm sure it has something to do with the sewing machine. That's all it can be. Maybe she thinks you are going to push her out." He stroked Penny's cheek with a gentle finger.

"I thought the same of her, but then I figured . . ." She fell silent for a bit. The ham sizzled on the stove. The pop of grease on the stove itself brought her to her feet. "Oh no, now I'm going to have more mess to clean up." She pushed the frying pan to the cooler part of the stove and stood staring at it. "I thought about Goodie taking away my business, you know, if she put in cloth and such, and I started to get all het up about it. But then I figured that I've got enough other things here, so if she wants to sell the machines and all that goes with sewing, so be it." She turned to face her husband. "I was going to tell her that, but I didn't take the time, and . . . and then she didn't—wasn't home, I think, and now this." She raised her hands in the air and dropped them again. "You think it could be such a simple thing as this?"

"Could be. It's a shame to let business get in the way of neighbors and family. You want we should go talk with them?"

"But what if she—I mean, I . . ." She took some already cooked potatoes and began cutting them up into melted butter in another pan.

"If we're going to go, we better go now." He stood and folded the paper he'd been reading until she had smashed it in his lap. "Good thing I was done with that."

Penny looked at the wrinkled paper and shrugged. "Sorry." She pushed both pans to the back of the stove and took her shawl off the peg by the door. "I'm ready." *Not really. All I want is things back the way they were before Drummond came. And I really like the sewing machine, but I hate all this.*

They knocked on the back door of the Wold home. And knocked again. But no one was home.

"Do you think they're just not answering the door?" Penny asked as they strolled back home.

"No. There were no lamps lit."

"But it's suppertime."

"So they are visiting someone else."

"Who could they be visiting? They need to milk their cow. You can hear her bellering."

"Maybe I should go do that for them." Hjelmer leaned forward and opened their back door. "You go on in and finish supper, and I'll go do their milking." He turned to leave, then looked over his shoulder. "We got a bucket?"

"In the pantry." She brought it back and handed it to him. *Why should he do this when Goodie acted so terrible, and at church even?*

Supper was ready and waiting when Hjelmer finally returned. "I left the milk on their counter," he said in answer to Penny's abrupt question.

She set his plate in front of him with a little more force than necessary, then took her own place. Light from the kerosene lamp in the center of the square oak table left shadows in the corners of the room but a warm glow over the table. Heat from the stove kept the room comfortable, while the soft plop of a falling wood coal sounded loud. So did the clink and scrape of silverware on the plates. Even their chewing sounded loud. And the rustle of their clothing.

Penny picked up her plate and scraped the leftover bits into the slop bucket to throw to the chickens Hjelmer housed back of the barn. They didn't keep a cow, depending instead on the Wolds or the Bjorklunds for milk and cream.

"Done?" At his nod she picked up his plate, scraped off the leavings, and set them both in the enameled dishpan. After pouring hot water over them, she slivered in some soap and set to washing and rinsing the dishes and silver. She did *not* ask Hjelmer to help her. And if she slammed the kettles a bit harder than necessary, he didn't comment.

She could feel his stare on her back every once in awhile, but he sat in his chair, reading some banking information without a word.

Penny yelped, grabbed her finger, and held the end of it tight.

"What did you do?"

"I didn't do anything. The knife did." She raised her finger in the air and watched the blood drip down the side. Several other words came to mind, none of them on the Christian woman's approved word list. She was glad Tante Agnes wasn't there to hear her.

"You need some help?"

"Hjelmer Bjorklund, if you value your hide, you will stay in that chair." Her teeth were clamped so tightly she could barely speak. She wrapped a rag around her finger and headed for her sewing basket, where she kept strips of leftover fabric. Right now muslin would be the thing or an old sheet. She turned her basket upside down with her left hand, muttering all the while. Some calicos, wool, dimity, but no muslin, no old sheeting. The entire thing fell on the floor, sending buttons and balls of fabric strips ready for rug braiding rolling across the floor.

She looked up to see Hjelmer standing in the doorway. "Go away! Just go away!" She fought the tears burning the backs of her eyelids and plugging her nose. She fought the blood no longer as it ran down her finger and stained whatever it touched.

She fought Hjelmer when he gathered her into his arms.

She lost all around. The tears rolled as he bandaged her finger, and she couldn't quit crying. She cried for the hurt from the morning, she cried for the snubs the day before, she cried for the cut finger and her bad language.

And when the tears kept on falling, she knew she was crying because she'd started her monthlies again, and there was no baby in store for the Hjelmer Bjorklund family—if two people could be called a family. Why had God deserted her like this?

Tuesday passed in a whirlwind of cooking, serving, finding things for store customers and ordering supplies. By late afternoon when the mail came in, Penny felt as if three days had passed instead of one. She sorted the mail into the slots and handed it out again to those who stood waiting. The good part of having people waiting for the mail was that they usually picked up something to purchase. The not so good part was that sometimes they were impatient.

"Mail was late today, eh?" Mrs. Valders laid some lace on

the counter. "Seems to me they ought to be able to keep the trains on time, don't you think?"

"That would be better. How much of this did you want?" Penny held up the lace-wrapped card.

"Can I get my mail? I gotta get home for chores," Mrs. Johnson interrupted, the note of impatience in her voice grating on Penny's nerves.

"Let's see, I need it around the neck, the arms, and I think I'll do a trim around the skirt too. What do you think?"

"Excuse me a moment, Hildegunn, let me get the mail. How full is the skirt?" She reached for the mail slot as she asked. Handing out mail for three of those waiting, she smiled at the others in the line. "Let me go get someone else to help here."

She checked in the bank room. No one there. Had Valders already gone home? She went out the door and to the blacksmith. While there was no Hjelmer in sight, Ephraim was sweeping up straw and horse droppings.

"Can you please come help me? The store is full, and I can't keep up."

"Sure enough." He leaned the broom against the wall.

"You better wash first." *If you move any slower, you'll be going backward.* She knew better than to say such things, but oh . . . She pasted a smile on her face and hurried back into the store. "Sorry."

"Now, Hildegunn, how much did you decide?"

"I think I'll wait on it until I measure. Hate to buy too much, you know."

Penny gritted her teeth and kept on smiling. "All right, then that will be twenty-five cents for the needles."

Mrs. Valders dug in her bag for the change and counted it out a nickel, a dime, and the rest in pennies.

A sigh came from farther back in the line, and several shuffled their feet.

"Thank you. Now, who was next?" As the lady turned to leave, she greeted those behind her and wished them a good day.

Ephraim tied on his apron and slicked back his damp hair as he joined her behind the counter. "Who do you want me to start with?"

"I'm next." Mr. Johnson plunked a box of shells down on the counter. "And I need five pounds of nails." The two men headed for the end of the store, where all the tools and such were displayed, to weigh nails out of the keg on the floor.

Within the next few minutes Penny sold all the remaining cheese, several candy sticks, the last loaf of bread, and the final can of allspice.

"I have to finish the headcheese, you know." A customer nodded and studied the row of spices. "Why don't you give me the bay leaf too. Sometimes I wonder why we don't grow some of the things ourselves. You think they don't grow here?"

"I don't know. Maybe if we got the seeds, we could try it next year. I'll look in my catalogues for herb seeds and see what I can find. I know Ingeborg planted parsley this year. She got some seeds from someone. I asked her to let it go to seed so we can all get some."

"Some things do better with starts. Why, my rose, the red one you gave me a start off, was just beautiful this year."

Penny sent an apologetic look to those behind her current customer. The line seemed to be growing rather than getting shorter.

Hans Peterson Wold waited for his turn. "Can I get our mail, please?"

"Sure enough. How's your ma?" Penny almost didn't ask.

Hans shook his head. "She's sad, I think, but I don't know why." He eyed the jar of peppermint balls.

"You want one?" Penny lifted the lid.

"I don't have any money."

"That's okay, here's one for you and one to take home to Ellie." Penny tucked them both into a folded paper.

"Thank you, Mrs. Bjorklund." Eyes shining, he darted out between the grown-ups still waiting.

"That was a kind thing to do." The older man smiled at Penny.

She returned his smile and waited. Not too many strangers came in at this time of day when there was no train coming or going.

"I saw some folks going out with cheese and bread. That's what I'd like."

"Sorry, but I'm plumb cleaned out of both. I have crackers

in the barrel, but no bread until tomorrow. I'm not sure when Ingeborg will bring cheese in again."

"You have anywhere in town a man might get a meal and a bed?"

She shook her head again. "I serve dinner but not supper. You can ask Olaf Wold over at the sack house about spreading a pallet in by the grain sacks." She glanced at the cigar in his hand. "But there won't be any smoking allowed there."

"That's all that's available?" One eyebrow disappeared under the brim of his limp fedora.

"You could ask at the soddy by the church. Pastor Solberg sometimes takes a person in. Otherwise, one of the farmers might let you bunk in his barn." *We've got to get that board-inghouse built.* She wished she'd been keeping track of all the requests.

"Anyone around here need a hired man?"

"You know how to handle a team, machinery?" Ephraim looked up from wrapping several packets together with brown paper and string.

"Pretty good."

"You might go on out to Gustafsons'." Ephraim gave the directions, and after buying a packet of tobacco, the man headed for the door.

"Thanks."

"Why did you send him out there instead of to Haakan?" Penny asked in a voice meant to be heard by her helper only.

"I don't know. There was something about him that bothered me."

"I wish I hadn't told him about Wolds' then." Penny watched the man turn left and head up the street. "That's where he is going."

"Don't worry. Olaf is a good judge of character. If he thinks like me, he'll send him on his way."

The thought of the Wolds brought back the hurt of Sunday morning. *Whatever had possessed Goodie to be so hateful? What if . . .* She cut off the thought, appalled that it had even entered her head. *Lord, what is the matter with me? With her? Please help me to . . .* To what? She didn't know.

Since the store was empty for the first time all afternoon,

she untied her apron. "Can you watch this while I run next door?"

"Sure."

I'm going to take care of this right now! She headed out the back door. Now, if Goodie would only let her in. Or at the very least talk with her through the screen door.

15

Open it quick, Tante Kaaren."

Kaaren smiled at Thorliff as she reached for a knife to cut the string on the parcel wrapped with brown paper. Carefully, so as to save every bit of string and paper, she unwrapped the package with the New York postmark. *Who would be sending me something from New York?* The thrill of opening it made her go slower, much to the consternation of her nephew.

"Thank you for bringing it home to me."

"You're welcome. Tante Penny called over when we were coming out of school to say it was there for you. She was going to ask Onkel Hjelmer to bring it if she didn't catch me." He leaned forward as if to encourage her fingers to move a bit faster.

"Where's Andrew?"

"He went to Ellie's house. I have to go get him after a while. Mor said I could ride Jack the mule. We might get to ride to school sometimes." He looked around. "Where's the twins?"

"Out in the barn with Lars. He's got the girls sanding on something he's making. Since they won't tell me what it is and they giggled when I asked, I get the feeling it's a Christmas present." She folded the paper before slitting open the envelope that held a letter.

Far as Thorliff could guess, it was a book, but there was another wrapping around it. Whoever sent it wanted it kept nice.

"It's from Mr. Gould." Kaaren laid a hand against her cheek. "And he even wrote in Norwegian. He is such a nice man." She read through the short letter quickly and turned to Thorliff, shaking her head. "You unwrap it."

He looked up at her to make sure she meant it, then picked up the paper-wrapped parcel. Sure enough, it was a book. He read the title out loud. " 'Teaching Sign Language to the Deaf.' " He looked up. "Sign language?"

"He says he hopes this might help Grace and all of us to communicate with each other. He heard about it and thought of us." She sank down in a chair and rested her elbows on the table. "Open it."

Thorliff did and leafed through the pages. There were diagrams of finger positions to say the letters. He tried a couple and handed Kaaren the book. "Talking hands?"

"Kind of like when we tried talking with Metiz at first. Sometimes we showed things with our hands." Kaaren tried forming an *A* with her fingers. She flipped through the pages. "Look, some of the signs are for simple words."

With him looking over her shoulder, the two studied the pages.

"Grace will be able to talk with us," Kaaren said.

"And us with her. We could learn this at school, so when she comes she will be able to learn like anybody."

Kaaren patted his cheek, so near her own. "Leave it to you, Thorliff, to think of that. I thought I would teach her here at home, so she—"

"But Sophie wouldn't go without her. You know that. This way they can both go." He formed the sign for *M*. "This is fun." Paws barked at the door. "Oh, oh. I gotta go. I want to learn this too. You better talk to Pastor Solberg soon."

"I better learn it myself first. And the first step is to read the book and send a thank-you to Mr. Gould. What a true friend he is." She glanced at the letter again. "But he didn't say anything about how his family is doing since his wife died. I wonder how they are."

Thorliff waved again as he headed out the door.

⚘ ⚘

"So, did you talk with Goodie?" Hjelmer hung his hat on the peg by the door.

Penny shook her head. "Olaf said she was taking Andrew home. He came to play at their house with Ellie after school."

"You want we should go over there later?"

"Guess we could try again. She made supper for the two men sleeping in the sack house, Olaf said, so she should be back soon."

"Did you ask him what was wrong?"

She shook her head. "I wanted to, but it just wouldn't come. Like maybe I'm making things up or something."

"We'll just go over there like we usually do and everything will be fine."

"I sure hope so. I don't like this one bit." While she talked, she slid four full bread pans in the oven and shut the door. If Goodie didn't start bringing baked goods over or come and help out at the noon hour as she so often did, Penny thought she might crumble under the load.

"Yoo-hoo!" The call accompanied a jingle of harness and the snort of a horse.

Penny opened the back door. "Kaaren, what brings you out so late?"

"I just had to show you what was in that package you sent home with Thorliff." Kaaren leaped to the ground like a young girl.

"Where are the children?"

"With Ingeborg." Kaaren gave a little skip in her progress to the door. "Penny, Hjelmer, you won't believe this." She sniffed. "Something sure smells good."

"Bread. Now what is it?" Penny felt like taking Kaaren's basket and digging through it if the woman stalled any longer.

Kaaren sat down at the table and pointed to the two chairs beside her. "Come see." She laid the book out so all could look at the diagrams.

"What is this?" Hjelmer looked up, confusion rampant on his handsome face.

"This is the way Grace is going to learn to talk." Kaaren spoke the words reverently, as if she were praying. "We are all going to learn to sign so we can speak with her. Thorliff is already working on her name. See the *G*." She flipped through the pages. "Mr. Gould sent us this. Can you believe it? What a wonderful man. I wish now, more than ever, that I had met him in New York with Ingeborg." She traced the diagram for G. "He has given Grace a life." Tears filled her blue eyes and shimmered on her lashes. "How can I ever thank him?"

"Let me get this straight. You form the letters . . ."

"Not exactly, there are signs for sounds and some words too. But the entire alphabet can be signed. She'll be able to say 'please' and 'thank you' and 'pass the bread.' We won't need Sophie for an interpreter. The book says children learn this very quickly, and Thorliff thought they should all learn it at school, so when Grace gets old enough to go, the children will be able to talk with her."

Penny threw her arms around Kaaren. She'd never heard her talk so much at one time unless she was reading the Scripture. "This is the most wonderful thing. You've got to learn it quick so you can teach the rest of us."

Kaaren sighed. "I know. But first I have to mail this letter to say thank you. I just wish I had something to send him." She put a finger on the letter R. "He is so rich he can buy anything he wants." She dug the envelope out of her bag. "I need to buy a stamp too. I am all out."

But rich didn't keep the poor man from losing his wife. Sickness doesn't care how much money you have. But Penny kept the thoughts to herself. "Come, let's stamp this and put it in the mail pouch right now." She drew Kaaren to her feet. "I'd send it out tonight if I could."

With the letter in the mail pouch, Kaaren turned to Penny. "I've been wanting to come anyway. Pastor Solberg saw you leave church in a rush on Sunday, and he asked me to come see if there is anything I can do to help you with whatever is wrong." She stammered to a close. "I don't want to tread where I'm not wanted, but if there is something . . ."

Penny stared at her fingers spread wide on the counter top. The urge to clench her fists made her jaw clench instead. *Shall I tell her? Why didn't Pastor come himself? Would telling Kaaren what is going on be gossiping? I don't want to be a gossip.*

She looked up at Kaaren. "I-I know you mean well, but I think we better see if we can work it out on our own. Isn't that what the Bible says to do if you've been wronged?"

"Or if you wronged another."

"Why do you say that?" The words came out harsher than she intended.

"Just finishing your comment of before. Penny, I am not here to accuse you. I just want to help you work it out."

"Well, maybe you should go see Goodie then. Maybe she'll talk to you."

"Meaning she won't talk to you?"

"I didn't say that." Again the snap in her tone. "Sorry, but this really has me all tied up in knots and . . . and . . ." She looked up at Kaaren, resentment evident in every line of her body. "It's not my fault."

"I see."

"How can you?" Then the story came rushing out, starting from the arrival of Mr. Drummond to Goodie not answering her door and the horrid accusation at church. "She's never been gone so much."

Penny felt as though someone had pulled the stopper and all her venom ran out. "I wish Drummond had never brought that horrid machine in here." She paused, studying her hands again. "And here I was, so excited about all the sewing we could get done so much faster. Finally something for us women, like the mowers help on the farms."

"So, do you want me to go over there with you?"

Penny shook her head. "I think Hjelmer and me going over there would be better. Then, if that doesn't work, I'll let you know. You think that's all right?"

"Ja, I do. But keep one thing in mind. The Bible says, 'Don't let the sun go down on your anger.' "

"It already has, several times in fact. And each day gets harder."

"Maybe that's why God put those words in the Scriptures." Kaaren raised an eyebrow and drew Penny close for a hug. "You are so close to being my sister after helping us for those months when the twins were born that I must sound like a big sister to you."

"That's okay, since I never had one." Penny wiped her eye with the edge of her apron. "Thank you for coming like this."

"You're welcome, and see, you got to share our good news too."

After Kaaren left, Penny checked the bread and put a couple more sticks of wood in the stove. They couldn't go over to see Goodie now because the bread would have to come out too soon. And supper was ready.

After supper she had to start more bread for the morrow and bake pies.

All during supper she stewed about her predicament. Finally she said, "Guess I'll just have to go over there in the morning. Ephraim, you'll mind the store for me for a few minutes tomorrow, won't you?"

He shook his head. "Sorry but I have to be out to Odell's real early in the morning to help them butcher. I told 'em I would."

"I'll take care of the store," Hjelmer said, laying his knife and fork on his plate. "Very good supper, as usual. No wonder the train makes sure to stop here at noon."

In spite of her worries, Penny fell asleep as soon as her head hit the pillow. But not long after that, something woke her. She got out of bed, shrugged into her wrapper, and with slippers on went downstairs into the kitchen. She opened the back door. Smoke. She smelled smoke. And it wasn't smoke from someone's chimney.

She spun around and ran yelling up the stairs, "Hjelmer, go ring the bell. There's a fire someplace!"

16

Where is the fire?" Hjelmer pulled up his suspenders as he thundered down the stairs.

"I don't know. I can't see any flames, but I know something is burning." Penny was pulling on her boots as she explained. "I can just smell it."

Hjelmer paused at the doorway to sniff the air. "That's grain burning. You go ring the bell!" He sprinted across the field toward the sack house.

Penny ran to the front of the blacksmith and barn where they kept the fire bell. Pulling on the rope for all she was worth, she kept muttering, "Please, God. Please, God. Please, God." That's all she could think "Help them hear it."

When she began hearing rifles discharging to pass the word along, she knew the alarm was out. She charged back in the store and gathered up the stacks of metal pails that had arrived only the day or so before. Out to the well, she began winding up the bucket.

"Where is it?" Pastor Solberg puffed up beside her.

"In the sack house, I think."

Riders on two horses galloped into the yard and tied the horses behind the shed.

"In the sack house."

They grabbed full buckets and headed for the grain un-loading dock. The double wide doors were still barred from the inside, so they turned toward the office door.

"Where's the fire?"

"In here," Hjelmer hollered back. "But keep the door closed!"

Penny and Pastor Solberg kept taking turns turning the crank and emptying the oak bucket into the pails. While her arms and hands worked, her mind careened around corners and out of control. *Serves them right! Goodie . . .*

Penny Bjorklund. What's come over you? Father, forgive me. Please guard those inside. Keep Hjelmer and Olaf safe. Please, God. Please, God.

All Penny could see was the next bucket, even though someone had hung a lantern for them and there was another lit on the outside of the sack house. Crank and pour. Let the handle go so the bucket would drop faster. Crank and pour. She could hear men yelling and coughing—oh, the awful coughing. Was that Hjelmer?

Goodie and the children ran out of their house with arms full of quilts and bedding. Two more men arrived with shovels and buckets tied to their saddles. Harnesses jingled in the crisp air.

"There's buckets over here. Let's get the brigade going!" Solberg directed traffic, and the line formed.

Where are Hjelmer and Olaf? Are they all right? She could see red behind the windows, a flickering red that meant one thing—the fire was growing.

The large double doors to the loading dock burst open, and men threw burning sacks of grain out to the ground. One of the men took Penny's place at the well, so she moved up the brigade line where they handed buckets hand over hand to the next person in line.

"Let's get some water up here on the roof of the house, just in case." The line shifted.

"What's happening?" Penny took the place next to Goodie and passed her a bucket.

"Man fell asleep with a cigar, they think," she panted. "He must have been drinking too."

"God have mercy on us!" Penny's hands burned from the crank and now the pail handles. Already her shoulders felt as if they'd been pulled from the sockets.

More smoldering grain sacks were heaved out the door and doused with water.

Two men, hacking and choking, staggered from the building. Even in the flickering lamplight, they could tell it was Olaf and Hjelmer.

"Thank God." The two women spoke at the same time.

"Stop the buckets." Hjelmer bent over and coughed till he had to lean against the wall.

Haakan and Lars drove in with their wagons and all those big enough to fight the fire.

"Too late," Pastor Solberg called as they bailed out, buckets in hand.

"You got it out?"

"Ja, thanks to Penny here."

Goodie stood beside Penny, both of them still trying to catch their breath in the smoky air. The wind out of the west was quickly doing its air cleansing job. "You smelled it first?" she asked.

Penny nodded. "Something woke me, and when I stepped outside to check because nothing was remiss in the house or the store, I could smell something different burning. Hjelmer figured out what it was."

"Ma, is the fire out?" Ellie pulled on her mother's coat.

"I told you and Hans to go out to the cellar."

"We did, but they said it was all right."

"Ja, then you go back on home now before you catch your death. I'll be there in a little bit."

"Thank you, Penny." Goodie looked at her, shaking her head and wringing her hands.

"You're welcome. Anyone would do the same."

Penny and Goodie both wiped their burning eyes.

"Ah, but you listened to the prompting of the Holy Ghost." Pastor Solberg joined the two women.

Penny shrugged. "I don't really know. I'm just glad nothing much was destroyed."

"Uh, you don't know, then?"

"What?"

"The man who was sleeping in there was killed, by the smoke most likely."

"Oh, merciful God." Goodie patted Penny's arm. "I'll be right back." She took a bucket of water, along with the dipper that hung at the well, to the men by the doors. One by one the buckets were brought back to the well, and Penny turned them upside down to drain. She'd wash them in the morning.

"You're a hero, Tante Penny!" Thorliff said at her side.

"You mean heroine." Pastor Solberg corrected him. He shook his head and sighed. "Guess you can't get the teacher out of the man even in the midst of night and fire. Penny, we're all thankful for your nose."

Hjelmer made his way through the crowd to drink right from her bucket. "Thankful is right. The whole town could have burned to the ground." He dumped the remainder of the bucket over his head and shook water all over everyone.

"How did you know it was the sack house?" Solberg asked.

"Back in the early years when we ran out of coffee—" He sucked in a deep breath and went into another coughing frenzy. When he could breathe again, he continued. "We toasted whatever grain we had and ground it. I burned it once and never forgot the smell."

"The Lord does provide." Solberg shook his head. "And to think how long ago He put things in motion so you would know what was burning. He says, 'Before you call I will answer.' And so He did."

"Amen to that." Hjelmer started coughing again. "The smoke was terrible. If Olaf hadn't brought a lantern, we wouldn't'a got the body out. I near to fell right over it."

The group around them parted for Olaf and Goodie, arm in arm, to walk toward them.

"We want to thank you for saving the sack house and our house too." Olaf put out his hand to shake Hjelmer's. "Some of the wheat is gone, sure, but it coulda been so much worse."

Goodie reached for Penny's hand. She ducked her head, then straightened to look Penny full in the face in the flickering lantern light. "I got to ask your forgiveness for the way I been acting lately. I'm sorry, Penny. I started thinking crazy-like. And over that silly sewing machine. All I could think was that you had the store and all, and you didn't need more to do, and that I deserved to have the sewing machines to sell." She shook her head and blinked several times along with a sniff. "I went crazy is all I can say. Foolish old woman that I am."

Penny remembered back to the terrible thoughts she'd had. "I forgive you, if you'll forgive me."

Goodie shook her head. "Don't know what for, but sure enough." She looked over at the dark building. "Just think. Mr. Drummond coulda been sleeping there . . . like he did last week. Shame this poor man had to ruin it for everyone. Olaf said he's never letting anyone sleep in there again."

"I told that man there could be no smoking and we don't abide by drinking here, but some people never listen." Olaf shook his head. "Poor fool."

"I think we better hurry up and get that boardinghouse built." Hjelmer stood close enough to Penny for her to feel the heat of his body through their clothing. "Seems my mor has the right idea."

"As soon as I finish shipping the grain and the sack house empties, I'll start making furniture for it. Tables and chairs and such. I have plenty of wood curing up in the rafters there. Had the fire got up there, those boards woulda burned real hot."

As the smoke blew away, the people started to leave, bidding each other good-night and heading back for their beds. Several men said they would be over to help clean up the mess in the morning. Penny shivered as the wind cut through her coat. "Good night, Goodie, Olaf. Morning is going to come mighty early." She covered a yawn with her hand. Together she and Hjelmer turned back to their house.

Once inside the door, Hjelmer said, "If the water's hot, I'll wash before I come up."

Penny checked the reservoir. "Not hot but good and warm."

"That's fine."

She dipped him a basin full while he shucked his shirt and undershirt. After setting towels and soap beside the basin, she hung up her coat and removed her boots. Sniffing her coat sleeve, she made a face. "I'll have to hang everything we wore out on the line in the morning."

⚜ ⚜

Before noon the next day, Goodie knocked at Penny's door, pies in hand. "Sorry I couldn't get any bread done yet, but after dinner I can go put it in the oven. You need anything else?"

"I don't think so. Thank you."

"You want I should set the tables then?"

Penny nodded while at the same time handing Goodie a spoonful of soup. "Taste that. I think it needs something more."

"Salt and some of that bay leaf, if you got any left from making headcheese. Might taste good in that."

"Sure do." When she really looked at Goodie, Penny shook her head. "Are my eyes as red as yours?"

Goodie nodded. "No doubt. That was some scare last night. And all because the man *had* to have his cigar and liquor. I keep asking the Lord to forgive me for thinking it serves him right, but the idea sure keeps popping back in my head. But we're the ones who suffer too, and those whose grain was destroyed. Why, what if those buyers won't pay premium price because of the smoke smell? You know how they use any little excuse to dock the prices."

"I been thinking the same but keep reminding myself to be grateful it wasn't any worse. Who's going to notify the man's family?"

"How? All he had was a letter in his pocket with no address. He had twenty-five dollars, five of it in gold and some change, a gold watch, and a Colt six-shooter in his bag."

"I sure don't know how, but someone around here might have an idea or two."

Goodie shook her head. "His poor wife and children, if he's got any. 'Twere me, I'd sure want to know."

The two worked side by side as they had so many times before, both of them knowing what had to be done and taking each task as it came. Between getting dinner ready, minding the store, and answering a million questions from those who came in, the morning flew by.

Even the railroad men knew about the fire, so it was the prime topic of conversation around the tables, but when Goodie tried to describe the dead man, no one had any idea who he might be.

"We're having a meeting at the church after school is out," Hjelmer told Olaf as they and the women ate dinner when the customers had all gone, "to discuss what to do with the body. There's no ice left in the icehouse, so we can't keep him for folks to identify later. Just wish we had someone who could draw a picture of him in case anyone coming through might be able to recognize him."

"I 'spose I can do that," Olaf said, laying his knife down across his empty plate. "Leastways, I could give it a try."

"You can draw?" Goodie looked at her husband, astonishment arching her eyebrows.

"Some."

"People's faces?"

"Um. Haven't done it for a long time. Not much call for that workin' your way around the country."

"Well, I never . . ." Goodie shook her head again, a small smile lifting just the corners of her mouth. A light of pride glowed in her washed blue eyes.

"It figures. Anyone who is such an artist with a carving knife would be able to draw too." Penny smiled at the man across her table. Gentle was a word she always came back to when thinking of Onkel Olaf. While he was a distant relative of Kaaren's, he'd become onkel to all of them. Nearly every house in Blessing had something that Olaf had crafted, from oaken buckets to stirring spoons to fine furniture like tables or chairs or, in her case, the kitchen cabinet he'd given them for a wedding present. His hands bore the evidence of his work, with scars on the palm and across the back of his left hand. He'd told Thorliff that a knife slipped on that one.

"It just makes me angry that he was drinking and smoking after you told him we didn't allow such." Goodie set the coffeepot down with more force than necessary. "What could he have been thinking of?"

Himself was her silent response to the question that needed no answer.

"So, what do we do about Frank?" Pastor Solberg began the discussion after opening the meeting with Scripture reading and prayer. "All we know about him is that his name is Frank and his wife's name is Louise. They have two sons who are doing well in school." Solberg glanced around the group. "We know this from the letter we found in his breast pocket."

"Olaf said he would draw a picture of the man's face, and

maybe we could do like they do with those wanted by the law."
Lars motioned toward Onkel Olaf, who nodded in return.

"You mean put up Wanted posters?" Pastor Solberg's voice
sounded like his throat had been sandpapered. The smoke had
given everyone who fought the fire a case of raw throat.

"Not exactly. He weren't wanted for anything, far as we
know." Lars cleared his throat too. "But if something like that
went out to the bigger cities and towns, someone might know
him."

"Or we could just bury him and put his valuables in a bag
in the bank vault and see if anyone ever comes asking for a
Mr. Frank So-and-So," Joseph Baard offered. "Be far easier."

"True. But I keep thinking about his widow. She has a right
to know." Solberg pursed his lips. "No, she has a *need* to know."

"Maybe we should let the sheriff in Grafton know about
him. Wouldn't he be the one to get any missing persons re-
port? Surely his widow will turn in something like that."
Haakan leaned his elbows on his knees.

"Only if she wants him back." The men chuckled at Joseph's sally.

"Any other suggestions?"

"We could send letters to some newspapers, saying we got
this man's belongings, like maybe in Grand Forks and Fargo."

"You could include Bismarck and Minneapolis."

"I could ask Kaaren to write the letters. She writes real
good."

"All right, I get the feeling we want to send letters to the
papers, and I believe contacting the sheriff is a good idea. That
way no one here will be accused of murdering the man."

"I told him we didn't allow drinking and smoking," Olaf
repeated.

"No one in his right mind smokes around hay barns and
grain storage. We all know that," Hjelmer threw in.

"That was the problem. No man who's been drinking till
he's drunk is in his right mind." Joseph rolled his eyes. "Just
ask my Agnes. She'll tell you. Her and all the women. They
hate drinking worse than dust under the bed." Several of the
men chuckled along with him. Drinking at community events
had caused a real stir for a time, until the women got their way
and drinking was outlawed.

"Now, we don't know for sure he was drunk." Solberg earned a communal snort for that comment.

"If he weren't drunk, the smoke woulda woke him up, or at least his coughing woulda." Joseph leaned back against the chair and crossed his arms over his chest. "Drunk as a skunk he was. I'd bet on it."

"Be that as it may, I'm not going to include it in the letters." He turned to Lars. "Thank you for volunteering Kaaren, but I better do the letters myself. Sounds more official coming from the pastor." He looked at Hjelmer. "You going in to Grafton in the next day or so?"

"Guess I could."

"Good, then you'll talk with the sheriff?"

Hjelmer nodded.

"Anything else we need to discuss then?"

"I think we should have a funeral for him. That way if his widow or family comes asking, they'll know we did right by him." Haakan glanced around the room. "I know it might help me feel better if I was the grieving party."

"I'll make the box," Joseph volunteered, "first thing in the morning."

"Thanks." Olaf was usually the one who made the coffins.

"And we'll bury him here in the cemetery."

"What if he weren't a believer?"

"Since only God knows that, we'll do what we can." Solberg looked at each face. "Anything else?"

When they all shook their heads, he bowed his. "Let's close in prayer then."

At the "amen" they all stood. "See you tomorrow, then, those who can come. Otherwise, remember the debate here at ten on Saturday morning. The women have planned a dinner for afterward."

"To keep them politicians from talking all day long."

"And talking our ears right off."

They all left chuckling.

⚭ ⚭

That sunny Saturday people began arriving an hour before the debate, tying their horses and throwing down hay for them. The men started the cooking fire and helped set up the tables on the south side of the church while the women set out the food, all covered and ready for the noon meal.

Some had brought coffee in jugs they emptied into buckets to hang over the fire to warm. Huge coffeepots were hung on tripods and filled with water to make coffee later.

The church filled to standing room only, so they opened all the windows in order that the people outside could hear.

At ten o'clock Pastor Solberg stepped to the front and raised his hands for silence. As the crowd quieted, the younger children could be heard playing at the schoolhouse. "Welcome, everyone, to our first political debate here in Blessing. Let us ask our heavenly Father to bless this day and us." He waited until the shuffling and throat clearing stopped. "Father in Heaven, God of all the universe and God of this great country of ours, we thank thee for putting governments on earth to help and guide us. We thank thee for all the folks gathered here and our interest in being wise citizens who understand the issues and choose carefully the people we vote for. Bless thou this day and this meeting. Please grant us wisdom and peace. In Jesus' precious name."

The crowd joined him in the "amen."

Pastor Solberg waited until everyone took their seats again. "Thank you. I now have the honor of introducing to you two gentlemen who have come here to inform us of the issues as they see them. Please stand, gentlemen, so everyone can see you." As the two well-dressed men rose from the front pew and took their places on either side of him, Solberg nodded and shook their hands. "Now, on my right we have Mr. Walter Muir, who has a reputation as an excellent farmer from up near Pembina. On my left is Mr. Porter J. McCumber, who is known for his association with the railroads." A slight shuffling greeted that announcement. "I believe our two guests have decided who will speak first." Solberg looked to his right.

"Mr. McCumber will go first." Walter Muir nodded to his opponent, so Muir and Solberg took their seats, leaving McCumber in front.

"Friends, fellow citizens of this great territory of Dakota, Pastor Solberg, thank you for your kind invitation to share the floor with my esteemed colleague, Mr. Muir. Thank you also for coming today. I know you all have plenty of work to do, so I will keep this as brief as possible, yet there is much to cover."

Penny, Ingeborg, and Agnes left the debate several times to check on the coffee and the children.

"That McCumber must think we don't have a brain between us," Agnes grumbled after the first man finally sat down. "I wouldn't vote for him if my life depended on it."

"You don't have to worry. We won't be able to vote. I heard there's talk of letting the women vote in school elections, however." Penny shook her head. "He's pretty condescending though. Probably thinks that since we are Norwegians we don't understand English."

They returned to the back of the church in time to listen to the beginning of Muir's speech. He was one of the Farmer's Alliance leaders and knew how much he needed the farmers' votes. Looking around the room, Ingeborg knew right away who was the favored speaker here. The question and answer time would be downright interesting.

Noon came and went and still the discussion continued.

The audience began to cough, shuffle their feet, and raise hands to ask questions.

Finally Pastor Solberg stood. "We'll entertain a few questions now." He pointed to a man in the back. "Yes?"

"What I want to know is how they are going to regulate the railroads so they can't rob us blind!"

The more questions that came, the more obvious it was that McCumber was on the side of the railroad companies. Muir talked about the proposed legislation concerning shipping and elevators.

Finally Pastor Solberg called a halt as the tempers heated up. "You can talk with these gentlemen over the dinner that's all set up for us outside. How about letting our guests go through the line first? They deserve a good meal after sharing such important information with us. Let's give them a hand, shall we?"

The applause was less than thundering.

"And now we'll have grace before we dismiss." He said the grace, and some were out the door before the second half of amen.

"That man never did recognize one woman who had a question," Agnes muttered to Ingeborg. "I'm half tempted to—"

"Don't even consider whatever you—"

"I just thought to be the coffee pourer. Wouldn't be my fault if salt got put in their coffee rather than sugar."

"Agnes Baard!"

"Well?"

"They need plenty of sugar after the vitriolic talk I heard up there." They both turned at the same time to see the two candidates shaking hands. While men crowded around them, the two made their way to the tables at the insistence of Pastor Solberg.

"Uff da," Agnes said after listening to several men get into a shouting match. "If this is the way of politics in this country, I'm glad I can't vote."

"Not me," Penny replied. "I'm more convinced than ever that the women's vote is needed, to keep things sane if nothing else. Think I'll write to Elizabeth Preston Anderson of the Christian Women's Temperance Union and ask if she would like to come here and talk with all the women. If I hear anything more about how wonderful the Louisiana Lottery is, I swear I'll scream. Gambling and drinking are two things that should be outlawed for sure if and when we ever get to be a state, or two states."

"How do you know about her?" Ingeborg leaned over and picked up Astrid, who had again managed to escape her sitters.

"I read about her in the newspaper lots of times. She writes editorials better than most of the men, I can tell you." Penny held out her arms. "Come on, Astrid, let's go get something to eat."

"Eat." Astrid nodded as she went into Penny's arms. "Astid hungry."

Penny grinned at Ingeborg around the little girl. "Spoken like a true Bjorklund."

Ingeborg laughed and turned to Agnes. "I think we should send Penny to one of the meetings of the CWTU in Grand Forks. What do you think Hjelmer would say to that?"

"If you think he would let her go . . ."

"He would if someone went with her, I imagine."

"Inge, are you thinking what I think you are thinking?" Agnes tried to keep a straight face, but the chuckle won out. "Maybe a whole group of us should go and show our support. Women who can think for themselves don't live just in the cities."

"Maybe we should."

"You have that look in your eye."

Ingeborg shrugged. "Me?" She rolled her lips together and nodded. "I wonder when their next meeting is."

P*lease come home.*

Mary Martha read the line again. Her uncle Jedediah had written the letter, one of the two or three he'd written in his whole life. She scanned the page again, trying to read between the lines. How sick was her mother? She must be bad for Jed to write.

"Who's that from?" Katy came out of the bedroom rubbing her eyes. "Why did you let me sleep so long? I only needed a short nap." She glanced down at her slippered feet. "See, even most of the swelling in my feet is gone. I've turned the corner, just as I told you I would." She patted her rounded belly. "Young Zeb here has decided I should sleep more too. He's calmed down from whatever was bothering him."

Mary Martha studied her sister-in-law, the dark circles that gave her raccoon eyes were gone, her cheeks had color in them again, and she hadn't thrown up or mentioned spots of blood for over a week now. She finally did indeed wear the bloom of a mother-in-waiting.

Mary Martha breathed a sigh of relief. "It's from my uncle Jedediah. He lives at the homeplace. He says Ma is sick and I should come home. He wouldn't write unless it was serious."

Katy sank down on her knees in front of the chair where Mary Martha sat. She laid her cheek against her best friend's snowy apron. "I don't want you to go and neither will the girls, let alone Zeb. But if you must, you must." She raised tear-filled eyes to see that Mary Martha wore the same sad look. "I will miss you more than I can even begin to say in Norwegian, let alone English."

The little sally made them both smile, one no more wobbly than the other.

"I had hoped to stay until after the baby was born." Mary Martha's thoughts careened to the schoolhouse. Oh, how she would miss the children. Who would help them with her not there? If only she'd been able to talk her mother into coming west and leaving the homeplace to Eva Jane and her husband. After all, she was the eldest.

She could hear her mother's voice plain as if she were in the room. *"I was born not five miles from here, I buried two children and a husband here, and here I will die."* *Please, God, don't let it be that serious. Surely the doctor can do something if I am there to make her go. And beyond that, thou art the God of healing. The Bible says so. You promised.*

And Pastor Solberg, John as she called him in her heart. Were they becoming more than friends? Might that even be a possibility? But if she left, then what?

God, I don't want to leave!

"When will you go?"

"Tomorrow." The word sounded as empty as the Dakota prairie in the winter.

"You'll hardly have time to say good-bye to anyone."

"Maybe it's better that way. Easier at least." Mary Martha folded the letter and put it in her pocket. "I'll get the supper going and then go talk with the girls. When did Zeb say he'd be in?"

"Dark, as usual. He's trying to get that last section plowed before the ground freezes. Valders didn't get to it last year with his accident and all. We need to leave as much in pasture as we can and still raise enough grain for feed."

"Now I won't see the foals come spring." Mary Martha kept thinking of things she would miss out on.

"You can come back, you know. The train goes both ways."

"True. As soon as Ma is on her feet again, I promise I'll catch the first train back." With that said, Mary Martha got to her feet, dusted off her hands as if the sorrow were smudges of soil and, squaring her shoulders, marched into the kitchen. She only had to brush the moisture from her eyes once while she got supper started. After all, there'd be plenty of time for crying on the train.

She found Manda and Deborah in the corral with the horses, as she knew she would. Manda was leading one of the fillies around the ring with Deborah in the saddle.

"Now, you take the reins like I showed you, and I'll just walk beside."

Deborah picked up the reins lying crossed over the horse's withers. "Tell me when to pull back."

"Now, and very gently. We want her to have a soft mouth, and anyone sawing on the reins could ruin that." The trio stopped and started, and stopped again. "Good girl."

Mary Martha wasn't sure if Manda meant the horse or her sister, but Deborah beamed as if she'd been given the best compliment of her young life.

"You sure have brought her along fast." Mary Martha left the corner of the barn and put one foot up on the bottom rail.

Manda shot her what for Manda was a grin. "Okay, now forward again and turn her to the right along the fence. Lay the reins along her neck like I showed you so she learns to neck rein."

Mary Martha let her chuckle only show a smile. That filly would follow Manda right into the house if they let her. When Zeb sold this one, which would be soon, there would be a real broken heart here, no matter how much Manda knew that's why she was training the horse. She knew Manda was hoping Zeb would change his mind and keep the horse for a brood mare, but one as flashy as the chestnut in front of her and broken both to saddle and harness would bring in good money. Until he sold some horses, money was in short supply.

"Whoa." Deborah tightened the reins, and the three of them faced her. If a horse could smile, this one was. Both the girls glowed like candles in the dark.

"You about ready to put her away?"

Manda nodded. "What's wrong?"

"Nothing." She'd just told a lie. Mary Martha corrected herself. "I'll tell you as soon as you've put the horse away." She looked up to the little girl in the saddle. "Did you gather the eggs yet and feed the hens?"

Deborah shook her head. "Manda needed me."

Mary Martha knew that said it all. If Manda needed something, Deborah would walk barefoot through the snow to get it if she had to. And vice versa. In spite of the home they now had with Zeb and Katy, sometimes the girls still acted as if it were the two of them against the world.

Mary Martha had hoped to be able to make life easier for them. She sighed. How could she do that from a distance? Tossing out grain for the chickens, she thought of all the people in Blessing who had become so dear in such a short time. While gathering the eggs, her thoughts and prayers continued, the foremost being Pastor John Solberg.

She sat the girls down on a bench beside the cow stanchions. "You know the letter I got today?" At their nods, she continued. "It was from my uncle Jed. He says my ma is very sick, and I need to come home."

"But this is your home," Deborah said firmly.

"I know, but my other home needs me worse right now, so I will be leaving on the train tomorrow."

"I knew it." Manda clamped her arms across her chest.

"I don't want you to leave. Ma needs you here too." Deborah flung herself into Mary Martha's arms. She raised a tear-stained face. "Please say you'll stay."

"Don't go cryin' on her. 'Twon't make any difference." Manda took her sister's arm and pulled her away. "Grown-ups do what they gonna do, and nothin' we can do about it."

"I hope to come back sometime."

"Um." The sound wasn't very positive. Manda had had people go away before, saying they'd come back, and they never did. "I gotta get another horse worked 'fore it gets too dark." She hauled herself to her feet as though a ton of hay had just fallen on her shoulders and strode out to the barn.

"You want to carry the egg pail?" Mary Martha asked the little girl who'd buried herself back in her aunt's arms as soon as Manda let go of her arm. Stroking the fine hair and patting her back calmed Deborah down. She nodded and the two walked toward the well house to leave the eggs in the cool room.

Zeb took her around that night to the Bjorklunds, the Baards, and the Wolds, leaving the soddy by the schoolhouse until last. "So soon?" everyone asked. But she knew she left with all their blessings and many reminders to come back whenever she could.

Zeb pulled the team to a stop by the hitching post to the north of the Solberg soddy. "You want me to come in or wait here?"

"Come in. You'll freeze out here." Mary Martha shivered in a blast from the north wind.

Pastor Solberg already had the door open by the time they got to it. "Come in. Come in. Is something wrong? Katy? Is it Katy?"

Mary Martha felt her face freeze in that moment. Still, the first thing for him was Katy. When her heart began to beat again, she forced a smile over iced lips. "No, it's not Katy. I came to tell you that I received a summons home. My mother is ill." Her tone sounded as formal as her face looked. "I . . . I won't be able to help with the schoolchildren anymore."

"Miss MacCallister, why I . . . I guess I thought you'd be staying here forever." He motioned them in. "May I take your coats? The coffee can be hot in a few minutes."

"No, thank you. We need to be getting home so I can pack."

"Wh-when are you leaving?"

"On the noon train." She amazed herself at the coolness of her tone.

"So soon?" He rubbed a hand across his forehead.

If he hadn't asked for Katy first, she would have listened more to what sounded like a wound in his voice.

"I . . . I can't even think straight." He sent Zeb a look that pleaded for help, but Zeb shook his head.

"Ma needs her more'n we do right now. She'll just have to come back when she can."

"Yes, when she can." Solberg nodded. "Would you like to hear from m—the children?"

"Most definitely." *And you?* "I'll write right back."

"I—we—I guess that's it then."

"Yes. We better be going." She turned toward the door.

"Wait. I mean, can we see you off at the train?"

Oh, why didn't I just write a letter? I hate good-byes. "I guess."

"See you tomorrow then, Pastor." Zeb took her arm and steered her out the door.

The tears caused by the wind turned to crystals on her cheeks that shattered when she brushed them away. Just like her heart. *He still thinks of Katy first. Until now I never knew that would hurt so much. What difference does it make? We are just friends. And not even that really. I just help with the children at school. That's all.*

That's all. Two words almost as sad as *if only.*

The schoolchildren weren't the only ones at the sack house in the morning. If she heard "God bless" and "Go with God" once, she heard them each fifty times. Her arms ached from hugging, or was it her heart?

Keeping a smile on her face took every bit of backbone she had, and then some.

"This-s i-s-s for you." Anna spoke slowly, just as Mary Martha had taught her. The little girl handed her teacher a red apple that had been polished nearly through the skin.

Mary Martha blinked and blinked again, but the little girl shimmered in a kind of light made brighter through unshed tears. "Thank you, Anna. I wish I could keep this always." She squatted down so they were eye to eye. "You keep working like you have been, and you'll be the best speaker we have. All right?"

Anna nodded and flung her arms around Mary Martha's neck. "I don't want you to go."

"I know. Me either." *I didn't even finish sewing her dress. Now I'll have to mail it to her.* Patting Anna's back, she looked up to catch a sheen in John Solberg's eyes. Did it matter to him that she was leaving?

He picked up Anna and held her, murmuring to her as Mary Martha said good-bye to the others.

"I'll send you a copy of our Christmas pageant." Thorliff stuck out his hand and shook hers.

"Good."

Ingeborg pressed a basket into her hand. "Just some things we gathered up so you won't be hungry on the train and you'll remember us."

"Mange takk." Mary Martha brought out a few smiles with that.

"Come home soon," Katy whispered against her ear. Zeb held her close, and when he stepped back, his eyes too wore that brightness. Deborah clung to her, but Manda just nodded, her jaw clenched so hard it shone white.

"All aboard." The conductor shook his head. "Sorry, miss, but you got to board now, or we leave without you."

Pastor Solberg took her hand to help her up the stairs. "You'll write?"

"Yes."

"Promise?"

"Y-yes."

"God bless and keep you and bring you back to us."

Did he say "to us," or did she just imagine it? "You also." She let go of his hand and mounted the last step to turn and wave as the train began to chug forward.

"Blest be the tie that binds . . ." Solberg's voice began the hymn, but the others joined in immediately. "Our hearts in Christian love. . . ." Could angels sound more sweet? The train chugged louder. She could no longer see them, but her heart heard the words. "The fellowship of kindred minds is like to that above."

She found an empty seat and sank into it, the tears flowing at last, an apple clenched against her skirt. "Dear Lord," she whispered, "will I ever see them all again?"

18

Go tell your ma that Mr. Drummond is here with the sewing machines."

Hans tore out the door as if wolves were chasing him. Penny wiped off the counter and put away the last bolt of wool serge that she'd cut from. She had wanted to tell Mrs. Valders about the sewing machines but had waited. For what she wasn't sure. It was just that she and Goodie still hadn't talked about what they were going to do. Was Goodie going to sell sewing machines, or would they become part of the merchandise of the general store?

So many questions.

The bell tinkled as the man walked in pushing a handcart with several boxes stacked on it. He parked it by the door and came down the aisle to the counter. "How are you today, Mrs. Bjorklund? I brought your machine."

"All that is my machine?" She nodded toward the boxes.

"No, I got two extra and can have more in a matter of days, once you two ladies decide what you want to do. Now, where do you want me to set yours up?"

"I cleared a little more space back where you were before. Once you have it put together, it's not hard to move should I decide differently."

"That is true. And how is Mrs. Wold?"

"She should be here any second. I sent her son to tell her you were here."

"Then I'll just get started, and you can be sewing away before you know it." He turned back to his handcart and trundled it down the aisle, whistling an off-key tune as he went.

Since the store was empty but for him, Penny went back to the kitchen to pull the coffeepot forward. Ham and baked beans leant a delicious aroma, and the molasses bread she'd made special for the evening meal was near ready to put in the oven also. She could serve supper to both families if that would make the discussion easier.

What to do?

Lord, I'm stuck again. While Goodie and I are back to where we belong, there's been no decision on this. Please, what is it you would have us do? All the while she prayed, she adjusted the draft so the oven would heat up for baking the bread and put several sticks of wood in the stove.

A rap at the back door announced Goodie's arrival.

"So, he's here?" Her eyes sparkled. "Olaf said I should go ahead and buy one too."

"Goodie, we need to talk." There, it was out in the open.

"I know, but I don't know what to do." She hung her wool shawl on the peg by the door and pulled out one of the kitchen chairs.

"The coffee will be hot in a minute or two."

"Good." She studied her clasped fingers, then looked up at Penny. "What do you think we should do? I don't ever want to get in a stew like that one again. All I could think was that I was going to get rich selling sewing machines to every woman in Dakota Territory. I didn't sleep good, I snapped at the children, and poor Olaf. He didn't know what hit us. Then there's the way I treated you." She shook her head, her lower lip quivering. "I don't never want to go through such a thing again. Uff da."

"Me either. But we got to look at this with business eyes. Women *need* that machine. Mr. Drummond needs someone in this area to sell and maybe repair the Singer sewing machines. Women need a supply of different kinds of cloth—I got a few but not very many, really." She poured them each a cup of coffee and set a plate of sour cream cookies out on the table. After sitting down and dunking a cookie, she continued. "So, I can expand my store on the west wall, been thinking of doing that anyway, and put up shelves, set up a couple of machines, and see what happens.

"But, I've got about all the business right now I can handle, unless I hire someone full time to help me. When the boardinghouse is built, I won't be serving dinner to the railroad men like I been doing, but that won't be until spring, and winter is when women have more time for sewing."

"I could come work for you."

"Or I could hire Bridget. Or you could take over part of the sack house for the winter."

"Or I could set up store in my parlor. The sack house office might work too. The big room is too hard to heat. We'd freeze in there."

"Olaf could put in another window maybe. But it depends—what do you want to do?"

"What do you want to do?"

They both shrugged, tipped their heads to the side, and shrugged again.

"I been praying about it." Goodie munched on a cookie.

"Me too."

"Olaf says to do what I want. He'll help when and where he can."

"Hjelmer pretty much says the same."

"Either of them could fix those things in a minute. Just give them the instructions and away they'd go."

"True."

"You want I should come work for you regular?"

"If you'd like."

"I would. Then that's settled. For now, anyway. We can change our minds and do something else later if'n we want."

"All right. Let's go tell Mr. Drummond and get his suggestions on how to go about this. He has three machines with him right now, one for you, one for me, and one for whoever grabs it first." She put out her hand. "Thank you for solving this thing for us."

The two women put their coffee cups in the dishpan and headed through the curtained door just as the bell over the store door tinkled. "You go on and talk with Mr. Drummond while I wait on this customer," Penny said, guiding Goodie ahead of her.

"I really don't have any money to put into machines anyhow. Just the one for me, and I'll pay for that working for you," Goodie said.

If only we could solve the statehood issues this easily, Penny thought. *Thank you, Father, thank you.*

"Is Mr. Bjorklund here? I need to put some money in the bank." The man peered around the corner to the bank room.

"No, but Mr. Valders can take care of it for you." Penny pointed him the way, knowing she'd seen him before, but not putting a name to the face. Another customer came in, and she got busy enough to forget about the man setting up machines.

Until Ingeborg and Kaaren entered at the same time. "I brought you some more cheese," Ingeborg called, hefting a basket. "Could only spare half a wheel."

"And I brought butter and eggs." Kaaren had a basket on her arm too. They both turned when they heard Goodie laugh.

"Put those down here and let me show you something." Penny pointed to the counter. When the baskets were set, she beckoned them down the aisle, stepping aside when she came even with Mr. Drummond. With one machine set up, he was showing Goodie how to thread the needle.

"These are Singer sewing machines, ladies, the greatest invention yet for women of today."

As he went into his spiel, Penny watched Kaaren's and Ingeborg's faces. They swapped looks full of questions that soon shifted to delight as they saw the seams the humming machine made. Goodie tried it first, and once she got the treadle moving in the right direction with the right rhythm, the needle went up and down like a charm.

When Ingeborg tried, she had no trouble. "It's just like working the spinning treadle, only with both feet." When she guided the piece of material under the needle and watched the seam form before her eyes, she sat back and dropped her hands in her lap. "Well, I never."

When Kaaren tried, she got the treadle pumping and the needle going up and down, but for some reason the thread tangled. "Oh, I broke it."

"No, no. That kind of thing can happen real easy. Let me show you how to fix it." Drummond sat back down at the machine and had it whirring along again in no time. He motioned Kaaren to take the chair again, and this time, she sewed her first seam. When they tried to pull the two pieces apart, they realized how strong the stitching really was.

"Think how fast it goes." Kaaren stroked the machine as if it were a perfect rose.

"Reminds me of the first time I saw a mower work. The way the grass fell so fast. With this we could make a quilt in no time. Or a dress." Ingeborg fingered the bolt of gingham Penny had laid out.

"Or the sheets and tablecloths for Bridget's boarding-house," Penny said. "When I think of all I could do with this machine, I . . . I . . ." She raised her hands in the air and let them fall.

"So, where do we get these machines?" Ingeborg turned to Mr. Drummond, who had sat back and let the ladies sell themselves on the machine.

"From the store here. Mrs. Bjorklund will have one on display here all the time. We order them from Boston and can have them within two weeks. If you can't afford to buy this little jewel outright, Singer will let you sign a contract, and you pay a little every month. This is the newest way of doing business. A Singer sewing machine for every woman in America."

Within two days every woman in Blessing and from more than five miles out had been by to see the new Singer sewing machine. When she wasn't helping Penny in the kitchen, Goodie spent every minute she could on the machine. She sewed a log cabin quilt too, and they hung it behind the machine. The calico dress they hung on a hanger by the quilt. The children's coat and hat lay folded on the shelf, also the boys' pants and shirt. Napkins for the boardinghouse stacked up.

Penny let Goodie show others how to sew on the machine. Even her tante Agnes.

"I sew just fine," Agnes insisted when Penny pulled her back to the sewing area.

"I know you do. You taught me how, remember? But this machine will make your life so much easier."

"What, you want me to get lazy or something?" Yet Agnes listened and laughed. "Good for you, child. I hope this helps your store get better and better. But I'm just not going to learn to sew on that contraption."

Bridget took over Penny's machine. She came to help in the kitchen, and as soon as the meal was finished, she sat down to sew. She started with hemming flannel squares for diapers for Katy's baby, then progressed to blankets, quilts, and baby things. She sewed shirts for Thorliff and Andrew, a dress for Astrid, and matching dresses for the twins. Her stack of Christmas presents grew daily.

"Maybe I'll open a sewing shop instead of a boarding-house," she said one afternoon.

"Oh no, you don't. We finally got the boardinghouse approved, and now you change your mind?" Hjelmer shook his head.

"You did?" His mother smiled and nodded. "That is good. Now I start working on sheets."

Haakan and Lars came in and bought the first two machines. One would have to be ordered. "Now don't you tell Ingeborg and Kaaren," they said. "These are for Christmas."

"Pretty wonderful presents, if you ask me," Penny answered. "You want I should keep them here then?"

"Good idea! Now, you promised. No matter what, not even a hint."

The two men had just left, teasing each other as they went out the door, when another man entered. The scowl on his face sent a chill up Penny's spine.

"What you tink you doing?" he shouted.

Penny was sure they heard him over in the schoolhouse. "I have no idea what you mean."

"Dat . . . dat sewing machine ting. You make us to go in the poorhouse or someting? You vant all our money?" He shook his fist in her face.

Penny motioned under the counter for Goodie to go get one of the men. "No, sir, I don't want all your money, and I don't want you to go to the poor farm." She wanted to take a step back, the liquor on his breath made her gag. "I don't force people to buy the things I have for sale here in the store."

"My wife, she vant dat sewing machine. Say we pay little every mont." He leaned forward and raised his voice again. "Ve ain't got a little extra every mont, you hear me."

"Yes, I do." Penny wiped the spit off her cheek with her apron.

"My wife, she not let me in the bed . . ."

Hjelmer and Olaf came through the front door together, caught the man by his arms, and lifted him right off the floor. He was still yelling and flailing when they sat him down on the edge of the horse trough. He fell in yelling.

Penny and Goodie watched from the doorway as the man clambered out of the tank and sputtered his way to his wagon. "He'll catch his death driving home all wet in this cold weather." Penny spun around and ran for the chest where she stored extra blankets. Grabbing one she ran back outside and up to the wagon. "Here, wrap this around yourself."

The man looked down at her, looked at the wool blanket, and shook his head. "Well, I'll be a . . ." He took the blanket and did as she said. "Tank you, ma-am. I vill bring it back."

Penny watched him drive off. Give a man enough booze, and he turned into a raging bull. She shuddered again. He had looked as if he was going to hit her. What if Hjelmer and Olaf hadn't come when they did?

"Penny Bjorklund, if you don't take the cake." Hjelmer stopped beside her.

"You shouldn't have dunked him. Not as cold as it is."

"We didn't. He fell in himself." He tweaked her earlobe. "And you go giving away a perfectly good blanket to a man who looked like he was going to chew you up and spit you out." He looked over her head to Olaf. "What are we going to do with her?"

"Buy her another blanket?" Olaf patted her shoulder. "You got a good heart, young lady, that you do."

Penny shivered. "The look in his eyes, like he was half crazy. What if you hadn't come when you did?"

"I think it's time to keep a gun under the counter. Been thinking that for some time now, with the railroad traffic and all. Blessing isn't like it used to be, you know. Strangers coming through here all the time now."

"A gun? I haven't used a gun for years," Penny said.

"Just a little pistol."

"I never used one of those. What if someone got hold of it

who wasn't supposed to? Hjelmer, I don't want a gun."

"We shall see."

She looked up at her husband. He had *that* look on his face. *What are we in for now?*

19

Ma, when's Mary Martha coming back?"

"She most likely hasn't even gotten home yet." Katy reached up to take down the sheets she'd pinned to the clothesline earlier. The north wind made her nose and fingers tingle. Wouldn't be too many more days to hang clothes out to dry without them freezing stiff. Zeb said the animals had coats thicker than he'd seen for a while. That meant a hard winter. But if God provided extra thick coats for the animals, He surely would provide for them. Besides that, they'd all done their best to get food set by. She had yet to dig the carrots, but the longer they stayed in the ground, the sweeter they grew.

"I wish she coulda stayed here." Deborah folded the pillowcases and dish towels as Katy handed them to her.

"Me, too." Katy dropped the clothespins in the basket she kicked along in front of her and handed Deborah two corners of the sheet. "You want to help me fold this?" When their hands met, she dropped a kiss on the little girl's forehead. "You are such a big help. Don't these sheets smell good?" She buried her nose in the fresh-smelling linen.

"When do you think she's coming back?"

"I hope in time for the baby to come. Having her here would be such a comfort." She folded the last towel and gave the full basket a pat. "There now. One more chore done. This afternoon I'll heat up the flatirons, and you can iron the handkerchiefs. Would you like to do that?"

"And the pillowcases?"

"If you're careful." They each took a handle of the basket and carried it into the house.

"Pa said he had a looker for the filly." Deborah wandered over to the front window where she could see Manda down in the corral. "Manda wants to keep her."

"I know, but she knows the filly is for sale."

"She's not ready for a heavy rider yet."

Katy looked over at the little girl staring out the window. "How do you know so much?" But she knew how—Deborah listened. She flitted about like a little ghost, her ears always ready to tuck things away in a mind that never seemed to forget.

"So, how was school yesterday?"

"Sad. We all miss her. Anna cried. I din't cry, but my eyes wanted to."

Mary Martha had been gone two days now, and the house seemed empty without her ready laugh. Strange in that she'd been at school all day, but still—maybe it took two to make a house laugh.

Katy swooped over to Deborah and, grabbing her from behind, blew on her neck and snuggled kisses between her braids.

The little girl laughed along with Katy, and the room—nay, the whole day—seemed brighter. They were still laughing when Zeb and Manda came in for dinner.

"What's so funny?" Zeb turned from washing his hands in the dry sink.

"Ma tickled me." Deborah set the plates on the table.

"That's it?" He looked at Manda, who waited behind him to use the soap and water. She shrugged and handed him the towel. "How'd the filly go with the harness?"

"She's ready to team with old Jezzy. Thought I'd hitch 'em up this afternoon."

"I got a man coming to look at her, you know."

"I know." Her brows knit themselves together. "She ain't ready for a heavy rider yet."

Deborah and Katy exchanged looks that made them laugh again.

"Now what?" Zeb looked from one to the other, shaking his head all the time. "If I didn't know better, I'd think the two of you been chewing loco weed." That brought out another burst of laughter.

Manda rolled her lips and looked the other way.

"Watch out, Manda, you just might laugh too," Katy said over her shoulders as she set the kettle on the hot pad on the table. She glanced around the table one more time to make sure everything was in place and sat down.

"Manda, it's your turn to say grace."

The scowl returned in full force. Her sigh spoke of a deep-seated refusal that couldn't be spoken. "Thank thee for this food and for our house and our animals and please take care of Aunt Mary Martha and make her mother well again so she can come back." The words rushed forth so she wouldn't have to pause for breath. "Amen."

"Well, thank you, and I'm sure glad the good Lord can hear fast too."

The buyer arrived just as they were finishing the apple pudding. Zeb got up. "You coming?" He waited for Manda to answer.

"She ain't ready."

"I know that, but he can buy her, and we can finish her off, say it take another week?"

"At least."

The two of them went out the door, Manda cramming her old fedora down on her braids.

Manda took the filly through her paces under saddle and the harness. "She's just green broke," she told the man.

"I know. Yer pa already said that. You don't have another young one to team with her?" When Zeb shook his head, the man studied the filly. "What you asking for her?"

Zeb named a price that even raised Manda's eyebrows. "And we'll need another week at least to finish training her."

"That's high."

"She's worth it. Not many young horses, flashy like this, trained to both saddle and harness." Zeb winked at Manda. "You don't take her, I got someone else coming next week."

The man felt down the filly's legs and looked at her teeth. "You wouldn't try to cheat me now?"

"Mister, you ain't got enough money to make it worth me trying to cheat you." Zeb tipped his hat back. "Seein's you're not interested, I'll have Manda put her away."

"Now don't go gettin' in a rush here. Man's got to make up his mind."

At Zeb's nod, Manda led the filly around the corral again.

The man offered a hundred dollars less than the asking price.

"Put her up," Zeb said to Manda, stepping away from the corral. Then he told the would-be buyer, "Come on back sometime when you're really in a buyin' mood."

The man increased his offer by fifty dollars. Zeb shook his head. "You know, I was in a mood to dicker some, but you blew that away. Four hundred cash or nothing doing."

"All right!" The man dug in his pocket. "Half now and half when you deliver her."

"No, half now and half when you come get her."

"Mister, you sure drive a hard bargain."

"Didn't have to be that way." Zeb looked out across the pasture where the rest of his horse herd grazed the last of the green pasture.

Grumbling, the man slapped some bills and a gold coin and some change in Zeb's hand. "She better be worth that, or I'm bringing her back."

Zeb counted the money, looked at the man, and shook his head. "I'm not sure I want such fine horseflesh going to a man who can't appreciate it." He made to hand the money back, but the man backed up, brushing away the offered bills with shaking hands. "No. I said I want her, and that's that."

When the man mounted his horse and loped out of the yard, Manda came to stand beside her pa. "He don't deserve her."

"Maybe not, but we got a hundred dollars more than I'd thought. He just got my goat, he did." He folded the money and put it in his pocket, then pulled some bills out of the other pocket. He handed Manda two dollars.

"What's that for?"

"You did the training, so you get paid." Zeb dropped an arm over her shoulders. "Come on, let's go see if your ma has any more of that pudding left."

"B-but . . ." Manda stared at the money. "I . . . I ain't never had that much money in my whole life."

" 'Bout time then." He pulled her with him. "Come on, girl. They might eat it all without us."

That afternoon, Kaaren Knutson knocked on the door of the pastor's soddy, the book on sign language clutched to her chest. If he was gone, she'd have to come by later, but Thorliff had been after her to talk with him.

"Why, Mrs. Knutson, what a pleasure. Come right on in." He stood back and held the door open. "You are out on such a blustery day."

"I know. I have some things to take to Penny for the store, but I wanted to show you something."

"Can you stay for coffee?"

She shook her head. "Not today, thank you. Here, this came several weeks ago." She handed him the book

"Can you sit down for a minute at least?"

"All right, so I can show you what I've been learning. I wanted a way to help Grace talk with other people besides reading lips, which she is getting very good at, by the way. She never misses the word 'cookie,' for example. But then Mr. Gould, Ingeborg's friend from New York, sent me this book." She pointed to the one in his hands. "It tells how to talk with sign language."

Pastor Solberg studied the cover. "Hmm." Opening the book, he studied the pages, quickly flipping from one to another. "Amazing." He looked some more. "And you say you have been practicing this?"

She nodded. "Every day. I started with the alphabet. This is Grace." Her fingers quickly formed the letters. "Grace knows that too, as do Sophie and Trygve. Lars says his hands weren't made for talking, but he is trying."

"There are signs for some words too." She signed and smiled at him.

"What did you say?"

"Hello." Her fingers moved again. "Good-bye. See how simple it is?"

"So, why did Thorliff want you to show this to me?"

"Because he said if all the children learn it, then when

Grace comes to school, they will all be able to talk with her. I had thought I would have to teach her at home and had no idea how to get Sophie to come without her. This is truly a gift from God and just at the right time too."

"His gifts usually are." Solberg continued flipping pages in the book. "If we were to do this, would you come and teach it? I don't see where I have time to learn it myself, let alone teach it. I need another helper as it is."

I want to teach again. I could help you. Her reaction caught her by surprise. She'd thought she was over that desire to teach. Besides, how could she do it with four small children and another on the way? Surely Ingeborg would take them while she did this. Or Bridget.

"Maybe I could do this one afternoon a week? After I learn more myself." She sat quietly for a moment. "If this is God's will, it will work out, right?"

"That's right. I hear you were a very good teacher."

"I hoped so. I do love teaching the children. I did so in our soddy for a time, before we could form a school. Things are so much easier now than when we first came here." She paused again. "I suppose this is like teaching another language. Only with hands." She stared down at her own callused fingers. "Agnes and I taught English classes too, you know?"

"So I heard. I have a feeling you are a natural born teacher, and now God is providing you with another way to teach. Who knows what will come of this?"

"Ja, who knows?" The cat purred and wound along the side of her skirt. Kaaren leaned over and ran her fingers along the cat's back and rubbed behind his ears. His purring filled the room and brought another smile to her face. "Well, I best be going. Thank you for your time." She stood and reached for her precious book. "Maybe I better learn to draw fingers and signs too, you know. For the schoolchildren." Even she could feel the lightness in her step. *I'm going to be teaching again. Please God, let it be so.*

"Thank you for coming and say hello to Mrs. Bjorklund for me. Tell her to save me a hunk of cheese if she has any in."

"She will have when I get there." Kaaren nodded toward the baskets in the wagon. "I'm the delivery woman today. You want some eggs? I'll get them for you."

"No, that's . . ." But at the look on her face, he changed his mind. "I'd love some, but no more than six, thank you."

After delivering the eggs, Kaaren clucked her horse forward, waving good-bye to the man in the doorway. Her heart sang at a pace the horse couldn't begin to match.

"What brought the stars down to your eyes?" Penny asked when Kaaren carried the two baskets into the store.

"I may get to teach again." Kaaren set the goods up on the counter. "I showed the book to Pastor Solberg, and he said we could teach signing at the school to the children if I would teach it."

"So Grace will go to school like all the other children." Penny slapped her hands on the counter and did a quick toe and shuffle step. "Yes, Lord, you *do* have a plan for that child."

"Ah, Penny, I been thinking. Maybe I could trade eggs and butter for my payment for a sewing machine."

Penny shook her head. "I don't know how we could do that, since you send your payment right in to the Singer Company in Boston. Sorry."

"Oh well. It was just a thought. But then with teaching and all, I probably wouldn't have much time to sew on it anyway." But Kaaren's gaze strayed back to where the sewing machine was set up. Set up just waiting for someone to come along and buy or at least try it.

"Maybe after harvest next year Lars will let me buy it." She turned her back on the machine. "I need a packet of needles, and Ingeborg needs a pound of coffee and peppermint sticks for the children. I'm going to ask her to keep my three while I teach signing, but oh my, I have so much to learn first."

Penny weighed their goods in and their groceries out.

"Oh, and Ingeborg said to tell you she is trying a new kind of cheese. One that is soft, so it doesn't take so long to cure. You know she would raise goats to make goat cheese too, if we would let her. That woman . . ."

"I know. She'll try anything. But even if she produced twice as much cheese, I still don't think we could keep up with the customers. They come off the train begging for that Bjorklund cheese."

"She's making the well house bigger, with a huge long

LAURAINE SNELLING

trough for the cold water. Lars said we could keep live fish in
there, it will be so big."

Penny chuckled with her. "Now, if we can get Metiz to
bring in more smoked fish, that would be good too. After
Bridget gets the boardinghouse up and running, I'm thinking
of making sandwiches here and perhaps pie or cookies. Quick
things."

"You could put things like that on a tray and take it out to
the train."

Penny stared at her. "What a wonderful idea." She nodded,
nibbling her bottom lip. "Some people are afraid to get off the
train, like they might get left. We could most likely go right
into the cars." She grinned. "Wait until I tell Hjelmer this!"

"And those who want a full meal can go to Bridget's, just
like they came here."

"Kaaren, you're a genius." Penny finished wrapping the
bundle. "And now, what else can I get for you?"

"Nothing, I guess, unless you want to throw in the sewing
machine."

"I can invite you in for a cup of coffee."

Kaaren shook her head. "No, I better get on home. But
thanks." She gave the sewing machine another longing look
before she went out the door.

Penny ran back to where Goodie sat sewing away. "I could
hardly bear it." She clapped her hands over her mouth to stifle
the giggles.

"Now what?" Goodie stopped pumping the treadle.

"Kaaren tried to buy a sewing machine with her egg and
butter money, and Lars has already bought her one for Christmas."

"So what did you say?" Goodie fitted the words in among
her chuckles.

"I said that since she had to send the payment to the Singer
company, eggs and butter might not get there in very good
shape." Penny exploded with laughter. "I didn't lie. Not really."
She wiped her eyes with her fingertips. "I can't wait for Christmas to see her face."

"Oh, such fun this will be." Goodie shook her head. "Sure
glad it wasn't me she was asking. I can't think that fast and
would have given the whole thing away."

"Well, I have some good news and some bad news," Kaaren said after she'd greeted her children and been greeted by all those gathered at Ingeborg's. Metiz smiled from the end of the kitchen table, where she sat pulling a tanned rabbit skin back and forth over the table edge to soften the pelt.

"Let's have the good news first." Ingeborg laid down her wool carding paddles.

"God willing, I will be teaching signing one afternoon a week, as soon as I learn enough to do so." Kaaren clasped her hands to her chest. "I will be teaching again. Such a dream come true."

"You've been helping with the English classes. Isn't that teaching?" Bridget asked, her spindle continuing to turn.

"Ja, but not really. I love teaching the children." She sighed. "Thanks be to God."

"Now, the bad news."

Leave it to Ingeborg to want to get the hard part over with. "I . . . I asked Penny if I could buy a sewing machine with my butter and eggs, but she said the money has to go to Boston to the Singer Sewing Machine Company. So I guess I will have to wait until after harvest, like Lars said."

"Maybe not. I'm sure I have enough money in my bank account to buy a machine, one we could share. Haakan said I should wait until after harvest too, but harvest just got over with. I don't want to wait a whole year. Think of all the sewing we could get done in a year."

"Would you do that?"

"Without hesitation. In fact, I'll go in there tomorrow and order it."

I hope Lars won't get too mad, Kaaren thought on the short drive from Ingeborg's to her own home. *But it isn't as if I really bought it. Maybe I can make him a new jacket for Christmas with it.*

ᴤ ᴤ

The next day Ingeborg set her basket up on the counter of the general store. "I brought you some of the new soft cheese

I made. Tastes right good spread on bread or crackers. Thorliff says it is best right off the end of his finger, but as I told him, we aren't all as sweet as he is."

"What did he say to that?" Penny picked up the cheese and sniffed. "Um. Smells wonderful."

"He grabbed his throat and gagged a lot. Astrid thought he was choking and started screaming. Glad no company came right about then." Ingeborg chuckled at the thought. "What those young'uns don't think of."

Penny schooled her face to keep smiling. What she wouldn't give to have young'uns creating a mess at her house. The thought brought on another. Did any of her brothers and sisters have children now? Some of them might. Were any besides her one brother still alive, or was cousin Ephraim mistaken? And if they were alive, why didn't any others answer her letters? She reminded herself to be grateful she found one. But letters took so long between answers. Too long, in her opinion.

"So, what can I get for you today?" Penny weighed the cheese. "We need to decide on a price for this. Can't be as much as the aged, I wouldn't think." She looked over at the remnant of cheese she had left.

"You have to keep this cool. It spoils faster than the other."

"Hmm. Would a nickel a pound be agreeable?"

"The other is ten cents." Ingeborg nodded. "You going to want any hams or smoked goose? I got a few extra of those."

"The hams for sure. The geese closer to Christmas?"

"Sounds fine. Now, I'd like to order me a sewing machine. Kaaren and I can share it until those tightfisted husbands of ours agree to buy another."

"Ah, would you like to put that on the contract?" Penny stumbled for words.

"No, I'm taking money out of my account as soon as Hjelmer or Valders gets here. Where'd they go anyway?"

Penny thought fast. "Hjelmer is in Grand Forks—left on the early train—and Mr. Valders went home for dinner." She glanced up at the clock.

"So early?"

"Ah, well, he had something needed doing. I got to get in

the kitchen to finish dinner for the railroad men. Perhaps we can fill out the paper later."

"I really wanted to do it now, but I guess I can wait." Ingeborg frowned. "How come it is so difficult for a Bjorklund to buy a sewing machine?"

Springfield, Missouri

How many miles to home?

Mary Martha stared out the train window. Had it taken this long to get to Dakota Territory? So many train changes, so much waiting time. She withdrew her tatting from the bag beside her, the thread flowing freely between her fingers and the shuttle as she created the tiny patterns that were becoming a lovely lacy collar. She'd planned to have it done for Manda for Christmas, and now with all the train time, it was almost ready to mail. Through repeated admonishments, her mother had trained her to not waste time. Her mother—how much care would her mother need? Her mother, who never admitted to anything being wrong with her, her mother, who always took care of everyone else.

If only Uncle Jed hadn't been so terse in his letter.

If only she could have stayed with Zeb and Katy.

"Next stop, Bolivar." The conductor made his way through the cars, checking tickets and calling out stops. Two more until she could get off the train, be done with being rocked from side to side, her ears blasted with the screech of steel on steel and the infernal clacking as the train raced over the rails. She felt as if half the coals from the engine now nested in her hair.

While she had pinned it up again just a few hours ago, she could feel tendrils drifting down to tickle her neck. Her hat now lay beside her on the seat, victim to the curved seat back that hit her just wrong. Everything felt wrong.

Father, if I didn't believe you know what is going on, I most surely would have stayed in Dakota. Please watch over my family there and keep them safe. And my friends. And John Solberg. She almost didn't add that last, but God knew her heart, so she might as well bring their friendship out in the open. If that's what they were—friends. But she had other friends who were male, and none of them made her go hot and cold within the blink of an eye, noodled her knees, and tied her tongue in half hitches.

At least John didn't know of her feelings.

Was he beginning to feel the same way? She'd seen him blush, the red creeping up his neck. Such an endearing trait.

She closed her eyes, the better to see him.

"Springfield, next stop."

She blinked and sat up straight. Had she been dozing? Daydreaming? She brushed off her skirt and, after smoothing her hair back into its bun, set her hat firmly in place and anchored it with the pearl hatpin.

The picture of Manda's battered fedora flitted through her mind. Since it was one of the few things Manda had from her earlier life, she hadn't thrown it out. But she'd been tempted.

Mary Martha settled the things in her reticule and drew her gloves on over hands that showed the work she'd been doing. But then lily white hands had never been a dream of hers.

She'd sent a telegram so that Uncle Jed would know to come get her. That is if anyone had thought to deliver it, far as they lived from town. Thoughts of the homeplace brought a smile. It seemed as if she'd been gone for years, not just a matter of months.

As the train screeched to a stop, she gazed out the window. Sure enough, the slight man standing with one boot on the streetlamp pedestal looked familiar. Dear and familiar and older. She picked up her bag and made her way to the door, accepting the hand of the conductor to help her down the steps.

"Thank you. And my trunk?"

He pointed up the wooden platform. "Right up there. They might be unloading it now."

"Thank you again."

She stopped for a moment to let her feet get their bearings after being rocked day and night for the last three days.

"Well, missy, I sure do be happy you got on home." Uncle Jed stopped in front of her. "Looks like that Dakota Territory agreed with you."

She put her arm in his. "I'm glad to see you too. How is Ma?"

"Holding her own for right now. That your trunk?"

At her nod, he looked around for a handcart. "Hate to have to pay someone to haul your trunk, but I guess there ain't no choice." He beckoned, and a uniformed man with a face dark as a crow's wing came their way.

Mary Martha pointed to her trunk. "That one." She turned to her uncle. "Where do you have the wagon?"

"Off to the side, over there."

The porter slid the steel plate under the trunk and tilted the cart back to follow them. Once the two men loaded it into the wagon bed, Mary Martha gave the porter a few coins and nodded her thanks.

As soon as they'd left town, she unpinned her hat from her head and repinned it to her reticule. Then with swiftly flying fingers she removed the net holding her hair in a bun, along with the hairpins, and let her hair fall down her back. She shook her head and rolled it from side to side and in a circle, loosening the tightness in her neck and shoulders.

"Feel better?"

"I will in a few minutes." She dug in her bag for a ribbon, tucked it under the curly tresses, and tied it in a bow on top of her head. "There now. While the lady might be gone, the girl is back."

"Yer ma would say you should keep yer hair bound up."

"I know. I'm 'too old to act like a child any longer.' " She mimicked her mother's slow drawl and spare speech. Her face crumbled at the same time. "What is wrong with her? I know you wouldn't have written if it weren't serious, and I know she didn't want you to even then."

"Yer right there."

"Has she seen a doctor?"

He nodded and spit a gob of tobacco juice over the wheel. "Not that it done any good."

"And?" She waited, knowing Jed would answer in his own time. She had to remember she was back home where time didn't mean so much. The warmth of the air compared to freezing Dakota reminded her she was plenty warm. She unbuttoned her black wool coat.

"And whatever it is, it's eatin' her alive, that's all. She's wastin' away right before my very eyes, and nothing anyone can do about it."

"She been taking her herbs and such?"

"I think she been dosing on those longer than she let on. Don't think she woulda told me, but I found her one morning bent over the washbasin, hurtin' so bad she couldn't straighten up. That's when I drug her to the doctor."

He shook his head at her unasked question. "He gave us a bottle of laudanum, said to take it as needed."

"Oh, Lord our God." She breathed the prayer, guilt snatching her breath away. She should have been here. But she was needed in Dakota too.

"This weren't nothin' new. Been growing for long time, like I said."

"Even before I left?"

"Long time."

The bugling hounds announced their arrival before they topped the last rise. The house and barns lay nestled in the arms of tree-covered hills, bounded to the north by the curve of the river. The trees were in their final blaze of fall glory. A thin ribbon of smoke from the chimney announced that someone was to home. So different from the flat Dakota prairie, these wooded hills and warm golden light. Dry leaves danced across the dirt road in front of them and crackled under the horses' hooves. A rooster crowed, a red squirrel scolded from the oak trees beside the road, and the dogs picked up their howling, knowing the wagon and occupants belonged to them.

Mary Martha drew in a deep breath. Somewhere, someone was burning leaves, the tang on the wind announced. The earth was settling in for a slumber and sighed its redolent scent into the fall air. She sniffed again. This too was so different from the west. How come even the earth smelled different?

If only Jed would slap the horses into a gallop.

She leaped from the wagon before the wheels quit squeaking and bounded up the ancient board steps. Bursting through the door, she found her mother lying on the sofa in a patch of sunlight. The sun shone through skin so thin the bones gleamed white beneath it.

Mrs. MacCallister stretched out a shaking hand. "Ah, Mary Martha, you come home. Lord a'mercy, thank you. You brought my baby home."

Mary Martha sank down on her knees beside the sofa and laid her cheek against her mother's cold hand. "Why didn't you write for me earlier?"

"Now, no need to carry on. Ah knew you would come when you could."

The words stabbed the daughter's heart. She could have come home sooner, but she loved being in Blessing. *Admit it, you wanted to be with Pastor John Solberg. Katy was just an excuse.* She tried to still the nagging voice, but how do you quiet the truth?

Mary Martha brushed back the hair from her mother's forehead. "You'll feel better now and get your strength back while I do for you for a change."

"Maybe so." Ma turned her head to study her daughter's face. "You look different somehow." She stroked her cheek with a trembling finger. "The prairie agrees with you."

"It is some different, that's for sure. Right now they're most likely having their first snow of the season. The ground was already beginning to freeze, as was the river. You'd like Zeb's place. He's raising horses, you know, just like he always wanted."

"He never did like hoeing tobaccy and cotton."

"How'd you know that?" She continued to stroke her mother's hair, so thin now she could see the scalp through the limp strands.

"A mother knows the heart of her children."

Do you know then how badly I want to be in Dakota? I surely do hope not. Mary Martha continued stroking as her mother's eyelids fluttered closed and her breathing slowed. The quiver in it made Mary Martha think of an animal in pain, a forest creature that didn't want to let the harsh world know it was vulnerable.

When the younger woman finally stood, her back was stiff

with determination. She would do whatever it took to make her mother's last days as long and comfortable as the good Lord permitted.

"Lord willin'." So often she heard those words from her mother's lips. And now there was no one else to depend on.

She and the good Lord—were they fighting on the same side or not?

"You want this in yer old room?" Jed asked from the doorway.

Mary Martha nodded. "I'll help." She shucked her coat and hung it on the carved oak coat-tree by the door. Together they wrestled her wooden trunk up the porch steps and down the short hall to the small bedroom off the kitchen. While during the hot days they cooked out in the summer kitchen, today the wood stove in the kitchen had beans baking in its great oven. She sniffed appreciatively.

"She set the beans to baking in spite of . . ."

Jed nodded. "I got a mess a squirrels yesterday and nearly had to fight her to let me skin 'em. They et squirrels in Dakota?"

"Not so much. The boys snared rabbits, fished, and brought home deer and prairie chicken. With fall, folks were bagging plenty of ducks and geese. You should see the skies, almost dark at times with birds flying south. Zeb hasn't been hunting much. He's too busy with his horses and the rest of the farm."

"So why din't you go?"

"I was helping at the schoolhouse. A one-room soddy with too many children for one teacher. Besides, Katy wasn't well." She shook her head. "I was beginning to wonder if carrying that little one might not be too much for her, but she finally rallied and looked the picture of health when I left."

"So Zeb will have a son to carry on the MacCallister name."

"It could be a girl, you know." She found herself adding the *you know* like they did up north. So many things reminded her of the northland. "He and Katy adopted the two girls he found in that soddy near the banks of the Missouri River. Manda and Deborah. You'd like Manda, feisty as all get out, and Deborah, so sweet she'd like to break your heart."

"You'll be goin' back then?"

"You could come too."

He stared out the window. "Don't know as I can leave this old homeplace. My bones don't like bein' cold, and from what I hear, they got a whole passel o' cold up there."

"True, and I didn't feel the worst of it. But that north wind, it like to blow right through you. I heard tell of blizzards that lock folks in their houses for days on end. They string ropes to get to the barn and back without disappearin' in the snow. You can't see your hand in front of your face."

"Ah, yer funnin' me."

She raised her hand. "God's truth. I heard tell more than once."

"Good thing you come on home then to God's country." He headed on out the door. "I better get on with the wood cuttin'. Plowin's all done fer this year." He stopped and looked over his shoulder. "Ya might want to get on with the apples. She ain't had the stamina to do much preservin'."

That night after she'd settled her mother in a bed with clean sheets and pillows fresh from a hanging on the line, Mary Martha took out paper and pen and settled at the kitchen table. The kerosene lamp shed a golden circle on the oilcloth-covered table, and Uncle Jed in his chair whittlin' away made Dakota seem in another world, another lifetime.

She stirred the ink and dipped her pen.

Dear Zeb, Katy, Manda, and Deborah,

I made it home all right, the trains running fairly close to on time. How we forget the distances between this home and that until we make the trip again. I thank God for trains and also for letting me get off in one piece. Thought for a while I might be shaken to pieces.

She knew Deborah would get a chuckle out of that. How she longed already to hear the girls laughter and watch Manda working with the horses. Had the filly already been taken? So many questions to ask.

Ma is not admitting to any pain, but I can tell. She is so weak, but I think she hasn't been eating good, and I plan to spoon-feed her myself if I have to.

That's what she'd done in the afternoon and at suppertime.

Her mother had slept through dinner, and Mary Martha didn't have the heart to waken her. Jed said she needed sleep. He had often heard her up in the middle of the night and came out more than once to find her sitting in the rocker on the porch, just wantin' to see the sunrise, she'd said, but he figured it was the pain.

Mary Martha didn't include all of that. No need to make Zeb feel worse than he already did. She continued writing.

> The sun is still warm here, and while fall has stolen most of the leaves off the trees, we will go picking hickory nuts and pecans tomorrow before the squirrels get them all. I forgot to tell you that my Christmas presents for everyone are in a box under my bed. Zeb, you will have to ask Penny to tell you when your present arrives.

She thought about the boots she'd had Penny special order for him. She'd drawn around the pair he had patched and patched over the patches to make sure the size was right.

> Manda, your present will be coming in the mail, since I had to finish it on the way here.

She looked at the words. She hadn't been able to write home. *Father, if home isn't here and I'm not there, where is home? I mean my earthly home. I know you have a mansion there for me. And for Ma.* The thought brought the sting of tears to her eyes. *Please, God, don't take her yet. She's not that old, you know. Though I'm sure if I asked her, she'd say heaven is better than here. Am I being selfish?* She added some more news to finish off the page.

> Please tell everyone that I miss them, and while I know it is only November, just in case I can't write soon again, I wish you all the most wonderful of Christmases. Please light an extra candle for me and know that you are in my prayers all the day through.

> Your loving sister and aunt,
> Mary Martha MacCallister

She signed her name with a flourish and blew on the ink

to dry it. She had managed to keep the tear that fell from blotting the paper. Would they think to pass her greeting on to Pastor Solberg? Would it be proper to write to him before he wrote to her? If he wrote to her?

21

Blessing, Dakota Territory

S o, we can order my sewing machine now?" Ingeborg asked.
"I guess so." Penny looked toward the banking room,
wishing she had told Hjelmer not to let Ingeborg take any of
her money out. Now what could she do? "We need to go back
there. That's where I keep the contracts for the sewing machines." She pointed toward the area of the store now referred
to as the sewing room.

When they sat down to write, she leaped to her feet. "Sorry,
I forgot the ink." *What do I do? I can't tell her Haakan has ordered one for her, so I can't order another. And yet, there she sits
with the money in hand. Lord above, if ever I needed your wisdom,
I need it now.*

The bell tinkled, announcing another customer. "I'll be
back in a minute, Ingeborg. Why don't you go ahead and fiddle
with the machine there. See what it's like, you know."

Ingeborg sat down on the stool in front of the machine,
and within minutes, Penny heard it whirring away, the ka-
thunk of the treadle beating time.

"Now then, what can I do for you?" All the time she was
measuring gingham and weighing sugar, her mind kept leaping back to Ingeborg.

By the time she returned, Ingeborg had hemmed four
squares of muslin that were to be boardinghouse napkins.

"You know, you ought to keep diaper-sized flannel here to
practice on, that way you could be making diapers for Katy's
baby."

"What a good idea. Now, where were we?"

"The contract." Ingeborg jingled the leather drawstring purse that Metiz had made for her. She gave Penny a questioning look. "Is there something I am missing here? It seems like you do not want to sell me a Singer sewing machine." She stroked the smooth metal shape. "I'd take this one right here if I could have it."

"Oh no. I mean . . . ah . . . I promised Mr. Drummond I would always have one out here for people to try out. Here, you can fill this in." *She's going to catch on, and it's all your fault.* The voice in her head was surely right this time. If she didn't act excited because she was selling her good friend a sewing machine, Ingeborg would surely catch on. *Oh, Lord, what am I to do with that? You say you know all that goes on with us. Well, this is no joke. I cannot tell a lie—that is a sin. And yet I do not want to spoil the surprise either. Please, I need a big helping of wisdom here.*

Ingeborg signed her name and laid down the pen. "There now, how much do I owe you?"

"For the first payment?"

"No, for the whole thing." Ingeborg slowed her speech as though she was talking with a slow-minded child.

"Oh, that's right." Penny looked at the contract and named the figure.

Ingeborg counted out the amount slowly. "There now. You will let me know when the machine arrives?"

"But of course."

"Bridget is as impatient to get the machine home as I am. Between her and Kaaren and me, it will be running round the clock." Ingeborg drew her purse closed and got to her feet. "Good-bye and thank you."

Penny stared after her departing relative. "Uff da. Such messes I get into."

❧ ☙

December blew in along with the first snowfall that more than dusted the ground. This one drifted and kept on coming until over a foot of fluffy white covered the ground. As soon as Pastor Solberg said "Class dismissed," the children grabbed their coats and ran laughing out the door. Shouts told of the snowball fight that ensued, with shrieks from those victims who took the drubbing.

"I wish Mary Martha could see this." Pastor Solberg stood at the window and watched. When had he ceased calling her Miss MacCallister? He shook his head. Did it matter? The schoolroom had seemed dimmer than usual ever since she left.

The setting sun reflected red and gold, dazzling in its glory both on the ground and in the heavens. Did they have snow like this where she lived? Silly question. He knew they didn't. *Why didn't I say more? Like, please, do you consider me more than a friend? Or, I'm coming to care for our friendship more than* . . . He sighed and shook his head again. Nothing seemed right. But at least he'd said he'd write to her. She would write back, wouldn't she?

He rubbed the end of his chin with one finger, then nodded and smiled in spite of his gloom. That was it. She couldn't reject a letter from the students. Tomorrow he'd pass a paper around and let everyone write their own message. Then he could sign it at the bottom.

He banked the fire and, after checking to see that all was clean and put away, took his coat and muffler down from his peg and left the school. Just as he turned to make sure the latch caught, he felt the thunk of a snowball in the middle of his back. But when he spun back around, there was no one in sight.

"You better hide good, cause if I catch you, there'll be lots of writing on the blackboard." He waited, recognizing the stifled snort that came from behind the woodshed. Chuckling, he made his way home. He realized that he should shovel a path from the soddy he lived in to the soddy he worked in. Perhaps one of the Baard boys would like an excuse to be outside tomorrow. Or perhaps Baptiste?

The next morning, right after the morning song and the children were settled, he looked over his classroom with a smile. "I have a surprise for you today. If you can get all your work done this morning, then we will have the afternoon to do it."

"Is it about the Christmas program?"

"Anji, you forgot to raise your hand."

"Sorry."

"No, my surprise has nothing to do with the Christmas program, so let's get to work." He made the assignments and then motioned the first graders forward to read to him. Every once in a while, he glanced up to check on the bigger children. Swen wore a terribly innocent look. That was always dangerous. He continued looking around the room. Manda wore more of a scowl than normal. Most likely Swen had been teasing her again. How that boy could do it so well without a sound mystified him. Perhaps it was time for another woodpile chat.

Thorliff drilled the Erickson sisters nearly as well as Miss MacCallister had.

Why did everything have to come back to her? That was a question he could never answer.

"Did we do all right?" Anna asked much later, after having raised her hand. Dinner pails were stored back on the shelves and woolen coats and scarves shaken free of snow, so the room smelled of wet wool, not the most delightful odor.

"Yes, you did all right. Some of you need to see me privately, don't you think?" He looked directly at the back row of big boys who suddenly became smaller. "Now, here is the paper. Let's write a letter to Miss MacCallister." He held up the largest sheet he had. "How about if we draw a Christmas tree on it?"

The children all nodded their heads excitedly.

"And each of you write Miss MacCallister a message. You older children can help the younger. Make sure you sign your name so she knows you all took part."

"What about you?" Andrew Bjorklund asked.

Pastor Solberg blinked in surprise. "Why, ah . . . ."

"He's a growed up. He don't be a kid." Ellie nudged Andrew with her elbow.

"But he likes Miss MacCallister, I know." Andrew turned on her, his voice carrying to the corners of the room.

"Thank you for your concern, Andrew. I will sign the picture after everyone else is finished." He could feel his ears burning, and Mary Martha wasn't even there. "Now, who shall we have draw the tree?"

"Baptiste. He's the best drawer in the whole school." Anji Baard spoke as she raised her hand.

Several others murmured agreement.

"All right. Baptiste, the paper is yours."

Within minutes Baptiste had drawn a pine tree that filled much of the paper. The children clapped when he stood back and indicated he was finished.

"Did you sign it?" Pastor Solberg asked, every bit as pleased as the children.

Never one to waste words, Baptiste signed his name in cursive, not printing as was his wont.

"Is there anything you'd like to write to Miss Mac-Callister?"

Baptiste shook his head, handed back the charcoal, and headed for his seat.

"Those of you who aren't at the paper may read anything you would like. The bookshelves are open, or you may work on the Christmas presents for your folks." After a brief flurry, the room settled down again, and Pastor Solberg spent the time answering questions, encouraging the slow and cheering on the shy.

"We're done." One of the girls handed the rolled paper to their teacher.

"Good. I will fold this and make an envelope big enough, then put it in the mail sack tomorrow morning before I come to school." He glanced at the clock. "You are all dismissed, and thank you for such a pleasant afternoon."

"You won't forget to sign it too?" Andrew stopped at the teacher's desk.

"No, I won't." He patted the boy's head and walked with him out the door. As if he would forget. He not only planned to sign the tree but to include a letter, a very personal letter.

It took him three tries before he got the letter right. Or as right as it was going to be. He breathed a sigh of relief and read it once more. It sounded friendly, newsy, and not too pleading when he asked her to write back. He signed it, "Sincerely, Pastor John Solberg."

While he wasn't much pleased with the last, he didn't want to copy the entire thing over again, so he left it as it was.

"So, what have you heard about my machine?" Ingeborg hoisted a basket up on the counter.

"N-nothing, but it's only been a week. I'm not surprised." Penny began to dig in the basket. "Oh good, more of that soft cheese. That has become really popular."

"If you want, I can make more of that. It goes quick. See the smoked goose? You think train riders might like to take one of those home for Christmas dinner?"

"I'll put it out and see. Some days they clean me right out, even after eating a full dinner. I think every one of them would buy a whole pie if I had it. You ever think of opening a bakery?"

"No, but Bridget considered it. They're cutting timbers for the boardinghouse. Got lots of the beams and two-by-fours and sixes. Haakan's wishing now they had dug the cellar before the ground froze." Ingeborg handed Penny one of Metiz' deer antler knives. "She says she'll have a couple more pretty soon."

"Good. I'm about out. Tell her to make more rabbit skin vests if she can. One man bought two, one for each of his boys."

Ingeborg leaned a hip against the counter. "You know the picture of that man you got in the window? Anyone ever inquire about him?"

Penny shook her head, adding up the column of figures in front of her. "You're going to have to buy more here, I owe you too much money."

"You want I should bring in less?"

"No, and I was teasing. I'll gladly pay you cash for the things you bring in."

"But they can't go on a sewing machine, huh?" The twinkle in her eyes said she was teasing.

"Once they tasted your cheese, those folks at Singer Sewing Machine Company would probably buy it by the carload. If they only knew."

"You seen Katy lately?"

"No, not since church on Sunday. Why?"

"I just miss seeing her, that's all. Think I'll go on over there. Any mail for them or anything?"

"Not right now, but the train will be in soon if you want to wait."

Ingeborg shook her head. "I'll be on my way. You let me know about the machine, now, you hear?"

"I hear." Penny breathed a sigh of relief when Ingeborg went out the door.

"Getting close, ain't it. You think she suspects?" Goodie came through the curtain that led to the kitchen.

"I sure do hope not. This is getting more and more difficult."

"You could tell her the machines are on back order, that the company is behind."

"But that would be a lie, and I can't do that." Penny looked to the sewing department of her store. "Not with their two machines sitting right there waiting for Christmas."

Goodie chuckled. "Wait until she finds out. She's going to bust up laughing."

"I sure hope so."

It wasn't long before the train whistle sounded far down the track.

Penny hurried to put a couple more things in the mailbag. "Anything for the mail, Mr. Valders?"

"No. I already took care of that," he answered from the banking room.

Penny took the leather bag stamped with United States Mail outside to hand to the man in the mail car. Two men who'd bought goods in her store waited at the other end of the platform. Olaf had the big door closed on the sack house, so he must not be shipping any grain today. After the fire in the sack house, he'd asked for a car to be left on the siding for him to fill, so maybe he'd gotten it all shipped.

The snow-blanketed prairie sparkled like freshly strewn jewels in the westerly sun. She shivered, even with her wool shawl around her shoulders. She could have hung the bag on the peg and come back for the full one, but being outside felt good for a change.

The heat of the steam engine had melted the snow along the tracks. Coal clinkers showed like black rocks against the white and the dirt both. She should ask Hans if he wanted to earn some money picking those up for her. The potbellied stove in the store devoured coal and wood like some ravenous beast. With the men having to haul wood so much farther now, perhaps she should switch entirely to coal.

"Good day to you, Miz Bjorklund," the green-shaded man from the mail car called. He jumped to the wooden platform and turned back to retrieve the mailbag. "You look all ready for Christmas with that red sweater." Handing her the new bag, he took hers. "You got any more of that cheese I got last time? My wife couldn't get over how good it was. She said she wished you didn't live so far away. She'd rather shop in your store than anywhere."

"Tell her I carry Singer sewing machines now too, and we will have smoked meats. I got a smoked goose right now for Christmas."

"I'll tell her, but you put my name on two of those geese. Let me know when they are ready."

Penny glanced down the line to see a black man climbing down from the passenger car. When he reached back up the steps for a valise, she realized he might be staying. "I'll do that," she said to the mailman. "Excuse me, please." She left the mailbag lay and walked on over to the newcomer. "Good afternoon, sir, is your name by any chance Sam?"

"Yes, ma-am, that it be." His soft accent sounded more like Zeb MacCallister's than anyone else around Blessing.

She put out her hand. "I'm glad to meet you. Hjelmer is my husband, and he will be delighted you are here. Come on, before you freeze to death."

He took her hand hesitantly, shook it once, and dropped it, reaching for his two bags. "Ah'm pleased to meet ya. Hjelmer tol' me plenty about ya."

When she bent to take the mail sack, he shifted his two bags to one hand and took the mailbag before she could get it. "Ah'll get that."

"Thank you. I can't wait to tell Hjelmer you are here. He's been getting further and further behind in the blacksmith, with all the traveling he's had to do with banking and now the Farmer's Alliance business." After the political debate Hjelmer had been asked to help talk other Norwegian farmers into joining the Alliance. While Haakan had been asked to travel also, he'd declined, due to the sawmill he had running and the ice cutting that would begin more toward spring.

When they entered the store, she pointed to the stove.

"Why don't you go stand there and get warm again while I sort this mail."

"Ah'd near forgotten how cold winter can be in Dakota." He shivered and held his hands to the heat.

"I can't tell you how glad I am you're here." Penny dropped her shawl on the stool behind her and pulled open the mouth of the mailbag, spilling the contents onto the counter. Even with the snow, she could hear people laughing and chatting as they made their way to the store. She had to hurry.

Taking a handful of envelopes, she began stuffing them in the slots with her neighbors' names on them. Without glancing at the return addresses, she put two in their slot and kept on distributing the mail. The doorbell tinkled and then again as the people entered.

Conversation drifted off and the room fell silent. Penny turned to see what was happening. All eyes were on the black man standing at the stove.

22

Springfield, Missouri

A nd *so we wish you a blessed Christmas.*

Mary Martha fought the burning on the back of her eyes. She sniffed once and blew her nose, then tucked the square of cotton back in her apron pocket. Tracing the outline of the tree with a trembling finger, she read the messages again.

They couldn't miss her any more than she missed them.

"Mary Martha." Her mother sounded stronger, much to the daughter's relief.

"Coming." She tucked the letter into her pocket and took the picture with her into the bedroom. "See, Ma, a Christmas letter from the schoolchildren in Blessing." As she held it up, she explained who each of the children were.

"Good of them." Ma studied the signature at the bottom. "This the man you left behind?"

"Pastor Solberg is a friend. That's all."

"But you wish more?"

"Sometimes yes and sometimes no. I mean, I like him." She stopped and rolled her lower lip between her teeth. "But sometimes he aggravates me no end." She knelt by the bed. "Ma, can you picture me as a minister's wife?"

Mrs. MacCallister stroked her daughter's hair with a gentle hand. "You will make a fine wife for any man lucky enough to win your heart. If this is the husband God has chosen for you, then it will work out."

Mary Martha didn't think she'd heard that many words from her mother at one time in years. "I know—I think." She laid her cheek against her mother's hand. "What's important right now is that we get you strong enough so that you can enjoy Christmas. Jed brought in a tom turkey, and I dug the last of the sweet taters. I haven't had sweet tater pie for far too long. How about you?"

"You know what sounds good to me? A custard pie, that's what."

"Then that's what I shall make first. I've got cornbread for supper and then for stuffing. You want to help me chop the onions? We could set you up at the table."

"Maybe after I rest a bit more. My eyes are mighty heavy."

"You do that. Jed is milking the cows, and I'll go pick the eggs."

Mary Martha threw her shawl around her shoulders, trailing her fingers over the long needles of the pine tree they'd set up in the corner. It wasn't as big as usual, but still the house smelled of cinnamon and pine, just the way it should for Christmas.

If only they could take Ma to church for the Christmas Eve service the next night.

She broached the subject to Jed as he finished stripping out the last cow down at the barn.

"We can put hay and lots of quilts in the back of the wagon, even the feather bed. I know some of the men would help carry her in, like in the rocker."

"Uncle Jed, you have the best ideas."

✕🐝 🐝✕

Late the next afternoon Jed padded the wagon just as he'd said. Mary Martha brushed her mother's thinning hair and fashioned it in the usual bun. Only this time she tied a red ribbon around it and anchored the whole with two carved wooden pins her mother kept for good.

"Pshaw. I don't need all that." But the color in her cheeks said otherwise, and when Mary Martha pinned the oval cameo at her mother's neckline, Ma turned her head to look in the wavy mirror. "Thank you," she said.

"You're welcome."

"And I don't intend to lie down in that wagon. I kin set in my chair just fine."

"All right, but we'll leave the blankets and things in case you feel like lying down on the way home."

Her mother fingered the cameo. "Seems forever since I worshiped in the Lord's house. Just not been up to it." She sighed. "I'm glad you come on home."

The queen of England couldn't have received more attention than Pearl MacCallister did when they drove up to the front door of the white steepled church. The men vied over who would lift her down in her chair and carry her into the sanctuary. Women greeted her, some with tears in their eyes, and all had hugs for Mary Martha and questions about her adventures in Dakota Territory. They asked about Zeb and his family, about life in Blessing, and said how thankful they were that she came home. Her ma needed her.

"Pshaw. They fuss so," Mrs. MacCallister muttered, but Mary Martha could tell she was moved by the greetings. The church glowed with candlelight, and the air was heavy with the fragrance of pine and cedar, which emanated from the branches that looped above the windows, around the pulpit and the altar, and festooned the ends of the pews.

Mary Martha sat with tears shimmering on her lashes at the beauty of the organ music. Old though it was, the minister's wife brought out the best in it, and "Silent Night" with the organ and everyone singing in harmony had never sounded so lovely.

The scriptures were in English, as was the sermon. Mary Martha found herself whispering the Christmas story as the minister read from the Bible. " 'And it came to pass in those days . . .' " what wonderful words, " '. . . that all the world should be enrolled . . .' " *Father, please let all of us be enrolled in your heavenly kingdom. . . .* " 'And Joseph also went up from Galilee with Mary his espoused wife . . .' " *How is my family out there? Is Katy well? Please keep her well. She wants to bear this child . . .* " '. . . because he was of the house and lineage of David . . .' " *That would be a good name for their son, a strong name. I wonder what Jo—Pastor Solberg's middle name is?* " '. . . the days were accomplished that she should be delivered.' "

Mary Martha took her mother's hand in hers and smiled at her sitting so proudly in the old rocking chair. "I love you,

Ma," she whispered. *Thank you, Father, for making this possible. It means so much to her . . . and to me.*

They sang "Hark the Herald Angels Sing" and "O Little Town of Bethlehem" before the pastor took his place in the pulpit.

"Brothers and sisters," he began, "we are gathered this night to celebrate the great love that our God, our heavenly Father, has for us, His children. Let us pray." He waited for the shuffling to cease, and then his deep voice rolled out over the full church with grace and peace. "Come to us this night as you did to those shepherds so long ago. Come to us in the stillness as you did to Mary and Joseph. Come to us in grace this night. Amen."

He looked over the gathered people, smiling at each one and nodding. "It is good that we are gathered here together, for He has said that wherever two or three are gathered together, He is right here, right in the midst of us. I see Him in your faces, I hear Him in your voices, I feel Him in the clasp of your hands, for we are His body here on earth, in this place and in this time. We do not know what tomorrow holds, but we know who holds today and tomorrow and all the days after that.

"He loves us so much that He sent His Son in the form of a tiny baby, not a towering king but a child. Jesus left the wonders of heaven and dwelled in a manger, in a small town in a small country. For you." He waited. If God had scooped them up in His hands, Mary Martha would not have been surprised. He felt that near.

"For me. For us. He walked this earth for thirty-three years, and then He died. On a cross. For us. He died that we might live, live forgiven of our sins. And all He asks is that you let Him come live in your heart, for He said, 'I will abide with you as you abide with me.'" He paused, then bowed his head, closing with a prayer. "Lord, come into our hearts to dwell there, to abide, that we might see thee face-to-face. Amen."

Mary Martha wiped away her tears and handed her hankie to her mother. *Abide with me, dear Lord. Please abide with me.*

The organ soared again and took her heart right with it.

Mary Martha was glad she'd come home.

That same night in Blessing, the bustle stilled, the children were all in their places, the last light extinguished. Joseph Baard lifted his fiddle to his shoulder, and the sweet notes sang forth for the gathering. "Jesu, Joy of Man's Desiring." As the final notes drifted away, light processed forward from the back as the children, starting with the smallest, carried lighted candles and filed up the center aisle, then took their places off to the sides.

"We come this night."

"With candle bright."

The sides took turns in unison.

"To praise the Father."

"And thank the Son."

Someone hummed a pitch, and they burst into song, all in the harmony Mary Martha had taught them, and in English.

Silence fell. Two voices could be heard from the back. "But, Joseph, when are we going to get there?"

"Soon, my dear, soon we will be in Bethlehem."

With Joseph leading the donkey carrying Mary, they made their way down the aisle.

Anna, Andrew, Deborah, and Ellie stepped forward in the front.

"Unto us a child is born," said Anna without a lisp. "Unto us a son is given."

"And His name shall be called Wonderful."

"Counselor."

"Almighty God."

"The Everlasting Father." Anna, Andrew, Deborah, and Ellie took turns on the names, then together all four said, "The Prince of Peace."

A sniff could be heard from the audience.

The child was born and brought out to lie in the manger. Anji, as Mary, treated the Amundsons' month-old baby with loving care, and like the angel he looked, little Carl slept through the entire program. Hamre played "Away in the Manger" with such heart on his harmonica that even Mrs. Valders sniffed and dabbed at her eyes.

The angels sang to the shepherds, and the shepherds found

the baby just as they were supposed to. Joseph, played by Swen, greeted the visitors and showed off his son as if he was his own, and Mary smiled sweetly.

The songs were sung, and the parents wept, and John Solberg had a lump in his throat, so proud was he of his pupils and so wishing Mary Martha were here to listen to them sing the song she helped them create.

> *Jesus, Savior,*
> *Love divine,*
> *Live within*
> *this heart of mine.*
>
> *Teach me how*
> *to love my brothers,*
> *Sisters, fathers,*
> *and all others.*
>
> *Give us joy*
> *and bring us peace.*
> *May our worship*
> *never cease.*
>
> *Jesus, Lord,*
> *Emmanuel,*
> *Almighty God*
> *with us to dwell.*

The plaintive tune stayed with him as he bid everyone God jul.

"Wonderful program, Pastor," Haakan said, shaking his hand.

"Ja, it should be. Your son wrote it. He chose most of the music too, and who should play what part. As I've said before, he amazes me."

"Oh. Well, in that case . . ."

"In that case, it was still a wonderful program." John clapped him on the shoulder, laughing at the consternation on his friend's face.

"You'll come for dinner tomorrow?" Ingeborg laid a hand on Pastor Solberg's arm. "All the family will be at our house, and we want you there too."

"How can I refuse? Mange takk."

When the last sleigh jingled off, he made sure the fire was banked and then shut the church door. Taking his lantern, he made his way back to his soddy, stopping at his door to rejoice in the brilliant flare of the northern lights. The stars shone so brightly, he blew out the lantern and stood in awe. If only he had someone to rejoice in this night with him.

"Father, care for her please and keep her safe." He could see his breath hang on the air in front of him. The night of the Savior's birth. What a wondrous night.

Entering his soddy, he took off his coat and hat, hanging them on the pegs inside the door. He lit his lamp from the coals in the stove and, taking out paper and pen, began to write.

"Dear Miss MacCallister. The program is over, and you would have been so proud of these children." He described the service and the program and how Mrs. Helmsrude had cried in her joy at Anna speaking so clearly. He told how the song she and the children composed sounded and found himself humming it again. After all, he'd heard it more times than he could count. He told how the angel's halo had slipped off and how Astrid called out "Andew," making everyone laugh.

He didn't tell her how much he missed her, but he signed the letter "Your friend, John Solberg." When he blew out the light and climbed into a bed warmed by the heated stone he'd placed there, it was already Christmas morning.

⚬ ⚬

Springfield, Missouri

When Mary Martha started her letter that night after tucking her mother into her bed, she planned to write only a short note. But by the time she told him of the awe and wonder she'd felt at church, how thankful her mother was to go, how at home she felt, the page had filled.

"And to think," she wrote, "that our Father has a heavenly home all prepared for us, so much brighter and more beautiful even than the stars I saw tonight. I felt I could reach up and touch them." *And wondered if you saw the same.* She told him that her sister and family were coming for dinner on Christmas day and of all the things she had prepared. She thanked him for the wonderful letter from him and the children and asked him to thank each one of them personally from her.

She didn't say "I miss you," but she signed her letter "As ever, Mary Martha MacCallister."

Extinguishing her lamp, she climbed into bed, the warm glow of the Christmas Eve service still lingering in her heart. *Thank you for letting Ma go to church tonight. And thank you for being there too.* She snuggled down under her quilt. *And please watch over Pastor Solberg, since he has no one but you.*

She didn't say "I wish I were there," but she knew God could see in the depths of her heart even better than she. *So much could happen*, she thought as she shivered.

23

Blessing, Dakota Territory

M erry Christmas. God jul!"

"Andrew, not so loud." Ingeborg made a shushing motion as she spoke.

"But it's Christmas!"

"I know, but Astrid is still sleeping."

"No, she isn't."

Ingeborg heard hesitant footsteps padding down the stairs. He was right as usual. Astrid was awake.

"Where's Pa and Thorliff?"

"Out milking. Christmas or no, the chores need to be done." She sliced the julekake, the fruit-studded Norwegian Christmas bread, and arranged it on a plate. "You get your coat and boots on and go feed the chickens. Pa said there's cobs of dried corn in a bucket by the oats that you can rub together. Give the hens a treat of corn kernels."

She looked down to see Astrid trailing her blanket from a thumb that seemed permanently attached to her mouth. The other hand tugged on her mother's apron.

"What is it, baby?"

Astrid lifted her arms, the corner of the blanket dusting across the floor.

"I know you want up, but can you not see I am busy?"

"Ma-a-a." The plaintive cry tugged at Ingeborg's heart. Astrid was getting so big she didn't ask to be picked up much anymore.

"Brr, it is cold out there." Bridget came through the door from her room out in the soddy, stamping the snow off her boots on the enclosed porch. "But thank the good Lord we have no blizzard. People will be able to visit around without fear." She took off her boots and slipped her feet into the knit woolen slippers she kept by the door. "Here, why don't I finish with the breakfast, and you go get her dressed." She chucked Astrid under the chin. "Our little girl needs some extra hugs this Christmas morning."

"Stayed up too late, that's why." Ingeborg handed over her wooden spoon. "The mush is about ready, the ham is fried, so all that's left is the eggs. Come, baby, let's go back upstairs and get you dressed."

"Pesents today?" Astrid laid her head against her mother's collar. "Tholiff, Andew say so."

"Later, after church." Ingeborg turned back to Bridget. "Is Ilse getting dressed? Good. The geese are ready to go in the oven, and I thought she could start peeling the potatoes. It takes a lot to make mashed for as many as we have coming."

Even though everyone would bring food, Ingeborg knew every person there would eat way beyond his fill. She thought of all the krumkakar, fattigmann, and sandbakkels they'd made. Bridget had rolled enough lefse to feed an army, but Ingeborg knew it would all disappear.

Without the heavy child on her hip, she might have skipped up the stairs. All the family would be there, even Solveig and George were coming with their little one and Sarah Neswig, another immigrant who came with Bridget. It had been nearly a year since they'd seen her, because Ingeborg and Kaaren no longer supplied chickens, cheese, meats, and garden produce to the Bonanza farm or the St. Andrew Mercantile. With the coming of the railroad, they could hardly keep Penny's store supplied.

She washed Astrid's hands and face and helped her into her new dress. Thanks to Bridget and her nimble needle, it had been finished, but no thanks to the new sewing machine that never arrived. Penny had apologized for the Singer Company, saying they had so many orders they could not keep up, and it would be several weeks before hers would be delivered.

She'd been so looking forward to using it to make Christmas presents.

"Now let's braid your hair, and you will look cute as a bug."

"What bug?" Astrid looked around the room. Before the frost got them, she'd hunted up every bug she could find and brought them to her mother. Astrid liked bugs. Even spiders.

"An Astrid bug, that's what."

"Astid bug." She giggled and clapped her hands.

"How about cute as a button?"

Astrid pointed to the buttons on the front of her dress. Bright red, they made her so happy she petted them like she would a kitten. "Astid like buttons."

"Astrid, you sweetheart, you like most anything." Ingeborg picked her up again and nuzzled her neck, making the little girl giggle.

"Moe."

Ingeborg complied and the giggles turned to chortles of glee. Astrid put a palm on either side of her mother's face. "Astid love Mo."

"And Mor loves Astrid." She kissed the child's cheek and laid hers against the same spot. "Come. I hear Far coming in. Breakfast is ready."

"Fa, Pa, Pa, Fa. Mo, Ma, Ma, Mo." She leaned back and looked her mother in the eye. "You gots two names, Mo and Ma, huh?"

"That's right." Ingeborg leaned back against the child's shift in weight. "Here, you better walk down the stairs yourself, or we'll both be rolling down together." She turned and set her child on the top step. "Now be careful."

"Astid caeful."

You're also the most accomplished mimic I've heard in a long time. With Astrid behind, they stepped on down to the warmth of the kitchen.

The children sang their song again at church that morning, and after that it seemed as though most of Blessing made their way to the Haakan Bjorklund home.

Thorliff, Hamre, and Baptiste were kept busy for a time leading visiting teams into the barns and tossing them a forkful of hay. All the sleighs lined up reminded Ingeborg of the old country.

"Make sure you don't slight these two," Hjelmer teased, stopping his team beside Thorliff.

"Oh, I won't." Thorliff tried to keep his eyes off the black man who rode with his aunt and uncle.

"Have you met my friend Sam yet?" Hjelmer asked.

"No, sir." Thorliff unhooked the traces and latched them onto the rump pad.

"Sam worked with me on the railroad, and he and I and a couple of others shared a house in St. Paul for a time. He's come to help me out at the blacksmith. Wait until you see the carving he does. Helped keep us from starving by selling some of it."

"Did you bring some?" Thorliff asked.

"Yes, suh, but it's fo yo mama fo invitin' me."

Thorliff looked up at his uncle Hjelmer, then at Sam. "Baptiste carves good too. He'll like talking with you, Mister—I don't know your last name."

"You kin call me Sam."

"All right, Mister Sam. Merry Christmas. Oh, you have any children?"

Sam nodded. "A boy, Lemuel, 'bout yo age."

"Good. He can come to our school and—"

"He's not here. He's back home."

"Oh." Thorliff shrugged. "When he comes then. You all go right on in." He led the horses off to the warmth of the barn.

Penny stuck her hand in the crook of Hjelmer's elbow. "That is one fine boy, our nephew."

"You said that right." Sam lifted their baskets from the back of the sleigh and handed one to Ephraim. "He evah seen a black man befo?"

"Maybe on the ship or in New York, but he was only five. He just has a heart for strangers and wants everyone to be as happy as he is." Hjelmer patted Penny's gloved hand. "Though, far as Thorliff's concerned, there isn't a stranger anywhere."

Conversation only slowed a mite when the four walked in, and within minutes Haakan was taking Sam around and introducing him to all the relatives.

"How come his skin is black?" Ellie whispered to Andrew, loud enough to be heard back at the church.

"I don't know." Andrew motioned her to shush.

Sam hunkered down where the children sat on the bottom stairs so they wouldn't miss anything. "God made you with yellah hair, right." Ellie nodded, her eyes round as teacups.

"He made me with dark skin. That's all. He just made us all a little different."

"Oh." She thought a minute. "In the summer do you get sunburned?"

"Yep, ah do. But ah don't turn red like you do."

"Oh." She reached out a tentative finger, and he held out the back of his hand for her to touch him.

"I got a little girl too, but she's growin' so fast, I bettah git her out here befoe she's too big for school."

"Does she have black skin too?"

"Uh-huh."

"Good. I like you." Ellie looked at Andrew. "Want to play Hide the Thimble?" The two turned and raced up the stairs, laughing and calling for the others.

"Thank you, Mister Sam," Ingeborg said with a smile. "Please forgive their curiosity."

"It's just Sam, ma-am. Ah don't go by no mister."

Ingeborg smiled. "You might have to here, especially with the children. Mister is only polite, and so they will call you Mister Sam, unless you want to use your last name."

"I like the sound of that, thank you." He dug in his pocket and handed her a cloth-wrapped piece. "This is fo inviting a stranger to yo home for Christmas."

"The Bible says to entertain strangers, for thereby we might know angels unawares."

Sam laughed, the skin crinkling around his eyes. "Well, ah sure enough not an angel, but I am beholden to you."

Ingeborg unwrapped the gift and held up a carved Canada goose, neck arched for grazing. "Oh, how beautiful. I love to watch the geese. You couldn't have chosen anything more perfect."

"She likes to shoot them and bring them home on a travois too." Haakan stopped at her side. "That's what we're having for dinner." He touched the feather detail in the wings. "You are a master."

"No, suh, just a man with a lot a time on his hands."

"You most likely won't find much time for carving here. You can go to work with me on the sawmill any time Hjelmer doesn't need you in the smithy." The men moved off to talk among themselves, out of the way of the bustle in the kitchen.

"I think that's everything then," Ingeborg said, looking over the array of food.

"Looks to me like there's enough to feed the Norwegian army," Bridget said with a shake of her head. "Anyone goes home hungry, it's their own fault, for sure."

After Pastor Solberg said the blessing, the guests lined up with plates and helped themselves. Ingeborg had wanted everyone to sit down at a table, but since that would have had to be done in shifts, she bowed to the inevitable. Just having everyone in one place was treat enough. What a large family they had become.

After everyone was finished eating and the dishes done, they all packed into the parlor, where the tree Haakan and Lars had brought back from Minnesota shimmered in the corner. Very carefully, Haakan and Lars lit the candles that were clamped to the larger branches.

"Oh, pitty." Astrid and Sophie clapped their hands. Grace stared up at the tree, entranced. Ever since they'd arrived, Kaaren had been trying to keep Trygve from chewing on the branches.

Kaaren began and everyone joined in singing the Norwegian words with cheer. " 'Oh, Christmas tree, oh Christmas tree, how lovely are thy branches. . . .' " When they finished, she stood and, taking the twins by the hands, led them to stand directly in front of the tree. "We have something we'd like to share with you." She bent down and made a sign in front of Grace's face. The little girl smiled and held up her hands. Sophie did the same. Together, the three made a series of signs.

"How lovely," Penny said. "What does it mean?"

"We said . . ." Kaaren nodded to Sophie, who then signed with her, "Merry Christmas."

When everyone applauded, Kaaren and her two curtsied, and, before sitting down, Kaaren took the sleeping Samuel back from his father.

"Pwesents now?" Astrid asked, giving everyone a chuckle.

"Come on, Thorliff, you can help me." Hjelmer came to stand by the tree and beckoned to Thorliff, who was on his feet in the blink of an eye. Together they picked up presents, read the name tags, and Thorliff delivered them.

Each little girl got a new rag doll and the little boys a

carved train engine. There were books and shirts, hats and mittens. Metiz had made each child a pair of rabbit skin mittens. Trygve kept his on and stopped playing with his train every once in a while to rub the soft fur across his cheek. Manda's eyes shone at the hand-braided bridle Zeb had made for her, and Thorliff gazed at his stack of three books by Charles Dickens as though the minute he could begin reading couldn't come too soon.

Such riches, Ingeborg thought, remembering back to the early years when a peppermint stick was beyond her power to purchase.

Baptiste stood like he'd been struck when they handed him a new rifle.

"We thought since you'd been supplying all of us with game, we ought to make sure your gun was safe," Haakan told him.

"Who . . . who do I thank?" Taller now than Ingeborg, the boy stroked the rifle stock.

"We all pitched in. There's a box of shells under the tree too." Haakan pointed to a square box toward the back. "We had to hide it to make sure Trygve over there didn't chew on them."

That brought a laugh from everyone.

Baptiste looked from face to face. "Thank you. Thank you very much I will bring you more meat soon."

"Here, take this to your bestemor." Hjelmer handed Thorliff an envelope.

"What's this?" she asked, her eyebrows raised in question.

"Open it, so we can find out."

She withdrew a sheet of parchment and handed it back to Thorliff. "You read it."

"I . . . I think it says you now own an acre of land by Tante Penny's store."

"I do?" She snatched it back and studied the letters. "I wish I could read it."

"Here, Mor." Hjelmer stepped over children and around gifts. He read it aloud, and though it was said all legal-like, Thorliff had been right. The bottom was signed by Mr. and Mrs. Haakan Bjorklund.

Bridget cleared her throat once, and then again. "Mange

takk." She sniffed. "My boardinghouse. Land for my board-inghouse."

"We'll get it up as soon as the land dries out enough. I just wish we had started this fall." Haakan sat back down next to Ingeborg, and the two exchanged smiles before another present was given out, this one to Pastor Solberg. He unwrapped the box to find a cream-colored cardigan sweater with a snow-flake design in tones of black and gray.

And maybe if there had been a boardinghouse, that man wouldn't have lost his life, Ingeborg thought as she hugged Astrid, who was clutching her doll to her chest. *So easy to not make mistakes when looking back.* But then she had to remind herself that the man chose to smoke and drink before falling asleep. Thank God Ephraim had been off to the Johnsons, helping them, or he might have died too. She looked over at him, admiring the buckskin shirt Penny had asked Metiz to make for him. It was beautiful soft deerskin, with a fringe of quills and beads. She looked down at the beaded elk skin moc-casins on her feet, also made by Metiz. With the hair on the inside, she knew her feet would stay warm.

Looking up, she saw Metiz watching her, so she smiled and pointed to her feet.

Metiz nodded and smiled back, patting her red wool blanket.

Who says we don't all use sign language?

Pastor Solberg held up his sweater. "Bridget, I think I see your hand . . . er . . . knitting needles in this. How beautiful." He stood and put it on right then, giving everyone a chance to clap.

"Looks right good on you, Pastor," Zeb said from the corner he and Katy were squished into. The box beside her was filled with things for their coming baby: diapers, knitted sweater, hat, booties, soakers, and gowns. Her eyes glowed as she read the tag again, "From all of us," and the names of all the women.

Ingeborg sat wishing she'd gotten her machine, because the coat she'd planned for Haakan still lay within the folds of the heavy wool material she had bought for that purpose. It lay in her trunk, awaiting the arrival of the machine. She would have started on it much earlier had she but known.

"I'm sorry, Haakan," she said softly. "I planned on using my new sewing machine to make you a coat. If I'd known I had to wait so long, I'd have started your coat long ago. The material is folded up in my trunk."

"No matter." He held up his knitted knee-high socks and new gloves. "These are just what I needed. Now my others can go in the mending basket."

Thorliff carried a box large enough that he could barely see above it to his grandmother. "Here, Bestemor, you went from littlest to biggest present."

Bridget untied the bow made of a bit of red calico. "But what more do I need?"

"Just open it, Mor." Hjelmer shook his head and leaned forward with a smile on his handsome face.

"Ah, me." Bridget put her hands to her cheeks. "Look at all this." She lifted out tablecloths, napkins, calico curtains.

"For your boardinghouse, huh?" Thorliff knelt beside the box and peered inside. "There's even some kettles in here."

"Mange takk." Bridget looked around the room. "To whom?"

"All of us." Thorliff pulled out three wooden spoons. "I carved these."

"How did all this get done without me knowing?"

Ingeborg and Penny exchanged glances. "We'll never tell," Ingeborg said. *If I'd had my machine, there would have been even more, like another quilt or two.* "We hope it's enough to help you get started."

"Oh, it is." Bridget smoothed a stitched sampler.

"I thought you could frame that and put it on the wall," Goodie said. "Ellie did most of it."

When there were no more presents, Haakan and Lars stood. "We'll be back in a minute. Don't anyone go away. Thorliff, Hjelmer, come on with us." And out the door they went—snickering.

Kaaren and Ingeborg shook their heads at the antics of their husbands. The level of noise rose again as people thanked each other and admired all the gifts. They heard the banging of the back door and Haakan called, "Okay now, Ingeborg, Kaaren, shut your eyes, you two."

Kaaren and Ingeborg rolled their eyes at each other and did as bid.

What in the world have they done now? Ingeborg sat with her eyes scrunched closed. She felt Astrid slide from her lap and heard Haakan shush his daughter.

Giggles came from around the room, and when one of the little ones started to say something, the sound was cut off, most likely by a mother's hand across the youngster's mouth.

Ingeborg fought the desire to just peek through her eyelids.

"What is going on?" Kaaren asked.

"You'll see."

"All right, you two, I am going to count, and on three you may open your eyes." They both nodded.

"Oonnne."

"Haakan!"

"Twooo."

"You'll pay for this."

"Three."

"Oh, my!" Ingeborg stared at the Singer sewing machine in its cabinet with the black iron treadle. She looked next at Haakan, then at Penny. "B-but you said . . ."

Kaaren leaped to her feet and threw her arms around Lars. "Thank you, mange takk, oh, thank you." Then she blushed a brilliant shade of red, and everyone broke out laughing.

"You know when you were trying to buy your machine, and Penny kept putting you off?"

Ingeborg nodded.

"Well, this one was already in the storehouse, waiting for today." Haakan tapped a finger on the cabinet. "You didn't want two, did you?"

Ingeborg tried to keep a sober face, as if she was scolding them, but a laugh burst forth in spite of her. "You . . . you two." She stroked the wood of the cabinet. "Thank you. Oh, such a surprise."

"Ma like supise." Astrid crawled under the machine and sat on the treadle.

Ingeborg and Kaaren looked at each other and laughed again. "And here we were going to share one."

"You can share that one with me," Bridget said. "I already know how to use it."

"I should have just made you another cheese press at the rate you are making cheese. Maybe after we build the board-inghouse, we should put up a whole separate building just for making cheese." Haakan exchanged looks with Lars.

"Not a bad idea." Lars nodded. "Kaaren could churn the butter there too. Cheese needs two rooms, one cool room to age it in, like the well house now. You know, if we . . ."

"There he goes, he'll have it all planned by tomorrow." Kaaren picked up Trygve and took a rubber ball out of his mouth. "No, son, you don't chew on the toys." His scowl said quite clearly that he heartily disagreed with her.

"Looks like we better be heading home," Zeb said after looking outside. "Be dark before we get there now."

By the time everyone had gathered up their things and said their good-byes, dusk cast purple shadows across the fields of snow. The last of the sunset gilded the clouds and pinked the horizon. Ingeborg and Bridget stood in the doorway, waving and calling good-bye as the teams pulling the sleighs gathered up their loads and jingled off across the prairie.

"Such a day." Ingeborg finally closed the outside door and returned to the warmth of the kitchen. "This had to be the best Christmas ever."

"Tomorrow *we* go visiting, huh, Mor?" Andrew looked up from putting together the wooden puzzle Olaf had made for him.

"Right. Who would you like to go see?"

"Ellie and Anna."

"But you saw Ellie today."

"I know, but I like to see her every day. And Anna wasn't at church. You think she is all right?"

"Why do you ask?"

"Well, she's been coughing a lot, sometimes it makes her not breathe good."

"Yes, Andrew, we'll go see Anna and her family. Let's think of some things to take them, all right? We'll visit the Baards too, since Gus was sick and they couldn't come."

24

She's sleeping right now, poor little thing." Mrs. Helmsrude twisted her hands together.

"When did she get so sick?" Ingeborg asked.

"During the night. Woke up coughing like to tear her throat apart." She beckoned. "Please, won't you come in?"

"Just for a minute then. We brought you some Christmas things."

"Can I see her?" Andrew stood beside his mother.

"If'n you want, but let her sleep. It's almost a miracle to not hear her coughing."

"I will." Andrew tiptoed to the doorway Mrs. Helmsrude pointed. Anna lay in the bed, her face whiter than the sheets, the bones trying to poke holes in her transparent skin. He walked on over and stood beside her. "Please hurry and get better," he whispered. But Anna didn't move.

Ingeborg watched from the doorway as her son knelt at the foot of the bed and prayed for his friend. She watched his lips move and whispered "amen" along with him. He stood again and, after another long look, tiptoed toward the door.

"She's awful sick, Ma," he whispered, when he saw Ingeborg standing in the doorway. "You better ask Metiz to come. 'Tween you and her, Anna needs you."

Ingeborg turned to Mrs. Helmsrude. "Would you mind if Metiz and I came to help you with her?"

"Heavens, no. Would you really do that?"

"Of course. Let me go home and get my things, and we'll be back in a couple of hours."

"Thank you, Andrew, for coming. I'll tell her you were here when she wakes up."

"She knows."

Ingeborg looked at Andrew when they were back in the sleigh. "What makes you think Anna knows you were there?"

Andrew shrugged. "I just know."

"Like you know when Astrid is awake?"

"Ja, I guess."

She clucked the horses into a trot, and the sleigh flew over the frozen ground.

As she had promised, within two hours they were back, carrying in baskets filled with every healing simple they could think of.

The wrenching sound of Anna's coughing met them before they stepped up to the door.

"Come in. Come in." Einer Helmsrude pulled open the door, shrugging on his coat at the same moment. "I'll go care for your horses. You go right on in."

Ingeborg headed for the bedroom where she'd seen Anna earlier. Magda Helmsrude held her daughter in her arms, trying to spoon liquid into her mouth. The child gagged and choked, her stick arms flailing the air, her face bright red from the effort to breathe.

"I heat water." Metiz set her basket down and returned to the kitchen.

Ingeborg tossed her coat over another chair and stopped with a hand on the mother's shoulder. "Ah, Magda, so terrible this is. Have you tried tenting her with steam?"

Mrs. Helmsrude shook her head. "I just tried to give her some chicken broth. She has no strength to fight this."

Anna doubled over, and the terrifying whooping that racked her body make Ingeborg flinch. "Have you tried an onion poultice?"

"No. This just struck her so fast. Christmas Eve she was fine and coughed some on Christmas morning, but this . . . I ain't never seen anything like this, have you?"

"Ja, I have. We must clear the airway."

"Water heating." Metiz stopped at the doorway. "Blanket?" She pointed to the bed.

Magda looked up at Ingeborg. "What do we need?"

"We are going to make a tent over a steaming kettle on the stove. Metiz will put some herbs in it to help the steam. Then we will take turns sitting in the steam tent holding Anna."

Mr. Helmsrude came to the door in time to hear Ingeborg. "How will you hold the blanket up?"

"The backs of chairs. I wish I'd had Haakan build us a frame. I thought about it last year and then forgot."

"I will make something." He flinched as though struck when Anna started coughing again.

A few minutes later, with the coatrack and a pole from the barn holding up the tent, Ingeborg and the mother held the child over the steaming kettle. Soon they had sweat pouring down their faces, but Anna breathed better. When she coughed up great globs of mucus, Ingeborg could feel the child relax for a short time.

The three women took turns under the tent, with Magda taking time to put the other two children to bed shortly after a supper. The meal was fraught with tension as everyone listened for Anna to breathe again or to stop coughing.

Father God, help this poor mite of yours. Give us the wisdom to help her, Father, please. Ingeborg never knew where her prayers let off and her talking took over. The hours passed, each bout of coughing leaving the little girl weaker.

"I don't know how long she can go on so." Magda held her daughter close and rocked her in the steam tent.

I don't either. Father, please!

In the early hours of the morning Anna fell asleep in the steam tent in Ingeborg's arms. She felt her own eyelids drifting closed, and in spite of herself, her head tipped forward and they both slept.

Anna woke with a jerk and threw up, a green viscous mess shot with bright trails of blood.

But she breathed easier again for a time.

Mr. Helmsrude awoke, and after checking on his daughter, he headed for the barn and the morning's chores.

"I think we should send for Pastor Solberg," Ingeborg said when Einer returned with frothing pails.

"Ja, I go now." He looked across at his wife, who was bathing Anna again with cool water to bring her temperature down.

"How is she?" Pastor Solberg asked when he arrived some time later.

"Resting." Magda held out a trembling hand. "Ah, Pastor, she is so weak." She dashed away tears with the corner of her apron.

Solberg entered the bedroom, nodding to Ingeborg and Metiz, who sat on the floor against the wall. Ingeborg left her place on the edge of the bed and motioned for the pastor to sit there.

"We've had her under the steam tent for most of the night, and it helps." Ingeborg kept her voice to a whisper. Solberg squeezed her hand and took her place.

"Ah, little Anna," he said, gently placing a hand on her head. "Father in heaven, we lift this lamb to you for your healing touch. She has been such a light to all of us, a gift of love to her parents, such a gallant little spirit. We know how much we love her, and we know that you love her more. You love each of us and are right here present. Oh, God, we beg that you clear this poor child's lungs, that you take away the terrible coughing, and that you bring peace to this room and strength to those who nurse her." He took Anna's little hand in the two of his. "Please, Lord, we beg of you."

Ingeborg wiped her eyes and blew her nose. She could hear Mr. Helmsrude out in the kitchen dumping more wood into the woodbox. The door closed behind him as he went outside again. His steps sounded labored, as though the man carried a load on his shoulders that would fell a mule.

Anna whimpered, "Ma?"

"Right here." Magda took Solberg's place and laid a hand on her daughter's forehead.

"I . . . I hurt."

"I know."

Ingeborg motioned to Metiz, and they returned to the kitchen to set up the steam tent again. Metiz dipped some willow bark tea out of a kettle that they kept warm on the back of the stove and took it in to be spooned into the child's mouth.

She took two or three spoonfuls and gagged. The coughing

attacked her again, and they immediately moved her back into the steam.

"I'll come back later, after school." Pastor Solberg shook each of their hands. "God be with you."

"Did Haakan get it around that everyone should pray for her?" Ingeborg asked as she held his muffler for him.

"Ja, and we will pray in school this morning too." He pulled his gloves on and tucked them under the sleeves of his black wool coat. "Thank you, Ingeborg, and thank Metiz for me too."

"I will." Ingeborg leaned her head against the doorframe after closing it tightly behind him. She could hear him talking with Mr. Helmsrude outside, she heard the other children coming down the stairs, but more than anything, she heard the agonizing "whoop, whoop, whoop" of a little girl trying to get enough air into her lungs to keep on living.

The sound invaded her heart and mind and soul. *God, are you listening? How can you bear to see this child suffer so? I can't! I can't!*

"Ingeborg." Metiz touched her shoulder.

"Ja, I am coming." She dried her eyes again, then taking the child from the mother, she and Metiz held Anna over the steam kettle.

Pastor Solberg came and went. Other neighbors brought bread and cakes, beans and stew. Everyone said they were praying for Anna, nay for the whole family. Mrs. Johnson took the two younger children home with her to play for a while.

Daylight passed into night. The coughing grew less.

Ingeborg and Metiz exchanged looks across the bed they were changing again so that Anna would have dry sheets.

"You go rest for a time while Anna is resting." Ingeborg took Magda by the arm and started her toward the stairs.

"What time is it?"

"Some after midnight. We will come for you if there is any change."

"All right." Magda stumbled on the first step, righted herself, and pulled her way up the stairs.

A bit later Einer came down and asked, "Do you need any wood or anything?"

"No, you rest too."

He knelt at the side of the bed and laid a hand on Anna's forehead. "Rest, child, ah my little Anna." His tortured face streamed with tears. "Is there nothing I can do?"

Ingeborg shook her head. "We will call you."

Ingeborg sat in the rocker by the bed. Metiz, wrapped in a quilt, sat against the wall. In the quiet warmth of the room, the verses tolled through Ingeborg's mind. *"I am the good shepherd. . . . My sheep hear my voice. . . . I will never leave thee nor forsake thee. . . ."*

She jerked awake, not aware she'd been sleeping. Was that the wind whimpering at the eaves? Or Anna? She leaned closer to the child in the bed.

No more coughing or choking. The silence was deafening.

Tears streamed down Ingeborg's face as she drew the sheet over the child. "Go with God, little one. I know you are in a better place."

Her whisper brought Metiz to an abrupt waking. When Ingeborg shook her head, all Metiz said was "Ah." What else was there to say?

Ingeborg's chest hurt from trying to breathe for the little girl. "How will I tell Andrew?" she whispered, staring down at the still form. "And her mother?"

"Andrew knows. The mother, we will let her sleep. No more to do."

Ingeborg washed the thin little body, combed Anna's hair, and dressed her in a clean dress.

Together she and Metiz pulled rocking chairs up by the wood stove and sat without talking, letting the tears slip by until Mr. Helmsrude woke to begin chores.

"How is she?"

Ingeborg shook her head. "She's gone home."

"Oh, God. Oh, my poor Anna." He entered the bedroom, and they heard his knees hit the floor by the bed. When he came out, his eyes were red but dry. "Thank you for letting Ma sleep. Wasn't nothing more she coulda done anyway."

"That's right. We'll wait here until she wakes. How long before you'll be ready for breakfast?"

"Couple hours. Will you tell her, or should I? Anna, you know, she ain't never been strong like the others. But she is— was our first, and a better little girl never lived."

"I'll tell her if you want."

"Good." He blinked a few times, clapped his hat on his head, and left the house.

The other two children had been fed and dressed, the mister ate and went back out to clean the barn, and still Mrs. Helmsrude slept on.

"Is Ma sick too?"

"No. Just worn out." Ingeborg took the little boy by the hand. "Let's go wash your hands and face, then you can show me where your toys are."

"Toys are in Anna's room. Can I see Anna now? She likes me to come play on her bed."

Ingeborg shared a sad glance with Metiz. "No, not right now." *Should I tell him or wait for his mother to do that? Oh, Lord, how would I want this to be taken care of in my house? Please, tell me what to do.*

"Ma's awake." He tore loose from her hand and ran up the stairs. "Ma, we got comp'ny. They made breakfast, and . . ." His voice faded as he found his mother.

"I take baby." Metiz lifted the youngest child up from her chair. "Come, we rock."

Ingeborg nodded and made her way up the steep flight of narrow risers. Mrs. Helmsrude sat on the edge of the bed rocking her son. She looked up at Ingeborg, tears streaming down her face. "She's gone, isn't she?"

Ingeborg nodded.

"I knew it when I didn't hear her fighting to breathe. That sound has filled the house for almost three days." She blew her nose and wiped her eyes. "Better for her. Oh, my little Anna."

"Anna sleeping."

"Ja, that she is." Ingeborg put her arms around Mrs. Helmsrude, held her close, and let her cry until the tears dried for the moment.

"Ma, why are you crying?" The boy hiccuped between the words.

"Because, Petey, Anna has gone home to be with Jesus, and we shall miss her terribly." She kissed his cheek and smoothed his hair.

"But she lives here with us."

"Not anymore, son."

"But, she . . ." He looked up at Ingeborg. "She said Anna was sleeping in the bedroom."

Ingeborg sighed. "I-I thought you should be the one to tell him."

The mother nodded and turned her son's face up to look at her. "Remember when the kitten died?"

"The dog killed it."

"Ja, well Anna died from the whooping cough."

"Are we going to put Anna in the ground?"

Both of the women nodded. "Come spring."

"But that will be dark, and Anna don't like the dark."

"Ah, but you see, Anna's spirit is already in heaven with Jesus, where it is light all the time, and where she never has to cough again. She's all better now."

Tears rained down on the little boy's face. "Then why are you sad?"

"Because I already miss her so."

Ingeborg gave up fighting the tears.

With his hands crossed, Peter said, "I miss her too." He looked up at his mother again. "Will I go to heaven and see Anna when I die?"

"Yes, if you believe in Jesus."

"Good. Maybe I'll go tomorrow." He hopped down and walked to the door. "Come, Ma. Have a cup of coffee."

"He's some child," Ingeborg whispered. *And like he's learned from the adults, when things are good or bad, you have a cup of coffee.*

"I think I been grieving for my little girl a long time now. Somehow I just knew she was never going to grow up and get married. I had a sense of that and kept asking Jesus to make her well again." She looked up at Ingeborg. "You think I didn't pray with enough faith, so that's why God took her?"

Ingeborg sank to the floor on her knees beside Mrs. Helmsrude. "I remember thinking that when my Roald never returned from that blizzard. I thought maybe it was all my fault, and if I was any kind of Christian, God would have answered my plea and brought him home. But now I know that God doesn't work that way. I don't know why He took Anna home any more than why He took Roald, but I do know that He loves us beyond measure and promises to be right here in the valley with us. The Bible says His ways are higher than ours, and I believe this is one of those times we just don't understand 'cause it's too high for us." She shifted to the bed. "But I do believe Anna and Roald are far better off than the rest of us, that's for certain sure."

"I believe that too, but my heart hurts like there's a hole there bigger'n me."

"I know."

"Can I see her now?" Mrs. Helmsrude asked.

"Ja, you can." When they got back in the kitchen, they could hear hammering from the barn. Mr. Helmsrude was making the small wooden box in which to bury his daughter.

Ingeborg and Metiz left for home an hour or so later after promising to stop on the way and tell Pastor Solberg.

Dear Mary Martha,

I have such sad news to write that I would rather be anywhere than here with pen and paper in hand. Anna Helmsrude died of the whooping cough two days after Christmas. She said her part so well in the program you would have burst your buttons. There was no sign of a lisp in spite of her being so nervous about standing in front of the congregation. And the song you all worked on? Well, people, me included, have been singing it ever since. Such a catchy tune it is, and the words say so much. If I didn't believe in our Lord's promises that we will see our loved ones again in heaven, I would run screaming out into a blizzard and never return. That said, let me turn to lighter things.

Christmas I was at the Bjorklunds, along with most of Blessing. That house was some full, and a better time could not be had anywhere. Bridget knit me the most warm and beautiful sweater, and others gave me so much that I have no idea how to repay them. The joke of the day was on Ingeborg and Kaaren, as their husbands bought them each a sewing machine quite some time ago, and Ingeborg tried to purchase one herself. Penny was caught in the middle, but she played the game with finesse, even though she said her heart was in her mouth half the time.

The weather has been cold but sunny for the last several weeks, so I'm sure we are due for a real northerner any time. I hope and pray you are doing well and that your mother is improving in health with you there.

I look forward to seeing you again, hopeful that it will be sometime in the not too distant future.

Yours truly,
John Solberg

He laid the pen down and looked into the flickering lamplight. "Oh, Father in heaven, watch over your lambs here and protect us all from the ravages of disease this winter. I believe, help thou my unbelief."

The cat purred at his feet and started for the door as soon as it had John's attention. "Ja, you are right. Time for that and then bed." While the cat was out, he put two chunks of wood in the stove, turning the damper so the wood would burn very slowly, and moved the water bucket to sit on top of the reservoir so it might not have ice on it in the morning. As cold as it was, he was grateful to live in a soddy, for they stayed warmer in winter, especially now that the roof wore a two-foot-deep blanket of white. The drift covered the back of the house.

He let the cat back in and headed for bed, including all of his Blessing family in his prayers. For some reason, Katy kept coming to his mind, so he prayed extra for her. As had become his habit of late, he closed with prayers for Mary Martha. The letter would go out in the morning, forging one more link in the chain and keeping the distance from being unbearable.

Springfield, Missouri

Dear Pastor Solberg,

Thank you for your letter, but oh, how the message made my heart ache. Anna had become so dear to me, as you well know. My regret? I had planned to sew her a new dress for the program, and I didn't get that started, let alone finished. Now I shall never have the opportunity. I know her mother's heart must be near to breaking, and her father's too. Such proud people they are, and it is so difficult for them to ask for help. Please make others aware of their needs. I know you can do so in a way that will not offend them.

You asked of my mother. She is doing better, has even felt strong enough to pick up her mending and knitting of an evening, or in the afternoon, for that matter. She fusses at me because I will not allow her to do anything about the house, but I rejoice to see some color back in her cheeks. That makes everything I do worthwhile.

My sister, Eva Jane, was here with her family. Mama had sewn dolls for the little girls, and Uncle Jed made rocking cradles to hold the dolls. They were an immediate success. I plan to stitch up quilts for the cradles and maybe a dress or two for the dolls. It has been many a year since I sewed doll clothes.

Uncle Jed says he thinks he would like to see that flat plain that I try so hard to describe to him. When one has seen only ridges and hollers all one's life, prairie as far as the eye can see is hard to imagine. I tell him that Zeb dreams of raising some of the finest horseflesh in Dakota and would love to make a place for him there.

I hope and pray that this finds you in good health. Please give my regards to the rest of the folks of Blessing.

Wiping away the tears, I am your friend,

Mary Martha MacCallister

P.S. Please remind that brother of mine that while I understand he is very busy with the baby coming and all, the mail still goes both ways.

She blotted the paper and looked out at the drizzling rain. A shiver ran up her back. What was going on in Blessing?

February 1888
Blessing, Dakota Territory

S he's gonna die, ain't she?"

"Manda MacCallister, whatever gives you that idea?" Zeb clamped his teeth till his jaw ached. "Katy's just some tired, that's all."

"She looks just like my maw did, that's what."

Zeb glared at her, and she returned glare for glare.

"Well, just don't go sayin' something like that where she can hear. Or Deborah, either."

Manda shook her head and gave him one of her "if you don't beat all" looks. "What do you think I am? Stupid?"

Zeb had the feeling he hadn't really reassured her, but then what did he know about birthing babies. Unless it was just the same as with horses, cows, and dogs, he realized the depths of his ignorance. But he couldn't let her see that. "Watch your mouth."

She clamped her jaw shut, but he could tell what she was thinking. And he didn't like it one bit.

"Well, let's get these chores done so we can git on up to the house. How soon before that gelding can be sold, do you think?"

" 'Pends on how much you want him trained. He don't much like either harness or rider yet. I get the feelin' he'd soon dump me as blink."

"I was hoping for next week or so. Couple of men are coming."

"What they lookin' for?"

"Not sure. But I wanted something to show them. Why

don't you work him more under saddle and see if you can get him smoothed out some?"

"I could get a lot more done if I didn't have to go to that no-account school every stupid day."

"Manda, your mouth."

"That weren't swearin'."

"But no way for a young lady to talk."

"I ain't no *young lady*. So there!" She made the condition sound worse than measles.

Zeb sighed. "Just work on the horse every spare minute you got, all right?" He snagged a bucket off a hook where he'd hung it to keep clean. "I'll get the milking done. You take the pigs and chickens, since you already fed the horses." He stopped and looked over his shoulder. "You *did* feed all of them, didn't you?"

She gave him *that* look again, then dipped a bucket of oats out of the grain bin and huffed her way out the barn door. Caring for the chickens was Deborah's chore, but not wanting to leave Katy alone for a minute, Zeb had asked Deborah to remain inside. Besides, the little girl had been looking a mite peaked herself lately.

He brushed the cow's udder off, then set the stool beside her and sat down, leaning his forehead into her flank. The ping of the first streams of milk in the bottom of the metal bucket soon turned to the shush, shush of a filling pail. He squirted a stream into the mewing cat's mouth and continued milking. The sound of animals chewing hay or grain, the rustling of the hay, the plop of manure from one of the other cows, the crying of the barn cats all spoke of a well-run barn. Steers lowed from the outside corral, reminding him that he'd neglected them so far. A horse whinnied, answered by another.

What is going on up at the house? Thoughts of the black smudges circling around Katy's eyes ever since she had a cold made him want to wrap her in goose down and build walls around her to keep her safe. But the danger came from within.

On their trip to Montana she'd been an indomitable rider once she became accustomed to the daily routine. Her love of life and vitality were what drew him to her. No one in his entire life teased him and made him laugh as Katy did.

He smiled, recalling an incident on their trip.

"What's the matter, cowboy, can't keep up?" Her English-Norwegian language mix both confused him and made him laugh.

"I can keep up. I just don't want to wear the horses out." While the land seemed flat, the grade was always up, moving toward the peaks in the distance. He'd never seen such mountains as those far ahead of them, hanging like blue dreams in the distance and drizzled with snowfields on the tops like frosting dripping down a cake.

"We have mountains like that at home, the whole length of Norway. You should come see them sometime."

"Katy, *this* is home now." He nudged his horse to trot beside hers.

She shook her head, setting the broad-brimmed hat she wore to flopping. "No, Dakota is home. Montana is just a dream."

And the wild horses they caught were a dream come true. Along with the heavy stallion he bought in Ohio, he had the basics for starting a fine breeding ranch. But best of all, he had Katy.

Zeb brought himself back to the barn and the cow, who turned her head and looked at him, a question in her big brown eyes.

"Yeah, I know. We're done." He set the pail to the side, then stood and picked up the stool. The dream of a lifetime, that trip to Montana. And they'd found the perfect valley to homestead. Trees, pasture, creek—everything he ever needed or wanted. And Katy.

She was sound asleep when he got back up to the house. Manda had finished before him and begun the supper fixings.

"Sorry, Pa, I don't know how to fry the meat." Deborah looked up at him, her blue eyes shadowed with worry.

"But she peeled the potatoes and carrots." Manda was quick to stick up for her. She turned from working at the stove, where a frying pan sizzled forth the aroma of ham slices cooking. Another two pots bubbled on the back of the stove.

"Looks to me like you got everything under control." Zeb dipped hot water from the reservoir into the washbasin and took it over to the dry sink to wash.

When he no longer smelled like cow, he brushed back his

hair with damp hands and headed for the bedroom to check on Katy. She lay on her side, her distended belly making any other position impossible. If only she didn't look so pale, as though there wasn't enough blood under her skin to live with. The babe was surely taking more than his share. Zeb sat down in the rocker by the bed and leaned his elbows on his knees. This was becoming a familiar place. He had spent many hours sitting here praying, thinking, praying, dreaming, and praying again.

The words were mostly the same. *Dear Lord, keep Katy safe and bring her and the baby to full health again.*

"Hi," Katy whispered, stretching out her hand. She turned her head to glance out the window, then threw the covers back and started to rise.

He sat beside her on the bed. "Where you goin'?"

"Supper. I've got to get supper. Why didn't you wake me earlier?"

"Easy now." He pushed gently on her shoulder. "The girls have that under control, and if you go rushing out there, you might hurt their feelings, make them think they can't get a meal on the table."

"Zeb, that is a bunch of . . ."

He raised a finger to his lips. "Now, now, little mama, take it easy for little Zeb there. He doesn't like being awakened so fast, leastways that's what you tell me."

"Ooomph." She laid a hand on the side of her belly. "Did you have to remind him? That little guy can kick worse'n any mule I ever met."

Zeb laid his hand on hers atop her belly, and both hands bounced up. Zeb felt a thrill shoot clear up his arm and straight to his heart. That was his son in there, kicking like a wild kid in a dirt fight.

Katy lay back panting. "What if there are two in there dancing the polka or something?"

"Metiz says just one."

"I know. Zeb"—she stroked his dark wavy hair back—"I'm thinking of asking my mor if she could come and help me. She volunteered a few weeks ago, but I thought I could handle everything. I *should* be able to, but I'm so terribly tired. What do you think?"

"Can I go get her right now?" His slow smile brought one back from her.

"No, I think we can eat first." She lightly punched him on the shoulder. "I meant tomorrow."

"You know what I really think?"

"No, what?" Her eyes darkened, making him sorry he teased her.

"I think I am married to a very wise woman who isn't letting her pride get in the way."

"No room for pride with what I've already got in my way." She stroked her belly with both hands, as if she could calm the new life within. "Did you know he likes me to sing to him?"

Zeb looked at her and shook his head. "He's a smart one then, 'cause I know how much I like you to sing to me."

Her eyes grew wistful. "We do sound good together, don't we?"

"We do everything good together, and don't you forget it." He got to his feet and, taking her hand, helped her roll into a sitting position on the edge of the bed, then raised her to her feet. "You want your slippers?"

"Ja, if I could see my feet to slip them on."

Zeb knelt and slid the sheepskin moccasins on her feet, the fluffy wool inside keeping her warm and dry.

"Mange takk."

"Velbekomme."

⚘ ⚘

"Ingeborg, come to bed," Haakan said.

"I will in a minute. I just want to finish putting in this sleeve." While she'd gotten real good on the straight seams, going around a curve and keeping the seam the same width still took strict concentration. When she finished, her heartfelt sigh made him smile.

"All right. Now you try this on, and let's see how it looks." Ingeborg held up the coat of heavy brown tweed that was supposed to have been Haakan's Christmas present. She pushed her chair back and held the garment for him to put his arms in the sleeves. "I've got to line it yet, so it will fit a bit differently, but . . ." She arranged the lapels and tugged on the shoulders to make the garment hang straight.

Haakan smoothed down the front of the coat. "This is the finest coat I have ever had." He shook his head and stared at his wife. "You did this." The awe in his tone made her smile.

"You like it then?"

"Ah yes, I like it." He brushed down the sleeves and flexed his shoulders. "You think the cows will like it?"

"Haakan, you wear that out to the cows, and . . ." She sputtered to a close when she saw the teasing glint in his eye. He looked so handsome. She walked around him, tugging here and there, as much to touch him as to straighten the coat. "You think it is wide enough in the shoulders?" *Ax handle width, that's what they were.* The day he'd come striding across the prairie that spring flashed into her mind. He'd carried his ax across his shoulders then and asked if he could help her and Kaaren, telling her right away that he planned to return to lumbering in northern Minnesota as soon as the cold set in again.

"I have to put shoulder pads in, and that will make it fit better here." She lifted the top of the sleeves. *But he had stayed. God, I thank you every day for this man of mine.* Her gratitude held a tinge of sadness still for Roald, who'd gone to help the neighbors after a terrible blizzard and never returned. That sadness returned at any death, like that of little Anna.

"What is it, my love?" Haakan laid a hand along her cheek.

Ingeborg sighed and turned her face to plant a kiss in his rough palm. "Just thinking." She took his hand in hers. "I think you need some goose grease. Look at these cracks." She motioned for him to remove the coat, then hung it on a wooden hanger carved by Baptiste for her Christmas present. With the coat hanging, she pushed her chair closer to the sewing machine and put her precious scissors in the drawer along with the pins and needle and thread.

"There now, come." Taking his hand, she pulled him out to the kitchen, and after warming the can with goose grease in it, she smeared it on his hand and began to massage it in.

"Um, that feels good."

"Ja, and so you would think you would do this once in a while."

"Feels better when you do it." He leaned forward and nuzzled the side of her neck with his lips. "You smell good."

"Give me your other hand." The warmth of his mouth set her heart to hammering. A log whooshed in the firebox. Paws whimpered from his box behind the stove. She turned her head, and his lips captured hers. So much for the goose grease.

꿏 ꙮ

As soon as the boys were off to school the next morning, Ingeborg made her way along the shoveled paths to the well house. Four-foot banks of snow on either side of her attested to the shoveling the men had already done. She was constantly amazed at how quickly a snowstorm could drift the paths full of snow again. The poles with rope strung between them laid blue shadows on the pristine surface this morning, mute testimony to the blizzard that had blown through the area the day before. The wind howling around the house sounded even more vicious than around the soddy eaves, drawing her back toward the black pit that called her name.

Especially since Anna died.

The tears that sprang so unexpectedly froze on her cheeks before she could open the door to the two-room sod building. Haakan had kept the stove burning since the day before, when she set the kettles of milk to heat and set for curds. Today she would cut the solid curd and drain them, then fill the presses. The slightly sour smell of the dirt floor, the spongy feel of the curds, and the sun streaming in the one window quickened her step. Some she would set to drain in the cheesecloth for soft cheese. The rest would go in the presses to harden off and cure.

Humming a tune, she cut through the curd first all one direction, then crosswise, then at various slants. The smaller the curd, the better the whey drained away. The pigs would be overjoyed with their grain drenched in the clear liquid left from the draining.

She checked the back room where Haakan had built shelves along both walls to house the great wheels of cheese while they cured. Using a piece of charcoal, she had written a date on each waxed wheel so she would know when they were ready to cut or sell whole.

"Ingeborg?" Bridget called.

"In here." She returned to the main room. "We surely do need more storage if we keep those heifers and make more cheese." She wiped her hands on her apron and went to the stove in the corner to refill the firebox.

"Astrid wants to go over to Kaaren's. Do you mind if I take her? I'll be right back." Bridget sniffed appreciatively. "Smells good in here, despite the soddy smell."

"Ja, that never goes away no matter how many times I whitewash these walls." She poured the drained curds from the wood-slatted strainer into the wooden mold and set the top in place. "She can stay home if you don't want to go."

"No, I want to be outside while we can. I got me a feeling there's another snowstorm on the way, so we better enjoy the sun while we can. You think Haakan would make Astrid a pair of skis?"

"Or Lars. Check with Kaaren. There might be some short ones over in their old soddy. I think we been putting all the skis up on the rafters." Ingeborg cranked the handle down as she talked, more whey draining out the sides of the press.

"I will look. She's a good age to learn. She and Trygve both."

"Ja, we missed out on skating this year. There has been so much to do."

"I'll be back soon. Then I can work out here, and you can go sew if you'd like."

"Don't tempt me." The cold draft that blew in through the open door warned her that the wind was picking up again. Suddenly the room seemed darker again, even though the square of sunlight that moved across the floor hadn't dimmed.

"Ingeborg? Bridget?" Zeb's voice called her now. She went to the door and cracked it open.

"We're out here. Go on in and make yourself at home. Pull the coffeepot forward too if'n you want some. I'll be there in a minute." She refilled the kettles from the milk cans, added wood to the stove, closed the damper, and gathered the things that needed washing into a basket. There would be more to make tomorrow, but for right now, the cheese house was caught up.

"So, how is Katy?" Ingeborg asked after pouring the coffee

and setting out pieces of apple cake.

"I wish you and Metiz would come look at her. While she tells me all pregnant women feel this way, I look at her and just don't know. She's so tired all the time that she falls asleep in the chair at meals. She hardly eats because nothing tastes good to her. I thought women ate a lot when they were carrying. And her feet. She can hardly get them in the slippers Metiz made her for Christmas."

"How about if we all come tomorrow? Bridget can go home with you today. You did bring a wagon?"

He nodded and smiled at both her and his mother-in-law. "I didn't know if you rode astride or not."

Bridget shook her head and rolled her eyes. "Our work-horses at home were for pulling not riding, so I do much better in a wagon. However, if we had skis, I could probably get there faster than you can with the team."

"Really?" He looked to Ingeborg for confirmation.

"I should warn you. If she offers you a bet and it involves skiing, you'll lose every time."

The three of them chuckled, and Zeb studied Bridget. He knew she had to be in her sixties at least, but she hadn't slowed down a mite since he met her. He remembered Hjelmer saying his mother was too old to run a boardinghouse. While he thought that about skiing, he was glad he'd kept his mouth shut. He didn't need both these women after him, and they still teased Hjelmer.

Bridget touched his hand. "Zeb, you are worrying for nothing. Katy is a good strong Norwegian girl. Why, she was made for having babies."

Zeb nodded and looked to Ingeborg. "You'll ask Metiz then?"

"You'll have the three best midwives in Dakota Territory at your service, sir." Ingeborg and Bridget nodded at the same time.

I just hope that's enough, he thought. *Please, God, make it enough.*

26

A h, Mor, I'm so glad you came." In her relief Katy slipped
back into Norwegian.

"You wouldn't let me come sooner, remember?"

"I know. You always said I was a stubborn one." Katy rolled
up to a sitting position on the sofa. "Uff da. Do all women feel
like a clumsy ball this close to their time?"

"Ja, they do." Ingeborg took Bridget's heavy coat along with
her own and hung them on the coatrack by the door. When
she returned, she sat in the chair beside Katy.

Katy smiled at Ingeborg and Metiz. "Thank you for coming
too. It is so nice to have visitors. With the girls in school, the
days get long, since Zeb won't let me do very much." She
clasped her hands together over her distended belly. "I don't
even have anything baked to go with coffee."

"That's no problem. We brought plenty." Ingeborg indicated the basket. "For dinner too."

Katy leaned against the back of the horsehair sofa. Pushing
her hair back with her hands, she shook her head. "I don't
know how there can be any room in here for food, but the last
two days I been wanting to eat everything I can find. For a time
there, I couldn't bear to eat at all. Zeb made me eat."

All the while she talked, Metiz and Ingeborg watched her.
The pale skin, tremors in her hands, her feet and legs swollen
like sausage skins about to burst. While Katy had tried to do
her hair, the golden strands hung listlessly around her face.

"I'm a mess, aren't I?" She tried to smile at Ingeborg.

"I wouldn't say that, but I'm going to ask you to do something that might seem silly."

"What's that?"

"Lie back down flat and put your feet up on the arm of the sofa. We'll pad it with a quilt or pillows or something."

Katy looked at her mother, who shrugged. "They know things in this country we didn't do at home. Just do what she says."

Between the three of them, they quickly had her situated. Bridget took over the kitchen, washing the breakfast dishes and adding wood to a stove low on embers. Soon she had the coffee bubbling, and the smell of meat stew floated through the house.

They heard the jingle of harness outside, and within minutes Zeb came in the front door, clapping his gloved hands against his shoulders. "Welcome. Sorry I wasn't here when you arrived. That young gelding thinks the other horse should do all the work while he admires the snowdrifts. Old Jezzy set him straight, let me tell you." He hung up his coat and crossed the room to take Katy's hand. "Were you warm enough? I was afraid the stove might have burned low."

"The kitchen did but not in here. Mor is taking care of dinner."

"Good. I know you get tired of my cooking. Manda tried to talk me into letting her stay home again today."

"Leave it to her." Katy tried to sit up, but he gently pushed her shoulder back before Ingeborg could even say anything.

"I have a feeling you've been told to lie like this, and so you shall."

"I must look huge as that beached whale I saw once in the fjord at home."

"You look lovely to me, so don't complain." He kissed the tip of her nose, making her blush. At least that way some color rose in her face.

"Zeb, we have company," she whispered, catching a giggle in the same breath.

"You think they've never been kissed? Maybe I should take care of that right now."

She grabbed his arm when he started to stand. "Z-e-b."

With a voice that flowed like warmed syrup and flashing

eyes with more than a hint of mischief, Zebulun MacCallister had them all laughing with his descriptions of life in Missouri when they talked about Mary Martha. They ate dinner at a small table pulled up to the sofa where Katy remained flat out, much against her will.

"But I am making such a mess," she grumbled, brushing away the crumbs.

"Then I shall feed you." Zeb picked up her fork and trans-ferred meat and potatoes to her mouth.

"But I'm not a baby."

"No, that is for sure not, but soon you shall have one, and then it will be your turn to stuff food in another's mouth. Open."

Afterward Metiz handed Katy a cup of hot tea made from dandelion. "You drink this. Drink much warm water. Keep feet up."

Ingeborg turned to Zeb. "We could pack her feet in snow for a bit to try to take away the swelling."

"If it would help. Won't be hard to get a dishpan full."

A short time later, with snow packs around her feet and legs, Katy shook her head. "I sure hope this baby comes soon," she muttered, her feet burning with the cold. "Before you freeze my feet off." She groaned and shook her head. "And now I have to use the necessary."

"Good," Metiz said with a smile. "Tea working."

"I'm glad it's doing something, because it tastes awful."

After they had her back on the sofa and as comfortable as possible, Katy looked at her mother. "I'm an awful bother, Mor. Please forgive me."

"You shush about bother. Some babies take a bit more out of their mors, and that's just the way life is. You'll find it worth all the struggle when that baby is lying in your arms."

"I can't wait." Katy flinched as her belly bounced the blan-ket up. "This one surely is trying to let me know that he's in there and getting ready to meet the world."

It wasn't too long before Ingeborg asked Zeb to bring up her horses so that she and Metiz could head for home before dusk. "You come for us when you need us, no matter what time of the day or night."

"I will. Thank you for bringing Bridget. I know Katy will

feel better with her here." He looked down at his snow-covered leather boots. "Am I making up things to worry about, or is something seriously wrong with Katy?"

Metiz leaned forward, the robe slipping from her knees. "She not right."

Zeb raised fear-filled eyes. "But she will be—right?"

"I hope so," Ingeborg said softly. "I surely do hope so. Best thing you can do for her is spend more time on your knees, for this is all in the good Lord's hands." She rippled the reins, clucking the horses forward. "God be with you."

"And you."

Pastor Solberg checked the window of the sod schoolhouse again. The snow that had started out falling gently now swirled and slanted, driven by a north wind blowing right off the ice fields of the northern tundra. He shuddered at the cold he could feel coming in the windowpanes. He couldn't send the children home in this. Why, oh, why hadn't he dismissed them earlier?

He couldn't even see his own house. The church sometimes appeared like an apparition through the snow curtains.

"Baptiste, Swen, please go out and bring in more wood."

They shrugged into their coats and wrapped mufflers around their necks.

Why hadn't he been paying more attention? But then, the storm had come like a freight train roaring out of the north. One minute a snowfall, the next a raging blizzard. Thinking of that he asked Thorliff, Knute, Hamre, and Anji to help with the wood. That way they could touch hands. "Stand near each other and pass the wood in. That way no one will miss the schoolhouse." He buttoned up his coat and added. "Hold hands and we'll go on out like a chain, with Anji right at the door. Children, don't be afraid, we'll be in as soon as we can. Ingrid, you man the door." The wind tried to rip his hat and coat from his body, but holding hands, they stretched as far as they could.

Solberg squinted against the snow driving into his face. Could they not reach the woodshed? Had he passed it? He swung slightly to the left, feeling with his hand straight out in front of him, the other holding on to Baptiste. Swinging it from side to side like a blind man, he connected with solid wood.

"I found it." He turned and yelled so Baptiste could hear. "Tell everyone to stay right where they are, and we'll pass the wood." So shouting, he picked up a chunk and passed it to Baptiste, who passed it on.

We might need enough for all night and tomorrow too. How long can we do this without freezing? He passed the wood, one chunk at time, until he could see much was diminished. Since he was under the shed roof, he knew he was more protected than the children. He sent ten more pieces, then he took Baptiste's hand and started back, the children clinging to each other behind him.

Once they were all inside with the door closed again, he breathed a prayer of thanksgiving and surveyed his charges. *Please, God, keep all the parents home. They must know that I wouldn't send their children out in a snowstorm, let alone a blizzard like this.*

"Well done." He smiled at the younger ones gathered in front of him and gestured to the wood stacked at the back of the room. The older ones were gathered around the stove, still shivering, their teeth chattering as they tried to warm up. "All right, let's get moving so we can keep warm."

"When is my ma coming?" Ellie Wold wore the soberest expression he'd ever seen on her little face.

"Not until the blizzard blows away." Pastor Solberg squatted down and drew the littlest ones into his circling arms. "We're safe here, and your folks know that. We will keep warm and have warm water to drink."

"What will we eat?" Jerry Valders asked, his face sober too, the teasing light gone out of his eyes at the enormity of their situation.

"Well, does anyone have anything left in their lunch pails?" As each student shook his head, Solberg nodded. "I didn't think so, but we won't starve to death if we miss a meal or two." *Or three or four. Dear Lord, let it clear by morning.*

Dark came early, since the window was soon covered with snow and blocked out what light was left. They slid open the windows on the front of the stove to have some light, and Solberg gathered them around the stove.

"Let me tell you a story," he began.

"Oh, good. I want David and Goliath." Andrew crossed his legs in front of him.

Every once in a while, the teacher would have them get up and march around the room while he put more wood on the fire, but then they would gather round the stove again. The cold pressed in on them as the wind howled over the top of the snow-covered schoolhouse.

They played Twenty Questions, reviewed all the arithmetic tables, and sang songs. As the younger ones fell asleep, the older cuddled them close, every one pressed against another to share the warmth. Sometime in the night, Pastor Solberg filled the metal pail with snow and let it melt atop the stove so they would have something to drink.

Never had he spent such a long night. He recited Bible verses to himself, answered questions when one of the children awoke, and dreamed of Mary Martha. What was she doing? When would she come back?

What if the blizzard lasted longer than a night and a day?

"I'm really hungry," a voice spoke, penetrating the stillness.

Pastor Solberg jerked alert. Day must have come because the room was lighter. The wind howled the same as the children stirred like a pile of puppies coming awake.

"I know, Joseph. We all are," he said to the hungry boy.

"Pa coming soon?" Andrew asked Thorliff.

"Soon as he can."

"I'm cold."

"Me too."

Solberg eyed the woodpile. Would they have enough to last the day, or would they have to brave the killing cold and wind again?

Someone started to cry and another hushed the tearful one.

"All right. Everybody up, and let's get moving around. We'll warm up that way. That's right, swing your arms and stamp your feet. Hamre, do you have your harmonica here?"

"Ja."

"Can you play for us, and we will all dance?"

"Ja." He pulled his harmonica from his pocket and blew

into it. With his mittened hands, the music hardly came through.

"Come over close to the stove and have a drink first, that might help."

Hamre did as told, and the dance began. Everyone partnered everyone as they whirled and stamped around the room dancing polkas, the Hambro, and the Pols. If someone didn't know the steps, they skipped and clapped anyway.

When they tired of that, they gathered around the stove again for more lessons, the older quizzing the younger. Solberg smiled reassuringly whenever someone looked at him with questions or fear in their eyes.

"Come now," he said at one point. "Let's move close together and pray that God will take the blizzard away and keep all of our families safe."

The children gathered, snugged as close together as they could.

"Father God, we know that thou canst see us in spite of the storm. We thank thee for thy protection, that we are safe within this snug school, and that our families are safe in their homes. I thank thee for each child here, that we are all precious in thy sight. Please, we ask thee, calm the storm as thou didst on the Lake of Galilee, that we may return to our homes. In Jesus' precious name we pray. Amen."

"You didn't ask for food." Ellie frowned up at him.

"I'm sorry. You're right, I didn't. Would you like to?"

Ellie folded her mittened hands over each other and scrunched her eyes closed. "God, we didn't have any supper last night nor breakfast this morning. It must be dinnertime now, don't you think? Please send us something to eat as soon as y—thou can. Amen."

She looked up at Pastor Solberg. "I didn't say the right words, huh?"

"Ellie, you said the perfect words. Thank you."

They alternated moving around, listening to stories, and reviewing their lessons in the dimness. Time seemed not only to stand still but to trickle backward.

"Anyone want a drink? I'm going to refill the pail with snow to melt."

Several of the children took sips from the dipper and

passed it back. The dipper went around again, and Baptiste took the pail and headed for the door. When he cracked it open, the snow was packed solid against the door.

"Oh, look." Deborah's eyes grew round.

"My pa will bust through that," Knute Baard announced.

"Mine too." Thorliff nodded at the same time.

Baptiste filled the pail and, with the help of two others, slammed the door shut again and dropped the bar back in place to keep it closed. The bucket rang in the silence when he set it back on the stove.

"Children, listen!"

"I don't hear nothin'." Toby White shook his head.

"I know."

"The storm is over! The storm is gone!" With shrieks of joy they clapped their mittened hands and jumped up and down.

"Thank you, God." Never had Pastor Solberg offered a three-word prayer more heartily.

"How will they get in?" Thorliff stopped beside the pastor while the others continued their dancing.

"We will begin digging with sticks of firewood." He turned to the older girls. "You keep the stove roaring so they can see the chimney smoke in case the whole building is buried."

"Really? You think it could be?" Swen went to the door and swung the bar up again. "Where we gonna put all the snow?"

They took turns digging, piling the snow along one wall and packing it down. Slowly they packed and cleared until they were beyond the doorframe and tunneling on an upward slant. Each time they changed diggers, they packed a step to reach higher.

"It's getting brighter." Swen stood in the tunnel and scraped back the snow to Knute, who scraped it back to Baptiste, where it was picked up by the middle children and carried to the side, where the little ones tramped it down.

When Swen broke through into the daylight, everyone cheered.

"Thank thee, Father."

The bigger boys pushed back the snow so there was room to crawl out.

"What do you see?" Solberg stood in the school with the smaller children around him.

"The church roof and the store. Some of those mounds must be your house and barn. And the sack house." Swen bent back down to yell inside. "And here come the sleighs."

"See, God made the storm stop 'cause you asked." Ellie clung to his coat. "I bet they brung food too, huh?"

"Yes, Ellie, I'm sure they did." Pastor Solberg thought of his horse and cat. Would they still be alive or frozen to death? And what about all the range cattle?

Pastor Solberg helped each of the children up the packed snow steps and into the waiting arms of their parents. He banked the stove and, stepping into the tunnel, closed the door behind him. He'd come back later and shovel out the snow before the floor turned to mud.

"Come on, Pastor, we'll get your house shoveled out before we get on our way, unless you want to come stay at our house," Haakan offered as he and the other men shook Solberg's hand and clapped him on the shoulder.

"Thanks for the offer, but I need to take care of my animals. I'd be mighty grateful if you'd shovel a path to my house, though."

"Ja, that we can do," Haakan replied. "And thank you for taking such good care of the children."

"Thank God you are all right." Joseph Baard hugged Anji and clapped a hand on his boys' shoulders.

"Your children are all pretty wonderful," Pastor Solberg said, waving good-bye as his pupils were tucked in the sleighs under elk robes, quilts, and blankets.

"We'll never forget this, you know," Joseph declared.

"Nor I." Pastor Solberg shook his head.

⚘ ⚘

Dear Mary Martha,

You wouldn't believe the blizzard we just went through. It hit within minutes and trapped me and the children in the schoolhouse overnight. I couldn't even go to my house and get blankets or food or anything. We had a short break, and then the storm returned for almost a week. Some are saying it was one of the worst blizzards ever. Farmers lost whole herds of cattle, and people were taking to burning furniture to stay alive. All of us here in Blessing came through relatively unscathed.

But life is hard here in our little town right now. I believe we are all still sorrowing over little Anna's death and that of an older man who lived south of here. While death is always sorrowful for those left behind, Mr. Henderson had lived a long and full life, nothing like the snuffing out of our young candle. I know that our heavenly Father is doing what He thinks best, but sometimes we struggle with accepting His will. When Mrs. Helmsrude asked me why Anna died, what could I say?

I'm sorry to sound so down in the dumps, because I am really rejoicing that we lived through the night without anyone getting frostbite or starving to death, although I know that wouldn't happen so suddenly. I am thankful that none of the families tried to come get their children until the blizzard cleared, for they could have been lost forever.

Kaaren is almost ready to begin teaching signing here at the school, but we will wait until the weather lets up some.

I trust that your mother is improving. Have you thought of bringing her here to Blessing?

> I remain faithfully
> your friend,
> John

Springfield

Dear John,

I was so glad to hear from you. When I think of Anna not being there in school, the tears begin to flow all over again. How I ache for her poor mother and father.

It is hard for me to believe that a snowstorm can be so vicious as to keep you at the school. Thanks be to our God that you are all safe.

You didn't mention Katy, and Zeb never writes. How is she? Tell my brother that his mother would feel much better if she knew how he was. How are the Bjorklunds? How are the twins doing in learning their sign language? I have so many questions, please forgive me.

The Christmas rose is blooming and the crocuses are just beginning to show color. Mother loves the snowdrops and feared she would never see them again. I am looking forward to the furring of the oak trees as the leaves begin to unfurl. Uncle Jed says there are kittens in the barn, and when you see Zeb, tell him old Blue is heavy with pups.

I think of you so often, and I pray that God will keep you through the winter and bring spring back into your life and heart again.

Yours in Him,
Mary Martha

Blessing

The sound of a wolf howling woke Ingeborg during the night several weeks later. She lay still, listening and remembering the year the wolves tried to kill their sheep. Now they were all penned up in a snug barn and safe from both predators and the weather. Lambing would begin any day now.

She woke later to the sound of water dripping off the icicles. The March wind no longer howled at the eaves, and when she opened the back door, a three-foot-long sword of ice fell with a crash.

"Don't count on this lasting," Haakan cautioned when he brought a pail of milk to the house. "I filled the milk cans in the well house. There's enough for you to make cheese again."

"Good. I thought as much." She cracked another egg into the frying pan. "After breakfast, would you please start the stove out there then?"

"I already did." He hung up his coat and topped it with his hat. "The sun's so bright it hurts your eyes this morning. I saw wolf prints out around the corral. I think they belong to that wolf of Metiz'. One front foot is deformed."

"Wolf isn't hers. He is free."

"I know. Just easier to say Metiz' wolf. I haven't seen him around for a long time and was beginning to think something had gotten him."

"I'm glad he's back."

"Saw other prints with his. You'd have thought Paws would have warned us." He took his place at the table just as Andrew and Thorliff pounded down the stairs. "You boys running a bit late this morning, eh?"

"I know, Pa. Onkel Lars said he would give us a ride. Where's Hamre?"

"Changing clothes."

"You boys will have to take over the chores tonight. We'll be moving the lumber mill downriver. Got to have more trees to saw. 'Bout the last thing we needed was a thaw, but I promised Sedgewick we'd start cutting for him."

Ingeborg set the plate of ham and eggs in front of him. "You going to be staying up there?"

"For the next couple of days. Sam will be coming out to help around here. Since Bridget is over at Zeb's, I thought he could share the soddy with Hamre."

"Ephraim is going with you too?"

Haakan nodded, chewing a bite of ham at the same time. "I figure four days at the most, then we'll be home and start filling the ice house."

⚜ ⚜

Two nights later winter returned, incensed that spring had sneaked in and melted some roofs clear. He howled around the eaves and tried to force his way in under the door sills.

The pounding on the door came in the middle of the night.

27

Springfield, Missouri

"She's gone." Mary Martha stood at her mother's bedside.

"Died peaceful in her sleep, just like she woulda wanted." Jed looked down at the face of the woman on the bed. "Gone to be with her Maker and right glad, I'm sure." He sniffed. "Ah shoulda knowed when old Blue was howling during the night. I jist thought some critter had come near the dog run."

Mary Martha wiped her flowing tears with the corner of her apron. She'd been making breakfast quietly so as to let her mother sleep, and here she'd died in the night. *Ah, Ma, forgive me for not being with you. I slept too sound.*

"Now, don't you go feeling guilty that you weren't with her." He turned to study the younger woman. "From that look on her face, she heard the Lord call her name and just couldn't wait to git outa here. Up there singin' with the angels 'stead of hurtin' down here. Surely would be my choice. 'Sides, you said good-bye in countless caring ways, and she know'd how much you love her."

"I . . . I guess. But even as weak as she's been, I thought she would be here always. Already the house doesn't feel the same." Mary Martha sank down on the chair by the bed where she'd sat reading to her mother nearly every afternoon. They'd read all through the Psalms and talked about places in their lives when they felt just like David, crying to the Lord. And like David, they had found reasons to praise their mighty God.

"I'm thankful I had this time with her." Mary Martha laid her cheek against her mother's cold hand that lay on top of the quilt. Never again would that hand stroke her hair or turn the pages of the worn Bible lying on the stand by the bed.

"I'll go tell the preacher if'n you want," Jed said after a time of silence.

"Thank you. And we better send a telegram to Eva Jane. I'll write to Zeb. He's too far away to come for the funeral anyway." She sniffed and wiped her eyes again. "I thought I was prepared for this, but here I am bawling like a newly weaned calf."

"That's the way it's s'posed to be. Hardhearted you'd be if you didn't sorrow for your ma." Jed turned and left the room, his stockinged feet soundless on the worn floorboards.

What would she do now?

Return to Blessing, her errant heart whispered. *Now!*

"But what about this place?" Mary Martha looked upward, willing the walls to show an answer. But when she sensed nothing, she rose and returned to the kitchen to finish making breakfast. Jed would be hungry.

Once they were seated at the table, the words just slipped from her tongue. "Would you like to go back to Blessing with me?"

Jed stopped, his fork of ham and egg halfway to his mouth. He took the bite, chewed, swallowed, and looked her full in the face. "Now, why would I want to go and do that?"

"Well, I just thought . . . there's no one here to take care of you . . . and . . . well . . ."

"You think I can't care for myself?"

"No, but . . . well. . . ." If she could ever get her tongue untwisted, she might make some sense. "But this is a big place for one man to care for, and . . ."

She wound to a stop at the look in his eye.

"I take it you want to go back to Blessing?"

She nodded and shifted her knife and fork. The eggs on her plate had congealed in the gravy and stared up at her like two huge yellow eyes.

"I . . . I have a good life there with Zeb and Katy and my work with the children."

"And that preacher feller?"

She shrugged. "Time will tell."

"But you care for him."

She nodded again and realigned the coffee cup with the silver. "But I don't want to leave you all alone here either."

"Ah, missy, I been alone in the midst of the crowd all my life. I don't need much, and this place will more than provide it. It'll be here for you anytime you want to come home, and someday you might want to bring your young'uns back here to see where you growed up. Same goes for Zeb and Katy. You all got your own lives, but this old place will be here waitin'."

Mary Martha patted his age-spotted hand. "There's always a place for you wherever we are."

"Ah know that."

She blew her nose and cut a bite of meat. "Reckon we better get ready for the folks who want to come say good-bye. I'll wash and dress Ma so she looks good for company while you go tell the news." She glanced around the house that was already spotlessly clean. "No sense cookin'. They'll be bringin' enough food to feed Sherman's army."

⚜ ⚜

Dear Zeb and Katy and girls,

Ma went to sleep here three nights ago and woke up in heaven. We buried her in the churchyard this afternoon, as she wished. Everyone in the parish came to offer their condolences and share some story how Ma helped them in a time of need. While I knew she did things like that, I had no idea the far-reaching effects. She will be and has been missed around here since she took sick.

Mary Martha went on to describe in detail the funeral and the time of mourning at the homeplace, then came to a close.

I plan to pack my things and return to Blessing as soon as I am able. Give my love to everyone, and if there is anything you would like me to bring, let me know. Uncle Jed will stay on here at home. I tried to talk him into coming with me, but he says pulling up roots now might damage them so bad they won't go down deep again. I'll see you soon.

Your loving sister,
MMM

The letter to John—she could no longer think of him as Pastor Solberg—took longer as she described the people and the feeling at the church.

> Ma's death was far different from the death of little Anna. While there was sorrow, we all rejoiced that Ma had gone on to her reward. I like to think of the angels rejoicing over one returned home, and I know they sang a full concert when Anna arrived. It must be so hard to wait and have the burying in the spring like you must do. Like never an end to the grieving.
> While I am sad and miss my mother dearly, I can no longer think of this place as home and am impatient to finish clearing things away and board the train for Blessing. If there is still a place for me to help in your school, I will be most delighted to take up where I left off.

She wiped her eyes again, knowing that Anna would not be there to work on improving her speech.

> Your sorrowing yet still rejoicing friend from the southland.
> Affectionately,
> Mary Martha

When Jed left to take the letters to the post office and pick up a few things at the store, she wished she were in the wagon with him. Why did she feel such a need to be in Blessing—not in a few weeks, but *now*?

28

Blessing, Dakota Territory

P lease come. Bridget says to hurry." Zeb stood just inside the door.

"I'll be ready in a minute." Ingeborg stood behind Haakan, still tying her wrapper around her. "You go for Metiz, and I'll be ready when you get back."

"Right." Zeb spun and headed out the door like a man needing to be told what to do because his mind was elsewhere.

Ingeborg knew all he could think about was Katy and getting back to her.

By the time she was dressed and had placed a few more things in the box she kept assembled for birthing and other illnesses, the jingle of harness was back at their door. She kissed Haakan good-bye and let him help her up into the wagon bed still on runners. The cold bit deep, even before she could snuggle down under the elk robes Zeb had spread for them. While spring had shown its nose, winter had nipped it off and returned with a vengeance, as if to prove there would be no season of new life this year.

"Tell me, what is happening?" she asked as they flew over the drifts, not bothering with the road, since the snow had frozen enough to hold the horses again.

"The baby started to come in the afternoon, but no matter how hard she struggles, it just won't be born. Bridget has done all she can and asked me to come for you. Oh, Katy is so weak. I can't lose Katy." The last words roared from his throat as if he shook his fist at the heavens.

Oh, Father in heaven, please strengthen our girl. Hold her in the palm of your mighty hand and help this baby come into life, squalling and pink. Father, we beseech you on Katy's behalf, give Zeb the strength to bear what he must and give us wisdom to be your hands here on earth. She answered when spoken to but otherwise kept on with her praying.

As the horses raced across the frozen snow, Ingeborg went over in her mind what they could do to help. She and Metiz were out of the wagon bed almost before the team came to a sliding halt. They hurried into the house and into the bedroom, where Bridget shot them a look of pure fear.

"She's so weak already, she can hardly push."

Ingeborg shucked her outer things. "Let me wash my hands, and then we'll see where we are."

"Katy sleep. Good." Metiz scrubbed right beside Ingeborg.

"How do we give her the strength to bring this baby into the world?"

"Work. Talk to Great Spirit."

Katy whimpered as they reentered the room. Her eyes fluttered open. "Zeb? Where's Zeb?"

"He's out taking care of the team." Ingeborg leaned over the sweat-soaked bed. "How are you feeling?"

Katy flopped her head from side to side. "Why doesn't he come?" Her hand fluttered over her belly, so Ingeborg knew she meant the baby.

"I don't know. But you rest as long as you can, and then we'll push that baby out, and you'll be on your feet in no time." Ingeborg wished she felt as confident as she tried to sound.

Together she and Metiz checked to see how far Katy had dilated. Metiz shook her head.

Why isn't she pushing? What's happening here, Lord? "Let's get some pillows behind her and get her sitting up more. Bridget, how long since she walked?"

"Hours." Then she whispered, "She's too weak."

"I know, but between us . . ." Ingeborg nodded to Metiz, who came around the bed. "Okay, Katy, my dear, we are going to get you up on your feet so we can get this going again. Metiz and I will hold you up, and you just move your feet." Together they rolled her to the side of the bed and, laying her arms over their shoulders, put theirs around her and hoisted Katy to her feet.

"Oh, dear God . . ." Bridget reverted to Norwegian in her misery.

They walked Katy to the door and back around the bed. In the meantime, Bridget whipped off the soaked sheet and threw a clean one over the bed, tucking it in after they sat Katy back down.

"I sit behind her." Metiz took her place against the wall, and between them all, they pulled and pushed until Katy was propped against her in as much a sitting position as possible.

Watching the limp woman closely, they could see the contraction begin.

"Katy, push!"

Katy groaned, her fingernails digging into Metiz' legs as she struggled to birth the baby. When she screamed, the sound came more like mewling of kittens than a healthy birthing shriek.

"Has her water broken?" Ingeborg turned to Bridget, who shook her head.

"Ah." Ingeborg took a sharp knife from her box, and when the contractions forced the opening to expand, she stabbed the membrane, and water gushed into the towels they laid in place.

Within minutes, the contractions deepened and the time between shortened.

Zeb stood in the doorway. "How can I help?"

"You go on to sleep. This is woman's work." Bridget made shooing motions with her hands, never taking her eyes from her daughter's straining body.

"No! Metiz, I can do what you are doing. Katy, I'm here." He leaned over and brushed the sweat-soaked hair from her forehead. "Katy, love, hear me. We're going to bring this baby out, okay?"

Metiz looked to Ingeborg and, at her nod, shifted over, relinquishing her place to Zeb.

For a time he seemed to give her strength, but soon her pushes weakened.

"Come on, Katy. You've got to push. Now, here we go again . . . that's it . . . now push!"

"Come on, Katy, love, one more time. Come with a big one," Zeb chanted, picking up from Ingeborg what was needed. Tears streamed down his cheeks, and he wiped them on her hair. "Good, now rest a bit. You're doing fine, girl. Come on, Katy."

"I can see the baby's head." Ingeborg felt as if she was shouting, but didn't want the girls to hear all this, so she leaned closer to Katy to let her know.

But after what seemed like hours, the baby had not come any farther. Katy's pushing grew weaker and weaker, and Ingeborg's prayers grew more insistent. *Father, give her strength now. Father God, help us.* With no conscious thought on her part, the words streamed from her mind to God's ear. She hoped.

"We can't wait any longer." Ingeborg took the knife and nicked the thin skin surrounding the baby's head. Then on the next push, with gentle fingers, she tried to get them around the baby's ears, jaw, something to help him come.

"Now! Push!" The head cleared and with it a stream of blood. "Again. The head is clear." She turned the shoulders and eased the baby boy into the world amid a gushing of blood.

"Oh, God."

Bridget grabbed the baby, turned him upside down, and smacked his backside. Nothing.

Metiz massaged Katy's now flaccid belly, while Ingeborg tried packing to stop the flow.

"What can I do?" Zeb's voice cut through the air thick with the smell of blood.

"Help Bridget!"

"Breathe in his nose."

"He's not breathing."

Bridget and Zeb continued to work on the newborn, alternating breathing in his nose, rubbing his body, and slapping his backside.

Ingeborg mumbled to Metiz, to Katy, to herself, as they fought to stem the flow of blood that would not stop.

"Dear God, please stop the bleeding," she prayed over and over.

Katy never regained consciousness. Like the lifeblood flowing from her, Katy's spirit slipped away, never having seen her son. The son that never breathed.

"I'm sorry." Ingeborg dashed away the tears that threatened to drown her. "Oh, God, Zeb, Bridget, I'm so sorry."

Bridget crooned to the baby in her arms as if he could hear.

Zeb fell on his knees beside the bed, kissed Katy one more time, and left.

In her misery, Ingeborg heard the door slam. She glanced out the window to see the crack of gold in the east. With this morning, there would be no joy.

"She's gone, ain't she?" Manda appeared like a wraith in the doorway.

"I'm afraid so." Ingeborg reached for the girl, but Manda dodged her hand and came to stand by the bed. She stared down at the peaceful face on the pillows. "Just like Ma." She laid the back of her hand on Katy's cheek. "Good-bye."

Ingeborg tried to bury her sobs in her hands and blood-stained apron, but it did no good.

Manda looked up at her. "Told you that prayin' didn't do no good. God don't care about us." She spun on her heel and left the room.

Her words echoed in the room. *God don't care about us.*

Ingeborg sank down in the rocking chair. "Let me hold him," she whispered, as if speaking aloud would wake the woman on the bed. Bridget placed the blanket-wrapped baby in Ingeborg's arms.

She looked down at the round face framed with dark hair long enough to curl already. "He's so perfect." She gathered him to her cheek. "Why, oh why, couldn't you breathe for us? At least your pa would have had you to remember her by." Her tears washed his face, and she sobbed into the blanket.

Moving like a wooden puppet, Bridget gathered up the bloody sheets and rags and left the room. Metiz laid a hand on Ingeborg's shoulder.

"Could do no more."

"I know, but . . . oh, God, oh, God, why hast thou forsaken us?"

"He not leave. He here."

Ingeborg shook her head. Heavy, it felt so heavy. Was that a door she heard opening? "Where's Manda?"

"Went out."

"Oh, we must help her." She started to rise, but Metiz kept a heavy hand on her shoulder.

"Chores will help her. Cows, the horses, they help."

Between the three of them they had bedclothes boiling and breakfast cooking when Zeb and Manda returned to the house. Deborah clung to Ingeborg, tears leaking from her eyes no matter how much she brushed them away.

"The box will be ready in a couple of hours." Zeb muttered his first words since he returned to the house.

"Haakan will be glad to do that for you."

"No! And there will be one box."

Manda stared at the oatmeal in front of her before flinging away from the table and running for the porch. They could hear her retching over the slop pail.

As soon as the meal was finished, Zeb and Manda both headed back to the barn without another word. A few minutes later they heard the jingle of the harnesses, and Manda pulled the wagon up to the front porch.

"I'll take you home."

"I'll stay here." Bridget spoke for the first time since she had placed the baby in Ingeborg's arms.

"Ja." Ingeborg reached for the older woman, and the two clung together, their tears saying all that words could not convey.

"Mange takk," Bridget whispered. "The Lord giveth, and the Lord taketh away. Blessed be the name of the Lord."

"Ja, I guess." If she closed her eyes, the black pit yawned at her feet. "I will come back later and help you with washing her and all."

"No." Bridget shook her head. "I will do that. She is my daughter."

Manda never said a word all the way to the Bjorklund farm. From the look on her face, Ingeborg almost doubted the girl would ever speak again.

How were they to help Manda and Zeb and Deborah? *I'll think about that later*, Ingeborg promised herself as she fell into the arms of sleep.

But even in sleep's arms, she could see the blood, bright red, that flowed over her hands, over the edge of the bed, and pooled on the floor. *No, no, oh, God, make it stop!*

"Inge. Ingeborg."

She stepped back from the black pit that yawned at her feet, turning to the man who called her name with such love and concern. "Wha-what?"

"You were dreaming." Haakan stroked her hair from her forehead.

"No." Ingeborg shook her head. "No, it was not dream. Oh, Haakan." She raised up to clutch his shoulders with both hands. "She bled to death right before our eyes, and there was nothing we could do." The last words burst forth like the howl of an animal caught in a trap.

"Ah, my Inge." He wrapped her in the protection of his arms and cradled her against his chest. "You try so hard and you do the best you can, but my dear love, you are not God." He kissed her forehead and let her cry.

"But why—why does He turn His face from us?" She hiccuped between sobs. "Zeb, the girls, they need her so bad, and still she is gone. And the baby, ah, Haakan, he was so perfect, and he never even breathed. I cannot bear this. I cannot." The bed shook with the force of her sobs.

Haakan let his tears wash her hair and gave her the only comfort he could—the warmth of his arms and the strength of his love.

Finally, she wiped her eyes on the bed sheet and gulped in a deep breath of air. Her head felt as if it was far too heavy for her neck to uphold. Her nose ran and she sniffed. The steady beat of his heart under her ear, the scratch of his wool shirt against her cheek, brought a lassitude that she had no will to fight.

"Sleep now, my Inge, and when you awake, all will be better."

"Where are the children?"

"At Kaaren's." He wiped away another tear with the pad of his thumb.

"Don't leave me alone." She moved over. "Please."

Haakan drew her into the curve of his body.

"They were going to call him Gustaf."

"After Katy's far?"

"Ja. I should go to Bridget and . . . and the girls."

"No, you shall stay here." He cuddled her even closer. "Sleep now."

She yawned and kissed his hand. "Mange takk." *I wonder...*

29

Springfield, Missouri

S omething terrible has happened, I know it has."

"Now, girl, you can't know that for certain." Uncle Jed leaned forward, his elbows on the table. He studied her face as if memorizing every inch. "But your ma could tell sometimes too. Guess it's a family gift."

Mary Martha started to close her eyes, but every time she did, the sense of doom deepened. "I wasn't planning to leave until next week, but I think I better be ready in the morning. Could you please go to town today and check on the train schedule? We need a few things at the store too." She looked deep into her uncle's faded eyes. "Are you sure you won't go with me, or at least come later?"

Jed shook his head. "Can't do that. I'll put in what crops I can. Hate to let too much go fallow. Sure wish Eva Jane's man wanted to farm this place with me."

"He's not much of a farmer." Mary Martha rolled her lips together. "Good thing he's helping his daddy, even though Eva Jane doesn't like living that close to her in-laws. Least they got a good roof over their heads and plenty to eat."

"They'd have that here too. If I had my druthers, I wish Zeb would come home."

"I know." She got up to pour them another cup of coffee. "But he likes Dakota, and I think if he left there, it would be to homestead a ranch in Montana. He sure did love the mountains out west."

"If everybody leaves, who's going to take care of the land here?"

After Uncle Jed had left for town, Mary Martha thought about his last statement while she gathered her things to pack in the trunk. Not really much she wanted from the house besides her mother's Bible and her book of recipes for both food and medicinals. Eva Jane had taken their mother's quilt from her bed and the rocker their father had made before he went off to war. Even though she'd moved furniture around in the front room, without the rocker, there was an emptiness there now.

With the trunk half packed, she stepped outside with a sharp knife and took starts from the white rose bush that smelled so sweet, the snowball bush, and the lilacs. After wrapping them carefully in a packet of damp earth, she wrapped them again in a bit of canvas and nestled them, along with seeds saved from the garden, in a corner of the trunk. If they took, she'd have another remembrance of home.

Old Blue announced Jed's return long before she heard the horse. When he tied up at the house, she knew something was wrong. She met him at the door.

"Here." The telegram he handed her near to burnt her fingers. Her hands trembled so hard she could barely read the print. *Katy and baby died in childbirth. Stop. Come soon.* She raised stricken eyes to her uncle. "I told you."

Blessing, Dakota Territory

The train wheels couldn't turn fast enough. She peered out the dirty window, willing the train to hurry. Every time she thought of the fun-loving young woman who'd so quickly become her dearest friend, the tears started again. She'd asked *Why, God? Why Katy?* enough times that she figured her heavenly Father must be weary of her cries. Her prayers took up rhythm with the train wheels and *Please, God, please, God* clacked over and over in her mind. She was no longer sure who or what she prayed for, knowing only that they all needed His succor.

"Next stop, Blessing." The conductor stopped at her seat. "You been here before, miss?" At her nod he continued with a broad smile. "You ever had dinner at the Bjorklund store? That Missus Bjorklund serves some of the best food west of the Mississippi. I heard they were starting a boardinghouse come spring."

Mary Martha ordered her mouth to smile in return. *Come spring. Hard to believe it's even near with all the sparkling snowdrifts that ridge this flat land.* Even as short a time as she'd been here, she'd forgotten how flat it was. "Yes, the Bjorklunds are good friends of mine."

When the train stopped, a black man stood on the station platform holding a tray of sandwiches, pieces of cake, hunks of cheese, slices of pie, all ready to serve. As soon as the passengers stepped down, he nodded to the conductor and took his wares aboard.

Mary Martha checked to see that her trunk was unloaded and pulled her coat more closely around her. This was a far cry from the spring warmth burgeoning at home. Though the sun shone, there was little warmth to it, and the wind pierced her coat as though she wasn't even wearing it. She'd just begun to wonder if they'd received her telegram when Pastor Solberg came trotting around the corner of the sack house.

"Miss MacCallister!" He panted to a stop. "Sorry I'm late. We had a problem at school." He grinned at her, then snatched her hands and held them both. "You . . . you look wonderful."

"I'm glad to see you too, Pastor Solberg." The name felt strange upon her lips. She'd been thinking of him as John for so long now. She felt tears burning on the back of her eyes. "How is Zeb? What about the girls?" *How are you? Deep down inside, how are you?*

Solberg shook his head. "Zeb has closed himself off to everyone. Bridget is caring for the girls. And Manda, well, Manda is why I was late. Deborah looks more like the lost waif we saw when she first came, but of the three, I'd say she's handling this the best. It has been really hard on Bridget too, but she keeps a good face on for the girls." As he talked, he tucked her hand under his arm and led her toward the store. "We'll get your trunk later. Penny has dinner ready. She's already served her *rush*, as she calls it."

Mary Martha wanted to smooth the deepening lines from his forehead. He too looked as though the times were hard, with the sheen of moisture in his eyes. After all, he'd once loved Katy. That thought made her swallow hard. Was that why he'd taken this death hard? Was he still in love with Katy? Or had he been? And if so, was he even aware of it himself?

The thoughts rushed pell-mell through her mind like children just let loose from the schoolhouse. But when she tried to withdraw her hand from his arm, he clamped his other hand over hers. The sensation of warmth sent her doubts scurrying. This was indeed the man whose written salutations had grown progressively warmer through the months of correspondence.

"Who was the Negro that brought food on the train?"

"Oh, that's Sam, friend of Hjelmer's from way back. He's come to stay. Plans to bring his family out this spring." Pastor Solberg pushed open the door to the store, setting the bell to tinkling merrily. "She's here!" His shout brought Penny and Goodie running from the kitchen.

"Oh, Mary Martha. I'm so glad you're here." Penny started by taking her hand but ended with a hug before passing her on to Goodie, who did the same.

"Land, missy, you are a sight for sore eyes." Goodie reached to help her with her coat. "I'm sorry to hear about your ma passing on, but it's hard to doubt the good Lord's timing in all this. We surely do need you here."

"Soon as we eat, Hjelmer and I will take you on out to the farm." Penny turned the store sign to Closed and led the way back to the kitchen.

"I have to get back to the school," Pastor Solberg said, setting Mary Martha's carpetbag on the floor. "I thought of closing school today, but we've missed several weeks due to the blizzards, and the children are trying to catch up. If circumstances were different, I'd wish you could stop and see them on the way. They've missed you too." He'd taken her hand again, this time without gloves. The ripples of delight were still racing up and down her arm.

Did he feel them too?

When he finally released her hand and headed out the door with a final wave, she felt as if the sun had blinked dark for a moment. She turned back to the conversation flowing around her as they sat her at the table and began bringing food.

"So, tell me, how is everyone?" Mary Martha looked from one woman to the other.

"Been bad." Goodie shook her head. "Hard enough losing little Anna, but then Katy and the baby . . . Makes one wonder at times, 'deed it does."

"Can't have the burying until the frost goes out of the ground, and I think that makes it even harder. Several others died too, but not anyone you knew personally. Those two boys that the Valders adopted been leading Pastor Solberg a merry chase, but he persists, and they are settling down." Penny passed the bread plate around.

"They done took all we had, Miz Bjorklund." Sam pushed the curtain aside. "Now ah'm needed out at the smithy."

"Fine, Sam, and thank you very much."

Sam tipped his hat and let the curtain to the store drape back in place.

"We sure have been fortunate to have Sam here, with Hjelmer out speaking for the Farmer's Alliance. There's talk of him running for the legislature." A little frown cloud passed over Penny's face. "I do wish he'd stay home more."

"Oh, and Kaaren received a book on sign language to help little Grace speak. She's going to be teaching it at the school, so next year when the twins go to school, all the kids can talk with her. Land, you can't believe how fast those children learn it." Goodie leaned forward. "Why Ellie and Andrew already move their fingers real fast, and then giggle, even in church. Makes me want to know what they are saying."

As the two caught her up on the news of Blessing, all Mary Martha could think of was the MacCallister farm and the schoolhouse.

A knock sounded at the back door.

"Come in." Penny didn't bother to get to her feet.

The door cracked open and Manda peeked around the edge. "Pastor Solberg said we could leave school early to . . ."

The door slammed open and Deborah pushed past her older sister. She flung herself across the room to Mary Martha, who gathered the little girl close.

"My ma is gone to heaven and the baby and Anna." It was difficult understanding her with her face buried in Mary Martha's skirts, but the tears that streamed down her face when she looked up brought answering ones from the women.

"I feel like a sodden old dishrag half the time." Goodie pulled a square of muslin from her apron pocket and blew her nose.

"I know, child, I know." Mary Martha pushed her chair back from the table so Deborah could climb up in her lap. She hugged her, patting her back and rocking at the same time.

"Did you come back for good?" Deborah leaned back to look her aunt in the face.

"Yes. For good." Mary Martha looked up to see Manda staring out the window. Glancing from Penny to Goodie and back to Manda, Mary Martha raised an eyebrow in question. Both the other women shook their heads and shrugged.

"Manda, you want some dessert with us?" Penny got up to pour the coffee.

"No." One word only, but it clearly showed the walls she'd put up. John had been right in his observations of the two girls. Was Zeb, too, in as bad a way as he'd written?

Mary Martha wanted to ask, but refrained since the girls were there.

As soon as everyone was done eating, Penny turned to the girl who still hadn't left the window. "Manda, would you please run to the smithy and ask Sam to harness up the horse and sleigh?"

Only a nod answered her as Manda slipped out the door, barely disturbing the air in her passage, so silent was she.

"No, you just sit back down," Penny said when Mary Martha started to rise to help clear the table. "For today, at least, you are company."

"I'll take care of the store then while you drive them out?" Goodie spoke to Penny as she held the hot coffeepot above Mary Martha's cup.

"No, thanks. I'm about floating now." Mary Martha answered the unspoken question.

Penny nodded. "That would be good, thank you. The mail hasn't come in yet, so there'll be that to sort. And if you run out of things to do, you could always bake cookies. Those train passengers sure do like our cookies."

"Molasses?"

"Or sour cream." Penny smiled at Deborah. "Would you like a cookie?"

Deborah nodded. Manda knocked on the back door and came in at the same time. "He said ten minutes. He has to finish shoeing a horse first, but he is on the last hoof. Unless you want me to do it."

"No, that will be all right. Manda, can you think of anything you need from the store—sugar, flour, anything?"

Manda shook her head and returned to staring out the window.

"Well, I'll take some of that soft cheese along, and let's see . . ." Penny strolled into the store, mumbling to herself.

Deborah snuggled closer to Mary Martha. "I'm glad you are here," she whispered.

The ride out to the farm passed in a blur as the cold and wind made everyone's eyes water. Mary Martha squinted against the brilliant white, amazed at the difference in the land since she'd seen it. "How much longer will the snow last?" she asked.

"Into April probably, unless it all melts too fast. We usually get a late snowstorm after weather that tricks us into thinking spring has really come. You warm enough?"

Mary Martha didn't answer. She shivered instead and pulled the elk robe closer to her shoulders. *What is warm enough? Each mile north, I've gotten colder it seems. No wonder everyone up here wears long woolen underwear. I should have bought some at the store.* "How are the horses doing?"

Manda shrugged. "Okay."

Mary Martha waited, hoping for more of an answer. "How many are you training now?"

"She ain't done so much since the blizzard. We have to finish shoveling out the corral for her to work them." Deborah ignored the glare from her older sister. "That blizzard was some awful. We had to spend the night at the school, and there was no food. But we didn't starve to death like lots of cows and horses did."

Death seemed to tag along with every conversation.

Smoke curling from the chimney at Zeb's farm said that someone was at home. A dog barked when Penny stopped the sleigh by the front porch.

"Did you get a dog?"

"Uh-huh. Pa brought it home last week. Thinks the poor starvin' critter musta come in on the train or something. We been feeding him good."

"What's his name?" Mary Martha reached for her carpetbag. Sam had promised to bring her trunk out later. Manda took it from her and strode up the front steps that had been swept clean of snow.

"Spot, 'cause he has a spot over one eye."

"Oh, thank you, God." Bridget met them at the door. "Praise be. You came about as fast as your telegram." She wrapped Mary Martha in a hug that smelled of yeast and molasses and warm grandma. "Come in, come in. The coffee will be hot in a minute."

"Where's Pa?" Manda asked after setting Mary Martha's bag on the stairs to the second story.

"I'm not sure. But he said . . ."

Manda left out the front door before she could finish her sentence.

Bridget looked from Mary Martha to Penny and back. "I just don't know how to help that girl. Neither does Zeb." She reached out and drew Deborah into her floury apron. "Neither one of us do, huh, little one?"

Dusk had near darkened to night before they heard Zeb's boots on the porch. He brought in a pail of milk and set it on the cupboard counter before reaching for his sister with both arms.

Mary Martha hugged him close and whispered in his ear, "Zeb, I'm so sorry."

"Yeah, me too." He stepped back and with one arm hugged Deborah to his side. "Sure smells good in here."

"Supper is ready." Bridget set the pot of ham and beans in the center of the table. "Manda, did you wash your hands?"

They took their places and Mary Martha bowed her head for grace.

"We don't say grace no more," Deborah whispered from beside her.

Father, help them, and help me, please.

She gulped. "Well, I do," she whispered back, not daring to look at her brother. She could feel his cool disapproval as she'd felt the cold in the sleigh. She murmured her prayer and looked up with a smile.

Zeb was not smiling. He and Manda wore matching scowls. They'd already started eating.

I guess manners died here along with Katy. She looked to Bridget, who shook her head.

Later, after the kitchen was cleaned up and the girls had finished their homework and gone to bed, Zeb and Mary Martha sat at the table, nursing a last cup of coffee.

"I can't seem to . . . to . . ." Zeb studied the swirl of coffee in his cup. "Mary Martha, it's like the sun has gone out, and I can't find it again. I can't stay here. I can't."

"Where will you go?"

"Down south to check on the homestead that ought to belong to Manda and Deborah. I've been meaning to get down there and either see about proving it up or buying out the time remaining before some claim jumper takes it. Although I don't know why anyone in his right mind would want that parcel of land. But I promised Kat—er anyway, I promised that I would do that, and this seems as good a time as any."

"But Zeb . . ."

"If I tell the girls I'm going, they'll insist on going too. I can't do that." The light that had been so absent from his eyes flared for a brief moment before flickering out. "Besides, they've got school."

"Zeb, God will . . ." She stumbled to a halt at the look he gave her.

"Will you go back to helping at the school?"

"If Jo—Pastor Solberg wants me to."

"Bridget will stay here if you like. I've asked Ephraim to help with the chores, and Manda can keep working with the horses." He glanced up at her. "I'll take the train both ways as far as I can, so that should shorten the time I'm gone."

"Looks like you've got it all thought out."

"Thank you for coming. The girls need you."

"And you?"

"I'll manage." He stood and took his cup to the dishpan. " 'Night."

Zeb was gone when they all awoke in the morning.

Mid-April

You think spring will stay this time?" Mary Martha asked.

Penny looked up from the letter she was reading. "I hope so, but we could get another snowstorm or two. Sometimes those late ones are vicious." Penny and Mary Martha were sitting on the bench in front of the store on a Saturday afternoon, soaking up the warmth that melted snowbanks so fast it was like magic. Green shoots were already thrusting through the dark earth, as if racing for the first touch of sun on their tips. The spring symphony of ducks and geese flying north, robins serenading their mates, and sparrows cheeping in the eaves swelled around them.

"It's hard to believe that could happen." Mary Martha lifted her chin so the sun could reach her neck. "After going south and then coming back, it seems the only time I'm warm enough is when I am right next to a hot stove, and even then I keep turning to warm the other side."

"Will you stay now?"

"Most likely. At least until Zeb comes home." She didn't add, *If he comes home,* but she thought it.

"What about Pastor Solberg?"

Mary Martha no longer needed the sun to warm her throat, or up to her hairline for that matter. "What about him?"

"Come on. He's as sweet on you as you are on him."

Surely she was experiencing sunburn. She shielded her eyes. "Is that the train I see coming?"

"What else would be on the tracks? Now don't change the subject. Admit it. You're in love with him."

Mary Martha drew circles on her skirt-covered knee with a fingertip. "So?"

"So, I take it he hasn't declared his intentions?"

"We're good friends."

"So are you and me, but that's not what I'm talking about."

Mary Martha let out a sigh that had been festering for some time. "I told him I couldn't make any decisions until Zeb makes up his mind what he wants to do."

"What difference does that make?"

"Well, I'm taking care of the girls, and Sam is taking care of the farming. Manda has two more horses ready for sale, we have mares due to foal, and I can't leave all that until Zeb comes back." Much as she wanted to. When John had talked about caring for her, she'd wanted to fling herself in his arms and let all the rest go. But they were both still grieving for Katy. Sometimes she wondered who was grieving more.

"If he comes back? I can't believe he stayed gone this long. Surely a trip to check on that homestead can't take two months."

"Six weeks."

"What if something happened to him?"

Mary Martha jerked around to face her friend. "Don't say that!"

"Sorry." Penny raised her hands as if she needed a barrier. "But sometimes you have to think about those things."

"Look who's talking. How long did you wait for Hjelmer?"

"Too long. Seems I've spent half my life waiting for Hjelmer. He better be on *this* train if he knows what's good for him." She glanced up the track in time to hear the whistle blow. "You know my letter?"

"Um."

"It's from my sister. One day I'll get to see some of my family again. She said they might make the trip out here and look into buying land or going farther west to homestead. Thanks to cousin Ephraim, I found two of them, my brother David and my middle sister Rose. Only two more to go. Isn't that something?"

"That's pretty wonderful all right. Don't know what I'd have done growing up without Zeb to mother. Ma was too busy making sure we had a home and food to do much for him. I'll never regret the time we spent together." She sighed again. This seemed to be a day for sighs. "I better go. The girls will be worrying about me. We have plenty to do at home. The work is just getting away from us, I'm afraid. I don't see how I can keep on helping at the school much longer."

"Why don't you wait and see if you have any mail?"

Mary Martha settled back down. "I guess." When it came right down to it, she didn't blame Zeb a bit for not coming home. Sorrow seemed to permeate even the walls of the house. But she knew he'd be back in time for the fieldwork. He wasn't a quitter by any means, even though Manda said this was just like when her real pa left them and never returned.

Zeb will come back. She'd repeated those words to herself more times than she wanted to count.

The train screeched to a stop, steam boiling out from around the wheels. The conductor stepped down and set the stool by the stairs. Hjelmer swung down, bag in hand, and Penny rose to greet him.

The sight of the smiles they shared and the way he took her arm made Mary Martha flinch at the stab of jealousy she felt in her heart. *Mary Martha, just like the women in the Bible, always taking care of someone else. When will it be my turn?*

Sunday after church, Mary Martha waited until most of the other church members had left and then approached Pastor Solberg. "Can I speak with you for a moment?"

"Of course. Oh, oh. I don't like the look on your face."

"Me either. But I've had to come to a decision. I will be able to help at the school only one or two days a week, and then I'll have to quit entirely. There's just too much to do at the farm. We can't keep up." *And I can't keep up being just a good friend forever. I want more.*

"I . . . I'm sorry to hear that. We—the children, ah—things have been so much better since you have come back." *When will I see you? I can't come calling every day. That's not proper.*

"Well, I have been glad to help." She turned when Manda called her name. "I must go."

"You will come this week?" *Please say yes.*

"Yes, Tuesday and Thursday." *If only he seemed more . . . more—was sad the right word?*

◦◦◦

The weather turned even warmer, and each day the roads grew soggier. Horses' hooves picked up twenty pounds of gumbo each, and wagon wheels groaned under the extra weight. After talking it over with his deacons, on Thursday Pastor Solberg sent a letter home with his pupils saying that Saturday would be the day for burying. All of the coffins were in the ice house, awaiting such a day.

"Ah, Zeb, you got to come home by then." Mary Martha read the letter to Bridget.

"We can't bury Katy and the baby without him here."

"I know, but we can't—I mean, the bodies are . . ." *God, I can't abide this. Waiting so long to bury a body, and now we can't wait any longer. Please bring Zeb home, please, for his sake and ours.*

Zeb and his horse, Buster, got off the train the next afternoon.

"Pa's home!" Deborah came shrieking into the house, eggs leaping from her clutched-up apron as she ran.

"Deborah! Look at the mess!" Bridget put both hands to her cheeks.

"Oh. Sorry." The little girl put the remaining three whole eggs on the counter. "I'll clean up the broken ones."

"You wasted the good eggs."

"I . . . I said I was sorry." Tears filled the little girl's blue eyes.

"I know but . . ."

"That's all right this time, Bridget. Leave her be." Mary Martha took one look at Deborah's apron and tried to keep from laughing. "That's a new way to scramble eggs, that's for sure."

Mary Martha hesitated to go outside to see her brother. Would he be himself again, or would the news of the morrow send him backward? "Let's pour this into the dog's dish."

"But Pa is here."

"All right, I'll take care of the eggs, and you go see him."

"Thank you." Never had an apron been untied so quickly, and Deborah scampered out the door.

Bridget had gone to the window, so Mary Martha joined her. They watched Zeb crouch down to catch Deborah as she flew into his arms. He said something to her, and she locked her arms around his neck.

Mary Martha searched for Manda. She was nowhere to be seen.

Zeb made his way to the house with Deborah perched on his hip and Spot leaping around his feet.

"Welcome home." Mary Martha met him at the door.

"Looks like I made it just in time."

"Ja, you are a good sight for these eyes." Bridget wiped her hands on her apron and reached for Deborah, who pulled away. "You're too big a girl to be carried like that."

Zeb set her down at his side. " 'Bout broke my back for sure." His smile made her smile back. But the smile never reached his eyes.

"Where's Manda?" Mary Martha asked.

"Out in the corral behind the barn. Said she'd be in after a while." Zeb hung his flat-brimmed hat on the peg by the door. He ran his hands through hair that now glinted with bits of silver. "Any coffee? I haven't had decent coffee since I rode out of here."

"I'll make some fresh." Bridget bustled away.

"I got the papers for the girls. The land is now theirs, held in trust by me. I leased it out to a rancher near there. Won't bring in much, but the well made it worth his while." He sank into a chair at the table and scrubbed his scalp with his fingertips. "Mercy, but I need a bath."

"We'll bring in the washtub and put extra water on to boil. Supper will be ready in a bit."

"Good." He took the cup and saucer Bridget handed him. "Mange takk, Mor."

"Praise be to God, you came back in time."

He sighed and sipped.

"That will have to make do until the new pot is ready."

"This is fine. Beats that mud I been making." He sipped his coffee and sighed again, staring into the brown depths as if that could keep him from looking around the house.

Mary Martha knew he could only think of Katy. Her imprint lay on everything in the house, her laugh echoed in the corners, and without her the house seemed to hover in expectation of her return.

She laid a hand on his shoulder, wishing she could make things different for him. All those years together she had fixed his toys, bandaged his wounds, and held him when he cried. And now, when he hurt the most, there was nothing she could do. "You heard then?"

He nodded. "I'll be grateful to get that part over with. Wish now I'd waited to come home."

"You can't mean that."

He scrubbed his scalp again. "Yes and no."

"Pa?" Deborah hung near his elbow.

Without another word, he put an arm around her and pulled her to him. If only he could do the same for Manda.

But when Manda came in, as usual she said not a word. She ate, helped with clearing the table, and got out her school books.

"Manda." His voice made her chalk falter on the slate.

She waited without looking up.

"Thank you for taking such good care of the horses and things around here." When he leaned over to touch her, she flinched away.

Zeb looked across the table at Mary Martha, who shrugged and nodded at the same time.

"G'night." The girl snatched up her books and headed up the stairs as if they were chasing her.

Bridget turned from washing dishes in a pan on the stove. "Your bath water is about hot."

"Good, thanks."

"I'll tuck the girls in, give you some privacy." Mary Martha held out a hand to Deborah. "Let's get you washed up, gettin' past your bedtime."

Deborah reached up and kissed Zeb on the cheek. "I've missed you, Pa. Manda said you weren't coming back, but I knew you would."

As soon as the dishes were done, Bridget dragged the tub in front of the stove and began pouring the hot water in.

"I can do that." Zeb got to his feet. "I'm so tired, I think I could sleep for a week."

"Bridget has been sleeping in your room, we can . . ."

"No!" Zeb waved his hands like she was a pesky fly. "I'll sleep in the spare room." He looked around like an animal seeking escape. "I . . . I can't . . ."

"Zeb, that's all right. I understand. I'll make up that bed then." She went softly up the stairs, aching for the man who sat as if he had no will to move—ever again.

⚜ ⚜

While the funeral for her mother had carried a sense of rejoicing for a saint who went home, the people gathered around the five pine boxes looked as desolate as the wind-swept prairie. She heard the ancient words as from a far distance, not permitting herself to look at John. His voice broke more than once, and someone behind her was sobbing. Manda and Deborah stood on either side of her, hanging on to her hands as to a lifeline in a tempest-tossed sea. Zeb stood like a wooden soldier right behind her.

One by one the boxes were lowered into the holes that had been dug for them.

Ah, Katy, I don't even have any flowers for you, and the laughter is all gone. Sleet stung their faces as Mary Martha held Deborah against her side. Manda had taken two steps away and released her hand.

Yesterday the birds were singing, and today winter is trying to blow us off the land again.

"Let us pray." John closed his Bible. "Heavenly Father, we do not understand thy plan and thy purposes, but we know that thou art our God, our Father, and our Comforter. We thank thee that thou hast prepared a mansion for us in the heavenly places, and that we will see our loved ones when we get there too." He stopped, blew his nose, and stumbled over the next words. "For all thy blessings, we praise thy holy name." He raised his voice and made the sign of the cross in the air. "The Lord bless thee and keep thee. The Lord make his countenance to shine upon thee and give thee his peace.

In the name of the Father and of the Son and of the Holy Ghost. Amen."

The wind clacked the branches of the cottonwood tree someone had planted in the cemetery. No more lonesome sound had ever been heard.

"Go in peace," John said, dismissing the group of mourners.

Mary Martha took Zeb's arm and turned to look for Bridget. She stood between Penny and Hjelmer, with Thorliff in front as if protecting her. That was as it should be.

"The ladies have prepared a meal for us at the church. Won't you all please come?" John announced to the crowd standing so quietly and soberly.

Mary Martha looked up to catch his gaze resting upon her. Oh, to be able to run to his arms and be held while she cried out her sorrow.

Instead she gathered the girls, and the four of them made their way back to the church.

They stayed only long enough to be polite. Mary Martha watched Zeb's valiant effort to accept the condolences offered, but she could tell that while he might be talking and breathing, there was no life in her baby brother.

By the time they came out, snow covered the mud ruts, the dead grass, and the fresh mounds of dirt in the graveyard. It stung their faces on the way home.

But in the morning it was gone.

Along with the girls.

Mary Martha threw on a coat and tore out to the barn, where Zeb was milking one of the cows. "Zeb, they're gone!"

"Who's gone?" He kept his head in the cow's flank, turning only enough to see her in the lantern light.

"Manda and Deborah."

"Gone where?"

"I don't know, but they aren't in their beds, not anywhere in the house."

"Go check the horse while I finish this cow."

Mary Martha checked the stalls and the corral outside where some of the animals stayed. Manda's horse was missing.

"Fool kids. What's the matter with them?" Zeb slammed his hand against the doorframe and flinched.

"I don't know, but I'm going with you."

"No, you stay here in case they come back."

"They won't come back. Not Manda. Once she makes up her mind . . ."

"I know. Like a bear trap." He handed her the pail of milk. "You fix us some food to take, and I'll saddle the horses."

Within minutes they were loping across the prairie, staying clear of the roads that were ankle-deep mud. They checked at the Bjorklund farms, Goodie's house, and the store. No one had seen the two leave.

"You go tell Pastor Solberg, and I'll go get Baptiste to help me track."

Haakan rode up with several others. "We can all fan out and search. Any idea where they might go?"

God, please help us. Protect our two errant ones, please. We can't do with any more loss around here. She opened her eyes and nodded. "I know where they are headed."

"Where?" Zeb looked up from adjusting his cinch.

"To their homestead."

"They can't get that far."

"No, but Manda will give it a try."

They caught up with the girls just before dusk, thanks to Baptiste, who had become as good a tracker as his grand-mother.

"Manda, Deborah, what in heaven's name is the matter with you?" Zeb clutched the reins of their horse as if he might strangle the leathers, since he didn't dare touch the two girls.

"We ain't stayin' where we ain't wanted." Manda wore her old slouch hat so low on her forehead, her eyes were invisible.

"Manda, darlin', where did you get that idea?" Mary Martha wasn't sure if she wanted to hug them or swat them first.

"Zeb don't want to stay here. You and Pastor Solberg are . . ."

"Manda MacCallister, for cryin' out loud . . ." Zeb took his hat off and scrubbed a frustrated hand through his hair, sending it flying every which way.

"If that don't beat all." Haakan shook his head.

"So, we're leavin', and that's that."

"That's not that!" The horse threw up its head at Zeb's roar.

"I'm your father, and I say you are coming home to where you belong. Now!" He climbed back on his horse and tugged on the reins of the other. "Come on horse, git up."

"Zeb." Mary Martha rode up beside him. "Please."

"All right."

Mary Martha dismounted and stood beside the girl's horse. "Look, Manda, Deborah, Pastor Solberg and I are good friends and . . ."

Manda's snort could be heard a mile away across the prairie.

"Whatever happens, you are our family, and families stick together. No matter how hard the times are."

"I told you so." Deborah slid to the ground and clutched Mary Martha around the waist. "I want to go home."

Bridget had a hot meal ready for them when they returned somewhere around midnight, thanks to a full moon that seemed to lead the way.

"Now, you got to promise me you won't do such a numskulled thing again, you hear?" Zeb looked Manda right in the eye. "You are my daughter, my eldest daughter, and one I expect to have some sense. You got somethin' to say, you just say it. MacCallisters don't run away, and I know the Nortons don't neither."

Manda looked from Zeb to Mary Martha and back. She locked her arms over her skinny chest and glared at them both. "I'll stay."

"Promise?"

"I said I would. That's enough!"

"And I know you don't go back on your word." Mary Martha laid her hands on Manda's shoulders. "Child, you gave us such a fright." She laid her cheek on top of Manda's head and felt the girl sigh and lean slightly back.

"I'd think someone smart as you would have at least taken a decent horse." Zeb wagged a finger at her.

"I weren't takin' nothing not my own."

"Manda, listen to me and listen right good. All that I have is yours. This place and all the stock and everything is *ours*. Do you understand? That's what family is."

Manda gave him her "I'll-wait-and-see" look, but her back

no longer looked as though she wore a suit of armor holding her upright.

⁂

The following Sunday afternoon, a day brighter than a shiny new penny, Pastor Solberg rode into the yard at the MacCallister ranch. He looped his horse's reins over the fence post and strode up the steps, knocking on the door with only the slightest hesitation.

"Why, J—Pastor Solberg. Come on in." Mary Martha stepped back and motioned him in.

"Later maybe. Right now I thought you and I could go for a ride, just the two of us." He stammered over the last words.

"Why, I guess that would be all right. Zeb and the girls are out at the corral."

Within minutes a horse was saddled for her, and Zeb held it while she stepped up on a block and slid her foot into the stirrup. Settling her skirts about her legs, she took up the reins. "Thank you. We won't be gone long."

"Take your time." Zeb winked at her.

She could feel the heat rush up her neck and wash over her face. The urge to pull his hat brim down over his eyes made her fingers twitch. Instead, she reined the horse around and trotted out of the yard.

"Where would you like to go?" She lifted her face to the sun. How wonderful it felt, and so different from a week ago.

"How about over to the Park River?"

"Fine with me." They kicked their horses into a prairie-eating lope, throwing mud up behind them. Reaching the river, they stopped side by side.

"Come, I have something for you." John dismounted and tied his horse to a low branch.

"What?"

"You'll see."

Mary Martha rolled her eyes and shook her head, then dismounted as he asked. "Now what is it?"

He beckoned her with one finger and eased his way down the bank. Quickly he snapped off a couple of willow branches and handed them to her. "See, the pussy willows are out. Spring is really here."

Mary Martha stroked the soft fuzz with a gentle fingertip. "How lovely they are." She looked up to see him studying her face. "Thank you."

"I wanted to find violets, but . . ." He shrugged. "They aren't in bloom yet, and I can't wait any longer."

"Wait for what?" Her fingers kept stroking the soft fur while she studied his face.

"For you."

The words hung on the air, light as thistledown. A bird sang in the branches near the frozen river.

She began shaking her head.

"Is it that you don't love me enough, then?" John gripped her hands with all the fierceness of his soul.

She shook her head. *No, it is that I am afraid you don't love me, that you still have Katy in your heart.* How could she ask him such a question? The tears he'd shed at the funeral—were they for all those he buried or for Katy? A lump blocked her throat. She wanted to reach out and smooth away the lines from his forehead, but she feared this last winter had written them there permanently.

"What then?"

Mary Martha pushed away the Mary side of her and let the practical Martha come forth. She sucked in a deep breath. *Now or never. If he answers wrong, I will return to my mother's house and take up my life there.* The thought brought tears burning in her eyes, making her sniff.

"Dear girl, what is it?"

She looked him in the eye in spite of her mother's voice, which she could hear accusing her of unwomanly behavior. A scandalized voice that knew of her intentions.

"Did you love Katy Bjorklund?"

John stood straight and inhaled deeply, as if she'd gut-punched *him*. His eyes bored into hers. "Ja, I thought so." She'd never know what the admission cost him.

"Oh." She started to withdraw, but he kept her hands in a bear-trap grip.

"You asked *did*? I did, but she never looked on me as more than a friend. She married Zeb, and I prayed that I could be her friend, their friend. And God honored that prayer. And then He gave me the desire of my heart. A woman to love in ways I'd only dreamed of. One who has a soul of such beauty that I am awestruck to think she might love me in return. One who makes me laugh, and when I watch her with the children, makes me yearn to have her caring for mine, for ours. Yes, Mary Martha MacCallister, I did love Katy, but that is in the past. Now I love you, and I want to learn to love you more every day for the rest of my life."

Tears trickled down her cheeks, turning her eyes to emeralds sparkling in the sun.

He wiped them away with a gentle fingertip. "So, now the questions are—"

"Qu . . . questions?" She sniffed and tried to smile, but her lips quivered in the action.

"Yes, questions. Number one: do you love me?"

She nodded.

"Say it."

She swallowed. "I love you, John Solberg." She squeezed his hands in return. "The next question?" Her heart fluttered like a bird learning to fly.

"Will you marry me?"

"Not today." Her smile went straight to his heart and nestled there. "Or tomorrow, but would next week be soon enough?"

He gathered her into his arms, raining kisses on her eyes, her cheeks, and finally he found her mouth.

"If I'd known you tasted so sweet, I would have done this plenty sooner," he whispered against her lips.

She sighed and leaned her forehead against his chin. "I still don't know what will happen with Zeb and the girls."

"If they need to come live with us, that's all right with me."

"Really?"

"Of course."

"In a one-room soddy?"

"Well, we might have to build a house. But there will always be room for one more at our table." He settled back against the tree bark, drawing her head down on his shoulder. "I don't ever want to say good-bye to you again, my love."

"But, as I said before, good-bye is not forever."

"Thank God for that." He kissed her again and leaned back to watch her sparkling eyes. *And thank you, Father, for your tender mercies in our lives—now and forever.* This time she kissed him.